The Judgment of Paris

BOOKS BY GORE VIDAL

Novels

WILLIWAW

IN A YELLOW WOOD

THE CITY AND THE PILLAR

THE SEASON OF COMFORT

A SEARCH FOR THE KING

DARK GREEN, BRIGHT RED

MESSIAH

JULIAN

THE JUDGMENT OF PARIS

Short Stories

A THIRSTY EVIL

Plays

VISIT TO A SMALL PLANET

THE BEST MAN

Essays

ROCKING THE BOAT

The Judgment of Paris

by

G O R E   V I D A L

LITTLE, BROWN AND COMPANY   BOSTON   TORONTO

Published simultaneously in Canada
by Little, Brown & Company (Canada) Limited

PRINTED IN THE UNITED STATES OF AMERICA

The Judgment of Paris

FOR JOHN LATOUCHE

PART ONE

"But what are kings, when regiment is gone,
But perfect shadows in a sunshine day."
Marlowe: *Edward the Second*

Chapter One

*SHE WORE HER TRAUMA like a plume. When she was
seven an elderly man attempted to have his way with her
in a telephone booth at Grand Central (her mother had been
buying a ticket to Peekskill). Although she was in no way
defiled, the shock was great and, to this day, she was so
terrified of the telephone that she was forced always to
compose innumerable messages on pale blue paper for the
instruction and pleasure of those acquaintances whom she
might otherwise, in a less perilous era, have telephoned.*

That was all there was to it, he thought sadly, studying
this one paragraph typed neatly at the top of a sheet of fine
white paper: there would be no more; he was confident of
that. "She" was lost to the world, trauma and all, and the
contents of those messages on blue paper would never be
known. She had emerged in his mind one day, clear and
precise, a lady of the highest, most Meredithean comedy,
with just a trace of something more racy, vulgar even, to
give her a proper contemporary relevance, but he had lost
her for good after that first paragraph, watched with helpless resignation as she sank back into a limbo of unarranged
words, convincing him that he would never be a man of
letters: not, of course, that he had ever thought too seriously
of becoming one; rather, it had seemed a pleasant way to
spend a life, composing sentences day after day with a tight
smile on his lips and a view of mountains, or the sea, from a
study window.

His failure was complete, however, and he knew with a
sad certainty that his lady of the blue notes (not a bad

1

title, he thought, wondering if there might not be a double meaning in it: something to do with music) would remain unrevealed forever, this paragraph her *alpha* and *omega*. But that is that for now, he thought, and he gave up literature as he had given up painting and music the year before, having composed one art song to a three-line Emily Dickinson poem, and painted one nonobjective painting in the style of Mondrian. "I am not an artist," he murmured to himself with some satisfaction, putting the paper back into his suitcase and ending forever a never too urgent dream of creativity.

The problem of what to do with his life still existed, of course; but time undoubtedly would arrange all that, he decided, removing the Hotel Excelsior, Napoli, tag which had only this morning been stuck on his new suitcase by a hotel porter whom he had never seen until that moment and who expected, but never received, a large tip for this superfluous service, thus further darkening the none too bright reputation of Americans in post-war Italy. There had been a scene as he got into the taxi but he carried it off well and at the station, as an act of contrition, he gave the cab driver a thick pile of torn and dirty *lire*.

He hated scenes, he thought, looking out the train window at the green countryside rippling uncertainly beyond the solid fact of glass, shimmering in the heat of a white spring sun.

Philip Warren sighed happily. He was here at last: Italy, Europe, a year of leisure, a time for decision, a prelude to the distinguished fugue his life was sure to be, once he got really to it, once the delightful prelude had been played to its conclusion among the foreign cities.

He glanced out the window again, looking instinctively for modern ruins which he hoped would not be there: the way one reluctantly examines the remains of a dead dog on a country road. Fortunately, there were no ruins in sight, except the ancient, the respectable ones. Bits of an aqueduct arched over the plains of Latium, brown-brick against the Apennines. . . . The Apennines, he murmured the name aloud, with reverence. Yes, he was on the march to Rome.

⌨

"This is your room," said the clerk, showing him a room as scrubbed and neat as the young clerk himself, a fresh-faced Swiss. A big balconied window looked out onto a

2

quiet Roman street of tall trees against the baroque façades of seventeenth-century houses—all embassies now, remarked the clerk, opening the window and letting in the sunlit air. Then after a quick briefing on the meaning and the uses of the various bells, Philip was left alone in this handsome room with its feather bed and numerous pillows, its old-fashioned bathtub hidden, along with a bidet, behind curtains. Very happy, he unpacked.

Now then: what does he look like? What sort of man or boy or youth is Philip Warren? Well, it is much too early to draw any conclusions about his character since he is hardly yet revealed. On the other hand, there is something to be said about his appearance. His face, certainly, must be described before he ventures out into the Roman afternoon and as he has not yet looked into a mirror (the usual device for describing one's protagonist), let it be noted that Philip Warren is twenty-eight and fairly handsome, slim, unembarrassed by overdeveloped muscles, flat-bellied (could one ever have a protagonist who was young and stout?) and though not tall, not short (all things to all all men obviously); he is, then, of middle height, his face more square than oval, his cheekbones prominent. His nose is unheroic, small and stubby, making him look even younger than he is. His eyes are a dark blue, not very interesting but, as one writer once said of another writer's eyes, interested. His skin is still boyish and taut and except for a deep line between fair brows he has no outward marks of age or experience or character in his face.

His body, for those who are interested in such things, was well formed and greatly admired by the not inconsiderable company which had, at one time or another (and on some occasions at the same time) enjoyed it. On the inside of his left thigh, near the groin, a small butterfly had been tattooed, a memento of the war when he had been a junior Naval officer on leave in Honolulu. His speaking voice was manly but marred by the faintest lisp, a defect which he hated although, unknown to him, it was his greatest charm for, instead of sounding sissy as he imagined, it made him seem very boyish and charming: a puzzled youthful man in need of a woman's protection. As a result his success with women was quite remarkable not only because of this boyishness but also because he genuinely liked them in an age and nation where, generally speaking, they were less admired than usual.

"Do you play bridge?"

3

"Why yes," said Philip, turning, as a stout bald man moved apologetically into the room from the hall.

"I'm so glad. I do hope you'll excuse my dropping in like this but your door was open and I live right down the hall and we do have so few people in Rome who even *play* bridge, much less *want* to play it. You do want to play?"

"Yes, not now, though. Some other time perhaps."

"Of course, of course . . . I was thinking of the future, not the present. You play it decently, I hope?"

"Rather," said Philip, meaning "rather decently" but, in the excitement of the moment, he found himself parodying the other's British accent.

"I'm so glad. Are you from home?"

"No," said Philip, already alerted. "I'm from America." He blushed as he said this unaccustomed phrase, as though he had begun suddenly to unfurl and snap, all red and white and blue in a chauvinistic breeze.

"Yes? Well, one never knows any more. The world is becoming one at last, is it not? Pleasant thought, or is it? Ah well, soon it will be a *fait accompli* and no concern of ours. My name, if I may introduce myself, is Clyde Norman." Information of this sort was formally exchanged and Mr Norman gave him a card, a very proper sort of card which declared that Mr Norman was a director of the Fabian Trade Mission, otherwise undefined. "I've lived in Rome almost all my life, you know. Stayed here all through the war. Very risky. Quite a story in all that, I suppose. If one likes stories, eh? But now I'm sure you have many things to do . . ."

They agreed, then, that it might be a good idea to have a drink together, to celebrate Philip's arrival.

◙

Mr Norman was splendidly knowing, decided Philip, as they strolled from the hotel to the Via Veneto, the fashionable street of Rome. He was able to say something amusing about almost everything mentioned, or at least he spoke as though what he said might prove amusing if one fully understood the various references.

Dingy youths stood on street corners, peddling blackmarket cigarettes, candy bars and currency. The streets otherwise were discouragingly familiar. The buildings were either severe and formal or baroque and formal, their stucco façades a weathered gray-gold, the color of Rome. The day was so very fine, however, that this momentary disappointment was succeeded by a sudden elation, a blitheness which he had seldom experienced since childhood. He controlled a sudden impulse to slip away from Clyde Norman, to run as fast as he could until he had reached the Forum, where he would sit among the broken marble and recall Horace and Keats and think how good it was to live, or to die, for both seemed equally desirable, the dark and the light, one meaningless without the other, twins and opposites. But he dared not mention this to Mr Norman who was, he gathered, more concerned with details than with abstractions.

"In thirty years one picks up quite a bit, you know. One comes to know the city *behind* the city, if you get what I mean."

"I certainly do."

"England is like a foreign country to me now. I hardly know how to act when I'm there, and the climate . . . do you know English weather?"

"By reputation."

"Damp, very damp. And from September to May everyone has a cold . . . ah, here we are, the Via Veneto."

They paused for a moment, surveying this celebrated thoroughfare. Mr Norman was somewhat proprietary while Philip found it not strange at all. The street reminded him of a minor avenue in Washington, D.C., except that it curved up a slight hill to a massive brick arch and fissured wall behind which could be glimpsed the rich green of gardens. The gardens of the Villa Borghese, according to his companion, who indicated various other sights of interest: the Excelsior Hotel, an outdoor café called Doney's where, presently, they sat in iron chairs at iron tables, the sidewalk between them and the main part of the café.

"This is the center," said Mr Norman. "So many cities have no center. London for instance has none, or rather too many: the Strand, Westminster, Piccadilly Circus, but no place where one can go and see everybody. No cafés like this one where, sooner or later, those one wants to see will come. I have always thought London must have been like this in the days of the coffeehouses." He ordered apéritifs with unfamiliar names. Then they sat back to watch. Philip felt as though he were sitting in a theater just as the lights had begun to dim, that expectant moment before the discordancies of an orchestra trying its instruments become an overture. Mr Norman, with a smile, figuratively tapped his music stand with an imaginary baton and the curtain rose as one of the late dictator's mistresses, a plump little woman

5

in black, walked slowly between the crowded tables of chattering people, accompanied by a plump little chow, its sad face a doggish facsimile of her own.

"I always thought mistresses were beautiful," said Philip who had thought nothing of the kind but, having been trapped in a role—naïve, youthful, American—had the good manners not to confuse the other by assuming a character closer to his own.

"They say she used to be," said Mr Norman, watching her as she nodded to numerous acquaintances who nodded back and then, when she was out of earshot, discussed her eagerly, her health, morals and current fortune.

"But then . . ." said Mr Norman, solemnly, pausing as though expecting an epigram on the nature of courtesans to spring sharp and original to his thin bluish lips; but as none came he took a sip of his apéritif instead. He was, Philip decided, one of those charming men whose way of speaking is so ceremonious and shrewd that they seem to be scoring one linguistic hit after another on the all too vulnerable target of human character while, actually, they do little more than repeat the clever sayings of other men . . . which takes a good memory, decided Philip tolerantly, not to mention a sense of timing and, finally, a style which was set if not by Dr Johnson then by Horace Walpole in the great days of aristocracy, after the perfect pearl of the Renaissance was misshapen by a rigid manner and the baroque was born of that tension between nature and artifice. Philip wondered if he would have an ópportunity to tell Mr Norman that the word "baroque" came from the Portuguese *barroco,* which meant a misshapen pearl. Later, perhaps, if they spoke of architecture (Philip was good at guiding conversations into home waters where, with infinite skill, he could scuttle the barks of others with some torpedo of esoterica, some bit of knowledge, properly timed; it was, he knew, the surest way to total unpopularity in a pretentious age).

"There are of course many different sets in Rome. The Church, the government (which isn't much these days), and the old nobility which is very fine and very distant, set apart. One hardly ever sees them. They live the way they've always lived in those *palazzi* and they are quite scornful, I suspect, of the rest of the world, of people whose ancestry does not go back to the Republic, as they maintain their own does, to the Republic and even further in some cases, to the gods."

6

"But then doesn't everyone go back that far?"

"Yes, but the descent is not recorded."

"Caesar traced his family back to Venus, didn't he?"

"Fully documented, too. Which proves I think that all genealogy is myth," said Mr Norman smiling, displaying two rows of British teeth in a state of only partial repair. "But tell me why you are here, Mr Warren, if I may ask."

"You certainly may," said Philip cordially. Then he paused awkwardly, destroying the illusion of cordiality with this ill-timed hesitation. Discreetly Mr Norman began to murmur, to back away from the personal until Philip, the reason for his hesitation still not clear to him, said at last, "To travel. I have a year, you see."

"A year? Is that all? I mean a year for what?"

"A year to travel in, to make up my mind."

"About your future?"

"Yes, about the future."

"I wonder if one can ever do precisely that."

"You mean come to a decision about life in a given period?"

"Yes, to make a positive, irrevocable decision. I shouldn't think it could be done, or should be done."

"I would like to try, even so," said Philip vaguely, distracted by the sight of a well-known American actor who strode quickly by, scowling like Cato and carrying under one arm a new and shiny book with its provocative title in bold black letters on red: *Decadence*. The actor disappeared into the door of the Excelsior Hotel.

"Accept the moment: there is nothing else."

"Perhaps not. Still, I am nearly thirty and . . ."

"You look so young! I thought you were a college boy."

"Thank you. And I feel I must decide what to do with the rest of my life."

"Even though, terrible thought, it might be, considering the state of the world (and pardoning the impertinence of my gloom), very short?"

"Or, considering my natural cowardice and cunning, longer than the average."

"Ah, now you exaggerate. I only suggested that your life might be shortened to convince you of the very real folly of making long-range plans: they are just *not* the thing to do nowadays."

Philip appeared to ponder this pronouncement while the waiter brought them more apértifs, pronouncing their name

"Cinzano" as he slopped the glasses before them on the table.

The day, Philip decided, was perfect in every way: clouds burdened the west, preceding the golden globe of the afternoon sun as it sank rapidly through the blue to the seven hills of the city, to the sea and to the new world beyond that. The day was warm, without wind but not hot, not the way he had been warned it would be in the spring. Conscious of weather and bemused, he said yes and he said no as his pleasant companion advised him to accept what was, since there would be, for all he knew, no more. As he had already planned to do precisely that, to live as he pleased for a year, he found that he could agree with the older man and, by agreeing, could establish a tentative friendship.

"What precisely to you plan to do with this year of yours . . . this climacteric in your life?"

Philip smiled. "I haven't the slightest idea. Sit at this café, perhaps. Or go and walk in those gardens over there. Or journey up the Nile to its source."

"You have no plan?"

"None."

"Wise! Very wise . . . and then you're so fortunate."

"In what way?"

"To be young."

"One doesn't realize it at the time. I'm not conscious of any serious blessing. Perhaps I will be one day."

"You will. How extraordinary though that you should feel that way. Are you really so detached? Or like so many of the politic young men nowadays, have you merely learned the proper responses?"

"You're too quick," said Philip, taken aback, not prepared for the other's shrewdness, for of course it was true: he had learned to say many things which got him easily and with no exertion the respect of his elders, statements which he knew well in advance would amuse or shock or please and which had little or no relation to what he actually thought. It was a schoolboy's trick and he felt a sudden shame to be playing again the brightest boy with the headmaster, as though he were still fourteen and ruthless, without a heart.

Mr Norman had the grace not to pursue his advantage; instead he remarked, "And then you are fortunate because you have money."

Philip laughed. "I have none," he said.

"But you are able to travel well . . . That's what I mean

by having money. You are not caught like me in a web of chicanery, trying to make your few pounds support you by doing all the squalid black-market things."

"In that sense, yes, I'm fortunate . . . I have the correct nationality."

"Indeed you have." Mr Norman drank his Cinzano moodily and Philip watched the street become more crowded as the golden light darkened and the evening star shone silver over the gardens. He was aware, after this discussion of currency, that he would be called upon to pay for the apéritifs and this thought did not sadden him for he was, after all, a young man with an income, a small one but sufficient for the traveler's purpose and he knew that he would entertain many strangers before he was done and though none of them might prove to be angels in disguise they had, he knew, a right to his hospitality since he had come among them to learn what he could.

Mr Norman suddenly got to his feet and shook the hand of a stooped middle-aged man with a fire-red face in which, shadowed by a bird's-beak nose, two watery blue eyes danced about seemingly unable to focus (although Philip was aware that he himself had been immediately comprehended by the newcomer in one quick intense glance).

"Sit with us, Ayre," said Mr Norman. "I want you to meet a young friend of mine, a new friend, only just arrived from America. His name is Philip Warren."

"How do you do?" said the older man in a curiously accented British voice, most of the stresses falling in unexpected places, a mock-Welsh voice as Philip later learned. "I can sit just a moment. I'm expecting Guido. I said I'd meet him here. He's late. Why is he always late? Why?"

"That's just his way."

"There is of course a possibility that *I* am late. I never know."

"I'm sure he'll be along presently," said Mr Norman with quiet authority and then he turned to Philip and said in a voice from which every trace of pride had been resolutely banished to accord harmoniously with a Stoic attitude: "This, Mr Warren, is Lord Glenellen." Since they were now all seated, Philip could only incline his head respectfully at the peer who was now insulting the waiter in faultless Italian, or what sounded to Philip (and to the waiter) like faultless Italian. Mr Norman watched his countryman with some satisfaction, smiling at the more colorful epithets and frown-

9

ing furiously when the waiter attempted a mild insult or two on his own.

"About the coffee," said Glenellen finally, as the waiter walked away, "coffee I had yesterday. It made me ill."

"What will you have now?"

"Not a thing. I think perhaps I'll go to the Excelsior for some decent coffee."

"And not wait for Guido?"

"He could wait for me, you know. There *are* worse fates."

"Of course, Ayre, of course."

"You're an American, aren't you?" The blue eyes, milky as though filmed by cataracts, turned on him disconcertingly, avoiding his eyes, though, concentrating instead on the line of his chin, the curve of his mouth.

"Yes, from New York, the state. . . ."

"Ah, I know. I know. Don't tell me. There's a state named that as well as a city. I was there, you see. Long, long ago. I adored Harlem. Is it still going?"

"Very much so."

"Do you visit there much?"

"No, almost never."

"Well, times change. Where do people go?"

"Nowhere in particular. There seems to be little difference now between one part of the city and another. The East Side is no different from Greenwich Village."

"Ah, I had forgotten the Village! Has it changed much? Is it still amusing?"

"I expect so. I don't live in the city, though. I live up the Hudson River, at a town called Hudson."

"All great civilizations," announced Mr Norman, checking in, "have flourished on the banks of rivers. There has never been a civilization of any importance on a lake, for instance."

"Is that so?" Philip was polite.

"Do you plan to stay here long?" asked Glenellen.

"I have no plans."

"A gentleman of leisure," said Mr Norman, with a father's smile.

"Fortunate boy . . . to have no plans. Now I, on the other hand, am burdened with plans. I have every day and every hour of every week outlined for months ahead. Dinner with this person and tea with that one. A week end at Ischia; a week in Vienna. I think sometimes I am over-organized because, in spite of all my activity, I have no time for work."

10

"Work?"

"Oh my goodness, yes."

"He composes," said Mr Norman, giving a brother's smile this time at the lean figure beside him. "He composes music," he added, "chamber music."

"When I have time," said Glenellen uneasily. "Tell me: where are you stopping?"

"He's at my hotel," said Mr Norman. "Isn't that a coincidence? I barged right in on him this afternoon and asked him if he played bridge. He does. Aren't you pleased?"

"I am pleased that he is here, Clyde," said the other courteously. "Besides, you know perfectly well that I seldom play cards."

"Ah, your barren life, Ayre. I had forgotten."

"I have my compensations."

"Yes, yes, indeed yes. Innumerable."

"And unmentionable!" They both laughed loudly and Philip looked from one to the other, puzzled as one always is by the private references of acquaintances newly met, the jokes which suggest vast unexplored areas of vice and virtue unrevealed to the outsider.

"But to consider you: you intend to follow your instinct, obey your whims, traveling here and there without a plan?"

"Exactly. I shall look at buildings I have heard about, absorb as much scenery as I can . . . I'm just a tourist, you know, not even a student like the rest. Then when I've had as much as I can take, I will go home and do something."

"Do something? Do what?" Glenellen leaned forward as though suddenly eager to know truth, to attend at a revelation.

But Philip was not equal to the moment nor for that matter was he in the mood to be examined, to speak of himself when for once there was so much outside himself that he wanted to see and to know: he suddenly resented the attentions of these two odd Englishmen who, for all he knew, were mocking him.

"Whatever I can," he said with a heavy attempt at lightness. "Take a job . . . I'm a lawyer, you know. I graduated from law school last June, from the one at Harvard."

"A lawyer?" Glenellen pronounced the word as though not quite sure what it meant. "How peculiar. No, I don't mean peculiar: I mean to say it seems so strange to find a personable young American who is not trying to be a painter or some such romantic thing among the ruins of our old

11

Europe. I suppose, Clyde, that we see only the romantic ones, the ones who have got away for a time."

"I think it most impressive, his being a lawyer. Original even."

"But, my dear Clyde, does one *want* to be impressed by young men? Isn't it far more agreeable to be *pleased* by them, charmed by their freshness and impracticality?"

"*I* am charmed," said Mr Norman, patting Philip's knee as the sun unexpectedly set: the light going from gold to gray, the air from warm to cool.

"Will you go into politics?" asked Glenellen.

"I may, yes. I've thought about it. My family is in politics, back home."

"You find it interesting?"

"Oh yes . . . but for a career, I don't know."

"And what are your politics?"

"Darkly reactionary, I suppose. In practice, however, I should, if ever in office, devote my time to staying there."

"No convictions . . . wonderful youth!" exclaimed Mr Norman, drinking the rest of his Cinzano. "How different you are from the young men of my day. How much more sensible. Tell me, would you like an ice or something? a little cake?"

"I don't think so . . . thanks."

Glenellen looked at him thoughtfully. "I would like very much to have a chat with you one day about European politics. I have certain insights which may interest you, certain schemes which . . . but more I cannot say, for now. Though let me add that when I was your age, I, like you, was interested primarily in the progress of my own life, my time given to hobbies. . . ."

"Hobbies?"

"A joke of Lord Glenellen's, Mr Warren," said Clyde Norman quickly, too quickly thought Philip, and he wondered what was not being said for his benefit.

"A joke, Mr Warren, yes, a joke . . . and here is the wicked Guido. Late! You're late! Hear me?"

The wicked Guido heard and he smiled a smile like polished bone. He was a slender well-proportioned Italian boy with a head like a Michelangelo and a body, as much as could be seen through his suit (a great deal), as fine as a Donatello.

"This is Guido," said Mr Norman urbanely as he and Philip rose and shook hands, while the high clear voice of the seated peer inveighed against the boy's character, accused him in English and Italian of monstrous crimes, denunciations which were received by the youth with a lovely smile.

"I was on my way stopped," he said, finally, when the querulous voice had paused for an instant; his English was good if original. "I find my brother has taken the only white good shirt of mine and so I went to my brother to receive the shirt once more for me. I want to look nice," he added simply, expressing his philosophy in five words.

"Shirts, suits, shoes, watches. . . ." Glenellen sighed and turned to Philip. "Those are the only things that really matter to these people."

"I like the motorcars, too," giggled Guido. "I like to drive very fast in *Alfa Romeo*. Oh good car, good car. I take cars apart. I know about things inside. Were you a soldier?" he asked all in one breath, noticing Philip as though for the first time.

"A sailor, for several years."

"In the war? In Italy?"

"In the war . . . in the Pacific."

"I knew many soldiers here. You might know some of them maybe. Nice men . . . very kind. I was fourteen years old so they gave me presents. A camera was given to me by one captain but it was stolen from me by one thief I know and he sells it."

"Come, Guido," said Glenellen, rising. "You can tell your stories to Mr Warren another time." He turned to Philip. "I would like to see you again one day soon, if I may." They shook hands. "Do you know the Baths of Nero?"

"I'm afraid not. I've only just arrived."

"That's so. Of course you wouldn't have had a chance. . . . Well, should you have a moment to spare, do drop by tomorrow afternoon around four. I always arrive at four and leave at five, like clockwork. . . . Marvelous for the figure, I've found. Not that you need to think of that quite yet, but we could talk. I have a plan which might interest you. Now I'm off. Many thanks, my dear Clyde, for introducing this young man to me."

Farewells were made and Glenellen hurried away, followed at a more leisurely pace by Guido, immaculate in his good white shirt.

"Splendid fellow," said Mr Norman as they watched the older man and the youth turn the corner beyond the Excelsior Hotel. "Difficult of course . . . one of the last of those eccentric peers my country used to produce with such abandon in the old days. The supply seemed inexhaustible but now of course, with currency restrictions and so on, Ayre is the last, the very last of a great line . . . and under a cloud, too."

"A cloud? But why?"

"Oh, for so many reasons. His life has been too colorful for one thing, too many hobbies. Then there was the scandal about his wife. I suppose you were too young to remember that."

"What happened to her?"

"I'm afraid he set fire to her at a party in the British Embassy at Berlin. There was the most terrible fuss made . . . relations were strained at the time and this was added fuel to the blaze, as it were. They got him out of Germany as quickly as possible. The Ambassador was furious and the party, needless to say, was ruined."

"And his wife?"

"Lady Glenellen was burned to a crisp. Fortunately they were able to get the Glenellen diamonds back . . . she had been wearing a good many of them at dinner, a number of quite important pieces too. The settings were badly melted, I believe, but Ayre had them remounted later in the Etruscan fashion, a stroke of genius as it later developed, for he started an Etruscan vogue in jewelry which lasted a number of years."

"Was he never prosecuted?"

"For making Etruscan art the vogue? Heavens no! He received a decoration from the Pope."

"I meant prosecuted for burning up his wife."

"Ah well," Mr Norman gestured vaguely, "she was an unpopular woman, a great hypochondriac and a bit of a religious maniac, too. Then of course there was some question as to whether the fire was his fault or hers."

"Who *was* responsible?"

"Who can say? All I know is that, as the ladies were getting up from dinner to go into the drawing room, he picked up the candelabra and hurled it at her, shouting, 'Be Joan of Arc, *if you dare!*' It was the addition of the 'if you dare' which saved him from more stern consequences since the phrase implied, you see, a certain choice in the matter. That she elected of her own free will to *be* Joan of Arc demonstrated a deliberate choice on her part and, as a result, he could hardly be held responsible for an act in which she so obviously concurred, perhaps even precipitated since

14

it was well known that she had always expected some sort
of martyrdom . . . ever since the day she married Glenellen,
in fact, fully aware of the extent and the nature of his
hobbies. Her life was one long expiation for the original
sin, as Catholics say, of having been born."

"You must tell me about his hobbies one day."

"I should be glad to, but best of all observe him yourself.
He will tell you all; show you everything . . . he has no
discretion, alas. You should go, by the way, to the Baths
of Nero tomorrow."

"Are they interesting?"

"I have always thought so. It depends upon one's taste, of
course." Mr Norman looked at him furtively and Philip
experienced a sudden weariness as he recognized the
ancient pattern, traditional and obvious, revealed perfunc-
torily, with little hope and less ceremony. He gave it back
to Mr Norman: gently, firmly, he folded it up and placed
it on the table before him; then, wiping the dust from his
hands, he guided the conversation to an end.

Mr Norman sighed. "I shall see you at the Baths then. I
often go there for the health's sake . . . to lose weight. I
get stout in the summer and slim in the winter, unlike the
rest of the world."

"Does Lord Glenellen live in Rome or England?"

"In Rome. He isn't allowed to enter England."

"Why not?"

"They disapprove of him. At least the Home Office does.
Being officials, they have no humor. They don't recognize
his very real value."

"Why do they disapprove?"

"Hobbies. But now it's getting very late. Where do you
plan to have dinner?"

"I hadn't thought."

"Then try the hotel. The food is very good there. I should
like to dine with you but I have a function I must attend
. . . dull sort of affair, part of my job, I fear." When the
waiter came there was a struggle for the check which Philip
won, as both knew from the beginning he would.

"Awfully good of you, really, but now of course you must
allow me to take you to dinner one night this week. Until
tomorrow then . . . the Baths of Nero. The hotel will
direct you."

They parted and Philip made his way alone through the
darkening streets to the hotel, elated and curious, aware
not only of himself but of the city, too. For an instant, he

15

was no longer separate but a part of it: an airy and fantastic bridge across the gulf challenged him and, deliberately, he moved across it, above the dark division, to the other side where strangers were.

Chapter Two

HIS FIRST DINNER in Rome was as good as Mr Norman had predicted it would be. He had dined alone with a volume of Byron's *Don Juan* before him on the table and as he ate antipasto and minestrone and chicken and drank chianti (the sort of Italian dinner that was served in America but seldom in Italy except at the better hotels, for tourists), he read of Don Juan's shipwreck and the hilarious account of the famished mariners who ate one another, beginning with Don Juan's tutor Pedrillo.

> "Part was divided, part thrown in the sea,
> And such things as the entrails and the brains
> Regaled two sharks, who followed o'er the billow—
> The sailors ate the rest of poor Pedrillo."

Excellent, he thought, murmuring the couplet to himself. Then feeling somewhat stuffed, he left the dining room, receiving the respectful bows of the maître d'hotel with a bemused expression which he hoped would be thought dignified but gracious. In the lobby the pink-cheeked desk clerk gave him a dolorous cocker-spaniel look and wished him a good evening.

A good evening? It was more than that: a splendid evening! warm and star-scattered. There was no moon, but he was too happy to object to this one omission as he strode down the Via Veneto in the direction of the *piazza* where he had been assured the Colosseum might be found. He hummed the only aria he knew from *Tosca* as he followed the curving Street of the Tritons toward the *galleria*. On the way he passed restaurants and *trattorias* all open, bright with undiffused light and loud with the noises of people eating and laughing and singing sad songs. Then he turned into the *galleria,* a massive arcade, not unlike a Gothic cathedral except, instead of a groined ceiling, it had dirty glass panels high overhead. Shops and bars like profane chapels edged the nave. Young boys and girls stood about

17

soliciting buyers, older youths sold drugs and *lire* and lovers with a sharp good humor, very different from the manner of such salesmen in other cities. Nothing was sordid here. The pimps, though shabby, were not at all sinister, and the boys and girls were cheerful, obviously more pleased than not to be making money in such an easy way. The young Swiss at the hotel had already instructed Philip in the current prices for girls, for virgins, for women and, with a blush or two, he had even quoted (from hearsay only, of course) the price for boys, and the one for men—there was a distinction, Philip had been amused to discover, but when he had pressed the young Swiss to define that difference he had only blushed all the more deeply and said that really he didn't know, he'd only heard tell, as everyone had.

But tonight Philip was not interested in finding a companion. He was on a mission of the spirit: to behold certain of the more profound Roman symbols by starlight. So, spiritually mighty, he paused in silence before the dark and rather unimpressive palace where, on a balcony, the fallen dictator had made so many appearances, burdening the newsreels of Philip's boyhood with a rock-jawed, insensitive face tilted with boundless assurance to a classic disaster. Few people frequented the square at night as though in deference to that battered ghost which still seemed, Philip felt, to brood over the palace, arm raised forever in a facsimile Roman salute; dwarfed, however, in death as in life by the fantastic marble monument across the square, the pillared white temple of the first modern Italian king, Victor Emmanuel, now a resident with the dictator in that limbo which some clever god has no doubt devised with the express purpose of maintaining the onetime great men of our world in a state of eternal discomfort, of perpetual desire and thwarted will. Philip, meditating comfortably on the folly of human enterprise, crossed the square, dodging the occasional cars which darted about, lights blazing and horns shrieking. He paused and asked a policeman where the Colosseum might be. Having had this one sentence already prepared for several weeks, he was confident that the other would be able to understand. The young policeman, with a gravely stupid frown, shook his head wonderingly and Philip said *"Grazie"* and turned down the street which seemed most likely to lead him to his goal.

It was the right street. He sensed that instinctively and he toyed with the idea of pretending to himself that he had been here before, that some atavistic memory was leading

18

him on to the center of the ancient city, over paths which in another life he had walked many times: a general returned from Parthia followed by his legions. He chuckled at the thought . . . more likely a prisoner from the island of Britain, a fair-skinned oaf with shaggy beard who'd probably fetch a better price at the slave market than an African, but not so good a one as an Asiatic.

Suddenly the modern buildings ceased and on either side he saw dark canyons a dozen feet lower than the street, and he could see dimly by starlight the ruins of the Forum, pale familiar shapes of broken buildings, shattered columns and arches, an occasional dark massive section of some government building still intact, reminiscent in style of nearly every railroad station in every American city. He walked slowly, quite alone. There were no other pedestrians and he wondered if perhaps the Romans had some feeling against frequenting ruins at night, the fear of ghosts, of all the bloody happenings which had taken place among this broken stone, the center once of a world of fine law and some order, an age of silver untarnished by that Christian blight which had coincided, somewhat suspiciously he'd always thought, with the dark ages.

The avenue widened and there before him, illuminated by several floodlights, was the Colosseum, far higher than he'd ever imagined it to be, solemn in its age. He paused, awaiting revelation. None came, however . . . he was aware only that his legs were rather tired from walking and that his left shoe was pressing too tightly against his little toe. There it was, though, precisely as he'd imagined it would be from the various photographs he had studied years ago in school, in the days when he had read with excitement the stories of Livy and the *Lives of Plutarch* and the splendid, trimming letters of Cicero. Now by the floodlights which managed to diminish rather than enhance this relic, he was able to regain in a rush that youthful fascination with the past which, like a sudden tide in the blood, returned: a love of the old not merely because the old was in itself romantic nor because the worst of the dull sad moments had long ago been winnowed out by chroniclers too busy describing great deeds to note that the human condition (how he loved this echoing phrase: the human condition!) was constant in its confusion, in its vulnerability to pain. No, he loved the past for another reason: continuity, that was it. He'd always known instinctively that when he died the poignant progress of one Philip Warren would end for good. He had

19

known this from the day he'd first been told about death: when he was four years old and his grandfather had died in the room next to his. War had only confirmed him in this knowledge. Men whom he knew became after an air attack so many torn limp carcasses to be put in canvas bags and dropped into the sea, their personal belongings sent home to a faraway family (equipment gone through carefully beforehand, however, to make sure that no unusual letters, lewd photographs or contraceptive devices would be sent on to shock the grieved family). Nothing remained of these warriors but fast-blurring images in the minds of friends whose primary interest is never the devout recollection of the good dead but survival. Somewhere Thomas Hardy had written a poem on this theme, he recalled. But Philip, though he acknowledged change, valued the past, his own and the world's. He became, as he pondered, all the more impatient with detail, more curious about the whole design of which only tantalizing fragments had been revealed by scholars, men not unlike himself, in temperament at least, all haunted by the fact of change which they attempted, in the only way they knew, to define, by fixing the near-true moment in the careful prose of history.

"'O, call back yesterday, bid time return,'" Philip whispered as he descended a deep flight of steps and approached the crypt-like building, eroded by weather and scarred by all the visiting Northern warriors. With a sense of one about to make a discovery, he entered a dark archway, pausing midway through the building, suddenly alert, as he realized there were people all about him in the dark. He could see no one but he heard breathing, an occasional whispered word. Finally the lighting of a match revealed a pair of lovers while, behind them, stepping hastily into the shadows, thieves and murderers forgathered to contemplate acts of violence. Although conscious of danger, he was unafraid, protected by his own conception of this battered place: no one is murdered in a dream, he knew, and like a dreamer he walked out into the open and observed with nostalgia and delight the tiers of seats which circled an arena whose floor had been torn up by archeologists to reveal the complicated passageways beneath. This was Rome.

"Do you think the ruins of Madison Square Garden will look as impressive?"

He started. The voice, a woman's, laughed pleasantly. He turned and saw that she was behind him, seated on a fallen column.

"Perhaps," he said evenly, moving toward her. "Have you been here long?"

"On this column? No, not very, a few minutes. . . ."

"How could you tell I was an American?"

"Only an American would come here at night and walk out into the arena. An Italian would have hid beneath the arches, doing business."

"Are we the only romantics?"

"It would seem so."

Was she young or old, he wondered, pretty or beautiful or plain? He could not tell. He moved beside her and caught the odor of her perfume.

"You're a student, aren't you?" she asked.

"In what sense?" he parried, remembering this stylized phrase so often used in intellectual debate when one warrior of the word, needing time to compose a new strategy, invites the other to lose his way in definition.

She laughed again, mockingly. "Now I know you must be a student. Scholarly young men always want to know 'in what sense' any question is intended."

He laughed, too. "I was stalling," he said, wondering whether he should tell her a lie or not. If she were old or plain he would not for a moment have hesitated to make himself sound as romantic as the occasion and the setting insisted that he be. If she were desirable he would of course be romantic about *her* and stick only to the facts, favorably arranged. Which should he do? What should he be? He paused, knowing that his decision would be irrevocable, that, if she were to be one day a lover, it would never do to begin by telling her that he was one of the heroes of the Air Force, now doomed to travel feverishly about until the cancer which had already begun to spread to his nerve centers (explaining that tiresome lisp) finally, and in great agony, brought him Icarus-like to earth. No, he would play it safe, he decided; and moving closer to her, he said: "I graduated from law school a month ago."

"How young you must be," she said, and his heart sank: he was positive now that she must be sixty with a strong resemblance to his mother. He backed away, wondering if it was too late to speak of his fatal disease.

"No, not so young," he said.

"Then you are one of the veterans who went back to school."

"Yes." He waited for an opening.

21

"What was it like, going back? Didn't you feel too wise to be taught?"

"I always felt too wise to be taught," he said, stumbling into an epigram, "but not, I hope, too wise to learn."

"Oh, I hope not." And again he caught the mocking note in her voice. Well, I earned it that time, he thought, grimly. "You're a lawyer now?"

"Yes . . . believe it or not."

"It doesn't seem so incredible. There have been other lawyers."

"But I never thought *I* should be one."

"Why not? what would you have rather been?"

"I don't know . . . probably nothing at all. I would have made a very fine dilettante in the eighteenth century . . . the sort that had theories on everything and wrote long careful letters to friends."

"You were born too late for that. Everyone must struggle now."

"A pity, isn't it?"

"I don't think so." She was now going to become serious, he could see, and the advantage would all be his. He had been on the defensive as long as she questioned or mocked him; but now she was vulnerable and he felt very much better. She said: "I suppose it's fashionable now to avoid responsibility, to speak lightly of Armageddon as though it were really of no concern."

"What can one man do, or fifty men, or even a million . . . if you could imagine a million men, or fifty of them for that matter, being united on any policy. What *can* they do? How can they alter the direction of life?"

"You sound so fatalistic."

"Not really," said Philip, wishing to get the conversation back to earth again, to himself and to the story he had planned to tell her of the sanitarium where he had spent the last year, and of this final fling before the end (had he not been warned that if he came down to sea level before the five years of his cure were up he would die?).

"Have *you* any interest in politics?"

"Only a spectator's."

"But you're a lawyer."

"What has that to do with it?"

"You know perfectly well what that has to do with it . . . the law is the first step in most political careers."

"So?"

"Have you money? Aside from what you earn?"

22

"I have enough. I've never earned anything yet . . . except my Navy pay."

"Are you married?"

"No, and I'm not likely to be." This was better. He was about to inquire into her status but she gave him no opportunity.

"Then obviously you have everything . . . and how you could enjoy yourself if you wanted to, in politics too."

"Talking to dull people all day? Smiling at my cretinous constituents and promising them all the things they have never had? It doesn't sound like fun to me."

"But can't you imagine yourself the head of state? making important decisions? striking an admired pose for your . . . cretinous public?"

"Too easily . . . I fight against the temptation."

"Then you *are* tempted?"

"Of course, but the fact that I'm reasonable now doesn't mean I should act reasonably if placed in a different situation."

"Then you *could* imagine yourself involved in politics?"

"I can imagine myself involved in anything . . . the one virtue of having served in a war is that one quickly learns nothing is unlikely. I can do anything."

"But would you like it?"

"I would have a real contempt for the whole business."

"But would you like it?"

"Probably." He qualified, partly from conviction, out of a desire to be as nearly accurate as words would allow and partly to see what she would say next, to determine, if he could, the reason for her curious urgency.

"Ah. . . ." She had got her way and for a moment she did not speak. Both stared across the trenched arena toward the tiers of seats on the other side. Stars shone large and white in the black sky. Beneath the dark arches of the building, struck matches, for brief instants, glowed like fireflies on a summer lawn. The air was still. There was no wind and, though he tried, he could not hear the sounds of the modern city which he knew must be all about them, outside this much-scarred oval of antique marble. An occasional voice, muffled and secret, came to him from the archways but, excepting those near-by voices, the rest was silence. What would she say? She asked him where he was from and when he told her, she laughed and asked him his name. He told her this, too, and she said, "I know your family."

"Oh no! I'll never escape, I see."

"Why escape? You have so much to do . . . Philip, and there isn't much time."

His name sounded odd to him, spoken like this in the warm Roman dark by a stranger, by a woman who apparently knew all about him though he knew nothing of her.

"What do you mean, not much time? Are you speaking prophetically?"

"Oh no . . . just relatively, I suppose. I was thinking how short lives are at best, and since you are thirty. . . ."

"Not quite."

"Not quite . . . and presuming you live to be seventy, your life at this moment is half gone."

"Nearly half."

She laughed and repeated, "Nearly half."

"Then, of course, you could so easily be killed in a new war. But somehow I feel you will survive it."

"So do I. But how did you guess I'd planned to avoid it?"

"I'm intuitive, I suppose."

"You must be. Yes, I've very elaborate plans for keeping out of the trouble. First, I shall have all my teeth taken out. . . ." He paused; then: "Where did you know my family?"

"In Hudson. My husband knows your father very well."

"And your husband, what's his name?"

"Rex Durham . . . my name is, as you probably know, and a poor joke it is after all these years, Regina."

He said nothing for a moment. He was surprised and amused and, against his will, more than a little impressed. All his life he had heard of Rex Durham and he still remembered, years ago, when Durham had married Regina: Rex and Regina. For fifteen years he had heard stories about them. Their parties, their deeds (both amatory and political). Durham was the boss of the party which was the boss of their state and the state, often as not, was the boss of the country. Philip's father had always been proud that he knew Rex well enough to call him by his first name, while his mother had always thought Regina lovely, "in a hard sort of way."

"No wonder," said Philip at last, "you're so interested in politics."

"No wonder," she echoed. "But tell me, have we ever met before? I must be honest and say I remember almost no one I meet, unless I've been briefed in advance."

24

"No, we've never met. But I was thirteen when you were married . . . I remember that very clearly. My parents were at the Albany reception."

"I remember, too. I mean, I remember your mother and father that day. I was twenty then," she added self-consciously.

"I know."

"Time passes," she said. "Shall we go?" She stood up, facing him in the dark. She was taller than he had suspected, not much shorter than himself, and her body was indeed slim. Her face he had imagined from the many photographs he'd seen of it: dark hair drawn severely back, thin mouth, arched nose, and black eyes with thick brows. He knew all the details, knew they made handsome photographs. He was curious to see how those familiar features looked in life.

Beyond the Colosseum, they both stopped as though by mutual consent beneath the first lamppost and examined one another with, he thought uneasily, that shameless eagerness which in the past had meant only one thing; and that one thing, he'd already decided, was out of the question for a number of reasons, all good.

As he looked at her he wondered if, perhaps, electric light was not in its way as false as photography. For this light was stark and dramatic and it made her face deathly white. It made the features bold as it cast dark shadows in all the hollows, emphasizing her large deep-set eyes. She wore no hat and her hair seemed pale and rather dull, not gray nor yet blonde but somewhere in between; not dark like the newspaper photographs, nor as severe. She seemed very young to him or, rather, ageless; a woman with handsome features and a tranquil expression.

"I thought you would look older," she said, smiling.

"I thought you would, too," he said, without thinking.

She laughed at this. Yet, suddenly self-conscious, she stepped out of the light. "You're not very gallant," she said.

"I'm sorry. I didn't think . . . one of those unfortunate sentences that don't mean what they say."

"Don't make too many of them or we'll never get you elected."

"Am I running for office?"

"Of course. Let's go back to the hotel . . . you must meet Rex, you know."

"Now? this very minute?"

"Why not? Are you afraid?"

25

"No, just uncertain. I never know what to say to politicians."

"He isn't like a politician. Besides, you'll have to learn how to talk to everyone easily. There's a trick to it."

"You'll really teach me all those things?" He was careful to disguise his amusement.

"Of course."

"Why?"

"For reasons of state," she said evenly, as though the phrase had been long prepared in her mind awaiting the proper moment to be spoken, to disguise, he was quite sure, her true intentions whatever they might be.

"I haven't consented yet," he said lightly as they approached the mammoth white confection which contained the martial spirit of that dull king who fathered the no less dull and now, thought Philip, fortunately defunct royal house of Savoy. A bat suddenly swooped across their path, circled in front of them and doubled back to the vast ruins of the Forum behind them.

"But you will," she said seriously. "You'll see, I think, that you must. For many, many reasons that I will give you one day, if you like."

"I should like to hear them."

"I should like to tell them to you. I wonder why you seem so much younger than you really are."

"Because I lisp, I suppose. It's my cross . . . before my voice changed I was considered the sissy of all time. After it changed I was considered very sweet and everyone wanted to protect me."

"The way I do?"

"I don't know. By the way, how am I to succeed in politics if I can't talk straight?"

"Stop finding difficulties."

"Tell me, do you know Lord Glenellen?"

"No, I don't think so. Why?"

"I only wondered."

It was almost midnight when they arrived at the Excelsior. The lobby was nearly empty as they turned to the right of the desk and walked downstairs to a crowded bar. As they walked between the red damask walls, he caught a glimpse of her in the mirror and saw her, he realized, for the first time. Among glass and damask and well-dressed people, she moved with purpose, pale and strange, foreign not only to this room, to these people, but in a sense to all that was familiar. He wondered with some amusement how she

26

managed to please her husband's political friends, for she was abrupt in a way sure to be resented. But then, too, it occurred to him that she might after all be a good actress and that the figure he saw crossing the room was an actress hurrying from her dressing room to the wings, mumbling lines to herself, oblivious of the supers who stepped aside, making way for the star.

Philip stepped forward like Ganymede prepared to meet Jove and, with a smile, he shook the hand of Rex Durham who had risen to greet them. The introductions were quickly and skillfully made and before the first Scotch and water had been brought, Rex had been told all that he would ever need to know of the past life and deeds of Philip, who said nothing while his protectress (or temptress, he was not sure which) instructed her lord.

Rex Durham was a tall man, heavily built, with a great head and large gray eyes, which, Philip noticed, could look either commanding or stupid, and nothing else. The brow was massive and deeply lined and his hair was a thick chrome-silver, while the square strong face was ruddy and healthy. He was just fifty, powerful, admired, and married to a remarkable woman, a combination of good things which, Philip reflected, might combine to destroy a lesser man. But Rex was in no sense a lesser man. He was a major one. He was, at this moment in his history, leader of the party and in rank a member of Congress. He believed, like all good bosses, that it was wiser to remain out of important office, away from the direct influence of the frivolous ballot box which could occasionally (though, he saw to it, not often) upset the most reasonable of combinations for the most irrelevant of reasons. He represented, Philip recalled, his own district on the melancholy-green banks of the Hudson River.

"Been waiting for you for half an hour, Regina," said Rex clearing his throat oratorically, trumpeting.

"I lost my way," she said. "Then, when I finally got there, I met this young man and we talked for a long time. He walked me back." Rex looked at Philip with the large gray eyes empty, not seeing. "He's one of your constituents," she added, "that's why I've been so nice to him. He's Judge Warren's son."

"Judge Warren! Old friend of mine, young man. I'm very fond of your father, very fond indeed. Do remember me to him when you write him next. We've been through a lot of campaigns together, the Judge and I. Wonderful old devil."

27

Rex's manner had changed and his eyes glittered as he reminisced. "But isn't that remarkable, Regina," he said, turning to his wife with an ingenuous air, "your finding a boy from our own backyard right in the middle of the Colosseum. . . ."

"In the middle of the night, too," she added. "I thought you would be pleased."

"Certainly am. So you're Judge Warren's son. You were in the war, weren't you?"

The catechism was then read through with a degree of simulated interest and vigor on both sides; Philip impressed by the older man's legend, while the older man, used from habit to flattering others, conducted the questioning with ease. It was soon done and they drank Scotch thoughtfully as the room suddenly filled with noisy young Americans, cheerful and handsome and a little drunk. The boys had crewcuts and wore seersucker suits. Their innocent faces were tanned from long drives through the golden country-side with short-haired, full-skirted girls. They filled the bar, four couples, collegiate and simple.

"They're really enjoying themselves," commented Regina with an inexplicable neutrality; he was disappointed that she did not share his pleasure.

Rex talked politics. He mentioned great names, many great names. He did not drop them to impress, the way an ordinary man might have done. No, he fired them in volleys. He was discreet for all his bluffness, and Philip knew the other was trying deliberately to appear frank while saying nothing that a reasonably dedicated reader of *Time* magazine might not have known. But the effect was all that could be desired and Philip listened with pleasure to a description of the Pope's views on the world's state.

"Grave, very grave."

Then he reported to Regina on his day and they spoke over Philip's head as though he were not there or were a child.

"Saw Jim this afternoon, after I left you."

"And he said?"

"Wouldn't be able to play ball with us . . . going to handle the whole thing through State . . . regardless."

"But didn't you tell him . . ."

"How could I? As long as they have confidence in him, I'm helpless."

"But not quite."

"No, not quite . . . the President . . ."

Their conversation at this moment became so very grand that Philip wondered if he should not tiptoe out of the room which had, with only a magic word or two, become, somewhat incongruously, a residence of majestic intrigue, despite the boisterous young people at the next table who were debating whether or not they should drive to Ostia that night and go swimming.

Rex Durham predicted a major war within thirty-six months.

"Let's not talk about that," said Regina uneasily.

"We must, though. It would never do to be unprepared again."

And here we go again, thought Philip: all his life there had either been talk of a war just ended or one about to begin or, and in a way best of all, a war in progress. Somehow the fact was never so terrible as the anticipation, as the gloomy predictions which his family in particular had indulged in all his life, confident as they were that they would some day be swept away by a common catastrophe, a major war or, failing that, a popular uprising. They belonged to that small class in America which regards itself as aristocratic, a wealthy class, nicely educated and as old in a tradition as the people of a new country can be . . . which is old enough, thought Philip, trying to recall the origins of the Durham family, deciding at last as he recalled some half-forgotten bit of gossip that Rex must have belonged to one of the new families, a self-made man or the son of one. But soon it would make no difference if his own father's prediction were to come true or not: the old man believed their days were numbered and that the old freedom their class had enjoyed was, with each year, being surrendered bit by bit as the taxes increased and the business of the government became larger and more oppressive, more concerned with the details of its citizens' lives in an effort, partly benevolent and mostly political, to sustain a majority of the voters in the gray and uniform security of a nursery where the eccentric and the private would not be permitted; and their own society, for the most part as stolid and as nearly virtuous as any reformer could wish, would vanish and their lawn-circled houses would serve to house girls' schools and asylums for the insane (the latter drawn more and more, Philip was certain, from the wise and the sensitive and the formerly free).

Rex had got to his feet. Rex was going to bed. Rex was tired.

"It's been a pleasure, young man. I hope we'll see a lot of you now that we're all here in Rome together. Far from home."

Tall elms, only somewhat blighted, black twisted locust trees, glittering copper beeches, green lawns and silver river: home was the same place for all of them. Philip bade the Durhams good-night or, as it turned out, only Mr Durham, for Regina said that she was not yet sleepy and that she would like to sit up a few minutes longer.

"Regular night owl," commented Rex, as Philip knew he would.

Then he was alone in the bar with Regina. The young people had, with a good deal of noise, departed just before Rex, their destination as far as Philip could determine still undecided.

"It's late," said Philip.

"Yes," said Regina, "very late."

Contemplating the lateness, they looked at one another across the table, aware of the silence in the room, empty except for a sleepy waiter on a high stool behind the bar.

"Do you like it?" she asked.

"Yes, very much," he said, not sure what she meant, willing to match her ambiguousness with his own.

"I do, too, very much. You'll spend a year in Europe, then? A year traveling?"

"So I've planned."

"Afterwards you'll come home?"

"I may come home, yes."

"But you may not."

"It's possible. The year has only begun."

"Only begun," she repeated thoughtfully, then: "You will be coerced, you know, by all of us."

"Am I as valuable as all that?"

"Of course . . . don't you think you are?"

"Naturally, but I wasn't aware that the world valued me as much as I do."

"But it does."

"A great responsibility."

"Of course. You *are* responsible . . . that is the meaning of the whole business."

"What business?"

"Being alive. Responsibility, action, to live usefully."

"For others?"

"Why not? Wherever the greater glory lies."

"One wants glory?"

"Oh, more than anything else! To live grandly, to shape the world!"

He laughed. "It's too rich a diet for me. In any case, I've already given you my opinion of politics."

"Shallow, smart opinions. You didn't mean what you said."

"But I did. Besides, I'm a shallow person. That's why I've come to Europe, to grow deep."

"You're making fun of me."

He smiled. "No, not at all. Only I don't think it's worth the trouble. You're wasting too much interest on me. Let's talk of something else . . . Mr Durham."

"My husband? What of him?"

"An unusual man."

"I think so. A political genius, if politicians can be said to have genius. I respect him."

"Will he be President?"

She looked at him without expression; as though she had not heard or had not understood. She answered elliptically, "Is he the sort, do you think?"

"I don't know. I mean, after all, he's your husband."

"Yes, he is. Would you like to be President?"

"I don't think so."

"It could happen."

"Nonsense."

"You don't know, you don't know," she repeated, shaking her head. The bartender, who had been asleep, fell off his stool. He got to his feet, blinking.

"Tell me something else," said Regina.

"What do you want to know?"

"Tell me . . ." she paused; then changed the question, "Tell me a story," she said.

"Any sort?"

"Yes, please."

"Once upon a time there was a mother who had five children. She was very proud of them in her way, but her way was very severe for she was ambitious. She made up her mind that she would make them the most successful children in the world and so every day she beat them until she had taught them how to fly. In time they got so they could fly very well indeed. They could glide and soar and do arabesques five thousand miles up; naturally, people thought very highly of them."

"Then what happened?"

31

"Oh, they flew away from home and joined a circus and became very rich."

"And their mother?"

"They never saw her again."

"Do you like that story?"

"Not very much."

"I don't like it either."

"It's getting late."

"Is it late?" She looked at a small diamond watch.

"Is there time?" he asked.

She nodded.

Chapter Three

THE ULTIMATE MOMENT. The splendid act. The joining of body and spirit in one breathing center about which
the earth and stars revolve, counter to all the established
laws of the empiricists who know only detail, and that
partly, while lovers know truth wholly. Or, to put it
less grandly, it is great fun indeed for the lighthearted,
solemn and emotionally edifying for the rest, the ones who
are aware of the tradition involved in the long duet, and
who approach it reverently, even fearfully, if the Puritan
spirit has by chance spoiled them as it has spoiled so many,
even now in these relatively enlightened days when most of
the fear has gone out of the act.

Union. An end of loneliness, exaltation, a moment compared to which all other moments are tedious and unbearable. What more can one say? Since Pindar, it has been said
all in a rush (and presumably before that in Babylon,
China, Egypt and the gnomic land of Crete), and so nowadays one must confine oneself to the peripheral rather than
to the central aspects of the business, the splendid game in
which we are all, to the best of our capacities, engaged.

Now, part of the pleasure one gets from reading novels is
the inevitable moment when the hero beds the heroine or,
in certain advanced and decadent works, the hero beds
another hero in an infernal glow of impropriety. The mechanical side of the operation is of intense interest to everyone. Partly, of course, because so few of us get entirely
what we want when it comes to this sort of thing and, too,
there is something remarkably exciting about the sex lives
of fictional characters. For one thing, there is so much
clear and precise talk both before and after the act. So
much talk that one feels far more clearly engaged than one
does in life where the whole thing is often confused and
clumsy. Also, there is a formidable amount of *voyeurism* in
us all and literature, even better than pornographic pictures,
provides us at its best with an excitation occasionally more
poignant than the real thing.

I have, of course, overstated the case, and Philip presents something of a problem at this point. Like most young Americans of his age and class, he has a tendency toward promiscuity, toward "emotional brashness," as an eminent English critic once remarked, rather sternly, of contemporary novels and their faithless, aimless protagonists. Philip is not, of course, aimless but his approach to sexual matters lacks the solemnity which those of us who care deeply for man's highest emotion demand of that most intimate union between man and woman. Taking all of this into account, it would, I know, be wisest to avoid the subject altogether and begin this new chapter as though nothing untoward had happened that evening in the Excelsior Hotel. One could indicate, perhaps, that the relationship between Regina and Philip had somehow magically deepened or, better yet, a fistful of asterisks tossed over the page might solve everything; and one would be praised for reticence since there are always a great many American ladies (of both sexes) who tell one that there are enough unpleasant things in the world without reading about them in books, lovemaking, significantly enough, being considered very nearly the most unpleasant activity of all. But, nevertheless, I feel obligated to reveal as candidly as I think proper what happened between Philip and Mrs Durham on the fourth floor of the Excelsior Hotel in a room separated from Mr Durham's by a sitting room and a locked door.

First, despite the essential beauty of the act, the union was not well made. There were a number of small frictions, tiny annoyances, which almost always occur between two people who are not yet properly attuned to one another and who are also overexcited by the novelty and the danger of what they are doing.

Philip had only half his mind on what he was doing. The other half was listening, somewhat frantically, for the sound of Mr Durham rattling the locked door and demanding entrance. Philip had placed his clothes on a chair in such a fashion that he could get into them with a speed which always did credit to his military training (shirt inside jacket, drawers inside trousers). Regina did her best, however, to put him at his ease, remarking that Mr Durham seldom demanded his marital rights, his energies, as far as she knew, being devoted to the greater business of controlling Presidents.

Now, one hardly knows how far to go in describing

34

precisely what happened. There is the brutal school, which uses the blunt words to get to the point. Then there are the incredibly popular lady novelists who titter and leer, describing the hero's great, rough (yet sensitive) hands and the back of his bronzed neck (for some unaccountable reason, the back of the neck has become, for the female at least, an erotic symbol of singular fascination). Then there are the sort to whom the business is very beautiful and very fine, the center of the book, tender and warm and serious, very serious. Much is described, as much is left to the imagination. One is moved and, should the novelist be a good one, the scene can have a remarkable immediacy. Yet, in this particular case at least, we must attempt another method. For Philip is not brutal nor is the back of his neck bronzed nor is he in love with Regina. He finds her attractive and desirable and it seems to him like a very pleasant way to spend his first night in Rome. In the words of that English critic, he is "emotionally brash," though it is to be hoped that in the year of self-discovery he has so wisely elected to embark upon he will come into a proper relationship with another human being, thus giving a certain emotional richness to the deed which, in Regina's cool arms, he lacks.

Cool arms. Now we come to it. At seventeen minutes after two o'clock they entered the bedroom. Regina turned on the light, took her rings and bracelets off and accepted his embrace. By two-thirty, more or less, they were both undressed and investigating one another with some pleasure. Regina's body was very fine. She was not too heavy. Her waist was slim and taut. Her hips were somewhat large but handsomely curved. Her breasts were not in the least unusual; they did not sag while, on the other hand, they did not point skyward like mounds of ice cream, the way the glands of girls in magazine advertisements are supposed to point. Her skin was rather brownish and quite smooth.

Philip has been described already in some detail. It should be noted here, however, that he had very little hair on his body, a characteristic which seemed to appeal enormously to Regina who caressed his chest and belly with some intensity. Genitally, he did not in the least resemble those lewd markings on the walls of public conveniences. He was properly and sturdily endowed, normally shaped and without any peculiarities. He was capable of a

35

spirited performance, guided by an intuition of the other's rhythm which often bordered on the miraculous. Tonight, however, because of nerves, his performance was violent and boyish rather than sensible and manly. Conscious of this tension, Regina helpfully murmured an occasional direction, but the stars were not right and the act, which lasted seventeen minutes, counting preliminaries of course, was not epoch-making in either of their lives. On the other hand, it afforded each some relief and the previous atmosphere of tension was succeeded by a state akin to euphoria.

The final details are not particularly relevant. Needless to say, Philip was anxious to leave, afraid of that locked door opposite the bed through which at any moment he expected to hear the rumbling of the husband's querulous voice. Regina turned on the light and they looked at each other with considerable interest, even critically now that desire was for a time allayed. Happily, they found that even under these somewhat exacting circumstances they were still charmed by one another and it was immediately apparent to both that they would, with some pleasure, repeat the act whenever in the future an opportunity should present itself.

Regina gave a number of dates and times when she felt opportunities would arise. They decided that, all in all, late afternoon was the best time to meet and his hotel the best place in which to reaffirm their passion. After a few more remarks (all whispered) they parted and Philip returned through darkened streets to his hotel where he slept without dreaming until noon the next day.

He was awakened by a gentle but insistent rapping at the door. "Come in," he said, sitting up, still half asleep.

"I can't," said a faraway British voice. "The door is locked."

"Wait a minute." Philip grabbed an enormous bath towel and wrapped it about himself like a cloak; then he opened the door and admitted Clyde Norman.

"Ah, you were bathing," said Mr Norman, rather pleased. "You Americans bathe every day, I'm told. Go ahead. Don't let me interrupt you."

"Oh, that's all right," said Philip vaguely, "come on in." Now that he was awake he did want to take a bath but modesty prevented him: there was no bathroom, only the curtained alcove which contained the bathtub and the bidet, this last an object of considerable fascination to Philip who thought it wicked.

"Don't you find it terribly unhealthy, bathing I mean? Doesn't it open up the pores dreadfully? I have a weak chest and so I take no chances. I never bathe."

"I'm afraid I've never thought about it," said Philip, getting back into bed. Clyde Norman went to the window and pulled back the curtains, admitting a flood of yellow light. In the street Philip could hear a newsboy shouting.

"You don't mind, do you? It's quite warm out."

"No, not at all. I've only just got up. I was very tired, you know . . . the train and all that."

"I should think so. Your first morning in Rome! How wonderful for you!"

Mr Norman sat down in the room's only armchair, crushing Philip's trousers beneath him. "I come," he said, making himself comfortable, "from Lord Glenellen, who would like you to play bridge with us tonight at his place. There will be only four people, counting yourself, should you come. Ayre, myself, you and Ayre's secretary, a pleasant Welsh boy named Evan Morgan who can't sing a note."

"Sing?" Philip was beginning to wake up at last.

"The Welsh all sing," said Mr Norman easily, "like your Negroes."

"Do they?"

"Of course they do. All except Evan, who doesn't sing one note properly though Ayre likes to listen to him. Ayre claims he's the only real interpreter of the Bardic songs . . . a minor peculiarity of his Lordship's and, to my mind, the only really insupportable one. The poor child is often called on to render a song or two after dinner and once every season there is a recital . . . all very sad, but then one must allow for human nature."

"I suppose so. Yes, I should like to play bridge. What time?"

"After dinner, at ten. I'm afraid we won't be invited to dinner . . . Ayre hates to serve food though he's one of the richest men in England . . . or, I should say, *out* of England."

"He seems unpleasant," said Philip sharply.

"Yes, doesn't he?" Mr Norman was bland. "It's very strange how unsympathetic people seem when described by a good friend. But of course in life all the unpleasant characteristics are blended in such a way that, to the friend at least, the result is most agreeable. To an outsider, Ayre must seem a monster. His reputation is not only frightful, it's frightening. Yet I find him one of the dearest people in the world."

Mr Norman paused sentimentally and Philip looked away uncomfortably, afraid he would find a tear on the other's sallow cheek.

Fortunately Mr Norman changed the subject. "What did you do last night?"

"I went to the Colosseum."

"But there was no moon."

"I know. I wanted to see it anyway."

"And did you? Could you?"

"Oh yes. It's lit up on the outside at least. Inside it was dark."

"Rather dangerous, too. You should be careful."

"I met an American couple while I was there."

"Of course. I should have known that the Colosseum at night would attract all sorts of Americans, as well as murderers and thieves and pimps. Who were they?"

"The couple? A Mr and Mrs Durham."

"Not the politician?"

"The same. Friends of my family."

"How very interesting! I've already met them, or rather I've seen them at the Embassy. There was a garden party given for them last week. It rained. Do you know them well?"

"No. I'd never met either of them before."

"How strange they'd be sightseeing in the middle of the night. He seemed such a hard, shrewd man . . . so very American."

"Anyway, we all went back to the Excelsior for a drink." Philip had a natural inclination to cover his tracks, an instinct which was at the same time usually undone by a need to discuss at length everything which had happened to him or might yet happen to him. He was sufficiently wise, however, to include Mr Durham in the starlight meeting, to allay any possible suspicion on the part of Mr Norman who, fortunately, had none at all along these lines but perhaps a suspicion along another, or at least a hope, faint but persistent.

"Then you must know them quite well by now."

"Not even Americans work that fast."

"But you'll see them again."

38

"Very likely, yes."

"I see." Mr Norman shut his eyes. It was a trick he had when he was about to make an announcement or to change the subject. Philip, wanting now to have his coffee and a bath, wished he would make his pronouncement quickly and go. Mr. Norman was capable of a mild surprise or two, however, for instead of some vague observation he asked a question. "You care much for politics?"

Philip moaned softly.

"I've heard nothing but politics for the past twenty-four hours. No, I'm not interested in them at all. I have decided that I'm going to be a water-colorist," he said inventively, surprising even himself with this choice of profession.

"How nice. Whom will you study with?"

"A Russian who lives in Paris. You probably don't know him."

"I see. Well, isn't that nice?"

"It's what I've always wanted," said Philip softly, gathering the towel about his neck and pointing his bare feet like a ballet dancer. Mr Norman watched the toes, an unpleasantly rapt expression on his ordinarily serene face. Philip wondered absently if perhaps Mr Norman liked boots.

"Do you approve of the Communist Party?" asked Mr Norman at last, with an effort removing his somewhat febrile attention from Philip's toes to his face, unshaven for two days now and covered with a golden stubble.

"No," said Philip.

"Do you approve of monarchy?"

"Why?"

"I should like to know. If I seem to pry, do tell me and I won't ask you any more questions."

"Yes, I like kings very much. In a decorative sense."

"I see I . . . I had to know."

Mr Norman laughed apologetically. "Fortunately, you said what I thought you would. You see, we've already looked into your history. Rather thoroughly, if I say so myself."

"We? Who's we? And why are you interested in what I think?"

"I can't answer either question yet," said Clyde Norman smoothly, enjoying the mystery.

"I'm not sure I like this at all," said Philip, sitting up

39

and swinging his legs over the side of the bed, the towel falling about his body in toga-like folds.

"Don't be alarmed. It's just that both Ayre and I were quite impressed with you yesterday and we may ask you to help us in something."

"In what?"

"I'm afraid I can't say. Ayre may tell you tonight. In fact, I can say almost certainly that he will tell you tonight, ask you to become one of us."

"Oh no . . . none of that," said Philip a little harshly, causing a blush to come to Mr Norman's usually pleasant face.

"I am speaking of a political movement," said Mr Norman evenly, retaining some but not all of his usual dignity.

"I know," said Philip, confused and embarrassed. "I meant . . ."

"I'm sure you will be interested in it. The fact that you know Rex Durham makes you all the more necessary to us . . . if you will but help us." He paused impressively, once again master of the dialogue.

"I'd like to hear all about it," said Philip contritely, eagerly, willing to do anything to erase the memory of his ungraciousness.

"Good," said the conspirator, getting to his feet. "I shall call for you at eight. We will dine in a *trattoria* I know and then on to our bridge game." He chuckled and, with the noise of Philip's good offices and protestations of friendship in his long hairy ears, he departed, well pleased.

Philip bathed. Then he had coffee sent up and he drank it thoughtfully. Finally dressed, with a minor anthology of major poetry under one arm, he set out for the Forum to commune with that splendid age to which he had always been mystically drawn, as though to a point of origin until now too obscured by distance to be more to him than a dream of home, a ghost or a shadow of a time of splendor. And so he came to the great pit which contained the squares and streets, the monuments and office buildings of that age, and after buying the inevitable ticket, he passed under a triumphal arch and walked solemnly down the grass-grown, moss-decked Sacra Via toward the hill where Capitoline Jove once sat in his temple and where today the tower of a building of state, the work of Michelangelo, dominates this marble wreck of a world which still contained for Philip, despite the shattered

walls and broken arches, a certain grandeur divorced
from reality perhaps but, in effect, in essence, no less valid
for that reason: a world which he wished to absorb
directly, the way he had, years ago, read the stories of
Livy and the poems of Horace, with the aid of a trot.

It was both more and less than he had expected. He
had not anticipated such vastness: the ruins of the various basilicas and public baths startled him with their
unaesthetic massiveness. They seemed too ponderous, too
calculated to overawe. He wondered what a savage must
have thought, coming from the foggy green forests of
Germany to this stern behemoth of a city, this center of
the world. He stood looking up at a dome still intact, the
work of the penultimate and gentlest dynasty, and he
tried to think of it the way it had been. He failed completely, as he always did. He had no visual imagination,
only an emotional one; he could simulate attitudes and
re-create forgotten moods but he could not with any success people the past with figures that seemed to him
visually convincing. His Forum was altogether too much
like Times Square on a Saturday night when he stared at
it very hard, trying to imagine it as it was, Cicero and
Brutus, Catullus and Julius, but he got only a double exposure of the jostling, noisy, sinister New York crowd
against these delicate columns which contained only sky
and summer air; tall umber walls emerging from green
unexcavated hills and cliffs where coins and urns and
marble heads lay buried in subterranean rooms, smothered
in the fine brown earth of violent and unremembered days.

Tourists wandered in and out of the Temple of the
Vestal Virgins, remarking upon their reflections in an
oblong pool of stagnant water greener than the Tiber,
like a pea soup which has sat too long and gathered on
its surface an iridescent scum. Thinking of the Vestal
Virgins, Philip crossed the atrium of their house, past
a series of statues which looked for all the world like
a conclave of club ladies, serious and benign; at the first
bench, an austere one of marble, he sat down between a
pair of Corinthian-capped columns which supported a
solid fragment of pediment on which a frieze had once
been chiseled, a design now lost except for a man's shoulder and arm, preceded by the tail and buttocks of a
prancing stallion.

He looked about him. The day was cool and the sky
was clear and yet, in spite of this total realization of an

41

old wish, he was neither excited nor content. He felt lethargic, the way he had always imagined a man who has come suddenly into a long desired place in the world must feel: this is it; the rest will be repetition. He shut his eyes and the sun was warm on his eyelids. He breathed deeply, wanting to absorb all this, to be all this. But he was himself, he knew, opening his eyes suddenly very wide and staring straight into the sun, going blind for a moment, lost in a green-gold world of Catherine wheels.

And then, as several American ladies, well dressed and confidently equipped with Baedekers, studied reverently the remains of the Ministry of Colonies, under the impression it had once housed the god Dionysius and his erotic mysteries, Philip read:

> "Oh rose thou art sick!
> The invisible worm
> That flies in the night,
> In the howling storm,
>
> "Has found out thy bed
> Of crimson joy,
> And his dark secret lover
> Does thy love destroy."

This suited his mood, he decided gloomily, reading it again.

"Do you really think that's what they did?"

"Of course, Claire. I have read all about them."

"Just think, it happened right here, right where we're standing!"

Philip glared at them, imagined satyrs sweeping them up in hot goatish embraces and bearing them off to catacombs, their hats, handbags and Baedekers scattered among the ruins as final witness to their impiety. But they moved on, unmolested, and he repeated, " 'Oh rose thou art sick!' "

Feeling a little ill himself, though not much like a rose bewormed or not, he wandered off toward Capitoline Hill and its memory of Caesar's death and of Jove and of *his* slow death at the hands of that Eastern mother and her mortal son.

There was a telephone message from Regina when he got back to his hotel. He called her, and after some trouble with a non-English- and possibly non-Italian-speaking operator, he got through to her at her hotel. She sounded very far away.

"What did you do today?" she asked as they made awkward conversation, behaving like strangers who have contacted one another reluctantly and at the insistence of a mutual friend. He told her where he had gone and what he had seen.

"Real sightseeing," he added, obscurely ashamed at not having been more like the other Americans here, the worldly ones who spent their days in the cafés talking and their evenings practicing hobbies with the cheerful and ever amenable Romans who, for money, were available for any activity.

"Are you free this evening?" she asked.

"No, I'm afraid that . . ." He told her where he was going, pleased that he could at least claim a certain social success for himself in this strange city where he had had letters to no one, except that unofficial one, a large draft on youth and charm which, in proper proportion and for a time at least, can buy the vitiated heart of the world.

"Perhaps another time then?"

"Tomorrow at five?"

"The day after at five."

"I should like that."

"So would I."

"Shall we meet here?"

"If you like. I have so many things to tell you."

"So many things," he repeated. And then, since neither could think of anything else to say, made shy by the intimacy of their short acquaintance, they said good-by to one another and the two tiny mechanical clicks emphasized the distance between them.

Philip went down to the bar of the hotel at seven o'clock, only to find Mr Norman was not yet there. Two cherubic American ladies were drinking orangeade in one corner of the rather bleak clean little room with its tile floor and odor of antiseptic: a "sincerely Swiss room" had been Mr Norman's comment on it and, perversely, he liked it and made it, after Doney's of course, his club.

One of the ladies said to the other, "Would you like a straw, dear?"

"No. No thanks."

"Oh . . . I *like* a straw."

Mr Norman wore a handsome dark blue suit with unusually narrow lapels which made him seem quite foreign, while the striped shirt with plain white detachable collar only added to his quaintness in Philip's eyes. He apologized for being late, allowed Philip to pay for a quick round of Cinzanos. Then they went to Mr Norman's *trattoria*, a small dirty place with a great many electric-light bulbs and an accordion-playing tenor who sang "Catalina" with a ghastly tenderness which cloyed Philip but pleased Mr Norman, who asked for a number of other songs all having to do with the fate of Italian maidens who love unwisely in Amalfi, Sorrento and Venice.

A very fine *pasta con burro* was followed by an entree which Mr Norman claimed was the specialty of the house: lumps of pink meat containing unexpected bits of bone served in a tepid white cream sauce.

"What is it?" asked Philip as he felt a filling loosen, his teeth having come down hard on a bit of bone.

"Goat," said Mr Norman with a happy smile. "It *is* good, isn't it?"

The Palazzo Mettelli was a large building covered with buff-tinted stucco and roofed with tile. The façade, as presented to the Square of the Mettelli, was as shabby and inexpressive as the fountain in the center of the square which was attributed to one of Michelangelo's students, the one who failed the course, according to Mr Norman, as they paused to stare at the dirty water which trickled from a number of unusual outlets placed frivolously in various parts of several marble ladies who were oddly involved with bowls of fruit and a dolphin.

The interior, however, was much more impressive, thought Philip, as they were led by an Italian youth across the long entrance hall whose ceiling was encrusted with gold decorations and paintings of heaven where various members of the Mettelli were prominently displayed, chatting with the higher-ranking personnel of the heavenly host.

"There is no electricity in the Palazzo," said Mr Norman as the boy led them through the great hall which, though handsomely tapestried, was not furnished. At the end of the hall they paused while their guide lit a new candle. "Ayre has never liked electricity."

"Why not?" asked Philip as they followed the boy up a wide marble staircase which curved into darkness, a place of unexpected drafts of air which made the candle flicker crazily. "I don't know. I never asked him," said Mr Norman. "I don't think he minds it in other people's houses. I'm glad you mentioned it, though. I shall remember to ask him."

They followed the will-o'-the-wisp flame down a long corridor to a massive door of carved oak. Bowing theatrically, the boy opened the door to reveal a small brilliantly lighted chamber with walls of carved wood and heavy brocade curtains. A table and four chairs were in the center of the room beneath a chandelier which glittered with many candles. A fire roared in the pink marble fireplace and before it, in leather armchairs, sat Glenellen and a plump young man with blue eyes and dark curly hair. Both rose as the newcomers entered.

"Behold the young American!" exclaimed Glenellen, moving forward in a stately glide and taking Philip by the hand; then, still ignoring Mr Norman, he led him to the fireplace where he was introduced to Evan Morgan, ". . . my secretary. An invaluable assistant. Invaluable," he repeated, looking at the young man solemnly. "When the truth is known one day, as it must be, he will be made a Chevalier of the Order of St Jerome of Padua. Mark my words and recall then at the proper time," he added, deepening the mystery by putting his forefinger to the side of his nose and winking.

"Did the meeting go well today?" asked Mr Norman by way of reminding the other of his so far unremarked presence.

"I don't know what you mean," said Glenellen blankly; then he smiled, revealing terrible teeth. "Ah, Clyde. You came after all. I was just saying to Evan here, I wonder if Clyde will come tonight and play a rubber or two of bridge with his old friends, and here you are. Do sit down by the fire. And you too, young man. I like a fire this time of year; these old palaces get so awfully damp. Fire dries them out. Dries me out, too, though I doubt whether that's such a good idea. Eh, Evan? Well, let's have a drink. Evan, ring for Guido, will you? And tell him to bring ice. Dreadful boy. You met him the other day, I think." Philip nodded. "If he doesn't learn to concentrate, I'm afraid I shall have to lock him up again."

"Lock him up?" asked Philip.

"Oh yes, often . . . with chains. He likes that best, he tells me."

Guido appeared with a tray of glasses, bottles and a silver bowl of ice. Philip studied him carefully but the boy's face revealed nothing at all. No scars attested to Ayre's grim reference and when he had set the tray down on a console he left the room. Evan mixed the drinks. Glenellen was disappointed to hear that Philip preferred Scotch to absinthe.

"I suppose I have the best absinthe in Europe," he said proudly, "guaranteed to make a weak head dissolve. But then nothing that is good is for the weak, is it, Clyde?"

"An interesting idea, Ayre," said the other noncommittally, turning to Evan. "Did you have a good day?"

"I think so," said the young man, glancing uneasily at Glenellen. But the peer was daydreaming, staring into the blue-gold flames of the fire as though anticipating the birth of the Phoenix or recalling his wife's death, thought Philip, suddenly remembering Mr Norman's story of the Embassy dinner.

"Did you hear from the Vatican?"

"Yes, the Monsignor came."

"The Polish?"

"No, the Austrian, the old one."

"And he felt . . ."

"That we would get considerable help at the proper time."

"From whom?"

"The Cardinal."

"Which one?"

"The fat one . . . you know, the River Po."

"Ah yes. But no news from above?"

"None. *He* must remain aloof."

"I suppose so, but perhaps at the proper time . . ."

"The proper time, and all will be forthcoming, or so the Monsignor indicated."

Evan turned to·Philip and asked, "Mr Norman tells me that you're a friend of Mr Durham's?"

"I know him slightly."

"He'll be in Rome another month, I hear."

"I'm seeing them day after tomorrow."

"Ayre," said the young man, nudging his employer who had so identified himself with the flames that his face had turned a sympathetic scarlet and his gaze was as abstracted and as flickering as the fire itself. But he responded to the nudge, his eyes focused on Evan. "Yes, my boy?"

"The Durhams. He knows the Durhams."

"And *who* are the Durhams?"

"You know perfectly well, Ayre," said Mr Norman. "He is the President's right hand."

"Which President?" His eye might be focused but his mind was not, thought Philip, wondering if this was the work of the absinthe he had drunk.

"The American one," said Mr Norman patiently. "Mr Durham is here on a mission to the Italian government. The President is relying on him. Our young friend has Mr Durham's ear. Isn't that enough?"

"Why didn't you tell me this before, Clyde?" said Glenellen, suddenly brisk and businesslike. "I could have made preparations. If I had only known I could have told the Monsignor when he was here today. Why, why didn't you tell me?"

"I did tell you, Ayre. Yesterday we discussed the entire thing and you suggested Mr Warren be brought here tonight . . . to play bridge."

"Bridge?" said Glenellen hopefully, clutching at the one reference which seemed most concrete. "I haven't had a good game of bridge in four years, since the German occupation."

"Ayre was here during the war," explained Mr Norman quickly.

"He was opposed to the Nazis . . ." began Evan.

"*Parvenus!*" interrupted Glenellen, throwing his glass into the fire. It shattered among the flames.

"But he had some friends from the old days, from the old German court. They protected him," finished Evan.

"You have influence with this Durham?" asked Glenellen suddenly, his foggy blue eyes on Philip's.

"No, none at all."

"He is being modest," said Mr Norman. "His family is politically very close to Mr Durham."

"How do you know that?" asked Philip, surprised.

"Oh, I know a lot of things about you."

"Clyde, this isn't the young man you told me about yesterday, is it?"

"The same," said Mr Norman wearily, appealing to Evan who was now at the other end of the room fixing drinks.

"I sometimes think, Clyde, that you try deliberately to

47

confuse me. Young man, how do you stand politically?"

"Nowhere at all," said Philip.

"But you disapprove of chaos?"

"I suppose so."

"You recognize the importance of human affairs?"

"Yes and no," said Philip, not understanding what this meant.

"Have you an adventurous nature?"

"Oh yes, yes," said Philip. Why else would he be here? he added to himself, intrigued though still confused.

"Do you play good bridge?"

"Fairly . . . I don't know. It depends."

"In that case, Clyde had better be your partner. I usually play with Evan anyway. He understands my bidding. The only other good player in Rome."

They rose and went to the card table and for two hours they played while hot wax from the chandelier overhead dripped on the table, and got in their hair, and Glenellen cursed but made no move to move the table somewhere else. Finally, when the game was over and the eccentric playing of Glenellen and Evan had triumphed over the more conservative game of their opponents, Ayre rose from the table and turned to Mr Norman. "It was good of you, Clyde, to bring this young man here tonight. We must remember, however, that discretion is of the greatest importance and that it is altogether too soon to admit him to our Order. Watch him, Clyde. Study him. Question him and if he seems trustworthy and valiant bring him to me next week."

"But the Durhams, Ayre . . . they won't be here forever."

"The Durhams can keep," said Glenellen sharply. He turned to Philip with a smile. "You must not mind being tested, my boy. We all are, every day, in one way or another, if not by man by God. I am sure you will not be found wanting."

"But will he *want* to serve us?" asked Evan reasonably. But this question was ignored. Clyde Norman sighed. "Very well, Ayre. It's your organization. Where shall we meet next week? And when?"

"Thursday will be the best day," said Glenellen. He frowned. "Not here, though. This place is being watched twenty-four hours a day. The Baths."

"The Baths?"

"Yes, Clyde. The Baths of Nero, at five o'clock."

"But, Ayre, I don't think . . . I mean." He gestured futilely in Philip's direction. But Glenellen was already ringing the bell for Guido to show them out.

Regina arrived on time, simply dressed, and Philip, when he met her in the lobby, thought her most desirable, more attractive even than she had been the night of their first meeting. They decided to take a walk in the near-by gardens of the Villa Borghese for both were a little shy at first and he hesitated about inviting her up to his room: he was not yet free of that American fear of desk clerks which has rendered the great game so depressing in his own country.

The day was fine, cool and at this hour golden, elegiac in mood, with rococo clouds arranged above the rolling meadows and dark woods of ilex trees which comprised the gardens, contained in part, along the Via Veneto, by a fragment of the wall of Rome and by a most heroic arch where, on either side, families lived like cave dwellers in the thick masonry. They paused by a silver pond beneath the dark green ilex trees. Priests strolled up and down; lovers sat together on the benches, silent and passive, watching with self-conscious eyes the children of others as they sailed little boats on the water and played tag between the trees.

"What can they mean?" he asked at last. He told of his evening with Glenellen. He had wanted to amuse and interest her without becoming too personal and since their supply of mutual reference was seriously limited, it was best, he decided, to stick to anecdote until they had known one another long enough to have a language in common, a world of easy familiar reference in which they could meet without resorting to the neutral or to the irrelevant.

"I'm not sure," she said with a frown. "It's a mystery. They all sound quite mad."

"I thought that, too, but amusing."

"I wonder if it's wise . . . your seeing them, I mean?"

"What harm could it do?"

"Well, one never can tell. The present government here isn't having an easy time of it, you know. Some think there may even be a revolution this year."

"But I'm just a visitor. I'm not interested in their politics. . . . I'm not even interested in our own." He smiled at her to see if she would take up the challenge as she had

49

at such length the first night. But today she was in a different mood; she turned away and walked to a bench near by. They sat down. A soldier with one leg and a face bristled like the back of a black boar came up to them and successfully begged a hundred *lire* from Philip.

"Be careful," she said, looking at him, her blue eyes serene; no matter what her mood, they never changed expression.

"I'll see them once again. . . . I promised Mr Norman I would . . . and that will be the end." He chuckled. "Well, at least I haven't got in with the usual group." Philip was suddenly conscious that his head was aching terribly. He shut his eyes and pressed his hand against the lids; inside his head the universe was definitely and brilliantly exploding outward, infinitely, and he with it. He opened his eyes and blinked.

"What on earth is the matter?" Regina was staring at him, alarmed. "Are you sick?"

"I don't know," he said weakly. The light hurt his eyes and he half shut them. "I have a headache. That's all. Came on me all of a sudden."

"Do you have them often?"

"Never."

"We'd better go back then."

"No, not yet. Let's sit here. It'll go away. I probably ate something that. . . . Oh!" He groaned, recalling the dinner the night before. "Goat!" he exclaimed, and he told her of the dinner. Then, when the pain was less acute, they got up and, slowly, as though he were an invalid only just arisen from bed, they walked down avenues of ilex to the Via Veneto and to his hotel where, at his insistence, she went up to the room. He ordered tea and aspirin and then, after this had arrived, sick though he was and in spite of her cautioning, they made love, the afternoon sun imprisoning the room with bars of light.

This time, it should be noted, all went well in spite of the fact the phone rang at the most important moment and continued to ring irritably for some time, as though the caller suspected he was being ignored deliberately. Then, when they were through, each knew (though neither was indelicate enough to mention it) that, in spite of his headache, it had gone very much better than the first time. Philip especially enjoyed it and he felt relaxed and easy when, finally, exhausted, they lay side by side on the bed and he smoked and she drank tea and the conversation turned once again to Glenellen.

"I'll find out about him, if you like," she said.

"I wish you would. And by the way, why should he be so interested in your husband?"

"I don't know. But the fact that he is means that he's up to something politically. If you want to do anything in this country you have to go to the Americans."

"And your husband is the American to go to?"

"So they think."

"I see." He blew a series of elliptical smoke rings. They watched the pale rings distend and vanish in the golden mote-scattered light of the room. When the last one had vanished, she sat up in bed and propped a pillow behind her head. He looked at her with interest and pleasure, relieved in a way that the novelty was gone (usually it went in the first five minutes) and that he could regard her without that distorting of perspective lust caused. What he saw now he liked and he could, he knew, in time and if all went well, love or at least grow accustomed to her in such a way that he might think himself in love: that grand nineteenth-century passion which had never, at this moment in his life at least, touched him with its burnished wing . . . although, if questioned, he would no doubt insist with some severity that he had loved and suffered in his day, adding as all philanderers do that the promiscuity of his more recent years had in no way atrophied his power to love one person wholly, should that person by some miracle materialize in his arms after the usual dalliance with a responsive stranger. Thus did he believe love would come, quickly, suddenly, utterly transforming some stranger into a creature as desirable and as unique as those goddesses who, in ancient days, would for love of a mortal become temporary exiles from the heroic beds of heaven.

But the transformation was not destined to be made that day. Regina, sensing no doubt what he was thinking, suddenly pulled the sheet about her and said, "Rex thought you very charming."

"I'm glad. But I prefer you."

"But he can do more for you."

"Oh no, not that."

"For someone who professes to hate politics you've got rather involved all on your own."

51

"You mean the Glenellen business? That's just idle curiosity. He makes me laugh."

"Do I make you laugh?"

"No. No, you don't, not at all. Should you?"

"I'm not sure." She sighed. "I must go now. Rex is waiting."

"When shall I see you?"

"Anytime you like. Tomorrow?"

"Tomorrow. The same time?"

"I'll be here. How do you feel now?"

"Rather odd."

"I wonder if you should see a doctor."

"No. I'll be all right. I'll sleep it off."

But the next day he was worse. The night had been terrible. He now had a fever as well as a headache and he tossed about unable to sleep until, shortly after dawn, he took a shot of brandy and at last slept fitfully, tormented by nightmares, by all the childhood monsters of the fever world. When he tried to sit up he grew dizzy, his head throbbed and his eyes ached, dazzled by the morning light. Convinced that he was going to die, he rang for some tea and some brandy to hasten the end. He wondered if they would bury him in the Protestant Cemetery, near Keats and Shelley. He could imagine the fuss his mother would make: his body would be shipped back at great expense and deposited with the other Warrens on the banks of the Hudson where he had, he thought lugubriously, played as a child. The idea of his own premature death, complicated by the very real discomfort he was in, so moved him that he was tempted to cry, not noisily but softly, in a manly way. The arrival of the waiter, however, immediately lessened the pain and brought him again into a proper relationship with the living as they exchanged greetings. Then Philip drank the tea and the brandy and felt somewhat better. He was considering whether to get up and take a bath, to try and draw the fever out of his aching joints, when Mr Norman entered the room, a friendly smile on his face.

"Do excuse me for barging in like this but I'm to tell you of a little change in our plans. Ayre has been called to Milan on business and so the meeting will be postponed for a week. I hope that's all right with you."

"Anything is all right with me," said Philip gently, beginning to die now that he had an audience.

"What *is* the matter with you?" Mr Norman was alarmed. "You look perfectly frightful."

"I am sick," Philip whispered and shut his eyes, feeling rather better for having drunk the brandy.

"Ah, you've caught it," said Mr Norman with some satisfaction, proud of his adopted city's treachery.

"Caught what?"

"We call it Roman fever, and everyone gets it. It lasts about a week. Possibly it's from the water, or perhaps it's just because the city is so low . . . used to be malarial, you know. There was a time when no one could stay here during the summer."

"But what do I do?"

"I'll get you a doctor. Nice chap I know, a German. He'll fix you up in no time. Meanwhile, you'll have to stay in bed and miss this splendid weather."

"I don't care. I don't care about anything."

"By the way, I telephoned you yesterday afternoon but there was no answer."

"I wasn't here. I was walking in the park."

"Now that's odd because the manager said you were in your room." Mr Norman chuckled maliciously.

"I take long walks up and down the corridor," said Philip, wishing Mr Norman would go away. His wish came true, for Mr Norman, after this final indication that he knew precisely what the other was up to, departed with the promise to send him the doctor immediately.

Illness becomes the young, in moderation, of course. It makes them pause in the midst of their physical euphoria and contemplate mortality. For young men like Philip the body is unobtrusive, something to be fed and washed like a motorcar and, from time to time, relieved in different ways. It gives no trouble and, served properly, can be the best of all possible toys. Philip's was no exception. He was vaguely fond of his body. He admired it dispassionately, without vanity though not without some complacency when he compared it to others and found it not only decorative but useful, equal to the admittedly not very rigorous tasks he set for it. But now after twenty-eight years of loving care, something had gone wrong. He had had the childhood illnesses but none had been severe, while his maturity had been marked by the most resolute health. Yet now, in an instant, he had been laid low and at first he wished he were dead; then, suddenly aware of what it would be like to die, he wished he were well and thousands of miles away from this city which had so gratuitously returned his passionate admiration with a well-aimed blow in the most unexpected quarter.

He convalesced slowly. He read. He sat on his balcony in the cool sunshine and surveyed the life of the street with a detached eye, aware that he was set apart from the busy men and women out of doors who did not know, as he did, that man is vulnerable and the flesh, after a certain age, corrupt and festering, preparing for its final dissolution. The morbidity of such conjectures appealed to him hugely and once the pain left he found that he almost missed the knowledge of the body it gave him, the sense of the secret actions and counteractions of the flesh which caused him to live and to be, which would cease all too soon when the mechanism, unbalanced at last, would degenerate into dust to be rearranged in time into other less sentient forms.

Regina came to see him every day. They talked of many things and she spoke often of politics, of his natural gift for them (though how she knew he had such a gift was never apparent to him). She tempted him in every way she could to go home when she did and to prepare for a great career. He was touched that she had such faith in him. Her calm assurance, however, was bewildering: she spoke of the winning of future elections as a fact. It all seemed easy when she spoke of it, so definite. She told him how elections could be won, which person could do what for him. Knowing her power, he could not, at least when it came to detail, doubt what she said. In his weakened state he found himself more receptive to this gaudy dream of dominion than ordinarily he would have been. And she, seeing that her companion was making some progress, pressed on until at last he was almost ready to agree to go back in two months' time and begin the ascent: wondering always what it was that she wanted from him, what he must give her in exchange. He did not like to ask and so he held back from the final declaration she so much wanted to hear.

One morning he awakened to find that he was well again. He stretched and unsuccessfully tried to recall what the pain had been like; but he could not remember, even the memory of the fever was gone.

Mr Norman, who had kept careful watch over him during his illness (he had even encountered Regina briefly in his room), arrived shortly after breakfast.

"You look very well, very well indeed."

"I'm going to go out today."

"By all means. Get more air . . . won't do you a bit of harm. Summer is here and the day is fine. I've been up since seven."

"It'll be nice to get out of this room."

"Has Mrs Durham called you yet?"

"No, I'm seeing her tonight."

"A lovely woman," said Mr Norman, looking in the mirror and combing his thin hair straight back. "She's quite a nurse, too, isn't she?"

"She's been very kind," said Philip, pulling the blanket about him and getting up. He felt strong and confident, ready for almost anything. Which was fortunate, for Mr Norman had, as usual, a plan to which Philip, with a number of unexpressed doubts, finally agreed. At four o'clock that afternoon he arrived, alone, at the Baths of Nero.

The Baths were in a small side street. A large, soiled plaster head of Nero hung above the door through which he passed into a dingy reception room. A man who spoke no English indicated the price, which Philip paid, wondering, as always, whether or not he was being cheated. He was then led down a spiral staircase to a large well-lit room full of cubicles with wooden numbered doors. Men dressed in sheets or towels padded up and down the corridor; when he entered several stopped their patrolling and stared at him.

Now, it should be remarked at this point that Philip was neither naïve nor innocent. He had had a varied and interesting life which had included a thorough indoctrination in almost every human activity. His own tastes were set when, at thirteen, he seduced a high-school senior, a much admired girl of eighteen and the object of his older brother's less virile attention. The excitement of this conquest had gone to his head and so, for fifteen years now, he had untiringly repeated that first experience with various partners, his enthusiasm and pleasure increasing rather than lessening as he grew older. Over the years, however, he had been offered any number of opportunities to explore other ways in the company of excited strangers. When he was fifteen an older woman, a respectable family friend, had tried to get him to beat her with the silken cord of her dead husband's dressing gown. He had refused her sternly. A year later, at prep school, he was invited to indulge in certain erotic ceremonies conducted by the school's leading athlete, a strong passionate boy who died in the fire of a bomber the year the war ended. In spite of his adulation for this young hero, Philip's natural modesty, combined with a precocious love of his own pleasure, caused him, with great politeness, to refuse the invitation. Later, in uniform, seldom a day went by without some form of adventure presenting itself. Elderly men bought him drinks and invited him up to their rooms for a nightcap. He refused them all, even though on occasion he would accept a drink or two at a bar. The lavatories of various railroad and bus terminals of the country were brilliant with generous invitations which he always declined pleasantly as he continued his own quiet and orderly progress. He was never outraged. In fact, everything interested him in the abstract, and several times when friends of his had tried to sell him on this or that variation he had admitted that it all sounded very interesting and that perhaps at some other time he might give it a try. But that other time never came and meanwhile Philip covered the field like a quarterback with good interference.

From time to time, however, he had become involved in situations which had he been less of a traveler, less curious, he might never have known about, much less become involved in—proving, perhaps, that he had an inclination toward forbidden vice; a very slight one, however; certainly not enough of one to render enjoyable this visit to the Baths of Nero where, after tying a small white apron about his loins, he timidly opened the door of his cubicle and stepped out into the hall.

Slowly, barefoot, not liking the thought of the dirty coarse matting under his feet, he walked down the hall toward a small sitting room where a number of middle-aged gentlemen were smoking and chatting and drinking apéritifs provided by the management. They paused in their conversation and looked at him very carefully. Several were noticeably aroused and one sighed audibly as Philip, blushing furiously, walked past them to the thick glass door of the steam room. He caught the words *"Inglese, Americano."* He wished he had not come. He had known perfectly well what it would be like: the world of the Turkish bath was no secret to him nor, for that matter, was the character of Mr Norman. Idle curiosity had brought him here, and now, he decided grimly, he would have to go through with it.

Hanging his apron on a peg beside the other aprons, he stepped into the hot room.

It was a large room with stained-glass clerestory windows which gave it a faintly ecclesiastical air. On three sides of the room a broad white marble shelf had been built and here, in Roman fashion, a number of figures reclined or sat. Off to the right was another door of glass, the door to the steam room. A fountain decorated the center of the hot room and cold water trickled from the fountain's mouth into a basin where the clients dipped their hands from time to time and cooled their faces. The most remarkable feature of the establishment was a number of unusually handsome Italian boys, with deep chests and velvet skins, who wandered about the room with preoccupied expressions, stopping here and there to say a few words to this or that person. They were, Philip could see, the quarry, the central attraction of the Baths.

The men on the marble benches were for the most part middle-aged though there were some very young ones, Philip noticed, as well as several incredibly old ones not yet free of Sophocles' cruel and insane master, though very nearly free of the flesh itself. They talked in all languages, laughing and joking like clubmen. There was a significant pause when Philip entered, and as he walked across the room to a vacant place on the bench he was aware that he was being judged, point by point, like a prize bull. Simulating indifference, he swung himself onto the bench and modestly crossed his legs. The conversation resumed, although there were many glances in his direction and one young man, a lean American with a crewcut, came over and asked him if he would like to go back to his room with him. Philip shook his head politely and smiled. "I'm meeting somebody," he said. Sadly the young man went away and Philip rubbed himself until he began to sweat, trying not to notice the various odd duets about the room.

In a great burst of sound, talk and laughter, Glenellen, red and leathery as a salamander, entered from the steam room, a towel arranged about his head in the fashion of the Pharaohs. He was accompanied by Evan, who looked handsome with his clothes off, and Mr Norman, who did not.

"Ah, there you are, my boy. Hardly recognized you.

57

Hardly recognized you, indeed," hummed Glenellen, inspecting him quickly, professionally. "May we join you on the slab?" They arranged themselves like corpses around him; Glenellen sighed voluptuously. "The heat, the heat," he murmured, "ah, the darling heat."

"We come here every day," said Evan, who looked as though he would rather have been anywhere else: he was sweating profusely, unlike the two older men who seemed to absorb the heat greedily.

"Good for the soul," said Mr Norman, hesitantly patting Philip's calf. Philip moved out of range.

"I should think you'd all get very thin," he said, for want of anything else to say. He had never felt so out of place and already he had begun to plan his escape.

"Source of life," intoned Glenellen, sitting up and looking at the youths who stood in decorative attitudes around the fountain, showing their wares to the would-be purchasers and talking in low voices among themselves. "Give me young lips that taste of fruit," said Glenellen, smiling, revealing his carious teeth. "What say you, young man?"

"Oh, by all means," said Philip distractedly.

"Aren't they lovely? Like young gods. Commercial young gods, but still divine."

"Very nice," said Philip, not wishing to give offense or to be thought gauche.

"Which would you pick?"

"I don't really know," said Philip beginning to blush, aware that Mr Norman was watching him with great amusement.

"You can have any one you like," said Glenellen with a royal gesture. "I will treat you to one."

"I . . . I'm afraid I'm not in the mood today."

"Nonsense. A healthy boy like you is always in the mood. Come now, don't be shy. Take your pick . . . my party, you know."

"Are they very expensive?" Philip stalled.

"Five hundred *lire*, that's all . . . *prix fixe*. Here, at least. On the street you have to pay more. Well . . . what about that dusky Venetian blond? Wonderful type! How Titian would have loved that skin, and Michelangelo that torso. I almost want him for myself . . . but after you. I will be generous. You are my guest today."

Philip did not know whether to reveal himself as a womanizer and a tourist, or to dodge the whole thing gracefully by going off with the boy for a polite length

58

of time. Mr Norman, a mound of white dimpled flesh, saved him by remarking, "Before we play, Ayre, I suggest we do our business. Besides, you must remember that our young friend has been very sick these last few days. He may not be in the mood for games."

"He looks all right to me," said Ayre suspiciously, "but you're right, we must set to work." He sat cross-legged on the marble. The heat, Philip decided, was good for him. Glenellen was far more alert than usual, even rational. "Evan, go take one of the boys and cool off. You look like a weeping willow."

Evan, obviously pleased, scrambled off the bench and walked over to the fountain, where he engaged a small sinewy Sicilian in conversation. They came to terms immediately and with a wave to the others, Evan followed the young man out of the room.

"He always likes those small muscle-bound boys," said Ayre peevishly. "He has no taste. No love of beauty. Poorly educated, that's the trouble, like all the Welsh. Where were we, Clyde?"

"Business. Mr Warren."

"Ah, yes. Mr Warren, we need you." His voice was urgent. He looked about furtively to make sure that no strangers were listening. "We've examined your record carefully, both of us, Clyde and myself, and we've decided that you can be of great use to us in our movement. But before I go into detail, I must impress upon you the need for secrecy. If you feel that you cannot for any reason respect my confidence, I wish you would say so now and I will not continue . . . my lips will be sealed."

"Well," began Philip uncertainly, torn between curiosity and a fear of involvement.

"I accept that, then, as your pledge," said Glenellen, rearranging his red, loose body upon the marble. "We know that politically you are in sympathy with us. Your comments on politics have been duly noted and interpreted. In short, Mr Warren, we recognize you as a fellow royalist and we wish for a short period to utilize your talents in our movement to restore the House of Savoy to its rightful place here in our adopted land."

It was out at last. Philip, who had long ago decided that Glenellen was the head of an international opium combine, gave a sigh of relief; pleased to know what it was all about, a little disappointed that the more glamorous alternative had not materialized.

59

"What do you think, Philip?" asked the suet-white lump on his other side, a flaccid, breathing shape which contained a soul as passionate as any other's.

"I don't know. I mean, I haven't any idea what you want me to do." Philip was immediately furious with himself for having taken the wrong line, for not having immediately opposed any suggestion that he join the cabal. He realized, however, that it was now too late, at this moment anyway, to back out; he had indicated interest and he was partly committed.

"Two things," said Glenellen promptly. "We need a courier to go to Amalfi next week. Most of our people are already known to the police and are being watched. We must send someone they cannot suspect and someone they don't dare touch. The fact that you are an American and new to Rome is all in your favor. You have never been seen with me. This place is safe, by the way. My own house, of course, is watched but if you remember, there was no moon the night you came. The second thing is the more difficult and the more important: we want you to try to enlist Mr Durham on our side. We feel that if he could present the true facts of the case to your President he would intervene and restore the monarchy. The Republic is a fiasco. Everyone knows it. Any day now, the Communists will take over and that will be the end of Italy. We have great resources behind us . . . great men are helping us . . . but we must proceed cautiously and not force an issue too soon. Above all, we must get the American government on our side. Naturally, we have any number of people at work in Washington but it has not been easy to interest your government. Since you are on the best of terms with Mrs Durham, you could, if you chose, exert considerable influence in that quarter, adding immeasurably thereby to the total effort in which we are all engaged." He paused, the foggy blue eyes beneath the Egyptian headdress alert, the usual vagueness replaced by an unfamiliar concentration which impressed Philip, against his better judgment.

"I'm afraid," he said at last, "that there isn't much I can do about the Durhams. They both know what they think and I'm sure they wouldn't take any advice from me on foreign affairs. After all, that's his specialty, you know. And, to be practical, even if I could influence him, that still doesn't mean it would be any help to you. The President and Congress don't respond to that sort of influence when it comes to a national policy . . . at least, I don't think they do," he added, suddenly appalled by the unexpected pedantry of his reply; it was not as if he knew what he was talking about. He persevered, however, covering up this involuntary expression of doubt by several more dogmatic remarks on American foreign policy.

"But that doesn't mean," said Mr Norman smoothly, "that one can't try. Every little bit helps, you know. Mr Durham can supply us with information either directly or indirectly. We can discover what his government is thinking, learn how to change, if possible, that thinking. Oh, there are many ways to accomplish our ends, many ways, and there are many of us at work on different levels. You could try, at the very least. If you wanted to."

"Perhaps," said Philip doubtfully, already intrigued.

"Will you deliver the papers for us?" asked Glenellen.

"What are they?"

"Very important documents. I can tell you no more. In any case, they must never fall into the government's hands. If there is any danger you must destroy them."

"Where are they being sent?"

"You will take them?"

"Depends on where you want me to go. I'm traveling for pleasure and I have only a year and many things to see. I don't want to waste any time."

"Waste any time! Young man, do you realize that at this very minute Umberto, our martyred king . . ."

"Amalfi," said Mr Norman quickly. "I'm sure you will like it . . . one of the loveliest old cities in Italy, and the bathing is excellent."

In a reckless mood, Philip accepted the commission. Both Mr Norman and Lord Glenellen profusely complimented him on his wisdom and thanked him for his wise partisanship to their high cause. Mention was made of several decorations which would be given him when a grateful king once more adorned the Quirinal Palace. Although Philip questioned them further about the movement, he received no new information. They would not tell him whether Umberto himself was involved or what stand the Vatican was taking. They suggested darkly that they had powerful friends who would, at the right moment, declare themselves king's men. As for his own role, instructions on how to proceed would be given him in a few days, said Mr Norman. He would not have to leave Rome before another week, in which time it was hoped he would have made some headway with Mr Durham. Philip agreed, dubiously, to much of this: he could already imagine himself in front of a firing squad of Republican soldiers.

This grim vision was cut short by the return of Evan, breathless but otherwise cheerful. The Sicilian youth also returned a moment later, unruffled and businesslike. He joined his confreres at the fountain and they conversed seriously, like a group of brokers on the exchange. It was obvious, even to Philip, that they were discussing the price of their commodity.

"Good?" asked Mr Norman.

Evan nodded, catching his breath at last. "Awfully."

"Better than Guido?"

"Well, Guido is Guido. I mean, there could hardly be another."

"No, I suppose not."

"We have forgotten our friend!" cried Glenellen, sitting up. "We've done nothing for him. Shown him no hospitality. Evan, go get that blond one over there, the Venetian beauty. I'm sure he will provide Mr Warren with a fine welcome to the Baths of Nero."

"But . . ." Philip got no further, for Glenellen then proceeded to celebrate in extravagant phrases the virtues of the baths and how, on more than one occasion, their existence had saved civilization. Even today, he implied, the serious work of Rome would be tragically affected if the lawyers and businessmen could not make an occasional visit to the baths on their way home to their wives and children. According to Glenellen, every Roman would be hopelessly frustrated and neurotic without this marvelously organized release.

Evan returned without the blond. "He won't come," he said, upsetting Glenellen's entire system.

"Won't come? And why not?"

"He says that our friend here is too young and too good-looking, that he only likes older men. He asked me to introduce him to you instead." They all laughed: Philip with relief and Glenellen with almost childish pleasure. Then the boy was brought over and presented to Glenellen who quickly, and in Italian, made the necessary arrangements. Philip, who only a moment before had congratulated himself on his narrow escape, was not yet safe, for Glenellen, with all the insistence of his monomania, summoned a powerfully built adolescent, with a body like the David and the face of a stupid angel, to be Philip's companion.

"A gift!" exclaimed the peer warmly.

It was too late for Philip to retreat. He submitted without a word, aware that Mr Norman was especially enjoying his discomfort. Led by Glenellen, they left the room for their various cubicles and those transports of commercial bliss which have ever engaged the highest talents of the finest poets but will not for once concern us here.

After making a date to see Philip in two days' time, Glenellen disappeared with his Venetian. Mr Norman, too, had engaged the services of a temporary friend, while the satiated Evan ordered wine.

When the others were gone, Philip turned rather hopelessly to the youth and told him, first in English and then in French, that he would get his money all right but that because of some fundamental perversity in his own nature he would rather forgo the pleasures of the couch. The youth knew neither French nor English. He smiled charmingly and said, *"Si?"* Then he followed Philip to his room.

It would be startling to report that the stalwart Philip succumbed to pagan vice, that the habits of his maturity were in an instant undone by this classic figure which, against his will, he found himself admiring. But we must remain true to the fact of Philip's character and report, truthfully, that nothing happened. When they got into the cubicle the boy removed his apron and hung it on a peg. Then he looked down at himself and smiled with an ingenuous vanity, as though to say: "Isn't this handsome?" Philip smiled back. They stood facing one another for a moment. Then, a little bewildered that no move had been made, the boy sat down on the edge of the bed. Philip, feeling silly, sat down too, several inches away from the smooth olive-skinned flank. The boy then asked for a cigarette. Each had a cigarette. The boy felt Philip's arm muscle and nodded admiringly; then he flexed his own arm and Philip gingerly touched the other's biceps with a forefinger. Another silence. The boy changed his position on the bed several times and Philip sat bolt upright beside him. Finally, the boy frowned and, indicating himself, suggested by signs that perhaps he was not Philip's type. Philip quickly put the lie to this by demonstrating with gestures that the young man's body was all that could be desired, but that (and here he made certain universal

63

signs in the air) it was not a woman's body. This revelation astonished the other. He talked a great deal, stating, as far as Philip could tell, that all Americans, English and Germans liked Italian boys and even Italian boys, though they didn't make too great a thing of it, liked Italian boys.

He then demonstrated graphically that he was all a woman could desire and that women were all that he desired even though he came every day to the baths not only for money but for the companionship of his friends, the other youths about the fountain. How could Philip understand all this? Never mind. He did. One of the first things one learns in traveling is that people understand one another if they want to, no matter how great the language barrier. And so, on a friendly note, their brief encounter ended. The boy put his apron back on, borrowed another cigarette, shook hands and left the room with, Philip knew, a hell of a funny story to tell the boys in the hot room.

"It is the most absurd thing I've ever heard."

"I suppose so . . . but then to me anything that has to do with politics is absurd."

"Well, you certainly won't go."

"I'm not so sure," he said stubbornly, waving to a waiter who responded as waiters do by distractedly going off in the opposite direction. They were seated in the open at Doney's, their backs to the street, facing the sidewalk and the afternoon display of new alliances and costumes, all rosy in the light of the setting sun.

"But Philip, you can get into trouble. Just remember the Communists may take over Italy any day now. There isn't a chance in the world of the monarchy being restored and even if there were, that madman Glenellen wouldn't be involved in it."

"So you do know who he is."

She grimaced. "I found out after you mentioned him the other day. Do be careful. He's really bad news, and mad as a hatter."

"But I want to see Amalfi."

She sighed. "That's another thing, of course."

"Is it really lovely?"

"Oh yes. I went there with Rex once, years ago, when we were first married."

Finally, a treaty was made after many speeches, border

64

disputes, hostages surrendered and compliments exchanged; their affair was, at the end, no longer the same, weakened by policy but like a fracture that has healed, strongest at the point where the break occurred. When two people are fond of one another the first quarrel, the first sign of wills in opposition, comes as a shock, destroying the vain illusion that two can be one: a knowledge that is saddening but, happily, soon obscured if the new alliance is intelligently refashioned, defined by sensible treaty. The covenant to which they both agreed was that he go to Amalfi, that he not mix in politics, that he await with mounting impatience her arrival some ten days later in a small English car called a Riley, very fast with a convertible top and room for only two people in it.

Chapter Four

"*I DON'T KNOW WHY*, but I can hardly believe that this is the room where Ibsen wrote *Ghosts*."

"Probably because this is *not* the room. It's over there, across the hall."

"But the manager said distinctly that it was the first room to the left."

"Well, dear, this is the first room to the right."

"So it is, Bella. I'm sorry. I was hasty."

"And there seems to be someone in it."

"Why, so there is. I wonder who."

"Not so loud, dear, he's asleep."

"Do you think it's an American?"

"Good heavens, how can I tell? I mean, he's asleep."

"Now *you* are talking loud."

"Come along, May. Let's look in the *right* room now."

"It's really terribly thrilling! I love Ibsen, don't you?"

"Oh yes, yes."

"What was *Ghosts* about, by the way? I've forgotten."

"Tuberculosis."

Philip waited until he heard them withdraw; then he rolled over and opened his eyes, unpleasantly aware that as usual in the heat he sweated more asleep than awake. Slowly he got to his feet and like an old man enjoying his discomfort, he crossed the room and shut the door, wondering why he had accepted this ridiculous mission. Pondering bleakly the House of Savoy, he put on bathing trunks and a dressing gown; then he left the room.

The hotel was a rambling, odd sort of structure on top of a steep cliff at the town's edge. In the center of a Moorish-style patio with delicate carved arches of yellowed plaster, ancient tiles, cracked and smooth from age, were arranged in oriental patterns about a lily pond, shadowed by a single orange tree.

He stood a moment blinking in the hot sun. Below him was the town of Amalfi, surrounded by steep cliffs and green hills, cut by a narrow ravine through which a slender foaming river ran, curving down through terraced stone houses to the luminous blue sea which sparkled a hundred feet below him, vivid in the noon light.

He crossed the street and descended the steps which had long ago been cut in the rock of the cliff.

He had had a brief recurrence of the fever coming down the day before on the train and now, today, he felt tired and irritable, obscurely despondent, without direction, conscious of no real center to his life. The thought of his secret mission depressed him further and he wondered if it might not solve everything if he drowned himself in that warm blue sea beside which he now sat in his bathing trunks, one foot in the water and his face turned blankly to the scorching sun, like a tired love offering to the occupant of the far-ranging golden car.

Then, bored with sunlight, he looked about him at the sharp brown rocks which edged the peninsula at this point; there were no beaches here, only cliffs and rocks. At the town's center, the ravine and the river were contained by wharves, the focus of Amalfi which, like some great pink amphitheater, fanned out over the green and umber hills at whose summits dead castles rose in solemn silhouette.

It was all very lovely, he decided sourly, giving up the idea of suicide for the moment.

"Are you American?"

"Yes."

"How nice, Bella. We were right . . . at least, I was."

He recognized the voices: the two ladies who had awakened him in search of Ibsen's *Ghosts*. They stood now before him in white dresses and wide hats, with cameras over their shoulders, each holding a great handbag containing pills and lotions, guidebooks and expensive cameos. They were American, plump, no longer young, resolutely cheery; mannerisms and costumes so alike they seemed identical twins, although he was sure that, examined carefully, there must be any number of differences easily remarkable to their friends.

Introductions. Bella and May Washington were sisters, teachers of English and Social Science, respectively, in the Bigelow Clapp High School, Council Bluffs, Iowa. Both were unmarried, they hastened to say, both virginal, he decided.

"Isn't it nice?" said Bella, sitting on the rock to his left.

"So lovely and warm," said May, perching on a rock

67

to his right. He pivoted to face them, the sun on his back now.

"We saw Pompeii, did you?"

"Not yet. But I passed near it on the bus from Naples this morning."

"Then you only got here today."

"A few hours ago."

"We've been here a week."

"We must really apologize for breaking in on you like that but May had been reading about Amalfi in the guide-book when lo and behold! she discovered that Ibsen had stayed at our hotel and that he had written *Ghosts* there so we hastened to discover which had been his room and the manager very kindly told us. By mistake we got into your room. May's mistake."

"Yes. Silly of me, wasn't it? I never seem able to follow directions. But it was so interesting, seeing the room. I asked the manager all about Mr Ibsen and he said that he remembered seeing him years ago when he was a little boy, when the manager was a little boy."

"Tell Mr Warren what he said about him."

"He said that he had whiskers and that he refused to eat *pasta* . . . isn't that interesting?"

"It certainly is," agreed Philip.

"Will you be here long?"

"About two weeks," said Philip, imagining those two weeks: A sun-scorched time of dazzling sea, of restless nights until Regina came. *"Dies irae,"* he murmured to himself as he was told what to see in Amalfi, which churches were lovely and which were tacky, which stores were expensive and which were reasonable and full, yes full! of fine cameos, old and rare. Would he like to see one? Yes? He was shown a large yellow cameo of Minerva, or was it the goddess of liberty? No, more likely Minerva. "I mean, after all in those days the Goddess of Liberty was rather *de trop,* as the French say. Not at all proper to reproduce in a monarchy like Italy," which reminded him again of his mission and thinking of it, he shuddered suddenly in the hot sun.

"And then he was killed by the Count's servants and eaten by wolves."

What on earth was she talking about? he wondered, aware that he'd missed an entire anecdote.

"How terrible!" he exclaimed. Then, to show interest: "Where did the wolves come from?"

"The forest, naturally. The castle was surrounded by a forest in those days and there were wolves everywhere. Certainly proves the legend, doesn't it?"

"I should say so." Philip was now ready to go swimming but they had other plans for him: they wanted to take his picture. So he posed for them against a rock, looking out to sea like a tired Hermes prepared for flight.

"Thanks so much. That's our hobby, you know, taking pictures. We have seventeen scrapbooks now."

"We travel a great deal. This is our fourth trip to Europe . . . the first since the war."

"Bella likes Italy. I like France." Their views were presented to him and he passed judgment as tactfully as possible and then, before they could draw him out, he rose and excused himself and with some style dived into the warm sea, narrowly missing a sharp rock which might have split his head, providing the sisters Washington with an unusual snapshot.

▣

He left the hotel through a back door, wondering whether or not he should have worn a cape. In his coat pocket, fastened with a safety pin, was the document which he was to deliver to the "organization." But before he could meet the "organization" he would first have to present himself at midnight at a certain antique shop where the proprietor, according to Glenellen's verbal instructions, would receive him warmly if he remembered to say *"O lente, lente currite, noctis equi."* He had been drilled in this one sentence by Clyde Norman and as he walked down the narrow street murmured it over and over to himself.

The street fascinated him: steep and only a few feet wide, a cobbled path between the windowless façades of buildings, broken here and there by deep-set bolted doors. The only light came from the fragment of moon overhead and from the lights of the town at the foot of the street. Feeling disembodied and faintly unreal, he walked like a ghost through the warm wine-odored darkness, the stale heat of the day lingering in the quiet air, and he wondered what would happen if, irrationally, he began to shout and batter at one of those metal-studded doors.

His mood changed when he stepped into the circle of dim electric light which illuminated the level part of the town, stage to the amphitheater. Men and youths stood

69

about on the wharves in groups talking, their shadows long upon the sea. In open cafés men and women were singing loudly and, Philip thought, melodiously on pitch. He was aware of curious glances as he walked in front of the main café. Tourists were still a curiosity in this country so recently conquered by the foreign armies.

In front of a pool hall he asked a policeman where the antique shop he wanted was and the policeman, an affable man, was able to tell him, in English. After thanking the man, he strolled up the main street of the town.

The farther he walked away from the sea the narrower the streets became, while the long dark shapes of the mountains on either side grew more oppressive by moonlight as they converged and the town continued on up the hillside, almost to the castle-crowned summits. Near the fast and narrow river, contained by masonry and spanned by medieval bridges, was the shop of Signor Alberto Guiscardo. A sign in Gothic script announced Signor Guiscardo's name and business. Philip pulled the bell; there was a loud jangling.

After a long wait the door was opened by a young boy who spoke rapid Italian until, seeing that Philip did not understand, he stopped abruptly and made a motion for Philip to come into the house.

The first room was the shop, large and musty, crowded with furniture and mirrors and paintings all jumbled together like a looted museum. The next room they entered was a modern drawing room, small, well lighted and airless. The windows were all shut and Philip wondered if he would be able to stand the heat and the odor of incense which burdened the torpid air. He was invited to sit down; then the boy disappeared. Philip had just picked up a book which someone had left open on a coffee table when the tinkling noise of a Mozart quartet filled the room. He put the book down nervously and looked about for some sign of life; there was none. The phonograph was in another room. He was about to pick up the book again when *it* appeared. Philip started with dismay. *It* was a fat middle-aged man in a Sulka dressing gown (mulberry with gold figurings) who wore over his face a rubber mask like the ones sold in American drugstores. This particular mask depicted, in the most lifelike manner, the rosy features of a plump somewhat vacuous hog.

"How do you do. How do you do. Please don't get up.

Sherry? Yes? I always drink sherry, too. I've nothing stronger, in any case." A glass of sherry was produced from the sideboard. Philip took it, still staring at the pig's face of his host.

"Now let us chat," said Signor Guiscardo, settling comfortably into an armchair. "You wonder at how well I speak English? So do I. I have never had a single lesson. I've never been out of Italy, in spite of my numerous . . . I repeat, numerous . . . friendships with Americans and English people. You are American?"

"Yes . . . just visiting."

"Have you been to Capri?"

"No."

"Do you plan to go there soon?"

"No. I shall probably go back to Rome when I leave here."

"You must under no circumstances miss Capri," said the Pig solemnly, taking the sherry through a slit under the snout.

"If it's very interesting, perhaps I will go there."

"Do, by all means."

There was a long pause as they sipped sherry and Philip sweated in the heat and looked longingly at the sealed windows. It did no good, however, for his host obviously had no intention of opening them. Finally, when the silence got too oppressive for him to bear, Philip said the magic words Ayre had drilled him in before leaving Rome. *"O lente, lente currite, noctis equi."*

No sooner had he pronounced the incantation than the Pig stood up abruptly, spilling sherry all over its mulberry dressing gown. Hands to his head, as though the piggish jowls might burst, he rushed from the room leaving Philip bewildered and a little frightened. He was nearly ready to make a run for it himself when his host reappeared. This time the dressing gown was of stiff brocade, dark green with a *mille-fleurs* design. On his face he wore a new mask, that of a goat, a pale astonished-looking goat with haggard features and unhealthy red eyes.

"I think this is more becoming," said the Goat quietly, returning to his chair and folding his hands in his lap.

Philip half expected to see cloven hoofs instead of hands. "So do I," said Philip, refusing to betray the very real alarm he felt.

"So much more in keeping with the tone of our discussion."

"I couldn't agree more."

"What were we discussing?"

"I had made a Latin reference. I had quoted a line of Ovid."

"Of course. In the excitement it had slipped my mind. Do you like the classics?"

"Very much. Especially Horace."

"Superb, superb poet. But I must say Catullus is more me."

"I'm not surprised."

"You're not despised?"

"No. I said that I am not surprised."

"Oh." There was a pause. The Goat looked at him thoughtfully; then it said: "How is milord Glenellen?"

"Very well. He sends you his regards."

"Send him mine, when you see him."

"I shall." Philip was relieved that the conversation had begun to take an anticipated turn. "Shall I give you the papers now?"

The Goat threw up its hands as though in terror. "Under no circumstances, my dear young man, are you to give me anything. Ever! Do you understand?"

"But I thought . . ."

"I don't care what you thought. You are not to give me anything. Do you realize that I am watched every minute? I can take no chances. There are a number of people who await with eagerness my downfall. I wish to disappoint them."

"Well, of course, if you . . ." The Goat had rushed to the window and was looking out into the darkened street, presenting, Philip thought, a dreadful vision to any passer-by, civilian or spy.

"I can advise, however," said the Goat suavely, satisfied that at the moment the street was empty, the enemy in hiding. "Not only can I advise, I will, with your permission, suggest." He looked inquiringly at Philip who nodded gravely. "In five days the moon will be full. You will proceed to the ruined Church of St Elmo on the slope above the St Elmo Bridge . . . you can't miss it . . . and there (you must arrive at midnight precisely, not earlier, not later) the committee will await you in front of what was formerly the high altar. Deliver your papers to them."

"Are you sure you don't want them?"

"As sure as I am that the House of Savoy will return

to its proper place among us," said the Goat with an intense piety, in keeping with its sacerdotal features.

"In that case, I had better go. I hadn't planned to stay in Amalfi quite so long."

"You're not going to leave without delivering the papers?" The Goat was anxious.

"No, I am going to leave you . . . I mean, I don't want to impose myself on you any longer tonight. You have been very kind."

"Not at all. I'm only sorry I couldn't have been of more help to you. But I'm sure that you appreciate my position in all of this."

"Of course. You must be careful."

"Not for myself, either," said the Goat with dignity, like a martyr discussing an *auto-da-fé*, "but for Italy and for our king."

The silence that followed this pronouncement was so long, so reverent, that Philip was tempted to steal quietly away. The Goat, however, was not finished. "Are you by any chance interested in antiques?" he asked in a different voice.

"No," said Philip cruelly, "not at all."

The Goat appeared to be depressed. "That's a pity. I have some exciting bits and pieces, you know."

"You see, I have no place to put them," explained Philip, relenting.

"I know how it is. In case you know of anyone who might care for some rather unusual items, do send him to me."

"I certainly will."

"I am sure you will enjoy yourself in Amalfi," said the Goat. "We have everything a gentleman needs."

"I haven't been well," said Philip. "I plan to rest here, to get some sun."

"We have quite a number of fair-haired people in this section . . . where do they come from? Ah, who knows? From those great barbarian armies that once ranged up and down this ancient realm, taking their pleasure where they chose, clothed in the rough skins of beasts like so many forest gods. Then, later, the Normans came, from whom I am descended on both sides, the blood of Plantagenets like some heady tide in my veins, pulled this way and that by the waxing and waning of the silver moon; and from the Normans a new vitality infused the old stock, and the kingdom of the Two Sicilies flourished for many years until it came under foreign dominion and corrupt houses reigned; at last, under a mongrel Bourbon, God willed that it cease to be and Italy accepted Savoy, as I do, until that glad day when my own nation is free again and I, my dear sir, am restored to my rightful place as the first prince of Europe, as the rightful King of Naples." The Goat stopped, one arm stretched out before him, upraised as though awaiting the anointing and the orb.

"May that day be soon," said Philip quietly, now very alarmed.

"It will come," said the Goat, arising and peering once again out the sealed window at the dark street. "It will come. In the meantime, I devote my days to the restoration of Savoy, knowing that once they have returned the task of Plantagenet will be more easy, that our day must surely come."

Philip rose. "Now I must really go, sir," he said, adding the "sir" as he'd always been told one must with royalty. The Goat-King got to its feet, too.

"We've enjoyed your visit. You must come back to see us soon, by daylight, on a mission of less state."

"I will, if I may."

"And should you perhaps want an interesting object or two, or know of a friend who does, why, bear my little shop in mind."

"I will, sir, I will indeed."

"I shall show you out myself." He led Philip down the dark hall of the dimly lit shop. Here they paused for a moment and the Goat rummaged through an antique Renaissance chest. At last he found what he wanted. "It is from Pompeii," he said. "Keep it as a little memento of our agreeable meeting."

"Thank you very much. I will," said Philip, pocketing the small metal object. Then he was led to the door, which was opened after a good deal of unbolting and unchaining, like a fortress Philip thought; he turned to say good-night to his host who had, in the meantime, somehow managed, between the shop and the front door, one final metamorphosis. The altogether too realistic face of a gray wolf stared at Philip, its green eyes glowing savagely in the dark.

"We must meet again. Remember your rendezvous: the Church of St Elmo the first night of the full moon." The wolf's teeth glittered.

"It has been a great pleasure," said Philip, backing out

74

into the street with an agility which would have done credit to Little Red Ridinghood.

◙

Two days later, at lunch with Bella and May Washington, he felt in his pocket for a handkerchief (the day was hot, the meal was a heavy one and all three were uncomfortably damp). The handkerchief was not there but the present from the King of the Two Sicilies was. He had forgotten all about it. While the two ladies were devouring chunks of hot fried veal, he examined the object. Then he tried unsuccessfully to hide it under his napkin but he was not quick enough, for the beady eyes of Bella Washington, like an eager raven's, had caught the shine of metal.

"A present someone gave me the other night. Nothing of importance."

"Oh, do let us see it." And there was nothing for him to do but hand them the small bronze phallus, executed in perfect detail by some long-dead Roman as an amulet to inspire fertility.

"What on earth is it?" asked Bella. "Is it very old?"

"Very. Roman, or so I was told."

"Let me see." May took it and after a quick glance she blushed, betraying a knowledge of mysteries denied the virgin. She looked at Philip accusingly, as though he had this on purpose to reveal her secret, to taunt her with memories, no doubt still vivid, of past events never to be repeated in this bleak world. She gave it back to Bella who asked what it was.

"An amulet, dear," said her sister, recovering her composure.

"Isn't it meant to be anything at all? It looks like something."

"A tree," said Philip helpfully, May glared at him.

"Do you know the Church of St Elmo?" asked Philip quickly, changing the subject, guiltily avoiding Bella's eyes.

"Oh yes," said Bella. "We loved it. So ruined."

"One of the more interesting examples of Romanesque," said May, her manner still constrained. "We recommend it very highly. Or have you already seen it?"

"No, not yet. Someone told me it was quite interesting. An antique dealer, a man named Guiscardo. Have you met him yet?"

Bella nodded. "We liked him," she said. "He sold us the

marvelous cameo you saw your first day here. I thought it
was a real bargain."

"Did he seem in any way unusual?"

"Oh heavens, no . . ."

"Of course he did," said May. "His English—why, I've
never heard an Italian speak such correct English. He was
a most fluent conversationalist and his grasp of the idiom
was firm. His remarks, too, were cogent and well expressed
on nearly every topic we discussed."

"On *every* topic," said Bella benignly.

"You are correct, Bella, as always. On every topic.
And he kissed our hands when we left."

The sisters Washington went to a near-by castle after
lunch and Philip, left to himself, wandered disconsolately
about the hotel bowing gravely to the other guests, a
dozen or so Europeans from the prosperous north of the
continent, red-faced and long-haired, demoralized by the
heat.

Then Regina, all in green, joined him on the terrace.
"Here I am," she said.

"At exactly the right moment, too," said Philip, standing
up, but not taking her hand or kissing her. "I was just this
moment thinking of the flesh."

"How flattering! A woman my age always enjoys being
thought of as flesh, a decorative cushion for the lust of
men. I knew that it was wise of me to come before I was
expected."

He pulled up a chair for her and they both sat down.
She was extraordinarily handsome, he thought . . . her face
darkened by the sun and her hair beginning to bleach.

"Has anything happened?" asked Philip, wondering how
long it would take to reconstruct their affair, for the days
that had separated them had provided each with a different memory of what had been at other meetings;
memories which had been further distorted by separate
ponderings: what one forgot the other treasured until at
last they met on a hotel terrace overlooking Amalfi, and
they were strangers.

◙

She had come away from Rome sooner than planned,
for Rex had suddenly gone on a tour of factories in western
Austria and she had used this trip of his as an excuse to
get away, to come to the seaside for a little bathing, to
escape the heat of Rome which reminded her, she said, of

76

that famous hymn by St Francis written during a terrible medieval summer and bedecked with sun images still vivid centuries later.

They spent the long days together, bathing in the warm salt water, boating, exploring caverns and listening to legends as old as the gods and as remote. At night, avoiding Bella and May Washington, who watched with eyes too interested to be disapproving, they strolled about the town visiting the waterfront cafés, drinking with the sailors and whores until, tired at last, they returned to the hotel and made love with an intensity that diminished as the moon grew great until, by the time the moon was full, Philip found his passion succeeded by a solicitousness which was more good manners than tenderness. Yet they needed one another and both knew that although there would soon be a change, this was not the time. He tried not to consider the future, unlike one of his idols, Stendhal, who always imagined the end of every love affair at the moment it began.

The afternoon of the day he was to go to the Church of St Elmo to fulfill his mission, he and Regina rented a rowboat and they rowed from the town to a grotto which could only be approached from the sea. They moored the boat to a large flat rock at the grotto's mouth; then they took off their clothes and swam nude into the cool dark blue of the cavern, away from the glare of the June day.

The water was warm and the air cool. For a time they paddled in and out among the stalagmites which supported, church fashion, a central nave from which dark forbidden-looking passageways extended into a watery darkness, sacred to old forgotten deities, terrible and proud. Finally, bored with swimming, they climbed up on a rock off to one side of the central nave and lay side by side together in the dim blue light and stared at the groined odd ceilings and Philip saw bats, hanging like furry fruit from stone branches, asleep, fearful of even this pale light. Regina took off her bathing cap and let her long dark hair fall free upon the stone.

"It's lovely, isn't it?" she said at last, her words echoing through the nave, repeated endlessly from wall to wall like the talk of gossips. They both laughed; they talked in whispers, not wishing to be overheard by the guardians of the grotto.

"If one could only prolong this," said Philip, wishing he had said something more spontaneous, less trite. But

insincerity seemed more and more to be his way in love
affairs as he tried always to please the other, to say what
the other expected him to say, his own true feelings sacrificed in the process: perhaps because I do not feel at all,
he thought gloomily, turning on his side to face Regina,
aesthetically pleased by the sight of their bodies side by
side, prototypical of their sex, the first man and the first
woman, or the last. He wondered what it would be like to
have no consciousness, to be, just that, a half with no
other function than to become, easily and blissfully, a
whole.

"But we can," she said, still on her back, her eyes shut
and her dark hair gathered under her head like a cushion.
"You can come on to Paris with us next month. We could
see each other every day . . ."

"What about Rex?"

"What about him? He has his own philandering to do."

"I thought you said he wasn't interested in such things."

"No . . . or at least I should have said he isn't interested
in me any more. He likes young silly creatures and I'm
just as pleased with the arrangement. I have no false
pride about my role in his life. You see, we're very happily
married. We have the same interests. We enjoy politics.
He'd be quite helpless without me, professionally at least."

"Does he know about me?" Philip, like all young men,
was eager to know everything everyone thought of him,
the more uncomplimentary the better. He liked to think of
himself as a ruthless buccaneer who strode across the
world shattering sensibilities and conventions with the fury
of his progress but he knew, of course, at the same time,
that most people thought him rather a lamb . . . a conception based on his small nose and his babyish lisp.

"Of course not." Regina laughed. "Why should he? We
never discuss our infidelities. As a matter of fact, he thinks
you're a promising young man."

"Promising what?" Philip was disappointed.

"A great career."

"In politics?"

"What else? Is there any other?"

"Of course, but since I probably won't pursue any of
them either, I can't throw an easel or a violin at you. . . .
Give me time," he said, suddenly serious.

"How long a time?" She sat up and looked at him. Her
body upon the dark rock was smooth and fine as the
white marble statue of that girl-saint who lies sprawled on

78

the floor of the catacombs near Rome, martyred beneath the cross and the fish.

"Give me my year. Then I'll know."

"You promise?"

"I promise. I must have the year first, no matter what I do." Then feeling the tug of sex, he took her and they made love on the hard rough surface as lovers before them had done since the days when the gods in human form wandered about the earth seducing mortals and rewarding them with curious gifts, with crowns and genius, with constellations in their image spangled across the black fields of night; or, if the mortals refused to yield to these passionate gods, they were struck down, destroyed, transformed to winter shadows or to summer flowers, their beloved forms becoming green laurel on the slopes of hills or wildflowers in the fields where the thunder sounded.

"Must you go?"

"I said I would. I promised Glenellen."

"But you promised me you wouldn't."

"I didn't really promise. I said I would try to get out of it. But it was too late. Besides, what harm can come of it? They are all perfectly harmless lunatics."

"I'm sure they are but you don't want to get into any trouble with the police."

"Why not? You can get me out."

"That's no reason to do anything foolish. Suppose they shoot you."

"Oh, for God's sake! and suppose I get run over by a taxicab? There's more danger of that happening, you know."

"Do as you please," she said. And he did.

He left her at eleven o'clock that night. They had dined with Bella and May Washington whose curiosity had finally got the best of them. May especially was eager to ferret out if possible the nature and the enormity of their sin. But Regina handled her beautifully, and, when dinner was over and Philip excused himself, the sisters Washington were fawning on Mrs Durham, eager to win her favor.

In the middle of the sky the white moon rode among black and silver clouds, blown north by the dry desert wind of Africa tempered with sea's salt but not much cooled from the long journey. The townspeople seemed more exuberant tonight than usual, as though celebrating unconsciously some old festival of the moon's fullness.

Philip paused a moment before the largest waterfront café. Inside men and women were singing and dancing. One tigerish, black-frizzy-haired woman (descendant of some Moorish or Carthaginian sailor) was doing a wild dance for the men, her skirt pulled up to her fat thighs, her legs moving like fleshy pistons in time to the music.

Philip, as unobtrusively as possible, slipped into the café and watched until, amid laughter and curses and cheering, the dancer stopped and the usual sentimental laments were wrung stickily from the fiddle and the accordion. Everyone was hot, sweating, flimsily dressed and happy, all that he'd ever imagined the joyful peasant to be. Yet he knew that if he looked close he would see what the outsider never saw: fear, antagonisms, envy, all the usual human characteristics accentuated by this summer land, the violence checked by pleasure in the evening, by piety and labor during the bedazzled day. Feeling much better, Philip left the café and turned into the street which led to the Bridge of St Elmo.

Even these ordinarily dark streets were well lighted, for the doors that were usually sealed against the night were open and townspeople sat on their own doorsteps or lounged about the cobbled streets beneath the full moon which hung, now rich and golden, swollen with summer, among its clouds, like a lantern in the dark.

On the other side of the bridge, all was quiet. A few houses were set back against the hill on terraces above the town, accessible only by foot. Set apart from these houses was the ruin of the Church of St Elmo, surrounded by olive trees and ilex, by giant cypresses, black and mourning in the moon's light.

But before he could get to the church he first had to climb many steps, each, it seemed to him, more steep than the one before and he was thankful for the south wind when he finally arrived, breathing heavily, at the top of the steps, where he paused a moment to rest. Amalfi was below him, its yellow light gleaming in a pattern as inscrutable as that of the white stars which shone everywhere, one beyond another, in the midnight sky. Far out to sea, a ship with blinking lights was making its way to Africa and, as he stared at the ship on the dark horizon, a star fell in the west, a delicate sudden arc of light.

He turned and walked slowly down a narrow flagstone

path to the grove of trees where the church, now black and silver, stood like a ship wrecked on a sandbar, roofless, its windows empty as idiot's eyes and its towers gone. He stood for a moment looking up at the cracked stone towers. Insects whirred drily in the trees and, far far away, he heard the faint tinkle of music, the echo of laughter in the town below.

Conscious of his danger, dreading ghosts more than police or Communists, he entered the church and stood in the roofless nave surveying the shattered arch beneath which the high altar, now a mound of rubble, had once been. As he moved down the nave the noise of the cicadas abruptly ceased. He stopped then, waiting for the ordinary sounds of the night to resume, but they did not; the silence persisted. He looked up at the moon, now bone-white, no longer golden, sailing through the black and silver clouds which separated solid earth from empty sky like an antique shawl from Spain thrown over that one-half world beneath.

He waited, trembling, before the mound where the altar had been. Minutes, hours, years, eras passed and still he waited, frozen by moonlight into a pallid facsimile of his living self. He saw the church as it once was: stained glass, wine-red and cerulean, filled with empty windows and translated clear sunlight into rainbows, while figures in vivid costumes moved about in ritual attitude and celebrated the ancient Mass. Then windows shattered and the roof fell; the towers crashed down the hillside and, as he stood there, even those walls which still stood buttressed all around him fell at last and he was alone in the dust, the burnt stumps of cypress and ilex and olive around him, and the sea where the town was.

He moved. The cicadas resumed their monotonous whirring and the moon was hidden by clouds. He looked at his watch and saw by its luminous dial that he had been there ten minutes, that it was now fifteen minutes past twelve and neither conspirator nor policeman had shared with him the ghosts and the constant shadows.

"Hello!" he said in a loud voice, which frightened him; but no one answered. Resolutely, he explored the church, pushing his way past the fallen masonry into chapels where wild grapes grew. He went everywhere except down into the dark hole behind the high altar where, he knew, the illustrious dead had once been buried in ice-cold crypts, the earth of their bodies now holding, indiscriminately, nests of scorpions and the roots of flowers, in decay, as in life, the fine balance between good and evil kept. Satisfied at last that no one living was in the church, he left.

As he stepped across the stone threshold he noticed something gleaming on the lintel. He picked it up, but since the moon was hidden he could not identify it in the dark; it felt like an empty balloon or a bag. He put it in his pocket, and went down the steps to the world again, his vision lost already.

Regina listened with amusement to his story of the empty church and his moment of vision.

"Then your time wasn't entirely wasted . . . you at least had a revelation."

"But of what?" Philip was irritable, conscious obscurely that he had been made a fool of in a way he did not understand.

"It would seem obvious from your description. I've always suspected, though, that revelations are valuable only in themselves, not for what, if anything in particular, they reveal. It would seem that you saw the life of one building from its beginning to its end, when not only the ruin will be destroyed but Amalfi as well. Nothing remarkable about that. Since nothing endures it's quite logical to conclude that Amalfi is not eternal, that one day the sea will make a bay of what is now a town. But since the exact date of this phenomenon was withheld, you do not qualify as a prophet."

"It all seems quite pointless, including your analysis," said Philip, tired and angry. "I'd like to get my hands on that antique dealer."

"Forget about it, darling. Why bother? Now we can go back to Rome. You've had your moment as a courier, a conspirator . . ."

Philip, remembering something, reached in his pocket and pulled out the rubber bag which, upon examination, proved to be a mask of a gray wolf's head, quite realistic, with green eyes which reflected light the way the taillights of automobiles do.

"This must have been Guiscardo's," said Philip.

"Do you think he was there all the time?"

"Perhaps. If he was, I wonder why he didn't speak to me."

"He wanted to see what would happen."

"Yet, what did happen?"

"You will never know now."

"I suppose not. Shall I return the mask to him?"

"No, keep it as a souvenir."

"Of what?"

"Of your monarchist days."

He snorted and shoved the mask into a wastebasket. They were in his room, seated in front of a tall window which overlooked the sea.

"Shall we go back to Rome?" asked Regina at last.

"I suppose so. I would like to see more of this country first."

"We can drive slowly."

"We might even go to Capri," suggested Philip.

She nodded. "It's lovely there this time of year. Crowded, though."

"I don't mind."

"You will see nothing but Americans."

"I've a feeling the best way to get to know them is to see them in Europe."

"You're right. But do you want to know them?"

"No, but for a budding politician I thought it the right thing to say." They laughed at one another. Then he took his jacket off. As he did, he noticed the safety pin which fastened Glenellen's documents to his inside pocket. He undid the pin and held the plain white envelope under the lamp.

"Do you think I should open it?"

"Of course. How will you ever know what's inside?"

"But I shouldn't really."

"Why not? Your mission is over. You'll have to destroy it anyway. Open it. I can't wait."

He tore the envelope open and took out a single sheet of paper on which had been written one word in Greek letters, a language he had not studied in school.

"What on earth does it mean?" he asked, bewildered.

"Let me see." Regina took the paper for a moment; then she handed it back to him, smiling.

"Well, what does it mean? Can you really read Greek?"

"Oh, yes. There's no end to my talents," she smiled.

"What does it say?"

"I can only tell you what the word means. You'll have to interpret it."

"Why?"

"Because it's a message, for you I think."

83

"But that's ridiculous. I was supposed to deliver it to the royalists here."

"Then perhaps it wasn't intended for you. In any case, *you* must decide. The word is *Asebia*."

"And it means?"

"Failure to worship the gods . . . a capital crime in ancient Greece. It was the principal charge brought against Socrates."

"I am very confused," said Philip.

"A confusing age," said Regina with a sigh. "How lucky none of us knows what will happen."

The vulgarity of Mrs Helotius was one of the few really perfect, unruined things in Europe; it was a legend and unlike most highly publicized phenomena, never a disappointment to the eager tourist who (properly sponsored) had got himself into any one of those five villas which decorated the spas of fashionable Europe like rough diamonds, bases for her considerable operations.

Officially she had never been born. That area of the world where she had first appeared fifty-two years ago had changed nationality so many times that all records had long since disappeared. But, as she freely admitted to her intimates (those creatures to whom she accorded precedence either because of birth or well-rewarded talent), she had started from scratch, as had Helotius, a Greek who had made more money than any honest man should out of figs in Asia Minor. Later, when he became British, he married Mrs Helotius whose family name had never been revealed to her intimates though all of them called her by her first name, Zoe.

Helotius was thirty-seven years older than Zoe at the time of their marriage. After twenty years together he died, leaving her the figs and a lust for position which until that moment had gnawed secretly at her vitals ever since, as a child, she had scrubbed the floors of her underprivileged home in that part of the world which, even then, was in the throes of being torn from one nation by another. Yet money itself was not important to her; clothes and servants and houses had, in themselves, no charm for her. She always said that a bit of horsemeat and a cold boiled potato was the best meal in the world and little did her fine friends know that she meant what she said. But Position was something else and fortunately she now had

84

the money to achieve it. Her career began two months after
Helotius died. She had gone to the finest couturier in Paris
and ordered a wardrobe which would knock everybody's
eyes out. It did.

There were those of course who laughed and thought
her in bad taste but everyone else followed her activities in
Vogue and *The Tatler* with feverish interest, aware that
money was being spent and that something must be done
about it.

She was vulgar. But she was rich, and the villas were
being bought at the rate of one a year. At the end of five
years she was a Papal Countess and her implacable design
was now fully displayed across the ravaged old world of
Europe as everyone came to her lunches, her dinners, her
ballet parties and her fêtes. The birthday of the British
king was always the occasion of her greatest effort: it
usually took place at night on the Eiffel Tower which was
acquired for the occasion. Unkind people said that her
observance of this particular day was because George VI
was the last holdout. She had never been presented at his
Court. The time she had invaded the Royal Yacht Squadron
at Cowes with a bouquet of roses, thistles, shamrocks and
leeks was not considered cricket, although she did get one
glimpse of alarmed majesty before the guards led her
away.

But even her enemies were now forced to admit that she
had won through and that, very likely, her vulgarity had
been more of an asset than not. Had she been more sensitive she could never have endured the contempt of the
established figures of this world; the fact that she had
ignored their hostility in the end gave her a certain moral
dominion over them. If she was really so sure of herself,
they reasoned, perhaps there *was* something to her after
all and certainly she entertained richly. Finally, almost
everyone came around; the ones who did not were considered stuffy and not in the fashion.

For Mrs Helotius the world was an enormous jungle
full of lions to be bagged and no one, not even a woman
as well equipped and devoted as herself, could hope to
assemble more than a fraction of them under her roof. To
add to her frustration new lions appeared every season,
and how was she to know if they were to reign for a
number of seasons and become legitimate or be devoured
in the first months of their maturity? Yet she did not make
many mistakes. She never read books but she was able

85

to skim reviews and study the authors' biographies on the dust jackets and determine with remarkable accuracy whether the gentleman in question was "there" or nearly there, or gone. She did not handle lionesses unless they were either royal or very noble. In science she was guided by *Time* magazine and the various selections of the Nobel Prize Committee. In politics and religion she was infallible. As for society, she had every Register, every Peerage and Almanac available while her secretary-companion, Lady Julia Keen, an impoverished daughter of a bankrupt Earl, presided over a portable filing case where everyone was neatly indexed according to age, general appearance, income, connections, with comments on the number of times they had been entertained at the five villas and the number of times they had entertained her at *their* villas. She was, as one ill-natured editor who had failed to be invited a second time to her house remarked, the Havelock Ellis of the social world.

Now she was in residence at Capri, and Regina and Philip lunched on the terrace of her house in the company of twenty brilliant creatures, the best to be had on Capri at that moment: a British Field Marshal, a Spanish Marquis, four American novelists (they were everywhere that season), a number of politicians, and a dozen men and women whose names are known to everyone who reads about the doings of the international set.

The house and the terrace, the day and the island were, Philip thought, marvelous. He'd never seen such vivid colors: burning green and blinding blue, flashes of flame-red and flame-yellow flowers among the green, stirred gently by the south wind, and by the more drunken guests who wandered off the flagstone terrace to look down the steep rock cliff at the sea below.

The house itself was not large: a dozen bedrooms, half as many baths, and the usual offices. Of the five villas it was the smallest but because of its setting, Mrs Helotius always spoke of it as her "jewel."

"You will so enjoy meeting the Field Marshal, Mrs Durham . . . and there are a number of people from your Embassy whom you must know. They will know *you*, certainly, and be so thrilled to meet you if they haven't already. Do come to lunch, both of you." She had said this last with a sharp rather puzzled glance at Philip. "The Field Marshal is so sweet."

And so they came to the lunch and the Field Marshal

was his famous self, not sweet at all. Regina knew a number of the Americans and all the Italians. It was a good way to spend his first day on Capri, thought Philip, who was thoroughly impressed, much more so than he'd been that morning in the main square of the town when Zoe Helotius, dressed in a Swiss dirndl and wearing dark harlequin-shaped glasses, swooped down on Regina, a hairy-legged Italian Duke in tow.

She was more elegant now. She wore one of her couturier's creations, a gossamer gray affair with emeralds the size of egg yolks at her throat. Her hair was a dark red, streakily dyed to give it the illusion of authenticity. She was a short lean woman, with no waist at all. Her features were tiny, except for the chin which was slightly undershot. She was always carefully painted and her face was lifted once a year until now it was almost totally expressionless, as though fixed for all time by some Medusa, in a mood midway between surprise and doubt. Her voice was harsh, very English, seldom betraying her obscure foreign birth.

They had dined at a buffet. Then, drinking champagne, the guests moved about a dainty gazebo which, banked by flowers, overlooked the sea below.

"Shall you be here long, Mrs Durham?" inquired Mrs Helotius, gazing over Regina's shoulder at the Field Marshal who was grimly tearing one of her finest yellow roses apart.

"I'm going back to Rome tomorrow. Then on to Paris."

"With your husband?"

"Oh yes. He has a job to do, you know."

"Indeed I do. All Europe knows. All Europe awaits his report with bated breath," she said dramatically, averting her eyes from the Field Marshal who was now heading purposefully toward a bush of white roses with much the same expression he'd undoubtedly worn on his face the day he had ordered one of his divisions into the worst ambush of the last European war, for which he had been raised to the peerage and sent to New Zealand to mobilize the Maoris in defense of those islands.

"I am sure his report isn't that earth-shaking," Regina said with a smile.

"Nonsense. He has the President's Ear," said Mrs Helotius intensely, betraying her near-Oriental origin by an exotic overemphasis which was very un-British and certainly not American.

"You must let me give a party for you next month in Paris," she said at last, gracefully accepting the fact that she would learn nothing of Durham's mission from his wife.

"We should like that very much."

"You come too, Mr . . ."

"Warren," said Philip, who was wondering just how Regina was going to explain him.

". . . met him just yesterday in Naples. His father is one of my husband's very good friends . . . a judge . . ."

"Ah, the Law," intoned Mrs Helotius, surveying the gazebo, wondering who was drunk and who was not. Lady Julia marked a minus after each name in the filing cabinet to denote one instance of drunkenness or bad behavior. Three minuses excluded all but the most eminent from the hospitality of the villas and the Eiffel Tower.

"Well, what do you think of her?" asked Regina as Mrs Helotius hurried away to defend her rosebush from the Marshal.

"Much better than I'd imagined."

"Quite up to expectations. I'm glad we came."

"To Capri? Or here?"

"Both. Aren't you?"

"I think so. I must go back to Rome soon."

"When?"

"Tomorrow, I think." For a week now they had been together growing dark in the sun and easy in one another's arms. Neither had referred to her plans or to his or to whether those plans would, after this week, coincide or not. It had been his idea to visit Capri. They had connecting rooms at the hotel and as she had predicted, everyone she knew was on the island. There were no secrets here, which did not disturb Philip much. He had nothing to lose and he was more pleased than not to be known as Regina's lover.

"Will you stay on here?" she asked, not looking at him, smiling pleasantly as a young American presented himself to her.

"A little while. I'll be in Rome before you go," said Philip quickly; then he said how-do-you-do to the young man whom Regina introduced to him as Robert Holton, of the State Department.

The three chatted amiably. Holton was one of those smooth well-educated youths Philip particularly disliked, not objecting to their smoothness or the fact they had gone to Harvard as he himself had, but rather to the way they

mixed opportunism, charm and earnestness in such a
fashion as to render (to him at least) their every remark
suspect. Young men dupe older and wiser men but never
their own contemporaries with whom they must compete
for the good places of this world. And Holton, carefully
dressed, beginning to go bald, cautious, no doubt sensed
the other's hostility for presently he went away.

"He used to be in Wall Street," said Regina, as though
anxious not to talk of themselves now that, in a moment,
a plan had been made for the next meeting, a promise
exacted, "but he got into the State Department this year.
I used to see him at Mrs Stevanson's in New York. You
know her, don't you? Blue hair? That one. He had an
affair with a charming Italian girl whose name I can never
remember. He treated her badly or she treated *him* badly.
I've forgotten which. Oh, here comes the Field Marshal:
the dullest man in Europe!"

And smelling of all the roses he had that afternoon
destroyed, the warrior bored them for twenty minutes
until Lady Julia Keen, under orders from their hostess,
led him away.

▣

"It seemed that Mrs Helotius was staying at Antibes
many years ago at the house of some very grand friends,
when some less grand friends at Cannes invited her to
lunch. She wired them she couldn't possibly make it. She
then received a card from them saying how sorry they were
that she couldn't come to lunch since the P. of W. would
be there. Lunch was nearly over, when Zoe arrived, dusty
and disheveled, her Daimler boiling in the hot sun. 'Where
is he?' she said to the startled host. 'Where is who?' 'Who?
Why the Prince of Wales, of course.' 'Oh, the Prince isn't
here. Just us and the Provost of Worcester.' "

Robert Holton was full of stories about Mrs Helotius
and Philip enjoyed them. Since Holton was staying at his
hotel they saw a great deal of one another after Regina's
departure and Philip's first unfavorable impression had
been succeeded by an amused neutrality. He did not like
young men. He'd never had a close friend among his
contemporaries and he thought it unlikely that he would
begin to care for one of them now. He enjoyed the company
of older men if they were civilized (his standards were
precise) and he liked women. Young men, however, always

brought out the worst in him, made him irritable and competitive.

But Holton was very nearly as neutral as he himself and they were able to spend the days together blandly, eating and drinking and bathing in the sea. At night there were various parties, expeditions to bordellos where everything was handled blithely and gracefully. The Italian pleasure in the natural communicated itself to these two Puritan youths who, nevertheless, felt all pleasure was evil and that only pain was good. Consequently neither could exact more than a temporary physical satisfaction from any act. Each would have been far more exalted by some calculated frustration and its attendant anguish. But the young and the unengaged in these fiery last days of the Christian era of which I write were not allowed the excuse of faith nor the rare delight of conscious martyrdom, rather, they were allowed to play any game they wanted, to invent the rules as they went along, to do exactly what they pleased as their culture approached its diffuse end and they themselves, though liberated from the arbitrary ways of the old church, from its superstition and dogma and bloody intolerance, had not yet managed to exorcise the mean devil of guilt, the sense of sin nurtured for two thousand years. Now though the churches themselves had died of their own victory long before the last of the wars of religion began, the fear of pleasure and the hate of loving persisted, a withering frost at the heart of summer, and all the martyrs, clinging upside down like bats from the rafters of heaven, no doubt felt that their work had survived the vicissitudes of knowledge better than even they might reasonably have suspected. Perhaps, though one must not look too far into the irrelevancies of the future, their great monument, that core of gleaming ice in each man's heart, might yet become once more the focal point of a new, more savage orthodoxy in which the dream of the martyrs would at last be fulfilled in the vast design of some new dogma from which there could be no deviation since the mind, as the late Christian scientists have discovered, can now be controlled: drugs will extract a truth or a fact from any man and no matter how strong he may be, he will recant on schedule with apparent calm, while virtue becomes the province of the state and the hero vanishes.

Does Philip know this? All men know it or rather feel it, in different ways. Were he examined he would say perhaps that he disliked the cold but whether he would choose the fire is doubtful. Yet neutrality bores him and, unconsciously, he does await the thawing of that spirit which was frozen by a long accretion of laws of conduct, empiric and mystical; to be unfrozen, if at all, by some act of loving outside the jungle that the flesh is, that the mind is, too. The beloved shrine of the false saints shattered at last by some central force, the glacier exploding into a million particles of ice, brilliant in the light of the fire outside, as the flow resumes, like a wide river in the spring or like those myriad galaxies of burning stars which, they tell us, are eternally flowing outward from some dark cold center to the void where nothing was before.

Chapter Five

PHILIP ARRIVED IN ROME on a hot gray day, windless and enervating. The Via Veneto was crowded with tourists who seemed very nearly as depressed as he himself. The chatter at Doney's was more subdued than usual and from time to time, anxious glances were turned skyward as though a storm or the Second Coming was imminent. Far away, beyond the Alban hills, thunder rolled. He told Clyde Norman that he wished it would rain.

Mr Norman had been sitting alone at a table gloomily chewing a meringue glacé, the whites of his eyes a liverish gold. He had greeted Philip cordially but without enthusiasm. He, too, wished it would rain.

"I haven't been well," he observed briefly as Philip sat down.

"What's the matter?" Philip tried not to sound as unsympathetic as he felt. The Amalfi adventure still rankled.

"Liver. And, for some reason, when I'm having a liver attack I eat all the wrong things. A demon drives me to larger and larger meringues, more and more curries and heavy veal . . . until at last I'm forced to go to the hospital for a few days and live on bread and water. The body! How I loathe it."

"I'm sure that mess you're eating will do the trick."

"Send me to the hospital? Very likely. But I can't stop. I just can't stop. By the way, have you tried the nougat here? It's splendid, but be sure to take the little bits of paper off—otherwise it has rather a nasty taste. Will you have something to eat?"

"I don't think so. A drink, perhaps." A drink was ordered.

"I went to Amalfi."

"I wondered. I didn't want to ask."

"Why not?"

"Well, Ayre is the one you must report to. I'm only a small cog in the organization. Did you enjoy Amalfi?"

"I liked the bathing . . ."

"Excellent water, so warm. I shouldn't mind going down there myself but the sun is the worst thing in the world for a liver complaint."

"But everything else went wrong."

"Wrong? In what sense?"

"In every sense. I wasn't able to deliver the message."

"Oh." Mr Norman sighed and looked distractedly about, as though for succor.

"And Guiscardo was no help at all."

"I don't know him."

"You know who he is."

"Who who is?"

"Guiscardo."

"Oh . . . I do wish you'd talk to Ayre about all this. I'm sure he'll make much more sense than I will."

"I can hardly believe that," said Philip, growing angry. "Of all the people involved in this idiocy, he is the one who has consistently made no sense at all."

"Hobbies," murmured Mr Norman.

"What are they, by the way?" asked Philip, deflected for a moment from his calculated denunciation.

"Oh, one thing and another."

"Such as?"

"Can't you tell?"

"The young men?"

Mr Norman blushed. "That too, of course. No, I meant the vagueness you referred to."

"What about it?"

"Narcotics, my boy. He takes heroin at the moment. But don't ever think he isn't making sense. He is. The difficulty is that when he's under the influence his tempo is somewhat different from that of a . . . civilian and consequently he tends to skip certain details in a conversation which, were they supplied, would make him very easily understood, even admired, for he has an excellent mind, you know."

Philip decided to postpone his scene. Obviously there would be no point in dissipating his wrath on Mr Norman who was not, so far as he knew, directly involved in the Guiscardo business.

"I suppose I'd better report to him, then."

"I think it would be a good idea."

"I shall also tell him that the House of Savoy can be restored without my assistance."

"Oh . . . I'm sorry." Mr Norman looked as concerned

93

as it is possible for anyone to look with a mouth full of meringue. He swallowed noisily and repeated, "I'm sorry. I had so looked forward to our working together."

"My connection with the movement wasn't intended to continue after Amalfi anyway."

"What about Mrs Durham?"

"Mrs Durham?"

"Yes. I thought you were going to approach her about our cause. I thought that was why she went to Amalfi."

"How did you know she was there?"

"One hears things."

"She came to Amalfi, and we did talk once or twice about your party and she was all against it."

"I was afraid of that. You weren't able to change her mind at all?"

"Not at all. As a matter of fact, I never tried. We only talked about it."

"Oh dear. This *is* discouraging. Well, I suppose everything will work out properly in the end. By the way, what did you think of Zoe Helotius?"

"How did you know I met her?"

"Someone saw you at a party she gave on Capri."

"You know everything."

"If only I did! But how did you like her?"

"She was pleasant enough, I suppose. I only met her once."

"Fabulous woman. I remember such a funny story they used to tell about her. It seems she was staying with some rather distinguished people at Antibes . . ."

Philip listened for the third time to this story, idly comparing its delivery to earlier accounts, finally awarding the prize for recitation to Mr Norman. When they had done laughing, an appointment was made for Philip to wait upon Lord Glenellen at his palace on the following day, to report the failure of his mission in the south. Refusing nougat and another Helotius story, Philip left Doney's and walking quickly, he got to his hotel before the rain in quick warm drops fell on the dusty streets, and thunder clapped above the gardens of the Villa Borghese.

Raindrops were in her hair and on her face. She had worn no hat. "Why wear a hat when the rain will ruin it?"

"I'll dry you off."

He took a towel and partly dried her hair and face, lik-

94

ing the familiar scent of rain on woman's hair, recalling once how he had made love on the banks of the Hudson during a summer storm and how, when the moment came, lightning had struck a near-by tree.

"I'm glad you're back," she said, when he had finished and they lay side by side on the bed.

"I got tired of Capri."

"I thought you would."

"I don't like that sort of thing."

"What sort of thing?"

"People who are interested only in people . . . or is that what I mean?"

"I don't know, my darling. *You* must know what you mean."

"Yes, I suppose I do. It's not that I object to malice and gossip. I'm capable of both myself, I know, but it isn't my principal interest."

"What is?"

He grunted. "Here we go again." He arranged the pillow behind his head. "Myself," he said at last, "but it's awful to admit."

"No one else?"

He paused. Then he repeated, not looking at her, "No one else."

"Sad," she said, with no inflection.

"Should there be someone else?"

"That's not what I mean, Philip," she said. "I'm not really very romantic either. I've had affairs. I have a husband. I've liked some men, adored others. But I will admit to you now that I have never loved anyone either, nor have I ever once put someone else's interest before my own." She laughed softly. "We're a fine pair, aren't we?"

Illogically, this hurt him. He did not care a great deal about her but for either to admit this truth to the other when their bodies had so recently been joined was a form of brutality which he had never before encountered. Seeing his momentary dismay, she kissed his hand.

"But I adore you," she said lightly. "Don't look at me as though I'd done you an injury."

He recovered. "I was just startled to hear you say something so frank."

"You don't think I'm ordinarily frank?"

"No . . . it's just that I've never known a woman to say anything like that, so soon after making love."

"Perhaps I merely said what you were thinking."

95

"No. That would have been childish. But then I'm not so sure anyone ever really sacrifices his comfort for another person . . . which is, I suppose, the ultimate test and definition of love."

"Oh, many people do."

"What do you want from me, then?"

Regina sat up and faced him.

"A great deal."

"But not love."

"Not what we usually call love, no. I don't want self-sacrifice, no grand gestures or frenzies. What I want is something else again. Something which has to do with our discussion that first night."

"But how could all that help you or, should I say, gratify you?"

"That is my business." She spoke more sharply than she had intended and for an instant Philip had a glimpse of another Regina, one like her name, cold, unfeeling, indifferent to everything but power and its impersonal logic; but the vision was brief. She was herself again. She apologized for the sharpness with which she had spoken but as she resumed her early role, he sensed with some uneasiness that the Regina he had seen so briefly might be, after all, the real one. And so, in that one instant of doubt, the affair ended. What might come after would perhaps seem unchanged and though they could still make love, talk intimately, affectionately, he was withdrawn, no longer committed or sympathetic, a stranger with all the privileges but none of the demands of the lover. If Regina was aware of his withdrawal, she did not show it. She talked of other matters.

"Did you see much of Zoe before you left Capri?"

"A quick and poignant meeting in the square," he said, selecting a number of artificial phrases to disguise his confusion, to give him time to recover. "She was guiding the Field Marshal about the town with a look of terrible triumph. I believe she thought I had written a book for when I said hello to her she told the warrior that he should read it. Unfortunately, the book must not have done very well because, before I could identify myself, they were gone."

"So like her."

"Why does everyone say 'so like her'?"

"Philip." He looked at her then.

"What's the matter?" She seemed puzzled, even defensive.

"Nothing's the matter," he said weakly. "Nothing at all. I'm just rather put out by the whole damned trip."

"I thought you enjoyed it."

"I did, parts of it." But he could not add the sentence she wanted to hear. He went off in another direction. "It got on my nerves, that's all."

"Have you seen Glenellen?"

"I go tomorrow for dinner."

"What will you tell him?"

"What happened, what I think of the whole thing."

"Do be careful." Then she got up and dressed. Philip put on a dressing gown and sat down in an armchair by the open window. Monotonously, the rain fell.

"Where's your husband?" asked Philip suddenly.

"Rex?" She paused, his hairbrush in one hand. "He's gone to Florence for a few days. I have to meet him there." She brushed her dark hair back, her eyes watching not her own reflection in the mirror but his.

"How does he feel about your . . . trip?"

"We never discuss those things."

"Have there been so many?"

She turned around, smiling, and faced him. "Now, Philip, for some reason you want to quarrel with me. Heaven knows why. But I'm not going to quarrel with *you*. If I've done something you don't like, then tell me what it is. But please don't be disagreeable."

Since there is no way to handle reasonableness when one is in a bad temper, Philip was forced, rather foolishly, to apologize, to say a number of things he didn't mean while Regina, the calm mistress of the situation, continued to arrange her hair.

"The rain is almost over," he said at last, examining the broken lines the drizzle made, as it slanted palely against the dark wet trees across the street.

"Would you like to drive with me to Florence next week?"

"I thought you said Rex was there."

"That's right. I'm joining him. We're going on to Paris the first of next week."

"I don't think it's such a good idea, my seeing him. Do you?"

"Why not? He likes you."

"But—well, after all . . ."

"Don't be silly. Besides, it's no concern of his what I do when I take a trip. I thought I'd explained all that to you. In any case, should he have been suspicious, he won't be if he sees us together. Obviously I would not travel to Florence with my lover."

"I don't understand."

"Oh . . ." She came over to him where he sat and looked down at him for a moment, smiling; then she said, "It's my plot, don't you see? Our going to Florence is part of it, the most important part. Do humor me. It's for you, after all."

"For me?"

"And for me too, in a way. But that's my problem."

"I'm not sure if I'll be able to get away," he said.

When the rain stopped, she left. He had given her no definite answer and he had been, he realized sadly, childish and hostile; this depressed him as all weakness in himself did, for as a rule he was at ease with everyone, especially lovers. But Regina was different; how different he could not tell, and because she puzzled him he felt, quite correctly, that he was at a disadvantage and he was undecided as to what course to follow: whether to break with her at once and for good or to go to Florence and examine the mystery close-to.

He stood in the window looking down at the street. He saw Regina get into a taxicab and drive away. The boys who bought and sold black-market money reappeared as the gray sky broke and the sun shone.

▣

"You will find Ayre somewhat changed," said Mr Norman, as they crossed the dusty parquet of the great hall and Philip noticed for the first time the threadbare ensigns of ancient battles which hung from the walls at regular intervals, between cracked and flaking portraits which stared darkly at him; the Mettelli in solemn conclave expressed their contempt for the dust and the new age.

"I always find him changed," said Philip. "Each time I see him he's a different person."

"Yet always the same Ayre, devoted . . ."

"To what?"

"Life," said Mr Norman grandly. The Mettelli looked aghast, while somewhere in the palace a large piece of plaster (or a body) fell crashing to the floor. Philip started, but the servant who was their guide smiled re-

98

assuringly and showed them into Ayre's study, the same room in which Philip had been received before.

A table had been set for lunch. Four places, Philip noticed, wondering who the fourth would be. Ayre greeted him effusively.

"So good to see you again, young man. We've missed you here in Rome. Missed you very much. Just the other day at the baths I turned to Clyde and said, 'Where could that nice young American be?'"

"I was in Amalfi, part of the time," said Philip precisely.

"I remember," said Ayre, and an expression which could only be called furtive passed over his lizard face. "We'll go into that in good time. But now let us dine, my dears." Fussing and chattering, he put first Clyde then Philip on his right. After that, the seating arrangement determined, they sat down.

"Is Mr Morgan coming?" asked Philip, indicating the empty place across from Glenellen.

"Of course not. He's in Wales, where I hope he'll stay."

"He *did* leave?" asked Mr Norman, interested.

"Yes, several days ago. I must say, too, that I feel well out of it. When I think of the sacrifices I've made, I could do someone an injury." He looked balefully at Philip as though he were an accomplice of the villainous Morgan. Then, collecting himself, he smiled. "You must excuse the outburst. I've been on edge lately. Very. Very on edge. But now here comes dinner."

A white-jacketed boy brought them caviar and blinis. A feast, Philip decided; his resolve to be stern and intractable wavered. Vodka was served in small chilled carafes and it was not until he'd finished the blinis and two glasses of vodka that he noticed Glenellen was wearing a fawn-colored tunic without pockets or tie. He was allowed no opportunity, however, to comment for between them Mr Norman and Glenellen controlled the conversation, moving easily if eccentrically through history, literature, medicine and finally politics. He was forced to wait until both Glenellen and Clyde were out of breath. Then, quickly taking advantage of this unusual hiatus, he said, "I saw Guiscardo."

Glenellen stared at him, his pale eyes glassy in the candlelight and his face red and shining from the vodka. "Oh." He looked at Mr Norman, who looked away, worrying a pickled beet with his fork. "Guiscardo, eh?" Glenellen cleared his throat. "Charming, didn't you think?"

"No."

"Trouble of some kind?"

"Yes. I wasn't able to deliver the papers."

"The papers? Oh." Glenellen looked puzzled. "I was under the impression that you did deliver the papers."

"Who told you that?"

"Guiscardo himself. He sent a message to me by a mutual friend, a man of the highest integrity."

"I went to the antique shop and Guiscardo was wearing a mask . . ."

Glenellen chuckled. "Just like the old days, Clyde, isn't it?" Clyde agreed.

"He told me to take the papers to a certain church a few nights later. He refused to touch them."

Glenellen's eyes opened very wide at this. He blinked furiously and a tear glittered in the corner of one eye. "But he said that you gave them to him."

"Are you positive?"

"Of course I'm positive. Not only do I have his word for it but later events, unhappily, proved that he *had* received my message. You see, he gave it to the police."

"The police?" Philip was frightened. "I thought he was one of your most important people."

"He entertained Republican sentiments in secret," said Glenellen primly. He poured himself more vodka. "Never trust a Plantagenet."

"What did the police do?"

"They sold me the papers. What else? Isn't all business done that way?"

"I'm afraid I don't know." Philip hardly knew what to say or do. "You didn't have any trouble, did you? With the police, I mean?"

"Of course I did. You don't think I enjoy giving them money, do you? I denounced the police captain to his face, told him a thing or two, but in the end I paid. One must, after all."

"And Guiscardo?"

"I am no longer in communication with him. I felt he'd let me down."

"I should think so."

"He sold me a bronze which he swore he'd authenticated, an Augustan piece. Well, of course, he hadn't. I don't know how well you know him but he is very nearly the laziest man I have ever known, and slovenly in business matters. I sent him a wire saying that one of the Vatican curators had proved this piece a forgery. Well, would he give me my money back? No. He sent me another bronze, a companion piece which was also fake. The man's perfidy is endless."

"But you are still fond of him," said Clyde sweetly.

"Of course I am. It's not his fault he is badly organized."

"But how did he get the papers?" Philip was dogged.

"You gave them to him."

"I did *not* give them to him."

"Then how did he get them?" Glenellen's voice was growing irritable.

"I don't know," said Philip, wondering if perhaps he had drunk too much vodka.

"What makes you think you *didn't* give them to him?" asked Clyde suddenly.

"First, because I didn't. I still can remember most things that have happened to me in the last month. And, second, because I broke the seal and read the message."

"You should not have done that," said Glenellen, unexpectedly mild. "It would have been much better to have dropped the whole business. After all, Guiscardo did have the real message."

"Which I could not deliver and so, having failed, I read what you had written."

"And what was that?"

"One word," said Philip, astonished at his own boldness. "A Greek word, *Asebia.*"

"I don't know a word of Greek," said Glenellen flatly.

"It would seem," said Clyde, "that you either delivered the message and forgot it (somewhat farfetched but possible) or Guiscardo got it from you without your knowledge."

"*Asebia* wasn't your message?"

Glenellen shook his head, his eyes bulging with indigestion, his hand on his stomach.

"It looks as though someone were playing a joke on you," said Clyde with his usual reasonableness. "Perhaps Guiscardo had a servant at the hotel substitute his message for the one Ayre intended you to deliver. There are any number of possibilities . . ."

"And none quite plausible," said Philip.

"Let's forget about it, shall we?" Glenellen motioned to the boy to take the plates away, to bring in the dessert. "I have a good reason for not wanting to remember."

"A very good reason," agreed Mr Norman.

"Things are not as they were in Italy," said Glenellen.

"Situation fluid—how fluid, none can say. There have been certain realignments which I believe you should know."

"There has been one particular alignment which may come as a surprise to you," added Mr Norman uneasily. "You see, Ayre has . . ."

"Seen the light! I have abandoned the House of Savoy to its fate. Yes, I have made the plunge. It wasn't easy, believe me. I weighed the pros and I weighed the cons. I went through the entire section on Italy in the Encyclopaedia Britannica and when I finished I knew that I had been wrong all these years, lulled to sleep by the decadent music of a dying order. But the awakening came; and not a moment too soon, for I can see that had I continued much longer to wander in the morass of reactionaryism I might have ended by losing all touch with the People, who are, we must admit, the only reason for political action, both here and abroad. On a Wednesday morning I realized with horror what I had so narrowly missed becoming. By afternoon I had acted. I canceled all my engagements for the next two months. Letters were sent to old friends and acquaintances, giving them fair warning of the change, allowing them, if they chose, to sever their relations with me. Many did. Some few did not, among them Clyde. Others I have not heard from. Their silence I interpret as a tacit disapproval, and so I have been forced to accept, stoically I hope, an abrupt yet necessary end to involvements which, in this perilous and exacting time, did afford me some pleasure. The Pope, among others less illustrious, did not acknowledge my letter, to my great surprise considering all that I've done for the Church. But I will not be petty. I want no one ever to say that Ayre Glenellen was petty in good times or bad."

"You see, Philip, Ayre became a member of the Communist Party last Wednesday." Mr Norman's voice betrayed not only melancholy but a certain pride in his friend's ability to do the unexpected.

"Sweet Jesus!" said Philip.

In one of the tall towers a thousand candles gleamed and flickered in the soft wind, as though alive, in contrast to the fixed constellations of electric lights which circled this old tower and defined the limits of the hill-rimmed city of Florence, crossed by a winding gray river, reflecting city lights and many stars.

Philip stood alone in the window looking down on the city, wondering whether the pleasant scent of the warm night was from orange or from lemon, from mimosa or from the rich gardens which had been carved in terraces out of the hills of Fiesole where he was now, in a villa, at a party, shortly before the moonrise and the end of the green summer, the beginning of the burning autumn, bright, intense and withering. A new season.

"I thought I'd lost you," said Regina, crossing the darkened library and coming out onto the balcony where Philip stood. "Oh, it is lovely. Look, the tower! They've lit all the candles. I wonder why? It must be some saint's day or rather the day of one of the old gods. The people are still faithful, you know . . . quite unchanged."

"They gave the gods new names?"

"Names change from age to age but the gods are constant. . . . Are you a Christian?"

This shattered him. He lived in a period where it was not polite for well-bred people to discuss their spiritual convictions or speculations, and for Regina, the great materialist, to ask him suddenly whether or not he subscribed to the official religion of his culture was almost as shocking as it would have been, a generation earlier, for her to have asked him if he had ever enjoyed sexual congress.

He laughed nervously and wondered what to answer. To say he was an agnostic sounded too much like everyone else and to say that he was an atheist would place him, socially, in the same class with undergraduates who had only just discovered to their horror that the rules of conduct they had always been taught were heavenly inspired were, after all, only a makeshift convenience, broken by everyone including their stern guardians. Yet the truth was somewhere between those two worn words. Philip said: No, he was not a Christian.

Regina leaned against the railing of the balcony, the party within forgotten. "Something will happen soon."

"What? A new messiah?"

"I'm afraid so."

"Has he already come, do you think? Marx? Freud? Lenin?"

"I don't know. But I feel it in my bones and I'm never wrong about such things."

Philip laughed. "You could hardly have had much experience. It's been a long time since the last one, you know."

"That isn't what I mean. I . . . but it's too hard to explain. I only hope the new one will respect the old gods."

"You prefer them, don't you?"

She nodded. The moon rose from behind the hills, red as blood, like a cold sun in the east. "They are different from the messiahs. They have nothing to do with philosophic systems. They are facts. Some are simple: the sea, the sun, the air. Some are more complex: violence, love, the mother, the father. It makes no real difference which is Queen of Heaven, Mary or Isis or Juno, as long as the idea of the mother exists, as it always will. Sometimes the mother dominates. Sometimes she does not and her son reigns. There are periods when war is regnant, or justice. . . ."

"Or love?"

"Can you see to the end already?" She looked at him oddly, as though he had frightened her, but she had no reason to be alarmed for he had not understood. He shook his head in bewilderment.

"I see nothing. Do you mean . . ."

"I meant only that there's a conflict between the natural gods who are, for the race at least, constant, and the messiahs who wish to rearrange the hierarchy of heaven, banishing this god, elevating that one, transforming some and murdering others, or attempting murder, for in the end it is the messiah who dies, a victim of the same forces he attempted to govern. No matter how appealing or ruthless his dogma, the old gods defeat him in the end; they change their names: Saint This-One, pray for me, give me wealth. Saint That-One, pray for me, give me strength. Hail Mary, full of grace—as indeed she was, and is."

He nearly saw the design, but a shadow before the moon hid the pale face beside him and the warm flower-burdened wind lulled him and he forgot what in an instant he had almost known.

"We'd better go in to the party. Your husband . . ."

"Is indifferent. But we'll go in. Are you enjoying yourself?"

"Yes, I think so. It's the first really Italian party I've been to. Something of a novelty."

"The host is very powerful in the government, behind the scenes. Rex says that when he wants anything done he goes to him rather than to the ministers."

In the drawing room, Philip stared a long time at this powerful man, wondering what it was that made him so

104

different from other men. But the problem was insoluble, as he had already discovered this last week in Florence in constant attendance upon Rex Durham who had, during all that time, not made an original or profound observation on any subject. Philip wondered if perhaps a certain type of energetic mediocrity might, after all, be politically more useful in a republican society than brilliance or wit or passion. Pondering the nature of power and earthly dominion from one age to the next, Philip sat in a chair between two sofas. Several decorative ladies and gentlemen shifted easily from Italian to English, and included him in their talk.

"We were discussing the Church," said one gentleman, with a brilliant smile, glossy mustache, and sporting in his buttonhole (as the late E. Phillips Oppenheim used to say) the discreet ribbon of some knightly order.

"And we were being so anti-American," said a thick vivacious lady.

"*You* were. Not I."

"We were talking Church gossip."

"What is the gossip?" asked Philip politely, pretending to listen, his eyes on Regina.

"The Roman hierarchy has come to a secret decision. I have this on the best authority. If the Russians conquer Europe they will make an agreement with Stalin that if he leaves the Church alone the Church will not oppose him. The alternative, the Romans feel, would be far more terrible."

"Alternative? What do you mean?" asked Philip, his eyes shifting from Regina to the white teeth and gleaming black mustache.

"Flight. The removal of the Church to America and an American Pope. The Romans consider the boorish Irish-American hierarchy more dangerous to the faith than an atheist tyrant who will fall, in time. The Church has survived worse catastrophes than communism. She might not, the Romans feel, survive the Irish-Americans."

"Suppose Stalin persecuted the Church?"

"Then there would be new catacombs and more saints in heaven."

On a signal from Regina, Philip excused himself and joined her and Rex.

"Enjoying yourself, Mr Warren?"

"Very much, sir."

"Good boy. We'll see a lot of you when we get back home."

Philip could never determine whether Rex's continual omission of the pronoun "I" was the result of modesty or merely a trick to make himself seem precise, direct, without fuss or frills.

"Regina, here. tells me you might want to take a fling at the great game. Think you'd like it?"

"Why . . . yes." He tried to get Regina's eye but she was smiling at someone across the room. "You're your father's son all right." Rex chuckled deeply and Philip recalled his father's contempt for politics.

"We've enjoyed seeing you these last few days. Glad to find someone Regina likes. Most people bore her to death and I'm tied up all the time."

"I've enjoyed . . ."

"She's shrewd. Never makes a mistake. Always take her advice when it comes to people. Thinks you've got a career. So do I. You're young. Unmarried. That's good at this point. You're a lawyer; a veteran; a judge's son. Can you make a good speech?"

"I . . ."

"It's a trick. You'll pick it up. Remember: tell 'em only what they want to hear." In short staccato sentences Durham outlined a political career for him. Then he stared at Philip with his small gray eyes, bloodshot beneath heavy brows.

"Give it a whirl?"

"I think so," said Philip, trapped.

"Leaving tomorrow, you know."

"Yes. Reg . . . Mrs Durham told me."

"Farewell party tonight as you gathered. Off to Paris first. Salt mines. Don't look forward to it. Can't do business with the French. Talk all the time about *la Patrie*, think all the time about money. Americans just the opposite. Will you be in Paris?"

"Not right away."

"Regina may stay over. I'm going back to Washington in a few weeks. Probably won't see you till fall."

"Or winter."

"That's right. Your year. Come see me in Washington, or on the river if we're there."

"I will."

"Good boy." Politicians swept him away from Philip and, for the moment, he and Regina were alone together.

"You see," she said, "how easy it will be?"

"Why did you tell him I was interested?"

106

"Because you are."

"You know I'm not and yet you insist I must be. Why?" He looked at her frowning. "I can't see why it should concern you so."

"But it does," she said lightly. "So there."

"And what do you want from me in exchange?"

"Nothing," she said evasively, not looking at him.

"I can't believe that."

"Is it so strange? Must every motive be selfish?"

"Yes and no. The word means nothing. I only feel . . ."

"What?"

"That you are not candid."

"When you tell me that you want a career I will tell you what you want to know."

"And name your price?"

"And name my price." She laughed. "Now I've confused you and I didn't mean to. I hate people who are mysterious, don't you?"

"I won't be able to answer you until my year is up."

"There's no hurry. I can wait."

"Where shall we meet?"

"Any place you like."

Addresses were exchanged and various geographical positions charted as they compared itineraries; then the party ended. The guests went home, carrying with them all the anxieties of the age: a beleaguered church, intellectuals in search of dogma, a barbarian horde poised upon the eastern marches, a materialistic giant beyond the western sea, neither civilized nor barbarians. Each age has its tyrants, thought Philip, preparing for bed. He was soothed by this knowledge as are all properly educated Americans when they come to Europe and visit ancient rooms in which all the fears of other days have been resolved by time or superseded by equivalent crises. He turned out the light and thought of what Regina had said about the old gods, and he wondered if she were right: were they constant after all? Would they reappear now that the last messiah's work had been undone? The son giving way to his mother and the father lost in heaven? He hoped so, knowing that when men are wise they love the natural more than dogma, more than revelation.

For an instant Philip was nearly convinced, as he hovered between waking and sleep. The Gods were alive again, for him at least; but then he recalled the solemn humorless religion of the barbarians, both Eastern and Western, and he saw with Virgilian clarity a new, more monstrous figure

107

appear, furiously denouncing the body and the spirit, re-fashioning history, casting a long shadow upon the future.

The moon set and the stars were drowning in the pale dawn when finally he slept. Near by, the wind put out those of the tower's candles which had burned all the night.

PART TWO

🙖🙖🙖🙖🙖🙖🙖🙖🙖🙖🙖🙖🙖🙖

"The life of the world is only play,
And idle talk, and pageantry."
The Koran

Chapter Six

PHILIP STOOD ON THE RIVER BANK looking down at the water gliding from south to north through the dry land. A solemn bloody sun was setting opposite him, its circle bisected already by the chalky mountains across the river. As he watched, the sun sank quickly, pulling the day after, bleeding the sky of light until when the sun was gone, the day was too. There was no time of twilight in this place, only day and night.

He lit a cigarette. The familiar brief glow of match fire reassured him as he turned away from the river and walked toward the colonnade beyond the row of dark palms. He wondered, as he walked, if those dead Egyptians had felt the same wonder in the presence of their new buildings as he experienced among the ruins of the same temples, cluttered still with all the debris of faith and glory. He decided not, for discounting their official preoccupation with death and the attendant details of dying, they must have been, all in all, more cheerful than not, too much preoccupied with family life and the never-ending struggle for political preferment, to brood too much upon that last journey from the east bank to the west bank of the river.

He thought of his own river, cold and broad, stately in summer, gleaming with ice fragments in the winter, as unlike this muddy turgid river as possible and yet, like it, a source of life. It soothed him to walk by a river, made him feel less strange, more at home, as if he were closer to the center of the world.

He entered the roofless temple and stood between two

109

thick high columns. In the darkness he could just make out various shrines, some still roofed, others shattered by weather and the wars. He stepped down onto the old pavement of the temple and proceeded to the center of the main court where he stood, awed by the dark and by the immensity of acanthus-crowned columns. Then far away, he heard the sound of automobiles and the shouts of street vendors. Thinking of dinner, he left the temple, crossed a field and walked several yards down a palm-edged road to the hotel where he was staying, a rambling stucco building on the edge of a town of whitewashed mud with tall striped minarets and narrow haphazard streets, a town oppressed, obsessed by the ruins on which it perched, like a living weed in a bone heap: the remains of the palaces and temples, markets and quais of what had been the greatest city in the world three thousand years before. Too long a time, thought Philip wearily, with a sense of having strolled out of time altogether.

The manager of the hotel, fortunately, recalled him to the present. Mr Koyoumdjian got not only his conversation but his love of America from the movies which he attended zealously, often seeing, he confessed, the same movie four or five times, each time learning new some expression he could add to his ever-lengthening American line.

No sooner had Philip entered the lobby than Mr Koyoumdjian was upon him, his face scarlet with crisis.

"He has done it! While you were out. Just after you left."

"Who has done what?"

"Your friend Mr Willys—with a gat. He tried to take his life. Such a caper!"

"What happened?"

"Shot himself. Except he missed—just nicked the top of one ear. The sawbones came and gave him something to make him sleep."

"But that's terrible."

"Real excitement! You can bet your life. I've got his rod in my safe. Want to see it?"

"No, thanks. Is he awake now?"

"Yes. I sent one of the bozos in with some tea and toast. Though why a man has just shot himself should be fed tea and toast I couldn't know. Maybe you'd better see him. Cheer him up."

The would-be suicide lay inert on his bed, a mountain of flesh behind the white mosquito netting; purple pajamas with white piping contained those rolls of flesh which composed the wretched Briggs Willys. A bed lamp was turned

110

on and the night table was cluttered with medicine bottles. There was a strong odor of iodine in the room.

"I hear you've had an accident," said Philip, attempting cheeriness. "How do you feel?"

"It was *not* an accident," said a thin voice, emerging from the still, fat center of the large iron bed.

"But I thought . . ."

"I tried to kill myself and I failed, as I have in everything else." A plump starfish of a hand pushed aside the netting and the bandaged head and shoulders of Mr Willys were revealed. He was not an ugly man nor was he old; he was just very fat. His features were small and rather indistinct, since one's examination of them was distracted by the full shining cheeks, the ripe tiers of chins, the splendid ruddy coloring which the white bandage emphasized.

"Now that's no way to talk," said Philip, sitting down in a chair near the bed.

"It may be no way to talk but it's the way I feel. Next time I won't fail."

"You're not going to try to shoot yourself again?"

A crafty expression rippled across the vast face and the tiny eyes disappeared altogether, until they resembled twin navels. "No, not shoot. Poison may be my next weapon."

"Surely you don't really want to die."

"And why not?"

"You have so much to live for."

"*What* have I to live for?"

There was no immediate answer to this. Looking at the matter dispassionately, Philip could see very little reason for Mr Willys to continue living with such an outlandish body, one that not only set him apart from the rest of mankind but one which gave him continual anxiety; for him to walk across a room was a physical effort not unlike a decathlon for someone of more ordinary proportions. But Philip was conscience-bound to be life's advocate.

"Any number of things. I don't know you well enough to be able to mention your pleasures . . ."

"Sleep," sighed the thin voice. "I love only sleep."

"Food, perhaps," hazarded Philip, tactlessly.

"Certainly not. I eat like a bird. I loathe food. A cup of consommé and a cracker is all I ever need. Just because . . ."

"I was only making a guess," said Philip, quickly. Mr Willys fell back against his five pillows with a gentle moan of exhaustion, his eyes shut.

"Still, there are so many things to do when you're alive

111

that you can't do dead," he continued, becoming more and more inane. Mr Willys was not listening. "You can travel, for instance. You don't have to work for a living. Think how other people envy you being able to travel anywhere you like. . . ."

"I came to Egypt to die," said Mr. Willys suddenly. "I was afraid I wouldn't have the courage to kill myself anywhere else so I decided to come up the Nile to the hottest town with a decent hotel and even if I lost my nerve, I should die of the heat. I can't stand the heat. My heart is not strong. My kidneys are bad. My liver is swollen out of shape. Yet I have been here in Luxor in this hotel for two months, unable to move, unable to sleep, unable even to shoot myself for my hand shook so I only scratched an ear. Oh, it's too terrible." Sobs convulsed the purple mountain like an earthquake. The bed creaked.

"There now," said Philip over and over again until the crisis had passed. "What you should do is go on a nice trip to the mountains, someplace where it is cool, like Switzerland, and take a cure . . ."

"Altitudes make me dizzy, and there is no cure. None at all. It's either wait until the heat kills me or else take poison."

"When?"

"When what?"

"When do you plan to take poison?"

"Well, I haven't picked a date yet. But soon. Very soon. Then it will be over."

"Have you thought what sort of poison you would take?"

"No," said the fat man dreamily, "I haven't. Something with a pleasant taste, I hope. Something quick."

"Will you do it sober or drunk?"

"Well, I'd planned it sober but now that you mention it, it might be easier to do if I had been drinking. Yes, that *is* a good idea. Thanks very much. I'd probably never have thought of it."

"That's all right. I just want to make it easy for you."

"I appreciate that, Mr Warren."

"Do you know much about poisons?"

"Not a thing. I did consider swallowing some iodine this evening but I'm sure it would burn like fire."

"No, iodine is out. What you need is something like strychnine."

"How do you happen to know so much about these things?"

"I used to read a great many detective stories," said Philip, quite carried away by the situation. He was alarmed, however, when Mr Willys asked him if he would bring him some strychnine the next morning.

"I suppose you can get it without a doctor's prescription?"

"Oh, I doubt that," said Philip. But I'll see what I can do."

"That will be splendid: to be out of this mess for good! By the way, I shall want to be cremated."

"Awful mess for the hotel, though, your taking poison in one of their rooms."

"Won't do them a bit of harm. The legal end of it shouldn't take more than a few hours. Besides, it will give that despicable manager something to talk about. He took my gun away, you know."

"You could hardly blame him."

"But I do." A barefoot servant appeared at the door and informed Philip his dinner was ready. After promising to go first thing in the morning to buy poison, Philip said goodnight and went downstairs.

He had the large airy dinning room to himself. French doors opened onto a garden. Flies buzzed about the electric light and fans suspended from the ceiling slowly twirled, hardly disturbing the hot air. A white-coated Negro, wearing a dirty fez, brought him a number of dispiriting courses of simple food, badly cooked.

The manager came by for a little chat as Philip was drinking the thick muddy black coffee.

"Did you see him? Was he green about the gills?"

"No, he was in the pink," said Philip, getting into the spirit of the manager's conversation.

"Why do you think he did it?"

"He seems to be tired of life and so he tried to kick . . ."

"The bucket," finished Mr Koyoumdjian with a smile of one Mason meeting another in the Libyan Desert. "I suppose it never occurred to him how disagreeable it would be for us if he killed himself."

"It was my impression that he didn't really care, that he was more interested in his own problems."

"Problems!" exploded Mr Koyoumdjian. "He has money, hasn't he?"

"A great deal, I think."

"Then what problems does he have? He can go anywhere he likes, do anything he wants. Buy any doll. . . ." The manager paused. "He isn't impotent, is he?"

113

"I didn't ask. But I wouldn't be surprised, with that weight."

"Weight has nothing to do with it. There's an old man here in town who weighs twenty stone and he's the busiest cat in Luxor in regard to the frails. He has a couch specially tilted so . . ."

"I don't think that would help Mr Willys," said Philip, not wanting to hear any more details.

"Maybe not. I wonder if I should have him moved to the Mission hospital, it'd be their lookout then, not mine."

"I'd leave him alone. There isn't much he can do without a gun and I don't suppose he has a knife long enough to penetrate all that flesh."

Mr Koyoumdjian laughed heartily at this grim conceit. "You got something there."

"Are there any more guests coming this month?" The last party, a group of cotton scientists from the United States, had left that morning and there was no one in the hotel but Mr Willys and Philip.

"Not for ten days."

"How on earth do you make enough in summer to keep a place like this running?"

"We don't. But the owner decided not to shut up this year. We usually close in May."

"Do you like having to stay here in this heat?"

Mr Koyoumdjian shrugged. "It's a living, Buster."

But the manager was wrong. The next morning after an early breakfast, Philip took a stroll in the garden and discovered that another guest had arrived in the night. She was seated on an iron bench at the end of a lane of magnolias or what Philip took to be magnolia trees: this garden was a strange one with flowers and trees he had never seen before, mysteriously set out in cabalistic designs, a maze of heavily scented green.

"Lovely morning," he said, approaching her.

"Yes. The only cool time of the day."

"May I sit down?"

"Certainly." She moved over and he sat beside her, conscious of the green world all about them. There was a hedge behind the bench and a sudden right-angled turn of the path in front of them gave the illusion of a roofless green-walled room, oblong and carpeted with grass, while flowers still

114

damp with night broke the solid areas of green with their bright colors.

"Did you just arrive in Luxor?" he asked.

"This morning." He liked her voice, which was cool and even, an educated American or perhaps British voice. He moved about on the bench so that he could see her more clearly. She was handsome, though not pretty in a contemporary sense for her nose was large, like a Julian portrait bust, and her skin was white and unpainted. Yet her eyes were extraordinary, pale gray with long dark lashes, and her hair was a fine auburn, drawn softly back from her face and gathered in a bun at the back. She was not forty, he decided; she wore no wedding ring.

"Not the best time of year to visit Egypt," he commented.

"I like Egypt any time of year," she said.

"You've been here before?"

"Many, many times. In fact, my father's family used to live here a long time ago."

"Then it must be like home."

"Yes, like home. Have you been here long?"

He told her he had been in Egypt for a month, in Luxor for a week, and that he was seeing everything there was to see in the company of an old dragoman named Said.

"I envy you, coming to it fresh like this even in the heat."

"I don't mind hot weather. The rest of course is wonderful. I've never felt so relaxed before. For the first time, nothing matters."

"The ruins," she said. "That's what does it, of course. It's very hard to dream of the future when the past is all around one, reminding one that what is has been before and will be again, over and over and over."

"Are you staying here?" asked Philip.

She nodded. "I always stay here when I am in Luxor."

"The manager told me he was expecting no one for a few days."

"We're old friends, Mr Koyoumdjian and I. He's never surprised when I appear without notice."

"Have you some business here?" asked Philip tentatively, realizing it was none of his business and that she appeared to be quite capable of reminding him that it was not. But she only smiled and said that she was interested in archeology: "Disproving, perhaps, my own theory that all is forgotten since I for one am devoted to seeing that nothing is forgotten, that every second of history is accounted for."

"History or, rather, legend is seldom wholly forgotten,"

said Philip with the studied diffidence of a man making an epigram. "Men always are." When this was said, as though by common assent, made reverent by pompousness, they rose and walked silently down the green path to the hotel.

回

"I see you've met Miss Oliver," said the manager, coming over to their table later that day at lunch, as Philip was toying with a number of vivid stewed fruits, all poisonous-looking and tasteless.

"Yes, we met in the garden," said Miss Oliver, whose first name Philip had already been informed was Sophia.

"A surprise visitor," said Mr Koyoumdjian. "You could have knocked me over with a feather when she walked in the hotel this morning as cool as a cucumber and asked for her old room. More investigations, eh?"

"Just one more," she said, removing a half-drowned fly from her coffee. "I may have to go out to the desert for a few days. I'm not sure."

"What's the desert like?" asked Philip, hoping this would lead to an invitation; it did not. He was lectured for several minutes on life in the desert, and by the time she finished an interesting account of the Arab method of divining the presence of water, the fly, which had been moribund, pulled itself together and flew away, heading directly, Philip noticed, for a coil of flypaper already nasty with the corpses of its fellows.

"Have you seen Mr Willys this morning?" he asked suddenly when Miss Oliver had concluded her remarks and was thoughtfully sipping coffee, her thoughts far away, no doubt in some distant *wadi*, her eyes narrowed as though against the glare of bright sun on sand.

The manager had indeed seen Mr Willys. "He seems in good spirits, keeping his pecker up. I think he'll be all right now. He spoke of coming down to dinner tonight. He asked to see you, by the way. Said you had something for him."

"Who is this?" asked Miss Oliver, the desert fading like a mirage as Philip explained the details of Mr Willys's obsession. She had, however, no comment to make on the situation other than a conventional word or two and a perfunctory expression of sympathy for the trouble the manager had been put to. Then she turned to Philip and, discovering that he was to go to Karnak that afternoon with his dragoman, asked if she might go along. Making a date for five o'clock when the sun would be less violent, they parted.

116

Philip found Mr Willys still in bed, but now quite nude, without even a mosquito netting to diffuse the horror. "Good morning," said Philip from the door, giving the other a chance to cover himself but Mr Willys did not have the energy or the desire. Instead he pulled himself up so that his stomach with its mottled pink flesh covered his genitals, giving him the curiously sexless look of a celluloid Kewpie doll. Philip found it difficult not to stare fascinatedly at this unusual display of one of nature's more bitter jokes.

"Good morning, Philip. Did you bring it?"

"Bring what?"

"The poison. You promised."

"Ah, the poison." Philip had no lie ready. He stammered. "I—I haven't been to town yet."

"You will remember it?"

"I'll see what I can do. I'll have to get a doctor's prescription, you know; and that may be difficult."

"You're not trying to get out of this, are you?" Mr Willys was suspicious.

"I'll do my best . . . but now I have to go out. I'll see you tonight. Mr Koyoumdjian said you were coming down to dinner."

"I have no intention of ever leaving this room alive. I only said I'd get up to put him off the scent. I was afraid they might try to move me to the Mission hospital. But now, if you'll do as you promised, I shall be asleep by dinnertime . . . forever!" And with a gusty sigh, Mr Willys began to turn over; the bed creaked; he groaned; the flesh sagged alarmingly and Philip fled.

◩

"Yonder wall," said the dragoman, in his King James Biblical English, "was builded by the children of Israel before their liberation by Moses. You see, some of the bricks are made with straw; others not with."

"This tree was brought back from the land of Punt by Queen Hatshepsut's fleet," said Miss Oliver. Philip was bombarded with information from all sides; some of it he absorbed, most of it he did not hear for he was too occupied with his own reactions. Like a man feeling his own pulse, he tried to define what he felt as he walked through the rooms and dusty gardens of three thousand years before.

When they came to the small Temple of Ptah, they sat down in its shade, out of the terrible light of the sun which scorched the temple walls and parched the earth as it rode like a disc of bronze in the harsh blue sky.

It is difficult to know how to deal with well-known landscapes when one is writing a novel. There is an impulse to describe everything literally, enthusiastically, giving dimensions, dates, distances and other pertinent information. This is the guidebook approach and the dangers are numerous: for instance, should one care to describe the Sphinx, one would have to record those dimensions which are available to any owner of an encyclopedia. Should one rely on memory there will inevitably be angry comments to the effect that the left paw is not worn away, that one haunch is higher than the other, that the bridge of the nose is still intact if one observes the face from the east, and so on. The impressionistic manner is somewhat better: to use the celebrated object as a point of departure, like Pater describing the Mona Lisa, or Henry James describing the Capitol at Washington, or rather Henry James describing Henry James describing the Capitol at Washington. Then there is the contemporary fashion of keeping away from celebrated objects altogether. In Paris the story, if it concerns artists, will all take place within a few blocks of the rue du Bac or if of high life, around the Crillon and the Ritz. While in a book about Egypt most of the action will take place either in a wealthy suburb of Cairo or else in a desert village with goats and lice-infested children running about, eating dates and drinking stagnant water. It would be pleasant to make some sort of compromise, to be able to give a thorough instructive tour of Karnak, the Valley of the Kings, and so forth, soaring every now and then with burnished wings into a paradise of lyric metaphor, getting around the object, as it were, translating its aura into a few balanced melodious sentences. But, reader, you will be spared even this. The movies have already made us so familiar with foreign countries that the novel, for its own good I am sure, can no longer be usefully employed in cataloguing details of well-known landscapes and so, except for an occasional odd glimpse of this place or that, travelogues and the monthly *Geographic* must still be our source material. But it might be useful to quote at this point what a well-known authority on Egypt had to say in 1887 of the country in general. After first remarking on the monotony of the scenery, the authority adds: "The monotony is relieved, however, in two ways, and by two causes. Nature herself does something to relieve it. Twice a day, in the

morning and in the evening, the sky and the landscape are
lit up by hues so bright and so delicate, that the homely
features of this prospect are at once transformed as by
magic, and wear an aspect of exquisite beauty . . . The
orb of night walks in brightness through a firmanent of
sapphire; or, if the moon is below the horizon, then the
purple vault is lit up with many colored stars. Silence profound reigns around. A phase of beauty wholly different
from that of daytime smites the sense. . . ." A beautiful
style, alas, is not enough, while generalities are always
treacherous; for as we have seen only the night before, the
sun set quickly without one single bright hue in evidence.

"The Arab women bring their babies here to bless them,"
said Sophia, as they stood in the close dark room, a life-
sized statue of a woman with a lion's head in front of them,
partly lighted by a shaft of light coming from a square
opening directly overhead.

"She has great power," intoned the dragoman, an untidy
old man with a grizzled beard and wearing the national
sheet-like robe, a fez on his head, sandals on his feet. He
was a true Egyptian, he assured Philip when they first met,
not like one of those God-damned Arabs in the north.
Proudly, he had shown Philip a blue cross tattooed on his
arm. "I am a Christian, a Copt," he had said.

"All the gods have power if one believes," said Sophia
firmly.

Philip, though he liked her, found her positive assertions
a little trying; she advanced every opinion as a fact of
nature. The dragoman, seeing his own position as an Egyp-
tologist endangered, had spent most of the morning attempting politely but tenaciously to disprove her observations
and theories. She, in her turn, was far more direct; she
contradicted him flatly until Philip was afraid there might
be trouble but they got through the day without unpleasant-
ness, and it was in a friendly mood that they rode back
to the hotel in a horse-drawn carriage, the top up against
the evening sun.

Men sat sleepily in doorways as they drove into Luxor.
Even the big-bellied, naked children sat or lay in the fly-
buzzing shade of acacias, hardly moving. Only the women
worked, preparing food, bringing water from the fountains,
nursing the children, cursing the men and the flies in their
deep harsh voices, cursing the fine dust which the foreigners'
carriage turned up in clouds as Philip and Sophia drove
through the dusty streets of the village to the highway

which led to their hotel, to fine modern bathrooms and cool rooms.

◙

"You failed me."

"But I tell you the doctor refused to give me a prescription."

"I counted on you. All day I've been happy. Happier than I've ever been before, thinking that never again would I have to open my eyes to see the morning, to look at this aching wreck and to realize that I must endure it for yet another day. . . . Oh, it's too terrible!" And he groaned piteously, the sheet which covered him rippling like a sea effect in an old-fashioned play.

"I did my best," said Philip firmly. "It's up to you from now on." And so, having divorced himself from Mr Willys's project, he left the room, ignoring the pleas, the anguished entreaties from behind the mosquito netting: "Oh, come back! I'm sorry. I didn't mean it. You *must* help me!"

In the lobby, Mr Koyoumdjian met him. "We have a surprise for you!" he said, smiling, his face breaking into a number of geometric shapes. "Another lady has just arrived—an American from New York City. You probably know her, Mrs Fay Peabody."

"No, I don't think I've met her. You see . . ."

"New York's a big town, I know. Babylon on the Subway, that's what they call it. I'm not green. What I meant is you probably know her books. She writes detective stories —hard-boiled. Seen some of them myself, but I have no time to read."

"Where is Miss Oliver?"

"In the dining room with Mrs Peabody. They're waiting for you."

Sophia was stately and cool in a pale blue evening dress which flattered her well-formed body, and yet, recognizing dispassionately all her physical attractions, he was in no way attracted to her; she was like one of those voluptuous figures carved in ice at a winter carnival in New England. Usually he had a difficult time explaining to himself why this person or that person appealed to him but now he was amused to find himself wondering why he was not attracted to this handsome, apparently available woman. When he tried to think of her in erotic terms, he experienced the same sort of embarrassment when, as an adolescent, he had speculated on the private behavior of his parents. He had

120

concluded that it was the enervating heat which had done this to him, heat combined with the mood of the place and a new knowledge of the ebb and flow of all of those generations whose debris, solemn and dusty, surrounded that garden which he now glimpsed, pale and shadowy, through the French windows of the dining room.

Sophia introduced him to Mrs Fay Peabody. The famous mystery-story writer was plump and soft, elderly, and though she had a slight speech defect (the result of ill-fitting dentures) she managed, nevertheless, to speak with very nearly as much authority as Sophia herself; she was limited however to fewer fields: the underworld, publishing and the law.

"Well, here we all are," she observed, after the introductions had been made and an American canned fruit cocktail was set before them. "Probably the only Americans in Upper Egypt."

"No, there are quite a few over at the Ponsoonah Laboratories outside of town."

"I mean, not counting professional people," clicked Mrs Peabody. "Although, perhaps, I don't quite mean that either since I, too, am a professional, *on a job*." There was a pause. Philip, aware that it was up to him to ask Mrs Peabody who she was, did so, neatly. She told him that she was Fay Peabody and he told her that he enjoyed her books. Sophia remained silent.

"I believe in doing my research on the spot, Mr Warren. None of this secondhand business for me. . . . Looking things up is all very well for most writers but, if I say so myself, I have quite a large body of readers who look to me for *the real thing* and that's what I give them. When I describe the inside of Leavenworth it means that I have been inside Leavenworth, as a *prisoner*."

"You must be joking," said Sophia mildly.

"I never joke about my work, Miss Oliver. Yes, I arranged with the warden and he allowed me to reside three days in a cell, just like any other prisoner, wearing man's apparel. You perhaps remember the prison scenes in *Red, White and Blue Murder?* well, those are *authentic* scenes based upon my personal experience." There was an awed silence after these remarks. Philip, toying with a bit of cold fried fish, wondered what to say next. He glanced at Sophia. She asked Mrs Peabody what she was doing in Egypt.

"I believe, Miss Oliver, that a *change of pace* is good for all of us. Even the best. I was never one to rely on formula,

121

although the Fay Peabody method may be considered, perhaps, to be a *kind* of formula. Yet I have been aware for some time now that there were certain limitations to the method. Not that I lack readers! No, bless them! each book sells more than its predecessor. Yet, in spite of such encouragement, one does have a duty to oneself and though I have written exclusively of crime in Philadelphia with, of course, related minor scenes elsewhere, I have never *thrown down the gauntlet*, you might say, and tackled a really big job elsewhere."

"Like Agatha Christie," said Philip innocently. The storm broke. Mrs Christie was flayed before their eyes and her corpse, like Hector's, pulled after Mrs Peabody's triumphal car from one end of publishers' row to the other. Sales were compared down to the last twenty-five-cent copy sold. Mrs Peabody had at her tongue's tip the exact sales of every mystery novel published since Conan Doyle, and while they ate the dry gray flesh of some mysterious beast, it became apparent to them that not only in quality but in sales, too, Mrs Peabody was tops. No, she was not going to do the Christie sort of thing in Egypt. She was going to do the Fay Peabody sort of thing in Egypt and, her jaw set, she looked from one to the other of her companions, challenging them to compare her with anyone, living or dead. Philip was impressed.

"Will it have J. R. Snaffles in it?" he asked, recalling the name of her detective, an ex-prizefighter with an aquiline profile and an appeal which reputedly drove women wild, not only in fiction but the ones in life who bought every book about Snaffles Mrs Peabody was good enough to write for them.

"Yes, Snaffles will be in it. I can't make too large a break with my fans. I mean, if you buy a Fay Peabody mystery you expect Snaffles. Isn't that right, Miss Oliver?" Sophia nodded and the denture-clicking words of Mrs Peabody continued, a thin trickle of saliva glistening at the corner of her mouth. "I can only give you the barest hint of my plot. To do more would be unfair to my other fans. Suffice it to say, Snaffles has been hired by the wealthy Greta Preston of the Main Line to accompany her and her brother on a tour of Egypt to ascertain, if possible, the whereabouts of her father who disappeared in Twenty-nine with most of his bank's available cash. (She has independent means from her mother.) Of course, *he* did not take the cash. . . ."

By the time coffee was brought, they knew a good deal

more about the next adventure of Snaffles than any Fay Peabody fan in the world, or at least in Upper Egypt.

"What a nasty taste!" exclaimed the authoress, after swallowing with difficulty one sip of the thick Turkish coffee.

"Oh, it's wonderful," lied Philip.

"You must get used to it," said Sophia. "*Everyone* drinks it here. Even your Mr Snaffles will have to drink it," she added maliciously.

Mrs Peabody sighed. "In that case, I'd better swallow it all, like medicine. Research! Never let anyone tell you it's easy. Take my word for it."

It was not until they were seated on the screened-in porch overlooking the garden that Philip had his marvelous idea.

"Tell me, Mrs Peabody, have you ever known a man who wanted to be murdered?"

"Certainly not, Mr Warren. The whole point to mystery stories is that people do *not* want to be murdered."

"Perhaps I should put it another way. A man wants to kill himself but he's afraid to."

"I presume you are speaking of suicide. I do not wish to sound intolerant, Mr Warren, but I do not approve of suicide. It is *unfair to the reader*. I know, of course, that you are a great admirer of Mrs Christie. . . ." And that poor lady's body was once more dragged the length of publishers' row.

"All I meant," said Philip, when she had stopped for breath, "is that there's a man staying here who wants to kill himself but hasn't the nerve. He tried to shoot himself a few days ago, but missed. Now he's been begging me to get him some poison."

"Good heavens!" exclaimed Mrs Peabody, for the first time interested in anything either Philip or Sophia had said that evening. Then, briskly: "Why doesn't he buy his own *lethal dose?*"

"He is very fat. He can hardly get out of bed."

"I see. You refused, of course, to do as he requested?"

"Yes, as a matter of fact I did, but I thought you might be able to help him."

"How could *I* help him?"

"I thought perhaps you might murder him, Mrs Peabody," said Philip blandly.

Mrs Peabody snorted dangerously. "If that is your idea

123

of a joke, Mr Warren, then I must tell you I think it in poor taste."

"But you said yourself that you are always authentic," remarked Sophia, joining the game. "How can you write about murders if you've never committed one?"

Mrs Peabody glared at her. "I don't think that follows at all. Besides, my novels are primarily concerned with the *detection* of the murderer, not the murder itself."

"In any case, Mrs Peabody, you could give him some advice on what poison to take—you know, some of the little tricks of the trade a layman might not know."

"But I wouldn't dream of such a thing!" She was outraged. "I can only hope that you're not serious, that this is some sort of private joke between you and Miss Oliver."

"I'm afraid he means what he says," said Sophia. "I haven't seen Mr Willys but I've heard all about his attempts at suicide not only from Mr Warren but also from the manager who took his gun away from him."

"What sort of weapon was it?" asked Mrs Peabody, in a voice suddenly precise and businesslike.

"A revolver," said Philip.

"You have no idea what make? Type bore?"

"I suppose Mr Koyoumdjian will let you look at it if you want to."

"No. It's not important. I'm always curious, however, about weapons. In my last book I had a murder committed with a sash weight attached to a medieval crossbow. Rather an original touch, I thought, since the murderer was able to prove he was next door at a party when the victim's skull was crushed by the weight. Fay Peabody books are noted, if I say so myself, for their *unusual weapons*."

"I think you should meet Mr Willys," said Philip, taking advantage of the authoress's change of mood. "I mean, it's really an interesting case."

"But I'm quite sure that in his present state he wouldn't want to meet me. . . ."

"Nonsense. In his present state he'd be thrilled."

◙

Philip put his head in the door to make sure that Mr Willys was still covered by the sheet; he was. The would-be suicide was propped up in bed, modestly tented, drinking Scotch and doing a crossword puzzle. Philip introduced him to the ladies.

"I've read a lot of those books of yours," said Mr Willys.

124

"I've a great deal of time on my hands, you know, and since I've nothing better to do, I read."

"Many great men read books," said Mrs Peabody gently, her ruthless material-gathering eye taking in everything: the whalelike body, the whisky, the bottles of medicine. "As a matter of fact, my most prized possession is a letter from the late President of the United States of America, Franklin Delano Roosevelt, saying that he thought *Red, White and Blue Murder* 'a swell yarn,' to use his expression." She talked on hypnotically, her eyes narrowed as though estimating a bullet's trajectory from different angles of the room, as well as places where a crossbow might be secreted, a sash weight dropped. "And I've heard that Mr Churchill also enjoys an occasional tale of detection when his mind is not occupied with the multifarious activities of state in which his high office involves him, not to mention his own *not inconsiderable literary activities,*" she said, moving over to the night table and, as though against her will, picking up the bottles and reading their labels as she talked. She was still talking when Philip and Sophia tiptoed out of the room.

"I wonder if I should have done that," said Philip, as they stepped out of the French windows and into the warm moonlit garden.

"I don't think much harm will be done. If what you say about Mr Willys is true, they have a great deal in common."

"You don't think she'll murder him?" He was half serious. Sophia laughed. "Don't be absurd. She's an idiot and he is a neurotic who'll never kill himself as long as he has someone to talk suicide to." Philip had almost forgotten about people who used such words as "neurotic" in conversation; he'd been under the impression that the private language of the mental therapists was becoming unfashionable, and that the cleverest people no longer talked about their psychoanalyses; but then Sophia would not bother to be fashionable; she would use whatever words she chose to make her point.

He often felt that he was with a foreigner when he was with her, someone who used the language intelligently but with no great facility or, rather, personal color: no tone, no habits of speech, no peculiar phrases or repetitions. It was all so clear and direct. For the first time, he asked her where she lived.

"I live in Paris now. But I travel a great deal."

"Why? Any purpose?"

"I like it. No other purpose. I have 'means,' as Mrs Peabody would say."

"That monster." Philip chuckled. They sat down on the tile edge of a small fountain. The light in Mr Willys's second-floor room burned brightly, a warm and yellow oblong in the dark wall of the hotel.

"Were you born in Paris?"

She shook her head but then instead of answering, she scooped up a handful of water and let it trickle back into the fountain. Water struck water with an unmusical sound.

"Why are you in Egypt?" he asked.

"You ask so many questions," she said: observation, not complaint. "Why are *you* in Egypt?"

"To see it. I've never been here." He explained to her about his year.

"Well, I'm here to see it, too."

"You've been here before."

"I like the ruins," she confessed. "I'm interested in archeology and I've occasionally put a little money into expeditions."

"Is there an expedition on now, one of yours?"

"Yes, in a way. I'm involved in the digging over at El Farhar."

"What are they digging?"

"They seem undecided. As far as I know it's a small temple built in the time of Seti the Second, an amiable young man who was deposed early in life, possibly because he was the son of Merneptah, the unfortunate bureaucrat who followed Moses into the Red Sea."

"How far away is this place?"

"About sixty miles to the south. We might go there, if you care to."

"I'd like to very much."

"El Farhar is a good-sized town. The excavations are near by. A group from the University of Berne are doing the work; thankless of course, since the Egyptian government confiscates everything of value, but then it's a mania, like any other, a passion for knowledge. Much more admirable than a passion for money or for position. I actually know of people whose principal interest it is to interfere in the lives of others, for their own good, of course."

Philip felt very close to her at that moment: two pure non-interventionists, seated in the jasmine-scented darkness of an Egyptian garden, each pursuing his own solitary way, paragons of human virtue and as just as gods. He could not

126

help but compare her with Regina. He even asked her if she had met Mrs Durham.

"Regina? Of course. I've known her for years. When did you meet her?"

"A few months ago. In Rome."

"Did you like her?"

This was a dangerous question obviously.

"Yes, I liked her," said Philip, deserting policy for a relative truth. "But she does answer your description: she's one of those people who want to govern others for their own good."

"I don't like her," said Sophia flatly. Philip changed the subject. They spoke now of the expedition to El Farhar.

"There's another reason for going there," she said; then she stopped suddenly, as though she had been indiscreet.

"Another reason? What?"

"I'm not sure I should tell you yet. I'm not sure myself what it is or, rather, if the rumor I've heard is true or not true. We'll find out soon enough."

Then she said that she was tired, that the sun had been very hot that day, that perhaps they should go in.

As he passed the door to Mr Willys's room, Philip looked in to say good night. Mrs Peabody had drawn her chair close to the bed and was saying excitedly, "There are four methods of making a hangman's noose. I always favored the traditional 'double coil and slip' noose . . ." Neither Mr Willys nor Mrs Peabody heard Philip's good-night.

Chapter Seven

THE CAR THAT THEY HIRED to take them to El Farhar ran out of water first, then oil, then gasoline, all of which Sophia patiently paid for even though the price for the services of the car was to have included everything. Fortunately, none of the tires blew out and they arrived at El Farhar in the late afternoon. They were taken to the town's only brick building, the Fuad I Hotel, and here they signed a register which was printed in French and they were welcomed by a manager who addressed Sophia in Italian, a language she spoke well.

Then they walked out into the glare of the day where not one sign implored them to drink Coca-Cola. A battered jeep parked before the house of the local administrator provided the only contemporary note in this hot dusty world of whitewashed mud houses and minarets with wooden balconies from which the faithful were summoned to regard the northeast and to contemplate the mercy of Allah and his dead Prophet's wisdom. The long-robed people stared at the two foreigners as they crossed the dung-littered market place where animals and their owners milled about, kicking dust into market stalls which were sheltered from the sun by a candy-pink and white striped arcade.

"I don't think they're very friendly," said Philip uneasily as they finally got through to the far side of the square, displacing a group of villainous-looking *fellahin*.

"No, I don't suppose they are," said Sophia, quite composed, her sensible heels clicking on the broken cobbles of a broad sycamore-lined street.

"But why? What have the Americans done to them?"

"They don't know we're Americans. All they know is that we're white and from the north, that we have money and eat pork. They don't dislike us enough to be dangerous yet," she added, comfortably.

The half-uncovered temple was at the end of a lane on the town's edge, not far from the dull snake-green river. To the west Philip could see the limestone mountains which separated the Nile Valley from the Libyan Desert, dead-white lunar mountains without water or vegetation. To the east, open country, dusty green where it had been irrigated and, where it had not, only dust and stone, broken here and there by clusters of slender date palms grown up about desert wells or, as Philip's authority, the Victorian George Rawlinson, M.A., Camden professor of Ancient History in the University of Oxford and corresponding member of the Royal Academy of Turin, in collaboration with Arthur Gillman, M.A., once wrote: "Egypt is a land of tranquil monotony. The eye commonly travels over a waste of waters, or over a green plane unbroken by elevations. The sky is generally cloudless. No fog or mist enwraps the distance in mystery; no rainstorm sweeps across the scene; no rainbow spans the empyrean; no shadows chase each other over the landscape. There is an entire absence of picturesque scenery." Egypt was not much like England and Mr Rawlinson missed the gray damp days, the homely pleasures of the common cold, the soft dampness which, as Mrs Woolf's Orlando discovered, stole over England shortly after Prinny's death, diffusing the bright sun of a more heroic age with veils of coal-smoke and fog, while high spirits gave way to probity and all the poets departed, following the sun to Italy.

But Philip, a child of the sun, was perversely attracted to Mr Rawlinson; especially now, while he sweated on the banks of the Nile, the foggy tones of Mr. Rawlinson were a breath of cool northern air. He could almost hear a phlegm-ridden voice intone that one bright sentence in *The Story of Ancient Egypt,* "Silence profound reigns around."

But there was no silence here, profound or superficial. The workmen chatted noisily as they went about their various jobs: some digging, others dusting blocks of stone with brooms.

Sophia and Philip walked slowly about the pit. The top of the temple just appeared above the surface of the ground. The excavators had dug down to the original level in front of the main colonnade. They were now engaged in completing a wide trench about the entire building. The roof of the temple had long since fallen in but the pillared façade was unbroken and though it lacked the familiar grace of Greek columns, it had a fineness of its own, despite squat proportions and dull earth color. Thinking of the bas-reliefs inside, hidden by earth and sand, he experienced some of the excitement which he knew archeologists must feel when

129

they finally enter rooms where no one for centuries has been.

You see? Quite against one's will the gray shadow of Professor Rawlinson falls across this discussion of Egyptian ways, making one almost agree with that contemporary English poet who once remarked that Hoboken not only has an evocative name but that just as interesting things happen there as in more exotic locales. Nevertheless, Philip has come to Egypt and there is a good reason not only for his sightseeing among the ruins but for this uncomfortable visit to El Farhar in the middle of the summer as well. For Sophia had a plan. There was a prophet in El Farhar. He had strange news.

That night after dinner, accompanied by an interpreter from the hotel, Philip and Sophia walked through the eccentrically twisted streets of the town. The moon had not yet risen but the stars were large and bright and in the open doorways lanterns shone, dull and yellow, flickering in the darkness. The high noise of Arab talk sounded in the streets as the sun-oppressed village of the day became secret in the warm darkness and lovers met and thieves fell out and murderers went about their bloody business, more like the slim shadows of palm trees than men by starlight, close to that shrunken summer river which was parent to them all.

Several children were playing a game of tag in the Street of the Date Palm. They stopped their game and stood back in the shadows, silent, as the three strangers passed them. In the Street of the Dead Camel, they paused before a tearoom where the men sat about inside, smoking water pipes, chewing hashish and drinking numerous hot cups of tea. But then one looked up and saw the foreigners standing in the doorway; he scowled and turned to his companion. The foreigners moved on, walking more quickly. "I always have a sense of danger when I walk about an Arab town at night," said Philip in a low voice to Sophia, not wanting their grim-faced, elderly interpreter to hear.

"It *is* dangerous, I suppose," she said equably, betraying no anxiety. "But I always feel nothing will happen to me."

"And I always feel something will happen to me," said Philip, realizing unhappily that the traditional attitudes of the two sexes were being reversed.

"I suppose I have the white man's guilt," he said nervously, as a man suddenly crossed the street in front of them, his robe making a rustling noise as he vanished into a dark doorway.

"Wait here," said the guide, stopping suddenly before a building like every other in the Street of the Dead Camel. He knocked on the door. After a long wait, it was opened by a small boy who stared suspiciously at them. The guide asked him a question in a low voice and the boy, impressed by his gravity and the presence of the two white people in the street, opened the door and told them to enter.

They were left alone in a long room with an earth floor, lit by a single dim lantern. Sandals filled the room. Some were carefully arranged in pairs on crude racks while others were piled haphazardly on the floor. The unpleasant odor of imperfectly tanned leather filled the air.

"Is the prophet a cobbler?" asked Philip.

"I don't think so," said Sophia, puzzled. "I can't think where we are." They were not left long in doubt. The guide and the boy returned with a message that the prophet would see them, that he lived next door, that they were in the house of his brother-in-law, Marouf the cobbler.

The boy was then paid off and they followed the guide across a courtyard where a goat was tethered, a rank, still figure in the yard. Behind the goat was a door through which they passed into a room where several silent veiled women sat playing dice. They did not look up as the strangers walked through their quarters to the next room. Here they sat cross-legged on a worn dirty rug, the only furniture in the room except for a battered lantern which sputtered and flickered, threatening to go out.

"He will join you shortly," said the guide, sitting a few feet away from his temporary employers, as though to disassociate himself from them.

"I hope he puts on a good show," said Philip, with a spurious casualness.

"I'm very curious about him. His claims, or so I've heard, are the most rational of all."

"And how many others have you visited?"

"A dozen. Some were Christ come again. Others were Israfel, trumpet and all. Still others were without precedent."

"Do you seriously believe a man can predict the future?"

"No. That would be granting too great an importance to the human race. But I think there's a significance in the *fact* of a prophecy. One often knows intuitively when one is in personal danger. Or one often knows that there is something seriously wrong with the body even when there's no pain, and a doctor can find no trace of the cancer whose presence the body instinctively knows. Well, I have a theory it is the same with prophecy. Some men feel more sensitively than others that some great event is pending. Usually the less educated, more simple man is better able to divine what the world wants than the educated man who relies too much upon logic, unaware of the simple need of the race which creates the messiah."

Before Philip could dispute this, the prophet entered the room. He was a small wiry little man, dressed in desert rather than town fashion, his head bare and his beard wild and tangled. His face was more Arabic than Egyptian, with a large beak of a nose and black eyes; the skin was dark and wrinkled and the only modern touch to this Biblical austerity was a pair of steel-rimmed spectacles through which the bright black eyes, somewhat magnified, stared at the visitors.

His name was Abu Bekr.

"The prophet greets you," said the guide, equaling the solemnity of their host, who made a salaam and then seated himself before them on the rug, in the center, Philip noticed with some interest, of a cabalistic design on the carpet. At first he was not sure if this was intentional or not but, when the prophet carefully pulled his robe within the circle, Philip was quite prepared for the carpet to ascend gently with all of them on it and float out the door to the land of Oz.

"We would like to hear the exact prophecy Abu Bekr has made," said Sophia firmly to the interpreter, who repeated this sentence with various ceremonial flourishes to the old man who mumbled a brief reply.

"Abu Bekr would like to know *which* prophecy you want to hear."

"Do you think he wants money?" asked Sophia of the interpreter.

"Certainly not. He is a holy man, inspired by Allah."

"I wasn't sure. Ask him what prophecies he has made."

The holy man's answer was a little longer than the preceding response. "He wants to know why you've come to see him and what you want to hear."

"We want to hear the truth and we have come to him to know the future. We have been told that he has had a revelation, that a new teacher is born."

The prophet answered at length, his voice growing louder, more excited as he talked, gesturng with his hands, molding the air as though creating out of nothing the figure of a

132

divine child. When he finished, the interpreter began his translation, haltingly, confusedly.

"The world is an evil place today, more evil than ever before. The men kill each other with machines and the women go without veils and act like men in the streets and bazaars, while both men and women have deserted the faith and the angel of Allah stands at the gate of heaven looking down upon the earth, ready to blow the trumpet which will put out the sun and shake the stars from the night and level mountains, cities in a sea of flame. But the angel's moment has not come, for a new token of Allah's mercy has appeared in a land to the west, a village by the sea. He will grow up a holy man and he will teach the word of Allah to all the world. The people shall hold him in reverence and call him great for he will teach them not to fear death." The interpreter stopped and looked expectantly at Sophia.

"*Why* will they not fear death?" she asked, looking directly at Abu Bekr, ignoring the interpreter. "What will he teach the people that will make them unafraid?"

The older man's answer to this was mumbled and he stared at the design in the rug while he talked, one hand wound in his beard. "Abu Bekr says he does not know, that he is not the teacher but only a man to whom part of the future has been revealed. He says the Koran says: a true believer need not fear hell."

"When was the saviour born?"

The answer was prompt: "Two months and nine days ago when the moon rose he was born and, the same night, an angel came to Abu Bekr in a dream and told him what had happened so that he might prepare himself and the men of his tribe for the cleansing."

"Will he be a king or a warrior or a priest?" asked Sophia.

"He will be a man," said Abu Bekr, rising. The audience was over.

All the way back to the hotel Sophia and Philip quarreled. The interpreter was silent as he led the way down the Street of the Dead Camel to the town's center and their hotel.

"You don't really believe such nonsense," said Philip, obscurely angry at what they had heard.

"Of course I do."

"But how can you? He's just an ignorant old man living in a godforsaken village on the Nile. He obviously knows the New Testament and he's made up his mind that it might

133

lessen the monotony of daily life if he were to become John the Baptist and attract as much attention as possible, which he seems to have done."

"He knows the Koran, too," said Sophia mildly. "The first speech he made us was a paraphrase of Mohammed."

"I'm still not impressed. I think it amusing and all that, like palmistry, but I refuse to take any of it seriously."

"But he gave us an opportunity to check what he had said. He told us the exact day of the birth."

"But didn't mention the place."

"We can find out easily enough. I don't think he knew himself where the place was."

"How can you find out?"

"There aren't too many sections of the world where the new moon rose in a country to the west, on the sea, on a day that we know."

"A line of longitude is several thousand miles long. I'm sure that a town on that line will be easy to find. Yet even if you should discover that the old man meant Tacoma, Washington, it will probably be thirty years or more before the mission becomes known."

"It's something to look forward to in our old age," said Sophia, laughing in the dark.

"Why do *you* care so much?" asked Philip suddenly. "Even if every word the old man said were true, what difference would it make?"

"A great deal to everyone."

"There's nothing you can do to affect it, is there?"

"No. Of course not."

"What would you do, if you *could* do something?"

"I would kill the child at birth," said Sophia. "But like Herod, I should fail. These things happen. No one can stop them from happening. We can only endure."

Chapter Eight

"*WELCOME HOME,* young man," said Mr Willys cheerily. "How were the ruins? Hot work, isn't it? Archeology, I mean."

He was sitting up in bed, his thin gray hair combed, the head bandage removed and the torn ear nearly healed. He wore a Chinese dressing gown of white silk with a blue dragon picked out in it.

"Very hot, and I'm glad to be back: the food was terrible. How have *you* been?"

"On top of the world." Mr Willys beamed. "I can never thank you enough for introducing me to Mrs Peabody. I never imagined any woman could be so wonderful. She knows everything, literally everything—in her field, that is. It's been a real education, I can tell you."

"Is she getting on with her book?"

"Oh, she's not *writing* here. She's just doing field work. Collecting data, that's all. She will later dictate the entire work in five days into a tape recorder."

"Prodigious," said Philip, sitting down beside the bed in such a way that the afternoon sun was not in his eyes. "Then you're taking a more cheerful view of things, I suppose."

"I certainly am," said Mr Willys. "I feel better than I have in years."

"You've stopped all of that nonsense about wanting to kill yourself?"

"Well—yes and no." Mr Willys suddenly looked as crafty as his open pudding face would allow. "If you mean have I given up hope of being able to kill myself, I will say yes, I have. I just don't have the courage to do it."

"That's good news. And that means you probably won't be staying here much longer."

"No. Not much longer." He smiled craftily.

"I'm afraid I don't understand you."

"Can I trust you?" Mr Willys narrowed his tiny eyes until they disappeared.

135

"Of course you can." Philip was curious.

"You'll try not to interfere in any way, if I tell you?"

"I promise."

"I know I shouldn't let on but I can't help it. I *must* talk to someone and you're the logical person since without knowing it, of course, you brought the whole wonderful thing about."

"What wonderful thing?"

"Fay Peabody."

"Well? *Is* she a wonderful thing?" Philip had a vision of Mr Willys and Mrs Peabody being married in a Hollywood chapel full of lilies of the valley. But his guess was wrong.

"You can take it from me, young man, that she's a mighty bright little lady, with her heart in the right place. She's consented to do it."

"To marry you?" Philip did not want immediately to give up this dream.

"No, to administer the poison. We've had a number of long talks and she's consented to do for me what no other person of my acquaintance would do and what, as you know, I couldn't do for myself. As a matter of fact, she's quite thrilled by the whole thing."

"You had no trouble in persuading her?"

"A great deal, especially at first. She had all sorts of scruples but when she saw how serious I was and how much I needed help she took pity on me. She has a heart as big as all outdoors."

"And she isn't afraid?"

"At first she was. But since then she has steeled herself to the task. Especially when I reminded her who she was: the greatest murder-mystery writer in America. You know what President Roosevelt said about her book *Red, White and Blue Murder.*"

"He said it was a swell yarn."

"That's right. I never cared much for him, by the way. Did you?"

"I hate all politicians," said Philip. "But how is she going to do . . . what you want her to do?"

"I don't know." He sighed. "Isn't it wonderful? I don't know how or when. Only why. The motive, as Mrs Peabody would say."

"You must be scared to death," said Philip tactlessly, carried away by the novelty of the situation.

"I've never enjoyed life more. If that doesn't sound inconsistent. To know that any day now it will be over for good. . . . Well, it's far more than I bargained for, believe me. There was a spell last week when I was going to go on forever like this, without relief."

"Is it to be a perfect crime, or will it resemble suicide?"

"She hasn't told me and I haven't asked. I don't want to pester her. I mean, what if she should suddenly refuse? No sir, I'm not asking any questions. I wouldn't interfere for a million! I figure that little lady has done pretty well in this field, the writing end of it anyway, and I don't want to put my oar in."

Philip wondered whether or not Mr Willys was quite sane. Perhaps the heat and the fat and the near-suicide had made him subject to hallucinations, made his dream of death seem nearly realized. Presuming that not a word of what he had said was true, Philip decided to humor him.

"I should think Mrs Peabody would be nervous, even if *you* aren't. After all, you want to die. But she, I suppose, wants to live and she is, you know, risking her very valuable life to satisfy a whim of yours."

"I should hardly call my wish to die a whim and although I may not have been very much in my life I think I should tell you that, as a citizen, there was a time when I was very highly regarded in Philadelphia: I was a director of the Quaker Greeting Card Company, before the Depression."

"I didn't imply your death was a matter of no importance. I only meant that it would be a real tragedy if Mrs Peabody were to be caught."

"Fay Peabody caught? Never! Even though this is her first attempt at this sort of thing she is a complete master of both method and theory. I wouldn't worry about her."

"But I do," said Philip. "For all her competence she is still only a theoretician."

"Well, have no fear, Mr Warren. *I* have none."

"I hope she pulls it off."

"I'm sure she will."

"When do you think—*it* will happen?"

"Sometime during the next week, I suppose. I haven't given it much thought."

"Poison?"

"I believe so. The only stipulation I made was that it should happen so quickly I wouldn't be aware of it until it was all over."

"Sounds like poison then."

"I should think so. To help her, I've taken to ordering enormous meals—all my favorite dishes: not that I have

137

much appetite, but I was something of a gourmet in my younger days so I've got that manager working his tail off. Tonight he's promised a *sauce béarnaise* made with his own hands. He's an amateur chef, he tells me. . . . Yet who knows *what* may be in that sauce?"

"Who knows, indeed?" said Philip, rising. "I hope everything works out for you."

"Thank you very much. You realize, what I've told you is in the strictest confidence? You won't repeat a word of it, will you? Not even to Mrs Peabody?"

"Of course not."

He did not see Sophia that evening until they joined Mrs Peabody for dinner.

Sophia was in a good mood. She had spent the day across the river near the Valley of the Kings and she had bought a contemporary cartoon of Ikhnaton which one of the natives had found the week before in the wreckage of an incompleted tomb. She showed them the fragment of plaster on which a cruelly sophisticated artist had, in a few strokes, sketched the long head and heavy-lidded eyes, the full mouth and sharp chin of the great monotheist, gratuitously adding whiskers, revealing Pharaoh as he looked when he had not shaved for a week.

"What a fool he must have seemed to his contemporaries," said Sophia, putting the sketch back into her purse.

"What a fool he was," said Philip. "From a practical point of view. He was given a first-rate country to govern and he wrecked it, all for the love of God."

"What did you say his name was?" asked Mrs Peabody, liverish in a gown of fever-red with garnets at her throat.

"Ikhnaton," said Sophia. "He ruled over three thousand years ago."

"Such a long time!" mused Mrs Peabody, toying with her fork. "You say he was a Christian?"

"No, Mrs Peabody. He tried to replace the old religion with a form of sun worship which various authorities have, ever since the nineteenth century at least, found singularly prophetic and attractive; actually, he was a mystic and he did the usual amount of harm those people do. His theology was soon forgotten but the damage survived him, as it always does."

" 'And the good is oft interred with their bones,' " quoted Mrs Peabody, under the impression she was reciting from the Bible. "How sad it all is! I am sure he must have been very fine. That face you showed us was sensitive. I can tell.

I know a thing or two about faces. When I was doing field work for *The Dark Pullman Car Murder* . . ." As she told them about her research, Philip examined her narrowly for any sign of anxiety or guilt, but she seemed much as ever and he decided that Mr Willys had indeed gone mad with the heat. In fact, the authoress was uncommonly animated tonight and dressed with more than usual care; she had even given her hair a fresh rinse and it was now a startlingly frizzled maroon by artificial light. When she had finished discussing faces, Philip asked her how her work was coming.

"Very well, all things considered: I don't care too much for the heat, you know. So I've taken to wearing an old picture hat with a heavy muslin veil, stuffy, but at least it protects me from the harsh rays of the sun."

"But you've done a good deal of work?"

"Ah, Mr Warren, that is something I can never tell until the moment I start to dictate. Then, if I have done my task well, the book takes form splendidly and another Fay Peabody work is born. But if I make a false start, I know that I have failed of my goal, that I have done insufficient spade work and so, willy-nilly, I am driven back into the field. At the moment, my guess is that my rate of progress has been average. I spent the morning with the manager studying the train schedules. That sort of thing is important, very important. How many a work of imagination has failed because of *faulty verisimilitude!*"

"How many indeed," echoed Philip and Sophia, in excellent humor.

"Get the facts, I tell you people who are contemplating a career in the field of detection writing. That and plenty of elbow grease *spell success.*"

There was very little to say after this until the dessert, an elaborate Arab affair of crushed nuts and thin pastry, was put before them. Then just as Fay Peabody, eyes glistening, had brought a large forkful halfway to her thin lips, Philip asked her how Mr Willys had been. She was obviously caught between delaying her answer for several awkward, perhaps even suspicious, moments while she chewed the longed-for confection, or disappointing her salivary glands by delaying the anticipated treat to answer him. She exercised her will. She put the fork down, swallowed hard and said, "Poor Mr Willys. I fear he is *morbidly inclined.*"

"He has very little to live for," said Sophia.

"Is not life itself enough, a precious gift?" Mrs Peabody chewed contentedly now, her dentures making odd little clicking noises.

"I should have thought that you, of all people, Mrs Peabody, might have sympathized with Mr Willys's attitude," said Philip, watching her face. She was admirably controlled.

"Come, come, Mr Warren. Merely because I have devoted my life to the problems of detection does not mean that I have, along the way, jettisoned that moral code which I learned long years ago at my mother's knee in Cleveland. Quite the contrary. My field work has dramatically demonstrated to me that *crime is bad*."

Philip waited a moment before he answered, not sure whether she had completed her statement or not; she had.

"I have never looked at it that way," he said humbly. "But I'm sure you're right. Still, a suicide is not precisely a crime."

"It is considered a major crime by both State and Church, far worse, morally, than murder. As a device in novels of detection, it is only to be deplored. It is not fair to the reader. Fortunately, most authors do not use it as a device, recognizing that it is not Fair Play."

"But I should say that Mr Willys could only hope for death to come quickly of its own accord or else to pray that someone will murder him."

The effect of this statement convinced Philip that Mr Willys had been rational after all; Mrs Peabody was indeed contemplating murder. A startled expression fluttered across her soft, ordinary face. Then she declared herself guilty when she said, "I shouldn't imagine he was in very good health, *with all that weight*."

"He might have apoplexy any day," said Philip, wondering whether to interfere or not.

"He has a bad heart, I believe," said Mrs Peabody, finishing her dessert.

"Perhaps nature will take care of him soon and solve his problems once and for all."

"I pity him," said Fay Peabody, as they left the table. She then excused herself, murmuring that an authoress's work *was never done*. Sophia and Philip wandered out into the garden where they discussed his discovery.

"Now the problem is what to do."

"But why do anything?" Sophia sounded surprised. They

stopped walking and stood in the middle of the path; palm trees hid the hotel.

"I think she should be stopped."

"Why? For one thing it's no business of yours and, for another, she's doing a good deed. If I were tempted to do a good deed, which I am not usually, I might have taken on the assignment myself."

"I'm afraid I must seem conventional to you," said Philip more from a sense of duty than from any real conviction.

Sophia laughed. "It's also the funniest thing I've ever heard! I could have sworn that woman wouldn't have been able to kill a fly."

"That bothers me too. Suppose she's caught?"

"Who will catch her? The authorities here aren't going to bother about the death of a fat man whom no one knows, a semi-invalid."

"Your attitude seems rather cold-blooded."

"Then let's go and tell the police."

"We can't do that either," said Philip.

"Let's wait and see," said Sophia. "Perhaps she won't go through with it. She may give up, you know."

But Fay Peabody did not give up. She did not lose her nerve. And even when the situation looked darkest, she was able to draw strength from the knowledge that she was, after all, the incomparable Fay Peabody, peerless in the world of detection writing, a woman whose field work was a legend throughout the civilized world.

The first attempt on the life of Mr Willys was made at breakfast the next day. Philip first heard of it when, somewhat late, he came downstairs to find Mr Koyoumdjian despondent, in what he called "a blue funk."

"That guy Willys ought to be in an institution like a hospital."

"What's the matter? Has something happened?" Philip's hands grew cold, as though he himself were the murderer.

"He got sick to his stomach after breakfast. The local sawbones is upstairs giving him the word. I told him I wanted Willys moved to the hospital but the doc said no dice. He stays here. Next thing he'll probably die on me."

Philip thought this very likely but he did not say so. "Where is Miss Oliver?"

"Up early and gone across the river for the day."

"And Mrs Peabody?"

"She's out in the garden. Says she wants to do some flower arrangements for the dining room. The gardener will be fit to be tied but the customer is always right, like they say."

Mrs Peabody, wearing her picture hat, gave a start when Philip came up behind her as she was leaning over some purple blossoms with a pair of garden shears.

"You startled me!" she said, dropping the shears. Philip got them for her. She sat down heavily on a near-by bench. "The heat," she sighed.

"Mr Willys is sick this morning."

"I should really look in on him. I plan to take him some of these gorgeous blooms after I do the downstairs arrangements. I hate untidy bouquets."

"Mrs Peabody, do you think it wise? Do you really feel you should risk your own life just to oblige Mr Willys?"

Mrs Peabody, now very pale indeed, dropped the shears again; neither made a move to pick them up. "What do you mean?" she asked, in a voice so tiny that had he not been sitting beside her, he might have thought a bee had sounded, or a cicada had whirred somewhere in the green foliage.

"I'll be frank with you, Mrs Peabody. Mr Willys once made me the same proposition he made you. Only I refused to help him. You, on the other hand, were taken in. Whether it was out of curiosity or out of a real desire to help him makes little difference. The facts are the same in either case. You agreed to murder him." Philip paused.

"Mr Willys told you this—fantastic story?" She got a grip on herself again. The panic of the moment was now succeeded by nonchalance. She picked up the shears and put them back into the half-filled flower basket.

Philip pressed his last bit of advantage. "And I also know that you poisoned him this morning at breakfast, but that something went wrong."

Mrs Peabody rose with great dignity and said, "Follow me." She led him to the far end of the garden where, in the shade of a gnarled eucalyptus tree, she said, "Since we are now completely alone and there are no witnesses, I will be candid, even though I vowed my lips would remain sealed until the day I died, but as the plot is already getting tangled, and you, whether you like it or not, are involved quite deeply, I will confess to you that I took on this perilous job and that I mean to see it through, *come hell or high water!* My motives were, and are, of the highest. My method has, to my own amazement, been faulty. I erred. I blundered. I took a hypodermic needle early this morning and filled it with a colorless, tasteless poison of local origin which I inserted into the soft-boiled eggs he had ordered for breakfast. The chemist had informed me, prior to my purchase, that the dose was not only lethal but that it would kill a host of rats. It failed, however, to kill Mr Willys. From my room I could hear the doctor talking to him and I gather he was only mildly nauseated."

"Which is probably just as well for you, Mrs Peabody."

"Let me tell you, Mr Warren, that should you attempt to go to the police you would only be laughed at since, obviously, I would deny having confessed to you while Mr Willys himself would never testify against me."

"I have no intention of going to the police. I was just reminding you of the risk involved, should you try again."

"I will take that risk, Mr Warren. Rome was not built in a day. I am not discouraged. *I shall strike again.*"

"I don't see how you have the nerve," said Philip, wonderingly; but then one look into the bright little eyes of Fay Peabody convinced him that she was a fanatic, and an artist. She would not be stopped by anyone until her demon was satisfied, until Mr Willys was dead.

"It proves," she said, in an ordinary voice, "that one can't rely on foreign products. If I'd had more time, I'm sure I would have been able to try the poison out on some creature to see if it were efficacious but, as you can see, I was forced to rely on the word of a native chemist and all my plans 'gang aft agley' as Bobbie Burns would say—like a false start on my dictaphone—yet when I fail to get the beginning right, I go back into the field with renewed vigor and I have never, never failed to *bring home the bacon,*" she said slowly, fixing Philip's eyes with her own serious ones, a loose flap of the muslin veil now shadowing her left cheek and eye, giving her a somewhat slovenly air.

"Well, I won't interfere, Mrs Peabody, beyond saying that I think that what you're doing is dangerous and that the morality of the thing is confused, to say the least."

"I will do my duty as I see it and though I appreciate your concern . . ." Suddenly she stopped talking and for a moment Philip was afraid she was going to faint. Quite pale, she made for the bench; with one last spurt of strength, she got to it and crumpled, her hand to her heart and her eyes wild with fear.

143

"What in God's name is the matter?" asked Philip, startled, positive that she was having a heart attack.

"*The hypodermic,*" she whispered, growing paler by the instant. "I left it in the pantry."

"Good Lord!" Then: "You must get it back immediately. Perhaps they haven't found it yet."

"It's been there several hours. How *could* I? How could I have blundered so? The plan was perfect. Oh!" She moaned into the muslin veil which now completely covered her face.

"There's no use in your losing your nerve now, Mrs Peabody. Go to the pantry and see if the needle is there. After all, Mr Willys isn't dead yet."

"That's right." This thought comforted her and she emerged for a moment from behind the veil. "We must hide the evidence."

"*You* must hide the evidence, not I. I'm not going to be one of your—what do you call them?—accessories?"

"After the fact. Only there's no fact yet. Come to the pantry."

The hypodermic was where she had left it and since there were no servants in sight, she hid the weapon in the flower basket; then with something of her old assurance, she went into the lobby, accompanied by Philip.

"Ah, flowers," exclaimed Mr Koyoumdjian brightly. "I hope you'll take some up to Mr Willys. Cheer him up. He's been asking for you."

"Poor dear man! Has the doctor gone?"

"He just now left. He's getting to know Mr Willys very well . . . it was him who patched him up after he tried to take a powder." Philip was pleased to find that the manager could make an occasional mistake in his well-loved vernacular.

"What did he say was wrong with our Mr Willys?"

"Nothing much, just stomach trouble. He picked up a bug in Cairo, I wouldn't be surprised."

"I have just the medicine for him," said Mrs Peabody, marching off, her flower basket swinging jauntily on her arm.

◙

The second attempt on the life of Mr Willys was made during the night when his bed collapsed; the iron crosspiece that held up the mosquito netting missing his head by several inches. Philip, when he heard the noise, thought to

144

himself: "That's done it" and went back to sleep, refusing to be even a witness to Mrs Peabody's plot.

In the morning, on his way to breakfast, he looked in to see what damage had been done. The room was the same as ever, however, and Mr Willys was sitting up in bed, glumly sipping water through a straw.

"What was all the racket last night?"

"The bed," said Mr Willys. "It collapsed. Gave me quite a shock. My heart's pounding so I can barely breathe."

"Mrs Peabody?"

"Mrs Peabody."

"She's failed twice."

"I know," said Mr Willys. "It's getting on my nerves. I had no wish to be hurt, you know. I can't bear pain. The thought makes me quite ill. And now the suspense! It's horrible. I tell you I don't know when or where she'll strike next."

"Make her stop."

"Oh, I couldn't do that. She's gone to such trouble. It would hardly be fair."

"I don't see that fairness has anything to do with it."

"But I still want her to pull it off. Only she's so damned sloppy. First of all, I knew those eggs were poisoned. She left enormous holes in the shells and they tasted god-awful but I ate them anyway and got sick. Then last night, the bed caved in. How she managed that, I'll never know. I suppose she loosened the top piece while I was taking a bath. I must say she's ingenious. What a mind that little lady has—like a steel trap!"

"A trap which won't close. If you weren't a willing victim, she'd be in jail now."

"Well, we must remember that this is all quite new to her: there's a lot of difference between writing about something and actually doing it."

"I could do a better job," said Philip scornfully. "Anybody could."

"You wouldn't take it on, would you? I'd be very grateful. I could make it worth your while. You can name your price, within reason."

"No, I'm afraid you're stuck with Mrs Peabody. It's a little like the medical profession. You engaged her and until *she* consents to call in a consultant it would be most unethical for you to replace her."

"This is *not* a joke."

"I realize that it isn't but there's nothing I can do about

it except tell the police you want Mrs Peabody to kill you and that she's trying to, without much success. No, I'm afraid you will just have to trust to luck and the Fay Peabody Method."

"You're not very encouraging."

"Now, why don't you be sensible and tell her to stick to her writing while you go to Switzerland and lose weight."

"I can't. Glands."

"Then take shots."

"They don't work on me. No, my mind is made up. Yet I keep wondering *what* will she do next."

"Probably drown you in your bath."

Mr Willys shuddered. "I hate the idea of drowning: strangling to death, that's all it is. Well, I'll keep the bathroom door locked. She won't be able to get in. Bolts on the inside. Besides, we have an agreement to the effect that the business must be done in an instant."

"But she's a desperate woman. Remember that. She's failed twice. Rather than fail a third time, she's quite capable of losing her head and setting fire to you."

"Oh, she wouldn't do that." He was alarmed, and Philip hoped that the fear of pain might yet force him to change his mind. "I'm sure the next time she'll be able to do it, easily, without any fuss."

"I think you're optimistic," said Philip darkly, and he left the room and went downstairs to join Sophia and Mrs Peabody who were already at breakfast.

"Did you hear the noise last night?" asked Sophia, cool in green, unlike Mrs Peabody who looked more dowdy than ever, her eyelids red and granulated from fatigue. Her hands shook as she drank the bitter black coffee.

"Mr Willys told me his bed collapsed on him in the middle of the night."

"Poor Mr Willys," said Sophia maliciously. "So many things seem to happen to him."

"He's very unlucky, poor man," said Philip, watching the murderess *manquée* out of the corner of his eye. She appeared not to be listening.

"One could almost believe in a malignant destiny. How could one man have so many things happen to him?"

"Foul play?" suggested Philip.

"It's possible. But who would want to hurt poor, harmless Mr Willys?"

"Mr Willys himself."

"Possibly. But no one else. The whole thing is so strange."

146

Then having made Mrs Peabody suffer for her projected sin, they changed the subject and spoke of the trip they were to make that day to some tombs near the Valley of the Kings and, to their great surprise, Mrs. Peabody asked if she might accompany them that afternoon because "I've never done those tombs." Since there was no polite way to refuse her, she was allowed to join the expedition.

After leaving the hotel, they went down the steps to the river where a rowboat and their dragoman were waiting. A number of naked boys stared curiously at the women who refused, pink-faced, to stare back. Then crossing the slow, warm river, they passed a sand island where donkeys were being raced to the delight of a large group of men. How the donkeys had got there and why they were racing one another Philip could never learn, for the dragoman, though he spoke English fluently, invariably expressed himself in such cryptic phrases that Philip preferred not to ask him questions.

The day passed pleasantly. They visited many tombs, small cheerful rooms cut in stone with bright wall paintings. The colors were new and fresh, preserved by the dry heat. They read in pictures of the lives of the dead and looked at representations of country houses, children, friends, all the activities of three thousand years before.

Mrs Peabody took many notes. She spoke very little but what she did say was to the point. They were, Philip decided, seeing the true Fay Peabody, the tireless master craftswoman giving her fans the best that was in her.

Once when Sophia and the dragoman were quarreling over a figure of Osiris, Philip got Mrs Peabody off in one corner of the tomb of the Second Chief Accountant to the Royal Household and asked her in a low voice why the last attempt on the life Mr Willys had failed.

"A miscalculation. I miscalculated the position of the crosspiece," she said bitterly.

"But it was clearly in the center of the bed. I don't see how you could have expected it to drop anywhere except in the middle of the mattress or on his stomach."

"It was weighted," she said, looking at him with undisguised malevolence. "It was so arranged that when he turned over the entire thing would drop, from a considerable height, onto his head. Had it done so, he would no longer be with us. I had not counted, however, on his head being at *the very edge* of the bed. The odds were ten to one it would be close to the center where the weight *did* fall, missing him."

"I think it's getting on his nerves, these false attempts of yours."

"Getting on *his* nerves!" She glared at him. "Do you think it a picnic for me? Do you? Do you imagine I enjoy making a fool of myself before all the world? Or at least before you and Mr Willys. You seem to forget that I embarked on this project for completely selfless reasons. I have twice failed of my object. I admit that. But I hardly feel that others should criticize me for not being able to do easily what they would never dare attempt to do in the first place. I want it clearly understood, by both of you and Mr Willys, that I will brook no criticism of my methods *and* if I do not have the fullest co-operation and confidence of Mr Willys, I may be forced to withdraw altogether. Do you understand?"

"Perfectly."

"You will repeat this to Mr Willys?"

"I will."

"What time is it, by the way?"

"Four o'clock."

"Ah! Then you will probably be spared the onerous task of repeating what I have said for, unless some unforeseen contingency has again arisen, Mr Willys is dead."

Here, among the tombs, the announcement lost much of its inherent awfulness.

"But how?"

She would not answer his question. Instead, she unpinned her veil, shutting out the world with muslin.

🔲

Mr Koyoumdjian was in a rage. "I'm going to have him moved today. I won't have him here another minute. The servants are thinking somebody has got the evil eye and they won't go near him. He's jinxed."

"Has . . . something happened to Mr Willys?" asked Fay Peabody, one hand on the corner of the desk as though to steady herself.

"Asthma!" Mr Koyoumdjian said with a moan. "He nearly choked to death. The doctor's with him. I'm going to get him out of this hotel if it's the last thing I do."

Sophia looked at Philip and smiled. Mrs Peabody, without a word, went to her room.

"What do you think she could have done to him?"

148

murmured Philip, as he and Sophia followed Mrs Peabody up the stairs.

"I haven't any idea. Do you think she tried again?"

"Oh yes. She told me so this afternoon. She intimated that he would be dead when we got back."

"Poor woman. She must be desperate. Let's hope she doesn't lose her head and blow up the entire hotel."

Mrs Peabody did not lose her head. That night she came down to dinner even more carefully dressed than usual, her garnets complemented by a double strand of pearls which were dingy enough, small enough, to be real. She was obviously aware that both Philip and Sophia knew her scheme and she carried the dinner off as well as possible under the circumstances, discussing fluently and instructively the large world of detective writers and readers among whom she was still a figure of the greatest magnitude, a thought which obviously sustained her now in her hour of defeat.

During dinner, the manager entered with the latest bulletin: "He's going in the morning. The doctor says he shouldn't be moved but when I told him I couldn't have any more of this monkey business in my hotel he said they'd send a car over tomorrow and take him to the hospital. I've never seen anything like it. My staff is just about ready to leave. They say a demon is loose in the hotel."

"Is he feeling better?" asked Mrs Peabody with an air of gentle concern.

"I think so. He stopped choking. But he looks green about the gills. Doesn't want to leave, of course, but I had the doctor tell him he would have to go in the morning."

"He's certainly an unlucky creature," said Sophia.

"I sure wish he'd be unlucky somewhere else," said the manager.

In the lobby, after dinner, Philip had another chance to talk with Mrs Peabody. She tried to avoid him, but he was too quick for her. "What went wrong?" he asked.

"I would rather not discuss it."

"You won't try again, will you?"

"It's no business of yours," she snapped. "But to satisfy your curiosity, no, I *won't* try again. Now, if you'll excuse me . . ."

"Do tell me what you did this last time."

"I placed a certain deadly, air-polluting poison in the pistils of a large number of flowers which I then set about his room so that, in a few hours, the atmosphere would be completely malignant. I had not, however, taken into account the fact that Mr Willys had an allergy to all flowers and the he nearly choked to death before they could be removed."

"Frankly, Mrs Peabody, I'm astonished you failed. I can't imagine anything simpler than killing someone who wants to die in a country where there probably would never be an investigation."

"I should like to see *you* try it."

"People do it every day. How can you explain that? Thousands of murders go undetected every year. I don't understand why you, with every advantage, can't do as well."

"Perhaps because *I* am not a criminal," said Mrs Peabody; and she went upstairs.

"How did she do it this time?" asked Sophia.

Philip told her and she laughed. "If only her fans could see her now."

That night before going to bed, Philip visited Mr Willys. He looked the same as ever but his thin voice was more weak than usual and talking seemed to tire him.

"It's all over with me," he said. "She won't try again."

"Just as well. I was always against the idea."

"I can't imagine her quitting now. After wrecking my nerves and health she refuses to finish the job! It isn't fair. It just isn't fair."

"I'm sure you'll be well in no time."

"I expect to be an invalid for the next twenty years. I can hardly move as it is. The strain of getting out of bed and going to the bathroom gives me such palpitations that I can hardly bear it. Oh, it's so terrible," and he moaned plaintively, his eyes tight shut, as though to blot the world out forever.

"Anyway it nearly worked last time," said Philip, illogically, hoping that this would please him, this reference to the plan which had failed; it did not.

"The fool! The incompetent fool!" Mr Willys turned on his former idol with a ferocity made all the more frightening because his voice was too weak to bear the passion of a denunciation. "Any half-wit Arab could have done better, if he thought there might be a plugged nickel in it for him. But the brilliant Fay Peabody, given every chance in the world, flops. She could have asked me about the flowers. But no, she waited until I'd gone to the bathroom, then she put them all around the room like a funeral parlor. It was half an hour before I could get enough breath to shout for help."

"Do you think that anyone suspected the flowers were poisoned?"

"How? They were thrown out right away, while I was strangling. I suppose if she had put a few more in the room, nature might have done the trick."

"Did she have any excuse to make?"

"She attacked *me* for having an allergy. Said it was the most ridiculous thing she'd ever heard of, that if she'd put it in a story nobody'd believe it."

"I hope you told her off."

"Don't worry! I said that if she'd ever. . . ." He began to wheeze alarmingly, shaking the bed, fat rippling dangerously as he gagged, tried to get his breath. When finally he did, he was pale and exhausted, too sick to acknowledge Philip's sympathy.

The next morning, refusing the litter which the doctor had sent over, Mr Willys dressed himself and slowly descended the stairs, supported on each side by a fragile native boy. It was the first time that Philip had seen Mr Willys on his feet and he was surprised to find that he was a short man, broader than he was tall, with ludicrously small hands and feet. He wore a crumpled white suit and a loud tie decorated with reindeer, a souvenir no doubt from his greeting-card days. He was very pale and breathing hard when, against the doctor's advice and the manager's wish, he insisted on joining the others at breakfast.

"Good morning," he puffed, as a place was laid for him.

"It's nice to see you up," said Sophia politely.

"I'm vertical, if that's what you mean. I am hardly *up*. I can hardly breathe in this weather. But a large breakfast does seem in order." And he had them bring him sausages, eggs and potatoes, as well as toast and coffee. "A real American breakfast," he said, eating as quickly as he could, his white face glistening with sweat.

"Do you think you should eat so much in this heat?" asked Philip, somewhat sickened by the other's unnatural appetite.

"I need a hearty breakfast," mumbled Mr Willys.

"I believe that toast and coffee is all *anybody* needs," said Fay Peabody. "Except, of course, working men who must *labor with their hands*."

Mr Willys snorted but made no answer as he speared a fried potato.

151

Philip looked out the French windows at the green gardens flickering in the heat. For several moments the only sound at the table was the wet noise of Mr Willys chewing and swallowing food.

Sophia mercifully broke the silence: "Where do you intend to go next?"

"Switzerland, if I can survive the altitude. Start taking glands and things. See if maybe they can do something. Doubt it, though."

This speech was dragged out to an inordinate length by long stops for breath and nourishment. Philip could not take his eyes off him, much as he would rather have looked anywhere else than at that gray shapeless face with the loose lips which quivered as Mr Willys gasped and talked and chewed, all at once. Philip almost wished, if only on aesthetic grounds, that Mrs Peabody had succeeded.

"Will you be in Europe long?" asked Sophia, who, of them all, was the only one not officially in on the conspiracy which had failed.

"Can't tell. May go back to Philly. Though it's hot there, too. Waiter, bring me some more toast. One place pretty much like another to me, except some are hot and some are cool. Want a cool place now." Then he did things to a soft poached egg which Philip never wanted to see done again.

"Did you get to see much of Egypt?" Sophia was intent on being polite.

"Saw the Sphinx my first day in Cairo. Then had a heat stroke and I've been laid up ever since. First there; now here."

"I'm sure you'd have enjoyed Karnak."

"Don't think so. I did want to see the Sphinx but outside of that I'm not so keen on sightseeing. It's hard on a man my size."

"Why did you want to see the Sphinx?" asked Sophia.

"Always heard about it."

"Did you like it?"

"Not much. Face all gone."

"At least you're able to get a bit of reading done," said Philip helpfully; only a few minutes to go.

"Don't read much. Eyes can't take it. I used to like detective stories." He put down his fork, swallowed noisily and stared at Mrs Peabody who had the grace not to stare back.

"I'm sure Mrs Peabody is pleased to hear that," said

152

Sophia. "I've never read a detective story, I'm afraid. A terrible confession to make in front of you," she said, turning to the authoress.

"Not at all. I am aware that the vineyard in which I have for so long toiled produces nothing more than a good table wine. At least so the connoisseurs in these matters seem to think; but it is good enough for me and for a great many other people as well, *both at home and abroad.*"

Mr Willys looked at her with loathing, but he said nothing while the others talked about Mrs Peabody's vineyard.

The manager came in just as Mr Willys was debating whether to have more coffee. "The car's waiting for you outside, sir. I've also got the bill for you and some other things out in the lobby if you'll be so kind as to take care of them for me."

"Let us go then," said Mr Willys, pushing back from the table; the two frail native boys moved forward, got him to his feet and escorted him out of the dining room and into the lobby. Mrs Peabody, with a bleak little smile, excused herself and left the room for the morning-fresh garden.

"Well, that's the end of that," said Philip.

"She seems rather crushed by it all."

"And he doesn't, which is suspicious. He seems almost cheerful."

"A great deal of attention sometimes has a good effect on people who are often alone. I don't suppose Mr Willys has ever been the center of attention before in his life, except as a minor curiosity in public places."

"All that food!" Philip shuddered.

"He could hardly walk."

"Let's go see him off," said Philip, and they went into the lobby where Mr Willys stood unsupported in the doorway, his baggage all about him and Mr Koyoumdjian, beaming with relief, was wishing him a quick recovery.

"Ah, there you are," said Mr Willys, as they approached. "This is it. I'm off at last."

"Have a good trip," said Philip, shaking the cold damp hand. "Are you going to stay at the hospital long? Are you going down to Cairo?"

"Cairo. Tomorrow. Then I'm leaving this goddamn country for good."

"I was going to say if you were at the hospital for any length of time, we would come visit you."

"Very kind of you, I must say. You've been wonderful about the whole thing . . . very kind. But now I must be

153

off. Good-by, Miss Oliver. Been a pleasure." Then, un-accompanied, he walked into the sunlight where he collapsed, a few feet from the automobile which was to have taken him to the hospital. His last recorded words were: "Get a doctor."

The sudden death of Mr Willys shocked them all. To Philip it seemed, somehow, grossly unfair while to the manager it was The End: he did not believe anyone could be as jinxed as he was. Several servants resigned on the spot while the remaining ones gave him a vote of no confidence but did not press for any immediate action, either on his part or theirs. The body was removed the moment the doctor announced that the anguished, flesh-burdened soul of Mr Willys had departed this vale of tears. Philip told the doctor that the deceased had wanted to be cremated and his ashes cast into the Nile. This last touch was Philip's own. The doctor thought they might have trouble finding a large enough oven for this purpose but that there was a possibility the brick kiln on the edge of town could be hired to do the job. Fortunately, Mr Willys had had sufficient cash in his pocket to make a fine cremation possible. Other details, such as the disposition of personal effects and the writing to the next of kin, were assigned to Mr. Koyoumdjian.

That night at dinner the two ladies wore black and Philip wore a blue serge suit.

"What did the doctor say he died of?" asked Sophia, after a long, lugubrious silence.

"A heart attack," said Philip, in a low reverent voice. "Excitement, the heat, and all that food he ate finished him off."

"What were his last words?" asked Mrs Peabody, softly, her hands folded before her on the table, as though in prayer.

"He asked for a doctor," said Philip; a sudden suspicion crossed his mind.

"It doesn't sound as if he was very *sincere,*" said Mrs Peabody, unaware of the suspicion in which she was held by Philip. "All that talk about wanting to die and then when he *does* get his wish, he is frightened. *A lack of moral fiber,* I should say."

"You . . . you weren't responsible?" asked Philip, for-

154

getting that Sophia was not supposed to know about the attempt on Mr Willys's life.

"No, I wasn't," said Mrs Peabody. "I debated whether or not to give it one last whirl. His rudeness to me at breakfast, however, restrained my essentially kind impulse and I allowed him to depart for what I hoped might have been a long life of physical distress and melancholia. Fortunately, for him, nature intervened."

The next day the manager brought Philip a shoe box which contained all that was mortal of Mr Willys. "You go throw them in the Nile," said Mr Koyoumdjian, "and do it quick because if the boys find out that even that guy's ashes are in the hotel, they'll leave me pronto."

Philip said that he would conduct the last rites immediately and so, accompanied by Sophia, he walked to the bank of the Nile and climbed down the rocky embankment to the water's edge. Sailboats glided across the water. Philip opened the box which contained some gray-black lumps of bone and ash.

"Who would have thought he could have been compressed to this?" he said, in an unconscious paraphrase.

"Give me the box," said Sophia, and she took it from the bemused Philip and emptied its contents into the green water. "You see how easy it is?" she asked, throwing the box away.

"How easy what is?"

"Dying."

"No, I don't."

Chapter Nine

HE PRESSED HIS EYELIDS and saw two black suns, two eclipses in the red darkness. His head ached from the glare and heat of the day which, fortunately, was very nearly over. He opened his eyes again and looked across the desert at the near-by pyramids: large buff-colored objects as meaningless as a child's toys upset in a sandbox. The sky was a pale luminous pink, cloudless and now, as the red disc slipped over the desert's edge, sunless as well. To his left was Cairo and to his right the desert. The green Nile Valley ended abruptly at his feet. One foot touched grass; the other brown desert: the line between was unnaturally precise, as though drawn by a giant. He turned and looked at the city, coral pink and white, divided by the Nile, edged by dusty green which was, in its turn, circled by the wide flat desert at whose edge he now stood, a few yards from Mena House where he had been entertained that day with lunch and a swim in the hotel's new pool. Thinking of his host, wondering if he should go back into the lobby and look for him, Philip strode slowly up the steep road which led to the pyramids. He was nearly at the top when he heard someone call his name. He stopped until, out of breath, his host and new friend Charles de Cluny joined him.

"I had things to do. The manager wanted to know about a party some friends of mine were giving. How I hate this hill! It's so steep. I'm quite out of breath. The sky. Isn't it a fine color? This is the time of day when I find myself really loving Egypt. Rose. Wonderful rose color, the sky, and cool without the sun. Here we are."

They were now at the top of the sand hill near the base of the great pyramid. Below them in the roseate distance was Cairo while across the desert, indistinct by twilight, were set the other pyramids, like so many broken metronomes.

"Magnificent sight. I never tire of it. I'm always staggered when I recall the age of these buildings. Think what they must have seen. Think!"

Philip thought and then de Cluny, shifting from con-

156

templation of the past to the scandal of the present, pointed to the only house in the desert, a small cube of a building with great windows and a soldier standing guard in front of it.

"His," he whispered. And from his tone Philip knew that he meant the King, a plump young Albanian, successor to those austere Pharaohs who had reigned before him over the same green valley.

"He brings his women here," his guide whispered as they moved toward the great pyramid. "A gloomy-looking place," said Philip, as they passed the sentry. "No trees, no garden, just sand."

"But the view! Think of it! Having the pyramids in front of you on a starlit night, with a beautiful woman beside you!"

"Do you think he enjoys it?" said Philip who often, in self-defense, liked to take the popular American view that the rich and powerful were hopelessly miserable with no whims left to be granted, no use at all of their wealth and even less for their power which was, of course, invariably attended by guilt and shame. The old woman who dies in a tenement house with fifty thousand dollars sewed in her mattress or the Texas millionaire who lives on cornflakes and weak tea are recurrent American folk types. But even Philip had to agree that the King of Egypt probably never suffered from much more than an occasional hangover or a moment's anguish at the lithe figure he had sacrificed to a robust appetite.

They stopped on the edge of a valley where, handsomely silhouetted against the sky, was, yes, the inevitable attraction, the Sphinx. To our authority, Professor Rawlinson, it is "among the marvels of Egypt, second to none. The mysterious being with the head of a man and the body of a lion is not at all uncommon in Egyptian architectural adornment, but the one placed before the Second Pyramid (The Pyramid of Shafra) and supposed to be contemporaneous with it, astonishes the observer by its gigantic proportions. It is known to the Arabs as *Abul-hôl*, the father of terror."

Philip stared into the mild, faintly smiling face and saw nothing at all, only an ancient monument; and yet, though what he saw was not in itself impressive, the associations of thousands of years affected him as strongly as it had at Luxor and he experienced once again that grave serenity, that secret knowledge of the endless flow of life, of genera-

157

tion and regeneration, never-ending, never-constant, the endless structure which contained all time and matter, the waking dream behind his own blue eyes, eyes which could if briefly hold it all.

Then the sky turned gray and silver specks appeared overhead; the ruddy-faced Sphinx turned the color of slate and Philip muttered that frightening name "Abul-hôl" to himself as he and de Cluny walked back to Mena House.

Later he sat in the dark rose-smelling garden of the hotel and drank whisky with Charles de Cluny, his friend of several days now, a traveler like himself but a knowing traveler, one who had been here often before. He was French. He had lived everywhere: in Central America, in Europe, in Africa. Now, for this month at least, he was in Cairo.

"When does she arrive, this friend of yours?" asked Charles suddenly.

"Miss Oliver? Next week, I think. She's in the desert now. I have no idea where; but I suppose she'll be here when she said she would."

"She sounds like a very intelligent woman," said Charles, disapprovingly.

"Very," said Philip. "She's good company. That's all."

"Ah. Then you're *not* in love?"

"Good Lord, no! She's the last woman in the world I'd be interested in."

"Do you think *she* knows that?"

"I doubt if she's ever given it a thought," said Philip, who sometimes wondered whether she had or not. His vanity often insisted that she *did* love him. Fire beneath cold surface, but his reason thought it unlikely.

"Is she wealthy?"

"I expect so."

"I wonder if she might want to buy some jewels. I have an impoverished cousin—as a matter of fact, I have dozens of impoverished cousins—but the one I have in mind has some exquisite pigeon's-blood rubies which she'd sell for nothing. Do find out if Miss Oliver's interested. It would be such a help if she were. My cousin, by chance, happens to be right here in Cairo."

"I'll ask her," said Philip, wondering how de Cluny himself earned a living.

"I should appreciate that."

After a long silence, de Cluny asked Philip if he knew Zoe Helotius.

"Only slightly. Is she here?"

158

"Just for the week. Out of season, too. But then there's to be a great party and wherever there's a great affair, Zoe's on hand. Amusing woman. When did you know her?"

Philip told him. A number of names were then exchanged. They had several acquaintances in common whom they had not, until that moment, bothered to discuss. They had met as strangers and neither had made the effort to fix the other's place in the world since the identity of each was so clearly apparent: a young American of apparent leisure and a French adventurer with a taste, but not a flair, for philosophy and a flair, but no taste, for a fashionable life on an income whose origin was obscure.

"If you care to," said de Cluny, when Philip's attitude and position had become more clearly defined after the naming of the names, "I will get you invited. It might interest you. A real Cairo affair to celebrate the wedding of . . ." And here he named both the host and the bridegroom, two Egyptian men so highly placed that they could have touched the throne itself if they had been so minded. "It will be a Western party, although we won't see the bride. Both gentlemen are enlightened, but not that much. Other women will be there, however . . . despite the Prophet."

⊡

There was too much of everything at the reception: too many people, too many flowers, too much food and champagne, and more jewels than Philip had ever seen before. The non-orthodox Egyptian women were especially gaudy in lace and damask with huge yellow diamonds, square emeralds, rubies like gouts of blood; their glossy black hair coiled and contorted by Paris hairdressers, dusted with gold and bright with diamond moons and stars. Philip had never before seen such display, as he walked from one large, airy room to the next, through Moorish arches while servants in white Western-style jackets served wine.

De Cluny was an excellent guide. He saw to it that they never remained too long with the very dull or missed meeting the occasional odd or interesting citizen of Cairo who stood, usually, at the center of a large group, receiving homage, constructing epigrams or diatribes or platitudes or whatever his specialty, applauded by the distinguished and decorative audience which moved from one point of interest to the next, like tourists in a museum.

The host, a large imposing man in a morning coat, welcomed them gravely in French, declaring that his house was theirs. That was the last they saw of him.

"And there," said de Cluny, as they crossed the largest of the rooms, "is a Russian spy, under the chandelier . . . calls herself Princess."

The spy was a small pretty woman in her forties, wearing an Indian sari. She smiled engagingly at de Cluny. "How are you?" she said in French, as he kissed her hand. Then, to Philip: "And how are *you?* I've seen you in Shepheard's, haven't I?"

Philip said that she had.

"Oh, let's find some chairs. Everyone stands. It just makes me wilt, standing in the heat." She went over to one corner where three gilt chairs were placed against the wall. Two of them were empty; the third was occupied by a small Egyptian. The spy gave a dazzling smile. "Princess would like to sit down," she said.

The small Egyptian looked puzzled.

"I said, *Princess* would like to sit down," repeated the spy, more sternly. The little man got to his feet and fled.

"That's better, isn't it?" They sat down. "They have such bad manners, Egyptians."

"Are you from India?" asked Philip, naïvely, not realizing that in Cairo no one asked the spies direct questions for fear of seeming gauche.

"My mother is Indian," she said, repeating the same dazzling smile that so confused the former occupant of the chair; then she began a long involved story about the peregrinations of her family and herself, a mélange of nationalities and resounding titles.

"But I am talking only of myself," she exclaimed, when both de Cluny and Philip were afraid she might never talk of anything else again all evening, holding them close to her with her brilliant smile and tiny gesturing hands which, every now and then, touched Philip's sleeve as she named yet another country in which she had lived. "Tell me about you."

"I'm an American," said Philip. "There isn't much more to tell."

"Come now. Princess doesn't believe that! I'm sure you must be a wonderful businessman building oil wells and making dollars all over the world." For a moment he was afraid that this might be a preface to an attack on capitalism but she meant it literally.

"No, I'm a tourist, just out of school," he said; her interest waned perceptibly.

"How wonderful for you to come see our old countries. To breathe the same air that Cleopatra did! Oh, history is my passion! How I should love to have lived in those times and gone to the sources of the Nile in a pleasure barge. Princess would like some champagne."

It took him a moment to separate the request from the rhapsody; by the time he did, de Cluny had clapped his hands and a boy came with champagne for them.

"Aren't you drinking, Charles?" she asked, noticing that de Cluny refused the wine.

"I'm a good Moslem today."

"Now you're making fun of me. Princess is a *real* Moslem but she believes the Prophet would not mind too much since he has promised us all the wine that we can drink in Heaven."

"Only the men were promised that," said de Cluny with a smile.

"You *are* old-fashioned! How are your cousins? I was at a dinner not long ago with one of them but I forgot her name."

"There are so many."

"How wonderful it must be to have distinguished relatives all over the world!"

"And all struggling to survive," said de Cluny.

"The old ways change," said the Princess gravely, and she walked off.

"I don't believe she's a Russian spy," said Philip, as they moved toward another large room where an orchestra was playing waltzes.

"I'm sure she's not either," said de Cluny agreeably, "but she's just like the ones they used to have here during the war. *That* was a time! Everyone was a spy and . . . Oh, look! There *he* is."

They stopped in the doorway of the ballroom where a dozen couples were dancing to the music of an orchestra which was hiding behind potted palms. The parquet floor had been newly waxed and from time to time the dancers slipped and stumbled, amusing those spectators who stood chatting, all eyes discreetly centered on a short burly figure in a tuxedo who was, de Cluny murmured to Philip in a low voice, the King of Egypt. Philip immediately recognized the curiously stiff figure and immobile face, half hidden now by dark glasses which made him look, more than ever, like an interesting experiment in taxidermy. The blonde with

161

whom he was dancing was a head taller than he and very beautiful.

"He's incognito," said de Cluny. "In other words, no one is allowed to fuss over him. But, on the other hand, no one can approach him without *his* consent. A happy arrangement. But here are the guards." Philip looked and saw that in each corner of the room stood a man in a business suit, hand in pocket, revolver barrel pointed.

Then they came to the last of the suite, a small Chinese room with carved teakwood furniture and crimson silk banners on the walls. Here a group of sedate Westerners were gathered, talking politics. De Cluny knew them all and he introduced Philip, saying the names rapidly and precisely. As there was no place farther to go, their journey ended, they sat down and de Cluny promptly talked politics with the severest and grayest of the men and listening to him, Philip could not help but feel that he was perhaps too fluent, too affable, too ready to see the other person's point of view and to argue it with even greater eloquence than the other person was capable of, at the expense of his own convictions, assuming he had any.

Zoe Helotius entered the room like some predatory bird of prey with white leather face, sharp beak, blood-red lips stretched in a vulture's smile. She attacked, surrounded by equerries, advisers, friends and enemies who spread out like an army, flanking the room, rounding up and sorting its contents until a series of concentric circles had been arranged, the lesser figures close to the periphery, important ones at the small center where Zoe herself stood, talking quickly, casting febrile glances around the room to see if she was missing anything. She was not. She was now the center of attraction; the main event.

"Ah, Charles, my dear. It's been a long time."

"Five years, madame."

"Too long a time. And how is X? and Y? I love them. I never see them. You must come pay me a call. Afternoon. At five. I'm staying with Z." A shudder of delight went through the circles, like waves from a stone cast in water, the circles ever widening until at last they spent themselves against the silk-hung walls.

"Mr Warren? Have we met? In Capri? Ah, Regina's friend. I remember now. You were attached to the Embassy at Rome. I love your Ambassador. Tell him I look forward to that dinner in Venice. He'll know what I mean. Is Regina here in Cairo? But of course not. I saw her in Paris a week ago. So much more like a queen than any of the queens one knows, if you follow me. Do you know her, Charles? Yes? No? Ah, you would love her. She has style and *he,* well, one defers to the most powerful man in the world, which he is nowadays. But," and she lowered her voice and opened her eyes very wide, her onyx irises circled now by white, "I hear *he* is going to divorce *her*." Philip was by now sufficiently used to the varying degrees of emphasis with which people in Cairo mentioned otherwise unidentified pronouns to establish the intended reference: *he* was Farouk; *she* was the heir-less Persian he had married.

"I hope not," said Charles, neutrally.

"It is what *they* say. But here is Anna Morris. Where have you been hiding? This is Charles de Cluny, Mr Warren."

Charles kissed the lady's hand. Philip bowed to the newcomer, a dark-haired girl, of his own age, with large hazel eyes and a husband who joined them a moment later, a burly, rough-voiced man with a limp. An industrialist, Philip gathered. In steel.

"Some party," said Mr Morris, in a tone which could easily have been hostile. "Never seen so much jewelry in my life. Build the Aswan Dam with one roomful of it."

"You have no love of beauty," said Mrs Helotius, who had, and who told them all about it while Philip talked to Anna, learning that she was originally European of mixed nationality and that she was now married to the industrialist with whom she was touring Europe and North Africa for her pleasure as well for his business: he had come to Egypt to sell steel. Philip was charmed by her voice which was low and melodic, faintly accented and appealing. He was also overawed by the bull-necked husband in whose broad shadow she now stood.

"It is too much," she said, in answer to a remark of Philip's about the reception. "Too heavy. I prefer lightness."

"The Petit Trianon?"

"Oh, I'm sure I would have loved that. So delicate, so false. Have you been there?"

He shook his head. "I've never been in France. Next month I'll be there, in Paris."

"I lived there a long time."

"Is it . . . ?"

"It is." She smiled. "You'll never want to leave."

"I'm sure of that."

"But when you do leave you'll not be the same."

He laughed. "Now, that's an exaggeration. I've known hundreds of people who've gone there, been enchanted, and returned the same as ever."

"But not you. I can tell." She looked at him gravely while he looked not at her serious, shining eyes but at her mouth instead, wondering at its Botticelli shape, like a bird gliding.

"I can believe anything," he said. "This is my year of belief. Until recently I doubted everything and trusted no one. Now the wilder, the more improbable the story I am told, the more eager I am to believe it. Tell me there are serpents in the sea and I will believe you; the next time I travel by ship I will see one a mile long, attended by mermaids with seaweed in their hair."

"There *are* serpents in the sea," she said, smiling, one hand touching the odd-shaped bit of crystal she wore about her neck on a silver chain.

"Then I shall see one."

"Mermaids, too?"

"A platoon of them, all wearing naval officers' caps." She laughed and then, aware that her husband was saying farewell to Mrs Helotius, she turned to Philip and gave him her hand. "Perhaps I'll see you when you come to Paris. Where will you stay?"

"I've no idea. Where do *you* stay?"

"We," and the pronoun was suddenly forbidding, "always stay at the Ida, a quiet place. We'll be there for several months, I think—this autumn. Or at least *I* will stop there while Vane is traveling about." The "I" was a promise; on that they parted.

Mrs. Helotius looked about the conquered room. Each person had been drained of information, catalogued and filed. She raised one arm slowly as though to adjust her hair. But this was no spontaneous gesture, Philip saw: it was a military signal, a cavalry officer's command to charge. Led by Lady Julia, mad in green watered silk, her cohorts assembled about her and swiftly the invaders withdrew, in a flood of sound.

"Did you ever hear the story about Zoe Helotius and Bernard Shaw . . ." began Charles.

"Many times," said Philip, sternly. "I have vowed never to hear it again."

"In that case I shall respect your wishes. There are too many stories about her anyway. Shall we move on?"

Not until they had regained the ballroom, now crowded with dancers, did Charles mention Anna Morris.

"I could see you liked her," he said.

"Why? Did I stare? Turn red with excitement?"

"You did indeed! I don't blame you. She's an attractive woman."

"Got a bad character, hasn't she?"

"Not as far as I know. Why do you say that?"

"I don't know. Isn't that what one always says about beauties?" asked Philip, wishing the orchestra would play no more Strauss waltzes, hoping Charles would have more to say; he did.

"You mean is she faithful to her husband? In that case, I can tell you, to your great delight, that she has been unfaithful on occasion; but she has good taste."

"In lovers?"

"In everything. Not that I know her especially well but I have followed her career with some interest these last few years. She has quite a vogue in Paris, you know. Less of one in America, I should expect. Too fine for them. That doesn't offend you?"

"Nothing offends me," said Philip, happily. But he spoke too soon. The Russian spy, her somewhat crumpled sari floating behind her, approached them, smiling stonily, like the Gorgon confronting two doomed mortals. "Princess has been looking for you," she said.

Philip was not surprised to find that Sophia and Charles had everything in common except mutual sympathy and so, after one grim dinner together, he kept them apart, devoting most of his time to Sophia who had arrived early in the week from her journey into the desert where she had inspected a newly discovered city of the Twelfth Dynasty and interviewed yet another holy man who had gloomily predicted the end of the world next spring, in the first week of Ramadan.

They kept mostly to Shepheard's, for Philip, once he had seen the great museum and a few of the mosques, had no real desire to explore Cairo, not liking the heat or the filth or the men and boys who followed them everywhere they went, begging and selling, their voices alternating between intimate whines and shrill cries of anger. He usually pushed past them, striking out at the brown hands which tugged at his coat: he hated being touched by anyone.

One afternoon he had tea with Sophia in the garden at

the back of Shepheard's and he asked her what had become of Abu Bekr and his prophecy.

"I never saw him again," she said, her gray eyes lovely, almost compensating for the thin mouth and square jaw. The wind rustled the branches of the tree overhead, scattering lozenges of sunlight across the white tablecloth. A Negro servant wearing a fez, tight jacket and bloomers leaned against the wall of the hotel, lazily trying to catch flies with one hand. An English family sitting at a table with a striped awning were the only other people in the garden. They looked red and hot, in white crumpled linen.

"I suppose he will stay there all his life, making prophecies as long as people will listen."

"They will always listen. Whether they believe or not is another question."

"Do you?"

"I'm not sure. In general, yes. Something is about to happen. Where and when and how . . . not to mention *what*, are all a puzzle. I look for keys."

"The keys are at Rome," said Philip obscurely.

"Rusty keys," said Sophia, pouring herself more tea. Philip put a whole scone in his mouth and chewed thoughtfully. Still leaning against the wall, the servant caught a fly; smiling happily, he dried his palm on the bloomers.

Then Philip told her that he would leave for Paris in a week's time. By plane, he added, assembling details as he spoke, pleased with the suddenness of his own decision.

"Oh, I'm sorry. I had hoped you would stay here another month. I thought you might be interested in some Ptolemaic things they've come across near Alexandria." If she was in any deeper way distressed or put out, she did not show it. She talked of ruins until the fact of his going had been accepted as immutable, a day of sure departure at last selected, a time of change.

"You'll be coming to Paris, too?" asked Philip politely yet not hypocritically, for he did like her.

"I'm not sure. My plans are seldom definite. How long do you think you'll be there?"

"A few months. Perhaps most of the winter. I'm not sure. I shan't know until I've tried it."

"If you're there several months, we shall see one another again." And the sentence came out cold and formal, which was obviously against her will for she smiled and tried, unsuccessfully, to be spontaneous. Her failure both surprised and embarrassed him. He covered it quickly, volubly, agreeing that they would see one another, pouring himself tea and inquiring quickly, irrelevantly about Mrs Peabody.

"Mrs Peabody? Ah, I'd almost forgotten that nightmare. She's gone back to America, I think. I saw very little of her after you left. She avoided me, too, for that matter. I think she was suddenly rather horrified at what she'd very nearly done. Last I saw of her she was going down the Nile to Alexandria on a freight ship. The regular passenger ships have been discontinued since the war but, undaunted, she found a place for herself aboard a terrible little freighter and, if she manages to survive that phase of her field work, she's probably at the very minute sitting, dictaphone in hand, composing *The Karnak Corpse*."

"That is *not* the title."

"Indeed it is. She told me so herself the day she left. Suggested I look for it when it was published next spring." They laughed. A bird chattered in the branches of a tree near by while another, like a scarlet shuttlecock, swooped in an arc from sky to flowers.

"Poor Mr Willys," said Philip, thinking back on those weeks at Luxor as though three years instead of three weeks had passed since they had stood on the edge of the Nile and scattered the ashes.

"Poor? He got his wish, didn't he? That's more than most of us get."

"What a terrible wish. What a terrible life!"

"I agree that the life was a piece of misfortune, a bad trick of chance but the wish was something else again."

"I don't want to die," said Philip exactly recalling vividly the horror of certain death dreams he had had from time to time all his life. When he was a child, he had often awakened alone and desperate in the impersonal night, trying to visualize what nothing must be like. The dream had changed very little over the years; the terror and the despair remained as he realized that one day he would die and *not* be. He shivered in the warm flower-scented wind and he touched the table, the cups, as though to prove to himself that he was still alive and that the present was all.

"Why should you want to, now? But one day—"

"I'm more interested in how to live than how to die," said Philip, feeling silly at the heroic ring of this statement: how often had he found a moment of true vision become, when reduced to words, a dusty bromide.

"There is only one way to live," said Sophia, pushing a strand of hair out of her eyes. "To do as you want, making

167

of course the obvious allowances for the rules your neighbors in place and time have established."

"And live according to the body," said Philip, wondering if he should accept de Cluny's invitation to visit a brothel that evening.

"That is part of it. But one comes closer to the way through contemplation. I feel a greater affinity to those men who built the temples of Luxor than I do to living men. The idea of the dead is pure and unconfused by the senses; we cannot see or hear or touch them . . . the irrelevant flesh has been swept away and only the idea of Thutmose or Amenhotep, Socrates or Plato, endures."

"I haven't the vocation to spend my life among the ruins."

"Then spend it with the shadows of men. Their books or attitudes which are so much purer than they themselves."

"But I've done that most of my life. I hate involvement in other people's lives. My serene disposition is a result of a childhood vow that I would keep my distance from all the trouble in the world . . . let no one touch me."

"And yet the further you seem to withdraw from the world of the living, the closer you come to life itself," she said urgently. "You see it dispassionately and, as they say, you see it whole. You see not a man but the idea of a man."

Philip looked at his watch. "I'm afraid I'd better go in and shave. I'm going out for dinner."

"Oh, I'd forgotten. With Charles?"

Philip nodded. "I believe we're going to the French theater afterwards."

"Give him my regards," she said, too wise to state her disapproval of the volatile Frenchman.

"I shall," said Philip; and he did, just as he and Charles entered the narrow dim alley which led to the brothel of the Three Sisters of Fatima from Beirut.

PART THREE

Chapter Ten

"IT USUALLY HAPPENS at twelve," said Glenellen.
"Seldom later than twelve-thirty. Well worth seeing, you
know. People come from all around but very few of us get
this close. Takes a lot of managing, believe me."

"I certainly do," said Philip, remembering the four locked
doors and the villainous *concierge* at the gate.

"You see the great thing is: *what* shall it be?"

"Does it vary?"

"Continually, from day to day. One never knows what to
expect."

"What will it be today?"

"How should I know? That's one of the reasons I came.
In any event, it's one of the seven wonders of Paris, if not
of the world."

"And the other six?"

"I was speaking rhetorically. I don't think you properly
appreciate the situation."

"I was only joking. I'm sorry."

"Americans always joke," said Glenellen, sulking. Philip
sighed and looked about the room. It was a cube, large and
shabby with a dusty gold throne at one end and a number
of scallop-shell Venetian chairs on two of which the visitors

169

sat while the chamberlain, a small dour gentleman wearing the rusty striped trousers and morning coat of a minor French civil servant, sat on a frayed wart-like, salmon-colored pouf. A door covered with green baize and studded with rusty nails led into the Presence, the shrine.

"Is there anyone else coming?" asked Philip, oppressed by the room's silence, by the lonely faraway sound of the traffic in the street below, muffled by heavy plush curtains which shut out light and air, made the cool morning a lowering twilight.

"How should I know?" Glenellen was petulant. "With considerable effort I have arranged this audience and now you sit and make jokes."

"I'm sorry," repeated Philip, tired of Glenellen, wishing that he had not accepted the invitation.

The chamberlain on the pouf answered him, however, in French. "We never know how many will attend the levee . . . seldom less than five. Occasionally as many as a hundred, in times of national crisis."

"It is also an expensive thing to arrange," muttered Glenellen. "One could dine at Maxim's for the cost."

"If you'll let me, I'll gladly. . . ."

"But you're my guest," said Glenellen, recovering his usual equanimity. "I wouldn't hear of such a thing."

There was a tinkling at the door and the chamberlain opened it to admit a beautiful young woman with short hair, wearing a shirt, necktie, tweed skirt and a pair of sensible shoes; under one arm she carried a swagger stick. "On the scene yet?" she inquired in a blurred English voice. "No? Not yet? I'll wait then." She sat down, ignoring Philip, who had risen at her entrance, and Glenellen who had not.

"She comes here every day," said the chamberlain in a low proud voice. "She . . ." but the tinkling of the bell sent him back to the door: this time a slim blond boy, unmistakably American with a crewcut and saddle shoes, entered, accompanied by an older man with steel-gray hair brushed carefully back from a smooth baby-fat face . . . the sort of man who had his nails manicured, thought Philip intolerantly, not moving as the newcomers were led by the chamberlain to chairs only a few feet away. The older man looked first at Philip with an expression which he had long since learned to interpret and not to resent; then, seeing Glenellen, he waved one of his well-tended paws and exclaimed: "Ayre! Why aren't you in Capri?"

"Edmond! My God!" retorted Glenellen, as though stunned; he rallied, "Haven't seen you since. . . ."

"The Baths of Nero . . . small world." He looked uneasily at the girl in tweed, as though unsure whether it was safe to speak out; obviously encouraged by the severe lines of her tailored back, he said, "But I hardly expected to find you here. You don't come regularly, do you?"

"No, this is the first time."

"Many, many friends of ours come here religiously, all the time. They find it soothing and I must say I have to admit that I do, too. I mean one shouldn't be ashamed of one's pleasures. . . . And is this the charming Mr Morgan I've heard so much about?"

"No," said Glenellen, "it isn't."

"But do introduce me. I like to know *all* the young Americans in Paris. My name is Edmond Twill," he said, warmly shaking hands with Philip, both leaning far out of their chairs, neither getting up. "And this is Jim, an American, too," said Mr Twill. The handsome youth with the crewcut nodded distantly at Philip, not speaking. "As a matter of fact, we're all Americans here today except Ayre . . . quite unusual, too, because as a rule Americans seldom come here. . . . I can't think why, can you?" he asked Philip, with a smile which revealed very even white false teeth, as clean and neat and expensive as his pearl cuff links, as well cared for as the round pink fingernails which now tapped out restless messages on the arms of his chair.

"I wouldn't know," said Philip. "I've never been here before."

"I'm sure you'll come again and again, the way many of us do. Would you like a cigarette?"

"Cigarettes are forbidden at this time," said the chamberlain who was now sitting cross-legged on the pouf.

"I must have lost my head," giggled Mr Twill. "I wonder why I haven't seen you around town, Phil. I thought I knew nearly everyone."

"I don't know," said Philip who knew perfectly well why they had not seen one another before. "I've been here since the first of August."

"A whole month! Well, we must do something about that. You and Ayre must come and have dinner with me one evening this week. Will Tuesday be all right . . . at seven?"

Philip shook his head, amused. "No, I'm afraid I'm tied up that night."

"Mr Warren has his *own* world," said Glenellen, in a

171

warning voice which Mr Twill, recklessly, chose not to understand.

"But how *special!* So few people have their own world any more. I had one but I gave it away . . . traded it in for the great one. But then we're none of us twenty, are we, Ayre?"

"Speak for yourself, Edmond," said Glenellen irritably, making various decisive gestures as though he could, with a wave of his hand, dismiss Mr Twill forever. But Mr Twill was not that easily discouraged. He renewed the siege. "In any event, you and Ayre must stop by my house one day this week for a drink. You'll love the place . . . only a few blocks from here. Used to be the hôtel of the Duc de Lyon et Grénoble. I have a floor in it . . . a really fine set of rooms."

"That would be very nice," said Philip noncommittally.

"Do see he comes, Ayre . . . like a good fellow."

Glenellen glanced at him, not answering. The ringing of the doorbell put a temporary stop to Mr Twill's offensive. This time nine thin young men of various heights and exotic arrangements of facial hair entered; the chamberlain ordered them to stand out of the way, against the wall opposite the bookcase where the girl in tweed now stood, reading the titles of the books to herself like a rosary, her mouth half open.

"*Messieurs, mesdames,*" said the chamberlain, climbing on top of the pouf, both hands raised to silence the room. "The moment approaches. Those of you who have never before been presented should take cognizance of the following ceremony. At the moment of Entrance, all must rise to their feet and bow very low until The Seating, after which you, too, may sit down, in absolute silence, however, until The First Statement of the Day. Is that understood by everyone? Are there any questions? Good." He jumped to the floor and paused for a moment, as though straining to hear some celestial melody. No one spoke. Then, from behind the Baize Door, came the unmistakable sound of an alarm clock going off, followed by the tolling of a dinner bell. Slowly the door opened and, preceded by the chamberlain, who backed into the room, a tall figure, with head erect, moved as though sleepwalking across the room to the throne. Philip who was standing like the others, his head bowed, caught a glimpse of the man, a tall pale creature with dark red hair, shoulder-length; and wearing a white undecorated gown which touched the floor. When he was seated, the

172

worshipers sat down and waited silently for the First Statement.

The figure on the throne looked straight ahead, the unseeing eyes glassy. Philip wondered if he were drugged. Then suddenly, remarkably, the eyes became focused, the pupils dilated and in a high toneless voice the man said, "Augusta." There was a round of applause.

"Oh, I'm so glad!" exclaimed Mr Twill. "I like her best, don't you, Ayre? But I forgot, this is your first time. Believe me, when I say it's a real treat you're getting. You just happened to hit it right. You'll adore her as much as we do."

Throughout the room there was a murmur of approbation following the applause. Everyone seemed pleased and there was a curious atmosphere of good fellowship to which Philip responded with some wonder, not understanding yet what it was these people were experiencing as they moved excitedly around the throne, making remarks about (but not to) the now smiling figure. The chamberlain disappeared into the sanctum behind the Baize Door; he returned a moment later with a large box which was placed on the floor to the left of the throne . . . a chair which looked to Philip like a discarded theatrical property, the gold paint mostly gone and the red tassels torn.

"Now comes The Robing," said Mr Twill delightedly. "The best part. I always lose my head during The Robing, don't I, Jim?" But Jim, too, was part of the vast conspiracy to snub Edmond Twill for he made no answer, only sat passively in his chair watching the others as they opened the large box and reverently removed a number of articles of women's apparel.

"What happens now?" asked Philip.

"Augusta is to be dressed," answered Mr Twill, eyes glistening. "*We* do that. It's part of the ritual."

"Who's Augusta?" asked Philip.

"She's sitting on the throne, silly."

"Oh," said Philip, his masculine pride suddenly pricked at being called "silly" by Mr Twill. He let it go, however. The ritual was now under way. The habitués were crowding about Augusta, each carrying some part of the ceremonial costume. Mr Twill had seized upon the hat, a toque somewhat similar to that affected by the stately dowager Queen of England. The young woman in tweed held a large frivolous-looking brassiere, ready to snap it in place at the proper moment . . . which soon came for, at a signal from the chamberlain, Augusta stood up, only to vanish in a sea of

173

clothes and chattering worshipers. All participated in this rite except Glenellen, Philip and the silent American boy.

It was soon over, to the sorrow of the worshipers who were now dangerously excited, shouting to one another in French and English, touching reverently the figure which they had robed with such speed and accuracy: Augusta now stood magnificent, if slightly rumpled, in a floor-length tea gown of apple green, a feather boa about her shoulders and numerous coral and amber beads attached to her person like decorations on a Christmas tree and with much the same logic and cheerful effect. Over one eye, at a jaunty angle, was the toque, Mr Twill's triumph.

"The Robing is completed," announced the chamberlain and the devotees withdrew slowly, admiringly, their eyes upon Augusta who stood for a long moment staring at the floor; then she sat down.

"Now wasn't that wonderful?" exclaimed Mr Twill, joining the nonparticipants.

"Very fine," said Glenellen, sincerely, his pale eyes interested. Could this be a new hobby? wondered Philip.

"Did you see me manage the *chapeau?* I do it the best, the chamberlain says, and he should know. I mean people do it every day yet on the occasions when I do it I add a little something, a nuance, or so he thinks."

"What does Augusta think?" asked Philip.

"Who can tell? I believe she appreciates it. One can tell a lot from the way she holds her head. When it is thrust slightly forward you had better watch out . . . she's on the warpath. When it's to one side, she is nervous . . . when the chin is held high, however, that means all is well . . . like now. She's always in a good mood when I officiate at The Robing."

"That's a very great honor," said Glenellen. "You should be proud."

"I am indeed. You must take part in the next one, Ayre. Tell the chamberlain you want to. He can fix it."

"How much?"

"Don't pay more than a thousand francs. That's all *I* ever paid. Some people, Americans mostly, pay as high as ten or fifteen thousand, which is outrageous."

"Does the money go to Augusta?" Philip was curious about the details.

"Who knows? It certainly goes into the establishment; then of course there are the missions."

"What missions?"

"Oh . . . missions," said Mr Twill vaguely.

"Is he booked up, do you think, for the next Robing?" asked Glenellen. "I would like to attend, you know."

"Oh, nothing could be easier, if you're properly sponsored and I would be very, very happy to sponsor you, Ayre. You know that."

"That's awfully kind," said Glenellen warmly, his former frosty manner quite thawed by the other's generosity as well as by the vision of Augusta seated on her throne, head back, eyes blissfully closed, absorbing the devotion of her worshipers like a lizard in the noonday sun.

"I suggest you come Friday. It is always Augusta without fail."

"When is it *not* Augusta?" asked Philip.

"Well, yesterday it was not Augusta. And it probably won't be tomorrow."

"What was it yesterday?"

"Augustus," said Mr Twill. "That's the whole point of the Hour of Meditation and the First Statement which precedes The Robing. During the hour, the First Statement is decided upon behind the Green Door. No one knows what agony of spirit racks that frail body during the lonely hour of decision. But always the choice is made; the facts are faced and the First Statement is delivered, calmly and unequivocally, no matter how difficult, how painful the decision behind the Green Door has been. Such courage!"

"Very real courage," murmured Glenellen, admiringly, "real character."

"Such mysticism, too!"

"Obviously. One can see that."

"The only functioning hermaphrodite in Paris, France," said the young man named Jim in a low Southern voice which, though the message was heard by no one except his immediate companions, sent a ripple of unanticipated sound through the room; hostile glances were turned upon them and even Augusta was seen to move uneasily, as though aware of a disturbing and unharmonious presence.

"Now, now, Jim," said Mr Twill, anxiously, smiling, looking about the room feverishly, exonerating himself, neutralizing with apologetic smiles the effect that that low voice had had on the Post-Robing Assembly. "You must not say such things here, not in the presence of Her. You are entitled to your opinion like everyone else but you must have the courtesy, not only to Augusta but to me, to refrain from outbursts like that."

175

Jim only grinned, pleased with himself. Philip rather liked him for this unexpected honesty. He wondered idly what he was doing here with Mr Twill. The obvious explanation seemed unlikely but then Philip never knew. His attention was distracted by Mr Twill who was discussing the lineage of Augusta. "You mustn't think that the influence Augusta has and the reverence so many intelligent and unsuperstitious people do her are entirely the result of the unusual condition to which Jim just now alluded. No, indeed! Augusta is directly descended from the goddess Venus and those volumes in that bookshelf prove it . . . and not on the male side (which is never accurate, due to the frailness of women) but through the female line so that there can be no doubt of her legitimacy."

"How do you know this?" asked Philip, squinting, trying to read the titles on the spines of the books.

"We know it because her genealogy has been traced back to Julius Caesar who, in turn, traced his own ancestry to Venus. Look, she even has the Julian nose."

And so she had, Philip saw, recalling those busts he had seen which were reputed to be of Caesar.

"Then she is Italian," said Philip.

"No, she is Augusta," said Mr Twill, bowing slightly in the direction of the throne. "But now comes the Naming of the Names." And, to Philip's horror, the names of every eldest daughter of the house of Julius in the one hundred generations since that great man's murder were pronounced, slowly and distinctly, by the chamberlain, to the obvious pleasure of the worshipers who grew more and more excited as the chamberlain passed from the Middle Ages into the sixteenth century, until, by the time the nineteenth century was reached, they were singing and cheering so loudly that they almost drowned out the final name which the chamberlain, in a religious ecstasy, shouted so that all might hear: "Augusta!"

"Wonderful, wonderful!" said Glenellen, mistily, his eyes tearful with excitement. "Wonderful! Absolutely wonderful."

"It is our best moment," said Mr Twill simply, wiping his own eyes with the back of a shaking hand. Philip and Jim looked at one another dry-eyed; then Philip looked quickly away as though he was in danger of being detected in a conspiracy.

After the last cheers had died away, Augusta rose and, attended by a profound silence, left the room, the Green

Door closing noiselessly behind her. The levée was over and the chamberlain went to the door through which the visitors had originally entered and opening it with a flourish, he bade them all farewell.

In the street, Philip and Glenellen left Mr Twill and his companion in a flurry of plans; dates and places were still being discussed when a taxi carried off Mr Twill and the silent Jim.

"What did you think?" asked Glenellen, as they left the rue des Saints-Pères and crossed the tree-lined Boulevard St Germain.

"Very unusual," said Philip, not wanting to dampen the other's enthusiasm. "I liked The Robing very much."

"Oh, it was magnificent! Really so! I must look into the possibilities of bringing all this to the attention of the world."

"I suppose their missions do that, don't they?"

"I am speaking on a grand scale. Do you realize that this could catch on? Like wildfire! Something the world has been waiting for: workers, intellectuals, everyone."

"I thought you were a Catholic."

"That has nothing to do with it. The two don't conflict, as I see it. One will complement the other splendidly. I shall wire the Vatican tomorrow."

"And the party?"

"What party?"

"The Communist Party. You were a member when I saw you last spring in Rome."

"Ah, the party . . . but that was Italy. This is France. Can't you tell the difference? The air is different. None of us is the same: even *you* are changed, in Paris."

"How am I changed?"

"Well, for one thing you had dark hair in Rome. You are now a blond; that is the principal physical change."

"I had blond hair in Rome, too," said Philip sharply.

"Oh, come now, you don't expect me to believe that, do you? Besides, you look very nice with blond hair . . . no reason to be ashamed. Many boys dye their hair these days."

Philip made no comment and in silence they walked down the rue du Bac to the river. In front of the white gleaming Pont Neuf they parted as casually as they had met the day before in the street. Glenellen hoped that they would see a great deal of one another; then he disappeared into the Metro while Philip crossed the bridge, enjoying the warm sun and blue sky, the design of the green gardens on the other side of the river.

177

One pleasant, aimless day followed another. The summer grew dry and dusty and the leaves darkened on the trees. Here and there, in the Tuileries gardens, an occasional vivid red leaf suggested autumn: the southerly flight of birds, the return of the tourists to the west, a cold time when Paris would become French again, the trees bare-branched and the winter skies as gray as the nineteenth-century façades of the buildings that lined the wide avenues the last Napoleon had carved out of the confusion of narrow medieval streets, avenues still green and gentle with the waning summer.

Neither Anna nor Regina was in Paris. He had inquired after both of them but no one knew when Regina would return. Anna, however, would arrive in six weeks, or so the desk clerk at the Ida Hotel had assured him that first day in Paris when he had moved in a happy dream through a silver afternoon, so different from the harsh hot country he had left behind early that morning.

He had been fortunate in finding a hotel for himself, a dark congenial place on the rue de l'Université, a block from the rue du Bac. Here he spent his time reading, when he was not sightseeing or meeting old friends from America who had come over to drink a great deal of cheap wine and to see night clubs where the girls took off most all of their clothes, so exciting the American boys that Philip almost believed the remark of a French brothel keeper who had once told him, quite seriously, that all Americans were *voyeurs,* except for the aviators who liked to be beaten.

But these old friends of his were in the minority that year for the city had been conquered by his homosexual countrymen, and he watched with wonder as the scandal grew, as mask after mask fell from familiar and ordinary faces to reveal the unexpected Grecian visage. Businessmen from Kansas City, good Rotarians all, embraced bored young sailors on the streets at night or paid high prices for slim Algerian boys at those bordellos which catered to such pleasures. College boys, young veterans, the ones Philip had always known in school or in the Navy, athletes and aesthetes both, ran amok among the bars and urinals in search of one another, the nice girls back home forgotten, as they loved or tried to love one another in this airy summer city.

Like most of his generation, Philip was tolerant of everything. It was an age in which, as a reaction to the horrors of the various European pogroms and experiments with genocide, his countrymen had been driven, somewhat hysterically, into the opposite direction, until the intolerance of intoler-

178

ance had become so remarkably virulent that one Jew or one Negro or one Italian not admitted to certain residential districts in America caused more disturbance in the newspapers than the gas chambers at Belsen. Fortunately, those people who must always have someone to hate could, if they chose not to be intolerant of intolerance, attack one another on grounds of sexual behavior. But this last cherished area for intolerance was suddenly declared out of bounds by a celebrated statistical report which revealed that one third of the nation's men had, at one time or another, committed a homosexual act. This survey promptly lessened everyone's guilt and, if only by weight of the numbers given, it made the idea of pederasty much less remote, no longer exclusively associated with managers of flower shops or with a fearful fumbling in the back row of a darkened movie house. Those sturdy youths who had been ashamed of their secret practice now took much pleasure, at least in Paris, in openly doing what they pleased and with all the enthusiasm of zealots, they proselytized furiously.

It amused Philip to think that his own puritan nation of Baptists and Methodists and good sound Americanism should, in its moment of empire, become so gaudily Roman, so truly imperial in one generation. Yet he disliked feeling out of things. The groups that gathered on the landing of his hotel would stop their intense conversations when he walked by and he was aware, or thought he was aware, of their real contempt for a countryman who, because of some basic duplicity or sexual inadequacy, refused to play the game. Nor did he enjoy being treated like a pretty young girl who could be rolled into bed at a moment's notice by a properly aggressive man. The tragic novel of the age, he decided irritably, would not be about the anguish of the sensitive neurotic youth who wanted to make ladies' hats but about the confusion of the undistinguished womanizing youth who came to the big city to make his fortune only to find that everywhere he turned men desired him and that the ill will his refusal to surrender his virtue created was so great that he was forced either to adapt himself to a life of pederasty or to go back home, not returning to the big city until age had so lessened his physical attractions that he was rendered safe from attack.

He had, however, two allies who felt the same as he did: apostates, for they had been lovers for seven years, first in high school, then in the Army, then in college and finally here in Paris, in a room next to his own. They were both twenty-five, robust, and charmingly simple. The following June, when they graduated from college, they were to be married to two girls they had known for a long time in their home town, Spartanburg, South Carolina, and their future was to be as simple and as well directed as their past, living next door to one another, working in the same business. They would even, they confided to Philip, name their children for one another.

"What will the wives think of all this?" asked Philip, putting his feet up on the bed. He was in their room, a small one with two big beds, an old bureau and a bidet hidden by a torn curtain. The single window was tall and the room was cool and full of light. Clothes were scattered everywhere: as well as tennis racquets, bathing trunks, even a pair of boxing gloves, for they were obsessed with their bodies, eating carefully, drinking very little, keeping their bellies flat with exercise. He could hear them every morning, doing pushups, puffing and straining. He had never heard them make love, however, even though the walls were thin . . . not that he had wanted to, quite the opposite, yet the idea had a real fascination for him, a morbid appeal, like the time when once, at a resort, he had slept in the room next to his parents and had heard everything until he could stand it no longer and had covered his head with a pillow. Unlike the other occupants of the hotel, these young men were quiet and well behaved. Regularly, often in Philip's company, they picked up girls and brought them back to the hotel, increasing rather than diminishing their love for one another on these occasions when, side by side on the same bed, they possessed the women, to use a good Victorian verb, an applicable one, thought Philip, since their devotion and respect for each other was essentially nineteenth-century: neither would have dreamed of humiliating the other, unlike most American combinations, orthodox or not. He was continually beguiled by the Southern courtliness with which they treated one another.

"I don't suppose they'll think anything about it at all," said the taller one, a fair-haired, dark-eyed boy named Stephen. "I mean, they've known we've always been good friends. They'd think it was unnatural if we stopped seeing one another after we got married."

"Besides, the girls get along," said Bill, a stocky young man with a boxer's figure and dark curly hair which grew low on his forehead. "I guess it would be impossible if they didn't like each other."

"You seem to have it all worked out," said Philip, not concealing his admiration for a long-range plan which had, so far at least, worked.

"We figured the whole thing out in high school," said Stephen with gentle pride, scooping up all the dirty clothes and tossing them into a corner.

"How do you plan to get away? I mean . . . see each other?"

"We'll be living in the same block and everybody knows we like to go hunting on week ends, when the weather's good. And the girls, they never go hunting. We'll have a lot of week ends together. Oh, there'll be plenty of time for everything."

"Well, you've done a good job," said Philip, sighing, thinking of his own loveless, aimless life which, though it usually pleased him, was obscurely incomplete: he could hear the beast in the jungle so clearly that he felt he knew what it would be like when, finally, at the end of a long difficult chase, he captured it. But he envied these lovers for having stumbled across it at an age when he had not even suspected that the jungle contained another living creature besides himself.

"I think so, too," said Bill, leaning back on the bed, stretching his legs till they cracked, his head against Stephen's thigh.

Philip was both envious and depressed. The trail had never before seemed so dark to him, or the quarry so elusive. He hated them for one ungrateful instant.

The evening was warm and windless when they arrived at the Café Flore and took their places at a table outside, close to the street where the curious and the fantastic stared at one another solemnly. Bearded young men wearing blue jeans and open red-checked shirts contrived to look more like Iowa than Murger, while the young women, their hair long and tangled, also wore open shirts and blue jeans, as dirty as the boys and quite as happy, as they too pursued the grand grim business of expressing themselves, imitating the French of that quarter who, with no effort at all, managed to be far dirtier, far more disheveled . . . in every way fine models for these children of the new world who had temporarily forsaken ice cream, Coca-Cola and the linoleum-floored new high schools of the West.

The two Southerners were amused, pointing out the various freaks to one another, without malice or condescension, examining with wonder the superficial variety of which man is capable. Every now and then a murmur went through the crowded café as a celebrity of some sort passed by or the rumor of a celebrity who might have passed by, and immediately all eyes turned in the same direction and two camps, one friendly, one hostile, discussed the poor creature freely, to his face if he was unwise enough to linger.

"Did *you* ever try writing anything?" asked Stephen, turning to Philip.

"Not seriously," said Philip, recalling Cyril Connolly's protest that he never again wanted to read a novel where, referring to a character who was an artist, another character asked, "How's his stuff?"

"I'm surprised," said Stephen. "You always struck me like you might be a writer or something."

"Just my pedantic manner," said Philip who had himself often been struck with the superficial resemblance he, on occasion, bore to those who fashioned the one bright book of life.

He was about to give them his considered views on contemporary literature in America when a slim familiar figure walked past their table, paused, and then came back. It was the boy who had been with Edmond Twill at Augusta's levée. He was very handsome, thought Philip looking at the golden hair and dark blue eyes. He was dressed like a conservative schoolboy in dark gray trousers and a sport coat. "You're Philip, aren't you? I met you last week . . . at that place."

"I remember," said Philip. "Stephen, Bill, this is Jim." It was like the Navy, he thought, the old anonymous days of first names. The three Southern boys gravely shook hands. "Want a drink?" asked Philip.

Jim shook his head. "I've got to go," he said, in his low expressionless voice. "You want to meet me here tomorrow at six?"

"Why . . . all right," said Philip, suddenly, surprised not only at the invitation but at his own prompt acceptance.

"I'll see you then . . . at six. Good-by." He nodded to the others and walked away.

Bill chuckled. "Looks like you got yourself a buddy."

"Do you a world of good," said Stephen.

"I'm sure it will," smiled Philip, who saw no reason to protest.

Under a violet summer sky, they met at .six. A storm

threatened and the leaves of the trees along the boulevard fluttered white and green in the sudden wind. The air smelled of sun and stone but there was a wet sharp edge to the hot wind which came from the northwest where night and the thunder were. An awning had been unfurled over the outdoor tables; here a few quiet tourists sat, waiting for Sartre.

"Let's get out of here," said Jim. "It's going to rain."

Philip, surrendering himself to the other's care, followed him across the square to the church of St Germain de Prés behind which was a narrow street, damp and shadowy, where above a restaurant Jim lived. "We can have a drink there," he said. "If it rains, we can eat downstairs."

Philip agreed, wondering a little uneasily what was expected of him.

"This is the dump," Jim opened a door, revealing two high-ceilinged rooms furnished haphazardly. A large carved bed of dark wood with four posters but no canopy stood in the center of the second room whose windows looked out on a gray court, littered with broken tile and discarded furniture. Unframed drawings by Tchelichew and Picasso were propped on the gray marble mantelpiece, a relic of the house's onetime splendor. To Philip's surprise, the drawings were originals and one of them, the head of a lean Picasso boy, was familiar to him and presumably of great value. There were no books anywhere except for a beautifully bound set of Balzac scattered carelessly on a plain kitchen table, as though placed there on arrival and never touched again.

"I've even got a bathroom," said Jim, as the storm broke over Paris with a sudden roar. "Oh . . . there she goes." They went to the window and looked out at the gray diagonals of rain which splattered in the street below. Gutters became rivers while the rain made sudden coronets of water in the puddled streets; men and women ran for cover with newspapers and umbrellas unfurled. The day was over and evening, dark and secret in the rain, moved across the wet city.

"I like the rain," said Philip, aware that someone always said that.

"I don't give it much mind."

"That's a Southern expression," smiled Philip, as they turned away from the window and went back into the dark room. Philip stumbled against a chair, Jim turned on a single lamp.

"I am Southern," he said. "Sit down and I'll get you some wine. Or do you want Pernod? I got both."

"Pernod. Where did you come from originally?" Philip found himself for some reason fearing silence, not wanting to be alone in the room with Jim with only the sound of rain against the windows; he was ill at ease, without words.

"From Virginia." He brought two wineglasses out of a cupboard and carefully filled them both. "Here you go." The apéritif slopped onto Philip's hand. "I'm sorry," said Jim. "Need a handkerchief?"

"I've got one." Philip wiped the stickiness off his fingers, slowly, deliberately, wanting to prolong the operation, to delay the moment of revelation which, he was sure, resided in the baroque clock on the mantelpiece: when the long and short hands came to a predestined conjunction he would be forced to handle with tact and severity his companion's suggestion. A moment later, Philip saw he had made a mistake: the clock was broken; both were spared. Relieved, he said, "I like Virginia, what I've seen of it . . . around Warrenton. I come from New York."

"I figured you were a Northerner."

"Have you been in Paris long?"

"Three years."

"A long time."

"A real long time. I like it here."

"You don't want to go back?"

"No, I can't go back, even if I wanted to."

"Oh . . . I'm sorry."

"Nothing to be sorry about. I got into trouble. Lot of people get into trouble. So I left. I've had a good time."

Philip was puzzled by the other's bleakness. He was curious about the trouble but his own years in the Navy had taught him not to inquire too closely into the lives of others, partly from fear of embarrassing them, partly because they might embarrass him with too complete an account of their lives. Mystery was often best.

"Are you working now? In Paris?" This was tactless, Philip knew, but he persisted.

Jim smiled at him, a slow engaging smile and with the first show of warmth either had displayed that evening, he said, "I don't work. You know that."

"Oh." Philip was stopped. Not knowing what to answer, he grinned foolishly and drank his Pernod in two long fiery swallows.

"I just drift along. It's easier."

184

"Do you . . . like Twill?" asked Philip.

"I don't like any of them."

"They like you."

"Yes . . . funny, isn't it? I've often wondered why."

"You're good-looking." This was not the sort of remark Philip liked to make to another man but having accepted the other's line, he was bound to it.

Jim made a face. "They can get a better-looking piece of flesh with a bigger thing for a dollar in any street in this town."

"Maybe they're attracted by your hostility."

"I've thought of that. But then I'm always very quiet when I'm around them . . . a real good boy who doesn't say much."

"And you get money?" Philip sounded to himself like a college boy talking to his first prostitute, asking her how she could possibly have become so degraded.

"I get everything." He waved his hand briefly at the apartment, the drawings, the set of Balzac. "One old guy settled a hundred a month on me for life."

"For his life, or yours?"

Jim laughed. "For mine. Get property . . . that's the thing. So many kids, when they start in, just go around chiseling drinks until they get fat and nobody wants them any more. But I get cash if I can . . . or jewelry or pictures: I've learned a lot about painting these last few years. I once spotted a phony Degas some old guy tried to get me to take."

"You make the deal in advance?"

"I'm not that crude. I get things without asking. That's what I mean when I say I don't know what it is that they see. I've often thought that if I knew what it was, I'd really be able to cash in."

"I suspect," said Philip, "that the fact you don't know may be your charm. Self-consciousness often produces great art but I doubt if many find it a lovable trait, in others. The secret to wide popularity is a kind of mysterious negativity . . . something that can't be imitated. Not that I mean you're actually negative, or mysterious (though you may, for all I know, be both), but you give that appearance."

"How do you figure that out?"

Philip, halfway through his spurious character analysis, suddenly realized the implication of his blunder. He had started talking nervously, affected by the rain and the dark, by the Pernod gulped too quickly on an empty stomach, and carried away by his own solemn attempt at analysis, he had managed to create a false impression on several levels at once, a considerable trick, he thought wryly, undoing the damage, reorganizing what he had said.

"I was putting it more in terms of the president of a high-school class," he said glibly. "When I was in school the handsomest and quietest boy in the class was always elected president. No one envied him, no one feared him; he was admired because of the strength of character his pleasing silence obviously hid. Boys who boasted were always thought liars; it never occurs to simple people that a loud, conceited person may be more competent than a modest quiet one." They were now a long way from the center and Philip examined the idea of popularity until, sick of it himself, he stopped suddenly in the middle of a sentence and stared at the Picasso sketch, the monotonous noise of the rain succeeding the equally monotonous sound of his own voice in the room.

"We'd better have another drink," said Jim, filling their glasses. Halfway through the second glass of Pernod, Philip's unease vanished and he talked about himself freely, and Jim seemed nearly as interested as he himself was. Yet the pleasures of egotism were brought to a rude halt when Jim suddenly asked him if he liked boys.

"No," said Philip, freezing, aware that a misstep would distress them both. "I never have."

"Not even once, in school?"

"Not even then. I have all the earmarks of a pederast, I suppose . . . or so a friend of mine at Harvard used to say; but I've never done anything about it."

"Would you like to?"

"No, I don't think so. I'm too old to change my habits . . . and they tell me it's mostly habit."

"You wouldn't like to try?" The invitation was abrupt.

"No, I wouldn't. I'm sorry."

Jim sighed, but not sadly. "You might have liked it."

"I wouldn't know what to do."

"You wouldn't have to do anything."

"I'm not that passive. I could never enjoy lying still while somebody else thrashed around."

"But you'd give me pleasure," said Jim, smiling, some of his early abruptness gone; he was almost gentle.

"That's the worst of it," said Philip, a new idea occurring to him; one which might be very significant. "I don't want to give anyone pleasure, especially a man."

186

"You want to give a woman pleasure."

"Yes . . . no. Consciously I do, for the usual selfish reasons; unconsciously, I want to take care of myself and go home."

"Even when you're in love?"

"I've never been in love."

"I'm one up on you."

"Did you like it?"

"That's a stupid question." Jim's voice was unexpectedly sharp. He apologized quickly. "I'm sorry. I didn't mean that."

"Forget it," said Philip, his curiosity aroused. But then, remembering his new idea, he worried it a bit. "I think maybe that's the difference between men and women, between men and certain kinds of pederasts; the man's instinct is to take his pleasure, the woman's to give it, to receive the man."

"That could explain the old guys in the latrines, looking for sailors. They get a charge out of that."

"Of course I know women who wanted men the same way men ordinarily want women, but there don't seem to be too many of them . . . yet who knows? Perhaps the difference in attitudes is only a social one."

"I don't think you know very much about it," said Jim, nicely.

"Am I wrong?"

"Damned if I know. I haven't got any theory. All I know is that it's one thing to love somebody and another thing to have sex with somebody you don't know or don't care about, the way I do all the time."

"Women, I know, often get their greatest pleasure out of the man's excitement. They ignore him. He's just so much sweating, heavy bone and flesh on top of them but when they realize that it is their own desirable body which has made an animal out of him, they are quite carried away by this vision of their own desirability and they reciprocate, loving themselves being loved in his arms." This very nearly said it, thought Philip, not wanting to see any cracks in the dike of his reasoning, pleased with the area he had rescued, if only for a moment, from the floor of a confused sea.

"You make it sound like acrobatics," said Jim mildly.

"Isn't it? It's often that in . . . well, in the other world."

"I don't think so. I suppose I've been mauled as much as anybody can be but in spite of all that I think it's possible to care about one person and to forget the acrobatics

187

and think just of him and not the two bodies. But I suppose I'm romantic because I'm just a whore and know how little sex has to do with loving. I got a theory that the more you do it, the more likely you are to love somebody when the time comes."

"When is that?"

"Only once for me, so far . . . maybe again. I hope so."

"Never for me, so far. But then, how can one tell? What's love for me may just be an ordinary experience to another person . . . or a leap into the abyss for still another."

"I've. . . . It's stopped raining," said Jim, who apparently disliked theorizing as much as Philip enjoyed it. "Shall we go across the street and have dinner? It's better than the place downstairs."

"I'd like to. I didn't have lunch today."

"They got wonderful snails across the street."

"I don't like snails."

"Have you ever tried any?"

"No."

"Well, how do you know?" They both laughed and Philip realized the crisis had passed. He was relieved. He was also surprised how callow and inexperienced he felt beside this youth whose life had been, or so he would have supposed, so much less than his own, so differently balanced.

He thought of Henry Miller's rhetorical title, "The Wisdom of the Heart," and, while he ate snails with Jim in the dingy restaurant, he wondered what, if anything, the phrase might mean: intuition? Possibly. And what was that? Accuracy in emotional matters achieved by chance, quickly, illogically, without recourse to any deliberation. That was intuition, he thought, not liking the snails. But what then was accuracy? Emotion was not a logic and one person's definition of a state of being or of a situation which involved himself and a lover, say, might not be remotely like his partner's: the wisdom of one man's heart could very easily seem like shocking ignorance to another's. Without ultimates it was impossible to define anything except in immediate and relative terms. Perhaps, he thought suddenly, the heart's wisdom was the knowledge that two people in a certain relationship *together* possessed, for that moment at least, in that one place, a special joint knowledge of mysteries which, separately, was denied them. He looked curiously at the snail-eating Jim, and wondered if he *knew*, if he had really *been*. . . .

After dinner, somewhat against Philip's will, they went

188

back to Jim's apartment. "Just for a moment," he said, as they climbed the damp-smelling stairs. "I have to practice my vice."

When they got to the front room, Jim turned on a lamp, an orange and black Japanese lantern; then he placed what looked to Philip like a Bunsen burner from a chemistry class in the middle of the table. A blue flame blossomed at the end of a lighted match.

"Have to be careful," said Jim, lighting the burner. "I don't want to set the place on fire." From a cabinet he took out a yard-long wooden pipe, brightly decorated with Moorish designs, and a thin metal spoon in which he placed a single dark pellet. "This is the tricky part . . . the cooking. Have to have a steady hand." Holding the spoon in one hand over the flame, he prodded the melting pill with the end of a safety pin. A strong odor like incense, like medicine, filled the room. "Now," said Jim, "here it goes." The hot viscous remains of the pellet were poured into the chimney of the pipe and quickly, all in one integrated movement, Jim turned off the blue flame, put down the spoon and raised the pipe to his lips and inhaled so deeply and so long that his face grew red and his eyes stared. Then, slowly, he exhaled a pale cloud of smoke. "Oh, that's good stuff," he said happily, smiling at Philip. "That's better than anything I know." He took several more lungfuls of the smoke before he offered the pipe to Philip who declined on the unusual but accurate grounds that, since he did not smoke tobacco, he wouldn't know how to inhale.

"Well, it won't work if you can't inhale," agreed Jim. "Anyway you ate the snails. That's enough for one night."

"How do you feel?" asked Philip, curiously.

"Like I'm dreaming . . . a little like a dream of flying."

"Better than love?"

"Wouldn't you rather fly than make love?"

"Any day."

"This way I feel like I'm doing both."

"Shall I go?"

"Oh, no . . . not yet. Stay with me until I'm way gone. It won't be long." He walked over to the carved bed and carefully, like a figure in a motion picture at half speed, he lay down, the pipe still clutched in his hand. "Sit over here," he said, pointing to the edge of the bed. Philip did, both of their faces in shadow now, the dull orange lantern far away in the other room, like daylight at a tunnel's end.

189

"Take my shoes off. I don't like to move when I get this far."

Philip untied the scuffed schoolboy shoes and put them neatly side by side on the floor, scrupulously careful not to touch the other's body, to avoid receiving the sensual shock of warm flesh against warm flesh, no matter what one's habit was. "Now I feel better," said Jim softly. "I can't think of anything unpleasant when I'm like this. Can't think about you."

"About me?"

"About the ones like you I've known . . . but it all seems fine now I'm flying." He inhaled again and again. The sweet heavy odor was making Philip sick; he wanted to go.

"I don't eat the dregs," said Jim suddenly. "Some people do, but not me. It's the worst of all. When you start to do that, you can't ever walk again, never touch the ground until they bury you in it. . . ." His voice grew softer and softer as he talked, now of flight, now of a river and one green day long ago in June. For a time Philip sat beside him in the shadowy room and listened to him talk. But then when he was sure that the other was no longer conscious of him, he got quickly to his feet and, blowing out the paper lantern, he left the apartment.

In the street, he paused. A thin gray rain was falling now and he was grateful for its coolness and for the fresh night air which he breathed in great gulps until he could no longer taste or smell the smoke on which, far away, Jim drifted, momentarily beyond the gravity which would, Philip knew, pull him back one day to the hard inevitable earth beneath that pale cloud which now maintained him, for one eternity at least, safe and dreaming above the land. The rain was cold in Philip's face, as he hurried down the rue de l'Université to his hotel.

"We were picked up," said Stephen, when Philip got back to the hotel.

"That's right," Bill chuckled. "Friend of yours, too. He said to send you his love."

"Who was that?"

"An old queen named Edmond Twill. We didn't know you were handling the carriage trade." They laughed, mockingly.

"I met him once," began Philip, feeling suddenly guilty.

"At a religious ceremony," said Stephen. "He told us all about it."

"I wish he'd told *me* all about it. I'm still confused."

"Perhaps he will tomorrow. There's a party and we're invited . . . you too."

"What kind of a party?"

"Can't you guess?" said Bill.

"We're going," said Stephen. "For the hell of it."

"He said he wanted some men for a change . . . I thought that was real flattering."

"Are you sure he wants me to come?" asked Philip.

"Sure," said Stephen. "He wants you special. He told me so. He also said that you were being kept by Lord Somebody-or-other, but that you had stolen his car and sold it."

Philip whistled. "That's a wild one."

"You didn't sell it, did you?" asked Bill.

"Never knew he had a car. I've only seen him once since I've been in Paris. I wonder who started that story."

"According to Mr Twill, everybody knows it. He said the only reason you weren't in jail was because you had too much on him, on Lord What's-his-name."

"That's quite a story," said Philip, more amused than angry.

"Anyway," continued Bill, obviously enjoying himself, "he's going to have the old guy at the party just to see what will happen . . . only I'm not supposed to tell you that he'll be there. Mr Twill wants a scene."

"I told him you weren't one of the boys," said Stephen. "But he wouldn't believe me."

"They never do," said Bill.

⬚

Mr Twill occupied a floor of one wing of the former Hôtel of the Duc de Lyon et Grénoble, a Marshal of Napoleon, who had grandly renovated the former town house of an aristocrat whose head had fallen into the basket during the Terror, to the cheers of the blood-minded women of Paris, one of whom had stolen it, according to legend, and rolled it all the way to the aristocrat's house, where, in a fit of poetic justice, she heaved it through a window, frightening the clerks in the government bureau which occupied the house at that time. A generation later, the Duc de Lyon et Grénoble, having robbed the quartermaster corps of a great many golden napoleons, restored the house to a point considerably beyond its original splendor. Traces of the Marshal's private vision of elegance were everywhere in the suite Mr Twill now ornamented, although two Watteau

191

fans and a heavenly stole occupied the place of honor over the mantelpiece where once the portrait of the Emperor had hung, beneath two sabers crossed by the baton of a Marshal of France.

Money was as much in evidence now as it had been during the years the Duc had lived in these high-ceilinged rooms with their white and gold walls, marble floors, resplendent (if dusty) chandeliers which were suspended like inverted frozen fountains from ceilings where cherubs and Napoleonic deities consorted archly with one another against a cerulean sky.

Mr Twill received them in the first of two drawing rooms. He looked much as ever, thought Philip, in spite of the feathered hat he wore and the white flowing gown which sparkled with brilliants.

"Do you like it?" he asked, giving Philip his hand. "I have the most wonderful little man who can copy anything. I don't suppose you recognize it, do you? It's from a Winterhalter portrait of the Empress Elizabeth. She was my ideal, you know." He turned to Stephen and Bill who were staring at him with alarmed eyes. "My two Southern lambs! How sweet of you to come. I've always said Southern boys are the loveliest. Don't you think so, Phil? But what have I said? You're not Southern!"

"South of Albany," said Philip, pleased with his own *sangfroid;* he was now prepared for anything. But anything proved only to be several middle-aged gentlemen in evening gowns and twenty or thirty young men in Brooks Brothers suits. They were gathered, for the most part, in the second drawing room, seated on Louis Quinze gilt chairs and fauteuils. On one wall a tapestry depicted Sebastian receiving, with a certain smugness, the arrows of his fate. Two Japanese boys in white jackets served champagne and brandy.

It was superficially like almost any party, thought Philip, yet in essence it was radically different, unfocused, even if one were to disregard the presence of the monsters in their elaborate gowns. In the other world, when men without women were together in the same room, an entirely different atmosphere was evoked: one that was louder, more fraternal, dull but easy, not like this decorous group of watchful creatures whose eyes never for a second ceased to shift from person to person, judging, calculating, comparing. Cats and dogs, thought Philip grimly, following Stephen and Bill into the room, aware of the excited interest which burst over them like waves over the bow of a ship leaving calm harbor for high seas.

Stephen and Bill were immediately separated by three young Frenchmen with narrow shoulders and pink healthy faces who moved between the lovers with all the cunning of a star basketball team in a classic maneuver. Philip, in his turn, was borne to the still center of the party by a nervous, hairy-chested Frenchman in a low-cut crimson gown slashed with gold, a large cameo about his neck.

"*Joli gosse, n'est-ce pas?*" he commented to two older conventionally dressed men who sat side by side on the largest couch in the room, a number of young men arranged around them, some speaking English, others French, their sibilants cracking like whips across the room no matter which language they spoke. Philip was introduced to everyone and he smiled amiably, taking his place on the couch between the two older men, one of whom was Clyde Norman.

"My dear Philip. It's been an age."

"Half a year."

"Ah, the year . . . the precious year. I see you haven't forgotten, have you? *Toujours fidèle.*"

"To whatever it is."

"But don't you know?"

"Three hundred sixty-odd days . . . no more."

"You still haven't decided?"

"No. I'm afraid you were right. It's not so easy. Nothing short of a major revelation will do it now. If anything, I'm more confused than I was. Too much experience is worse than too little."

"It wasn't experience you lacked, only conviction . . . and conviction takes a lifetime to come by."

"I hope not. I don't want to go on forever like this."

"Why not? Aren't you enjoying yourself? You're young and pretty . . . why live in the future?"

"Why live at all is the question I ask myself," said Philip, wanting to change the subject which, fortunately, a Japanese bearing champagne interrupted; when he withdrew, Philip was able to ask Mr Norman where he had summered.

"Torquay, of all places . . . the British Riviera. I stayed with a sister I'd forgotten all about. Now I'm on my way back to Rome."

"Is Glenellen here?"

"Not yet. He told me he'd seen you. He's got a new interest, you know. Augustus, or whatever his name is."

"I know," said Philip. "By the way, I understand I've been accused of stealing his car."

"First I heard of it," said Mr Norman. "But now, tell me all about Egypt."

Philip told him, his eyes as watchful as all the others, sizing up each newcomer, commiserating with Stephen and Bill who were being devoured alive by the bright-eyed little Frenchmen.

"What, by the way, are you doing here?" asked Mr Norman, after he had swallowed his third glass of champagne and could dare to be less delicate than usual. "You haven't by any chance. . . ." But three glasses of champagne were not sufficient to give him the courage to finish that sentence; so he merely gestured weakly with one hand and frowned.

"Oh, no," said Philip. "I'm just a tourist."

"I thought so. But, with Americans, it's often hard to tell . . . with the young especially."

"I met Mr Twill at Augusta's levée, a place Glenellen took me to," said Philip carefully. "Then I ended up here."

"In the secret shrine of the lodge, as it were."

"Where are the articles of worship?"

"There's only one . . . the sacred totem which each man carries with him and to which our *laus perennis* is addressed."

"There are, of course, deviationists," said Philip.

"Worse . . . schism! Since the very beginning there have been interventionists."

"Better to give than to receive?"

"Their philosophy precisely. But there is a movement afoot, not organized of course, to bring the two groups closer; for one to complement the other."

"Don't they do that now?"

"Often in individual practice but since the initial heresy, various interdicts have been hurled back and forth and the gap has widened terribly in certain countries. I must say, however, that we look to America for that third way which both of the traditional Western parties could accept . . ."

"And the third way?"

"All Americans know it," said Mr Norman roguishly. "It is the practice of the young nation . . . no matter what your interests, whether you belong or not, you know instinctively *the way*. That is a rule. I've known many Americans and all accepted, even if they did not *live*, the third way."

"I knew something fine and spiritual would one day come out of America," said Philip who was fast losing track of the conversation. "I never thought it would be that."

"Neither did any of us. One's first reaction to the idea of America is: look at all that money! those vigorous pioneers! uncouth fathers of thousands of children! But when they came over here during the last war, ah! we were surprised. Since the last century of course we have been used to the American exquisites, the careful New Englanders, the opulent New Yorkers who collected our paintings with the same energy that their daughters collected our titled men. They were too gentlemanly, too civilized to be endured, especially the bachelors who accompanied their mothers obediently from spa to spa, entranced by each new dowager, reveling in our old world of manners which might have expired sooner than it did had it not been for the heady and unexpected applause of our Western cousins. But the war . . . *that* was something else. Those lovely golden youths without guilt, like an Athenian army come to save an outlying province from the Persians. It was not until I'd come to know those youths that I realized what the frontier had been like. We'd forgotten in Europe what a world without women could be like. We grew up in rebellion against an old society, the organized world of our mothers, the elaborate conventions which contained, with remarkable success, the native exuberance of the young. We turned away from what we knew, not loving the other but rather hating what we had known. Then, suddenly, the children of that last frontier descended on us and showed us what it was, traditionally, to love one another: not out of hate or inadequacy but spontaneously, like the Moslems, like those Asiatics whom we call inscrutable. It was a refreshing experience, believe me. The third way. . . . Such a relief after the accretion of attitudes and fetishes which have so long burdened both our camps that our activities have become as formalized and as ritualistic as a ballet. *Le vice anglais,* that sort of thing was unknown to those frontiersmen who lived without women and who loved one another, men who needed men in every sense."

"We're several generations removed from the frontier," said Philip gently, thinking of the nervous pederasts on the beaches of Southern California, descendants of the forty-niners, their dyed hair carefully arranged as they searched

195

continually for those lusty youths who would tolerate them for a price, who often in a neurotic frenzy beat them, to their great delight: O pioneers! "We have our rebels, too," said Philip, "but our world is almost as rigidly stratified as yours. The frontier is gone, its myth ignobly preserved by Wild West movies."

"Where the hero never kisses the girl."

"Where the hero kisses the horse's ass," said Philip. "And speaking of horses, there is Glenellen."

The peer, wearing a plum-colored smoking jacket and a gold chain about his neck, the sort wine stewards in the better restaurants affect, approached the couch where Philip and Mr Norman were seated, the bleeding Sebastian behind them and the youths in a semicircle before them. "There you are. I'm exhausted, absolutely shattered." And he sat down heavily. "Such a day . . . there were a hundred this morning."

"Where? A hundred what?" asked Mr Norman.

"A hundred in attendance on Augusta at The Robing . . . you've never seen such a madhouse! Then I spent all afternoon at the new mission. We now have an abbot and eleven monks there. I am following the medieval church in my reorganization of the various missions. Such a task! Absolutely Augean! Doubt if I shall survive it."

"Where will it end, Ayre?" asked Mr Norman, no longer an ally.

"In a world conversion . . . I demand nothing less. I've been entrusted by Augusta with The Chain." He fingered the chain about his neck which, Philip saw, was indeed a wine steward's badge of office, for the small cup which was pendant to it bore the legend "Ritz Hotel" in a handsome engraved script.

"A very great responsibility," said Mr Norman.

"It makes one, somehow . . . humble, to feel the weight of such a responsibility on one's shoulders. I sometimes feel myself hardly equal to the task."

"About the car," said Philip, interrupting.

"What car?"

"I don't know. I heard some crazy story that I'd been accused of stealing your car."

"I don't think I *accused* you."

"But you're not sure?"

"Not entirely. I vaguely recall having drawn up a list of suspects for the *Sûreté*. Your name might possibly have been on that list."

196

"Even though I didn't know you had a car? that I had seen you only once, briefly, since I'd been in Paris."

"One can never tell."

"I would appreciate it if you told Mr Twill that I didn't steal it . . . told him right now."

"My dear fellow, you're taking much too pedantic an attitude about this. Besides, the police discovered I'd left it myself on a side street; *they* didn't make a scene . . . took it very well, as a matter of fact."

"You should exonerate Mr Warren," said Clyde. "It is only fair."

"Later," said Glenellen. "By the way, Clyde, I've arranged for you to attend the Friday levée. It's always the best."

"I'll be there. Any special costume?"

"We like a morning coat but, alas, so few people have them nowadays. Only the English Lesbians dress properly . . . vigorous crew: backbone of our missions, both here and abroad."

"Abroad?" Mr Norman's eyebrows arched. "Has it spread so far?"

"Indeed it has. Nicaragua, Germany and Norway all boast Missions, while we have Conveyors of the Word in England, Italy, Spain and Switzerland."

"Not in America?"

"Potentially our largest plum. I am leaving for New York September first, a trip which may change the history of the world . . . you realize that, Clyde?"

"It is possible. So many things are continually changing the history of the world that your journey could very easily be one of them."

Mr Twill swept over and they made room for him on the couch, between Philip and Glenellen. "Ayre, my darling, where did you get that ghastly thing about your neck?"

"If you'd been at the services for the last month, you would have known that it was presented to me by Augusta herself when I was made Guardian of the Green Door."

"But I had no idea! Do forgive me! That was nearly blasphemous, wasn't it?"

"Very nearly. Why haven't you been in attendance?"

"The crush," said Mr Twill, adjusting his white elbow-length gloves. "There are too many people there nowadays . . . too many of the wrong sort. But, although I may not be there in person, my heart is with Augusta."

"You are a backslider."

197

"Oh, Ayre, don't be cruel! I tried, God knows I tried to get there but I have so many appointments . . . and I don't get up till noon nowadays anyway."

"There is a story that you are ashamed to go back because of the time you dropped the toque."

"You are merciless, Ayre," said Mr Twill, genuinely if briefly wretched.

"It is only for Augusta," said Glenellen gently. "We must do everything for *her*. We must not let *her* down."

"I'll be there tomorrow. I'll move all my appointments up an hour so that I can attend. You are absolutely right: I've been selfish, headstrong, and I *was* upset when someone knocked the toque out of my hand. I confess now that I swore I would never go back . . . I was in such a pet. But you're right, this is no time to be small."

"You have made us very happy, Edmond, very happy indeed."

"Will I . . . be able to handle the toque?"

"You will indeed. And should it be Augustus instead of Augusta I think I might be able to get you assigned the Privilege of the Braces."

"Ayre!" Too moved to say any more, Mr Twill managed a high whinny of pleasure.

"By the way," said Philip, "I didn't steal Lord Glenellen's car."

Mr Twill looked puzzled. "But isn't this the one, Ayre, who was at the levée?"

"The same one . . . but it seems that I lost the car. No one took it after all; my suspicions were groundless."

"Oh, what a pity! I so hoped he had. I like a bold reckless boy!" He squeezed Philip's thigh; once out of sheer exuberance, a second time to corroborate the favorable impression of the first squeeze. Philip moved away. "Such a solid boy, isn't he? I love that combination, blond hair and violet eyes."

"He looked better in Rome," said Glenellen. "He had dark hair then."

Philip sighed but said nothing.

"Well, I'm glad he changed it." And he cast a sidelong flirtatious glance at Philip, his eyes small and bloodshot behind artificial beaded lashes.

Then, as though a stage manager had given a command, everyone changed his position: groups dissolved, reassembled in new combinations, presenting all sorts of possibilities. Large quantities of brandy and champagne were consumed

198

and the lights had been so dimmed that Sebastian had quite faded away, only the golden arrows still visible against the wall. In the next room the phonograph played the songs from the latest of Mr Cole Porter's musicals, and the doors to two bedrooms were already locked.

For one brief moment Philip found himself with Stephen and Bill, both bewildered and far less amused than he. "Don't take it so seriously," he said. "It's not so vicious, after all."

"I don't think it's very funny," said Bill, his face flushed and his dark curls sweaty from the room's heat and the brandy he had drunk.

"He's a big hit," said Stephen, the less outraged of the two. "That joker in the red dress has been goosing him all night. Just now he offered to take him on a Mediterranean cruise; then when Bill told him we were buddies, he said he would give us each a hundred dollars if we'd let him watch some time."

"Easy money," said Philip, enjoying himself.

Bill snorted and then, seeing the fat figure of the red-gowned man moving toward him, he walked quickly to the next room, Stephen close behind him.

"You're not so bad, either," said Red Dress, drunkenly, pausing in front of Philip, his breath hot and unpleasant with wine and garlic. "You want to take a little trip with me? Moonlight . . . Mediterranean. We could have a swell time, you and me. We could . . ." But Philip was gone before Red Dress had finished telling him what they might do together.

He crossed the room and stood for a moment between the ghost of Sebastian and the couch where Glenellen still sat, surrounded now by a group of young belles. Voices were growing louder and there were now over fifty people in the two dimly lit rooms. Amorousness in dark corners warned Philip that it was time to go.

"Excuse me," said a dignified gray-haired man, a Frenchman who spoke excellent English and looked exactly like Philip's idea of a Quai d'Orsay man, with the rank of minister at least. "You're American, aren't you?"

"This is my first trip to Paris."

"This is a part of the grand tour now, isn't it?" He indicated the room with a scornful gesture of his long white hand.

"A very interesting part."

"For a young man, yes, but not for me. I've seen too

much, I suppose. I'm bored with this sort of thing . . . so obvious, so feverish, so pointless."

"But worth seeing once."

The Frenchman raised his dignified brows. "This is not your *métier?*"

Philip shook his head. "I'm here under false pretenses . . . incognito, a spy."

"But how charming! You dabble, of course?"

"No. I don't dabble."

"But surely you plan to one day, don't you? You're not fighting that hard against it."

"I'm not fighting it at all," said Philip blandly. "I'm a grown man, perfectly contented."

"How rare! How refreshing! But then my instinct is always infallible in these matters. Placed in a room with twenty men who all look alike, who all share the same tastes except one, I will, unerringly, go to *that* one, to the incorruptible . . . my fate, alas."

"Isn't that rather sad for you?"

"Fortunately I live in Europe, where a gentleman can buy very nearly anything he wants, including the incorruptible."

"That is fortunate."

"Indeed, yes, but tell me, have you found a comfortable hotel?"

Philip told him where he was staying.

"How very nice, so Bohemian. Young people live that way, for a time at least, even though the facilities are not always of the best. Do you have a bath? That's lucky. So many of those places have no hot water. In which case I should have offered you my own place for bathing. . . ." He laughed and added, "Quite legitimate, as you people say. I never force myself on people. What about the laundry situation, though? That's always so difficult this time of year."

Philip, a little bored, said that he had had no trouble in getting his laundry done.

"I see. If you cared to, however, you could give it to my woman to do . . . she's quite marvelous, no starch . . . the way Americans like their shirts."

"Thank you very much but . . ." Philip declined his offer, looking around the room in search of Mr Twill; he was ready to leave.

"Tell me," asked his companion, "do you wear what the Americans call 'jockey shorts'?"

200

Philip looked at him startled. "Why on earth do you want to know?"

"But do you?" The other was insistent.

"I do."

"Are you wearing a pair now?"

"Yes, but why . . ."

"I will give you ten thousand francs for them."

Philip fled. In the black marble foyer he found Jim who was just arriving.

"What the hell are you doing here?" asked Jim, surprised.

"I'm beginning to wonder myself. I was just getting out while I could."

"Good idea." The boy's face was very pale and his eyes were half shut. "Can't stand the light," he murmured.

"Are you flying?" asked Philip gently.

"And how! I'm real gone. I'm never going to touch the ground again. Why, I can't even see you from where I am." He smiled at Philip, opening wide his silver eyes and Philip saw the tears.

Chapter Eleven

SHE LOOKED EXACTLY THE WAY he had remembered her that day in Cairo when Zoe Helotius introduced them in the room with the silken banners on the wall. She was sitting with Charles de Cluny at a table opposite the door. Philip looked at his watch: twelve-thirty at the Ritz. He was on time. With a smile, he went over to her table, suddenly self-conscious, aware that he needed a haircut, that his shoes were not shined.

"I'm so happy we found each other," she said warmly as he greeted her and Charles, and sat down.

"So am I," said Philip. "It's nice to see you too, Charles. How long've you been here?"

"Just a few days."

"Oh, do you know each other?" asked Anna.

"We're old friends," said de Cluny. "In Cairo."

She nodded. "Now I remember . . . at the party. This is an unexpected meeting, isn't it?"

"It certainly is," said Philip. "I checked with your hotel every week until they finally told me you were here." This was indiscreet, he thought, aware suddenly of de Cluny's knowing glance; but he carried it off. "They must have got tired of me."

"On the contrary, I was told that a gentleman with a very nice American voice had inquired for me and the manager was extremely solicitous, hoping, I am sure, that he would be allowed to assist at an intrigue. He couldn't have been more disappointed when I told him what a great friend Mr Warren is of my husband's. We saw each other quite often in Cairo," she said, turning to de Cluny; Philip admired her for the clear and sensible way she arranged the facts, confirming all de Cluny's suspicions.

"Are you in the steel business now?" asked Charles maliciously, his cigarette holder pointed at Philip like a conductor's baton.

"I'm *very* interested in steel," said Philip, suggesting by his tone innumerable secret committee meetings where wars

202

were decided upon and governments broken, all for the love of steel.

"Mr Morris is a giant among men," said de Cluny, placing the cigarette holder between his teeth, smoke for an instant hiding his narrow face.

"He'll be in Paris soon," she said as the waiter brought the cocktails.

"I hope you will all do me the honor of dining at my house."

The invitation was accepted with a friendly vagueness.

"Will you have lunch with us today, Charles?" she asked.

"If only I could! But I have to be with Hélène de Lyon et Grénoble. She's deaf and blind but she has an uncanny gift for divining whether one is talking to her or not. I don't know how she does it but when one is not at her house, she knows it and, though most of her faculties are gone, she is not yet mute. What a tongue! So, if you'll excuse me, dear lady, and you, Philip, I shall make my way to the Faubourg . . . regretfully. Don't forget about our dinner when Mr Morris has returned. Philip, I'll call you tomorrow."

More graceful words and then, with several bows and flourishes of the cigarette holder, he was gone.

"I like Charles," she said, not looking at Philip, as though she were suddenly shy at finding herself alone with him. "He's been acting the part of the courtier so long he has finally become one. The role has swallowed up the man."

"The courtier with no court?"

"That's his charm: he makes each of us the center of the world . . . he has a hundred *reines-lunaires* and though they realize how absurd he is they love him for his attentiveness, for his good manners. And where would we be without the snobs, without the people who value tradition?"

"Where would we be?" repeated Philip. "Well, I'm afraid we'd be exactly where we are now since all the old traditions are gone and new ones are still aborning."

"It's a pity, I suppose," said Anna, watching the bartender shake a cocktail so hard that the eye was confused and his hands and the silver shaker became a single blur in space, reflected by many mirrors. "But perhaps there is an advantage to living in a time of great change . . . though every time is one of change. . . ." They looked at each other for the first time and he saw his own face twice reflected in her hazel eyes.

"I called your hotel," she said, suddenly personal, her

voice changing as she discarded the eternal manner which became her not at all.

"Today?"

"Yesterday when I arrived. But you were out and I didn't leave a message. I wasn't sure you'd remember me."

"You knew I'd remember."

"Perhaps. I have a good memory, too. I remember your telling me that you would get your mail through the Embassy. I called them and they gave me your address."

"Would you have called today if I hadn't telephoned you?"

She nodded. "Yes . . ."

"I'm glad," he said and then to bridge the awkward moment, this time of shy and difficult declaration, he ordered two more cocktails. "I drink too much in Paris," he said. "I don't know why. I go for months at a time without taking anything; then, all at once, I find that I want to be amiable and relaxed and sentimental like other people . . . like some other people at least."

"I'm sure it's good for you," she said, hardly touching her own glass. "I don't need it, I'm afraid. Nature made me sentimental from the very start. I think that if I drank I should be maudlin."

"Or perhaps the opposite . . . very hard and aloof."

"Never . . . even though there are times when I should like to give that impression."

"But not with me, I hope."

"No, not with you."

They lunched in a small restaurant around the corner from the Crillon, a place with Chinese red walls, lacquered and gleaming and decorated with banks of roses and ferns not yet wilted, still fresh with morning.

"I see why you chose it," said Philip. "The Chinese room . . . with all the banners."

"The same mood, without Zoe." She laughed.

The day went easily, carefully. Each deferred to the other and their conversations alternated between a delicate formality and a loverlike intimacy: usual prelude to an affair. But Philip for once could not determine the nature of the work to come.

He was often able to see at the very beginning the end of an affair, with a painful clarity which had, in recent years especially, done much to diminish the intensity of his own emotions. Too fine an understanding was far worse, he knew, than the confusion with which most young men blundered into love affairs. He had always known, for instance, not only how far he would commit himself with Regina but also at what point his withdrawal would, imperceptibly, commence, and though this prescience was saddening, it gave him a sense of security, of power which made the affairs, at least while they lasted, singularly agreeable, lacking in the usual dissensions, the blind misunderstandings; then, too, as he grew older, he had become more kind; he prided himself now on having become an adept at the art of separation, the gradual retreat which left neither anguish nor rage behind. But, being a child or the grandchild of the Romantic Movement, living in a culture still dominated on a vulgar level by the high romantic poets of the nineteenth century, he longed instinctively for the flames, for the one attachment: "my last and only love," the love which increased from moment to moment until the lovers strangled for lack of air among those peaks which touch the edge of heaven, close to the consuming sun in whose fire, united at last, they perish to the accompaniment of French horns and frenzied woodwinds, the voice of Isolde, strong and pure, lingering in the vast golden dome of heaven where angels, out of sympathy, deluge the earth below with their pity. And in the back of his mind, each time he began the intricate ritual, he hoped that his own knowledge would be proved false by the unexpected conquest of that suspected but never before attained dimension in which he could indulge not only his secret passion for romance, for immolation, but also achieve that instant which each man awaits as though it were his due, inevitable, the moment of recognition that there is someone else in the world with whom the mortal's loneliness can be shared and finally overcome, the last of the fluttering moths from Pandora's box, caught and speared.

But I am a realist, said Philip to himself, disliking this self-estimate, aware that it was true: he was not a romanticist or a visionary.

Yet for Philip, for the realist who recognizes the more obvious limitations of both flesh and spirit, the hope of a great romantic experience is tempered always with the grim knowledge that nothing is constant and that even though a certain height might, temporarily, be attained, descent from it is inevitable and painful, unless one chooses to perish at the grand moment, a gesture which did not attract Philip although the rich, dark tragedy at Mayerling had fascinated not only him but others of his generation, as directionless as he, all of them like compass needles gone awry, awaiting the pull of some magnet to set their courses for them, true north no longer the center it had once been. But Mayerling or not, he had no wish to die. He would, he knew, go as far as his temperament would permit into a separate world with one other person but since it would not be his only world, since he was possessed by other demons, the pure expression he dreamed of seemed unlikely although, as he talked to Anna, he thought it would be difficult ever to become bored with her and that was more than he could ever have said of any other woman he had known, at this point at least in the ceremony of union. As he talked he recalled the loveliest of the *Minnesänger's* songs: *"Unter den Linden, an der Heide, da unser zweier Bette."* A bed for us on the heather would be very fine, he thought and, as it always had before, his desire drowned his love and he could only think of the act, the excitement, the mysteries revealed, a new conquest and as he succumbed to the familiar itch, Anna ceased to be, her face and character were veiled, only the body was real and immediate. But she countered him, to his surprise, for just when the moment seemed very nearly achieved, the way clearly indicated, she withdrew, leaving him staring angrily into his half-empty coffee cup.

"I promised to meet some people. I ran into them yesterday and they made me promise."

"Tonight . . ."

"A silly dinner. But tomorrow why don't we get Charles to give us dinner at his house. He has a lovely one, or rather some rooms in one, opposite the Isle de la Cité."

▣

"I've always thought there was a happy symbolism in the choice of St Germain's name for our left bank boulevard. He was a remarkable man, a Bishop of Paris at the end of the sixth century and having that rarest of maladies, ancient or modern, a Christian conscience, he went about Europe raising funds for the liberation of slaves. By the time he died, he had very nearly shattered that barbarous practice in Europe. Now the young people come from all over the world to live here on his boulevard, to lose their superstitions, to become emancipated. It is very touching." But nothing de Cluny said ever sounded as though he quite meant it, thought Philip critically: Charles had cultivated the ironic manner to such an extent that his most casual

206

words were redolent with self-mockery and double meaning. Yet he talked well enough, Philip conceded to himself, content with the dinner they had just eaten, with the view from an open balconied window of Notre Dame against the stars, with Anna who wore Chinese red like a Chinese bride, the curious fragment of crystal about her neck.

The evening had been perfect and they now sat in a book-lined study, neither shabby nor elegant, made unique by the view. Philip and Anna had talked little, pleased with the moment, not wanting to upset the delicate balance with irrelevant words. De Cluny, aware of this happy situation, seized the opportunity to speak of himself and while his guests looked at one another, he talked of his recent sojourn in a country of Central America.

"An incredibly lifeless place, all things considered . . . and in my dozen years there I did consider nearly everything, including suicide. Not that my job wasn't interesting . . . I was adviser to the President, Alvarez Asturias. You may have heard of him."

Philip and Anna murmured in unison that they had not.

"He was a dictator, one of the better ones. But he was deposed and I followed him into exile. Had he remained in private life all might have been well. We were very snug in New Orleans but he attempted a revolution in which I took part, a ghastly affair and disastrous for everyone concerned, except me: it galvanized me into a feverish literary activity. I had lain fallow for so long that I thought it unlikely I should ever bloom again. But I did. We escaped by helicopter . . . an exciting time, I might add, with government troops firing on us. Fortunately we got as far as Guatemala where we fell, for some reason no one has ever been able to determine, in the middle of Lake Atitlán . . . on a clear day, mind you. I have a theory that the pilot was drunk but we shall never know for he was knocked unconscious when we crashed, and sank like a stone. The rest of us were rescued by a fishing boat and I went back to France as soon as I could, where I had certain properties saved from the deluge."

The moment had come when the dinner must be paid for. Philip and Anna looked at one another. It was agreed silently that she request the reading. She did, graciously, with an air of real sincerity.

"I know what an ordeal it is to be read to, especially in French, but of course you, dear lady, *are* French and Mr Warren speaks it beautifully." And he shuffled papers on

207

his desk, assembled a staggering number of manuscript pages from which he read in a loud ringing voice, the cadence as regular and as monotonous as the alexandrines at the Comédie-Française, without benefit of scenery or of entr'actes or of talent.

Gently, Philip dropped off to sleep. He awakened with a start, aware that a question had been asked, that the others were looking at him intently, awaiting an answer.

"Fine." He croaked; then, clearing his throat, he sat up and said, with as much resonance as his light voice would permit, "Very fine."

"You don't feel that the scene in the park is a trifle grandiloquent?"

"On the contrary, I thought it remarkably muted, considering its theme," added Philip confidently, blundering into a trap.

"But what do you really feel *is* the theme? I mean the underlying motif at that point? I have kept it oblique, I think, awaiting the proper moment to develop it more fully; yet it *is* there, all the way through the scene, like an echo to what is said . . . a faint counterpoint to the obvious theme."

"Ah," said Philip, looking at Anna helplessly. She only laughed at him, silently.

"The echo I think is the broken statue," hinted de Cluny eagerly.

"A sense of loss, I should say," said Philip, gambling everything with a flourish. "A longing for what will never be."

"You have it! I *knew* it was apparent but I was afraid it might be lost. You have no idea how relieved I am! Shall I get you more brandy? Yes?" He left the room to find another bottle.

"Where shall we go?" asked Philip, suddenly, when their host was gone.

"Wherever you like, Philip. To the Ida?"

"No, that wouldn't be wise."

"To your hotel?"

"It's so . . . dark. I don't want that, do you?"

She smiled. "No, we must have light."

"Then we leave Paris. Go somewhere else."

"When?"

"Now . . . tonight."

"But where?"

"To the sea. What about Deauville?"

"But . . ."

"St Malo? That's better, isn't it? We could stay there."

"But how . . ."

"You have a car. We'll take that. Please. If we leave right now we'll be there before noon."

"Before noon," she repeated, taken aback; then she laughed. "Do you really want to take such a chance? You hardly know me."

"I'll take it, if you will."

"Oh, I will, of course." Her lack of hesitancy surprised and pleased him.

"But your husband?"

"He won't be in Paris until the end of the month. You are very brave, Philip."

"Shall we go?"

She nodded.

"Tonight?"

"Whenever you like. It will be a lovely night for driving."

"Where's the car?"

"At the hotel . . . parked in front. I have the keys with me."

"Let's not take anything with us. We'll go just as we are."

"I would like that," she said, surprising him for the last time.

"This brandy," said de Cluny, "has been in my family for fifty years. Look! Cobwebs!" He put the bottle down on the table and wiped his hands with his handkerchief. "One's voice needs a little . . . lubrication after a long reading, I find. The audience, of course, deserves a stimulant."

"A sedative," said Philip gallantly, exuberant, more pleased than he had ever been before. "After all you keyed us up."

"Now you exaggerate." De Cluny's face darkened slightly with pleasure; he poured the brandy.

"You read so well," said Anna. "Like an actor . . . your face is very like Jouvet's."

"Do you think so? Ah, that *is* a compliment, indeed! André Gide was most sympathetic the other day when I paid a call on him at the rue Vaneau. Most sympathetic."

"Did you read for him?" asked Philip.

"Alas, no. He didn't have the time. He's very old, you know, but he told me he had every confidence that I should maintain my old level . . . he was most encouraging. Such a vigorous man for his age, too. Physically, like a hard, barrel-chested peasant . . . not always kind either: when I made some reference to Claudel he said: who? Imagine! But then I suspect he dislikes discussing in his contemporaries or near-contemporaries. He talked for the most part about a delightful manuscript of pornography, handsomely and primitively illuminated, the work, I swear to you, of a retired Anglican bishop living in Italy. He had sent it to the master with a *dédicace* and, as the master said, it *was* fine but a trifle too literary in tone."

"He sounds very agreeable," said Philip.

"A fine manner. And isn't that, on a human level at least, the most important of virtues? Genius exists only in the work, not in the man, or I should say one can only approach it in the work . . . where the man is disembodied, as it were, made pure. Naturalness, of course, is supposed to be one of the most engaging of American virtues, but is it really what one wants? Is it truly civilized? A country of first names! Only the Negroes there have manners. They are most scrupulous in calling one another Mr and Mrs. The white people, especially the ones in business, at their first meeting with a stranger call him by his Christian name, even if he is old enough to be their father."

Philip made a great scene over the hour. What time did de Cluny's watch say? and the ornate clock on the mantel? the broken Dresden clock in the bedroom? his own often inaccurate watch? Was it really so late? and the evening, was it really gone? Then, the symposium on time concluded to everyone's satisfaction, Philip and Anna said good-night.

The false gray-pink Paris dawn had already begun to glow when they drove across the city through dark and silent streets; neither spoke until they were in the open country, the towns of eastern Touraine before them and beyond Touraine, the fields and orchards of Normandy and the northern sea.

"I'm glad I wasn't wearing an evening dress," said Anna as the day illuminated the dark sky with gold, with rose; then a ghostly yellow sun appeared over the green and misty land and the sky shone blue with morning.

"A few more hours," said Philip.

"Do you want me to drive?"

"No, I don't want to stop for a minute, until we're there."

"Neither do I."

"No breakfast?"

"Nothing . . . until we're there."

Three miles east of St Malo they stopped and got out of the car. In the distance, partly hidden by the sea mist, they could make out the pyramidal shape of the ancient castle, set far out in the sea. Half a mile away was a stone cottage with a thatched roof, the only building in sight. The land undulated, soft and green, white-dotted with rocks and grazing sheep. The clover-scented air was still and warm as they stood by the side of the car, looking upon the dark blue sea which broke on a dun-colored, rock-strewn beach at the meadow's edge. Then, without a word, they walked across the coarse turf to the beach and, finding a stretch of sand that was sheltered from the road by tall trees, they paused among the gray, smooth rocks, relics of an age of glaciers and still not speaking, the hot sun in their faces, they undressed. It was noon.

He took her in the cool sea, their lips tasting of salt, blue above and all around them except for the green land they had left behind. Gulls circled slowly overhead. Salt water stopped his watch, holding the sun forever in the center of the sky: high noon, as they moved to a sea-like rhythm in one another's arms until, at last, the tide drove them back to shore again and the sun fell in the west.

Between two guardian rocks, they lay on the sand, side by side, their bodies touching, creatures belonging neither to the sea nor to the land from which each had come to this beach between earth and water, the air above them and, far below, their own element fire, swathed in sea and air, earth, stone and metal, a smothered sun at the center of the world.

He sat up on one elbow and looked at her as she lay, white and perfect, upon the sand. He touched her carefully, as though she might melt like the snow princess in the legend. But she was mortal. She sighed and opened her eyes, her dark hair cushioned by seaweeds and shells, crystals of salt glittering like a powder of fine snow on her white skin, dried by the warm air.

"I was asleep," she said. "Were you?"

"I think so. Look, the sun is almost down."

"The day can't end." She shut her eyes again, her arms crossed upon her breast. He plucked the shells and seaweed from her long hair and, when she opened her eyes again, he half expected to see the pearls that were her eyes. " 'Full fathom five,' " he whispered to himself.

She looked at him a long time, her hand gently stroking his arms and his chest as she gradually followed the line of blond hair to the now limp and childlike origin of life; then they made love again, closer to earth than to sea, once more whole: a double star, a third sun suspended between the other two, the one below and the fiery one which now lingered in the western corner of the sky.

They lay together, joined, until the sun set and the pale gray sky was pierced by a single star, a gleaming point of silver in the nascent evening. "Ah, there it is," she said. They separated and got to their feet, unsteadily, like invalids or like children who had just learned to walk. "Have you made a wish?" she asked.

"I have," he said, his arm about her waist.

"Have you made the wish?"

"There is only one."

"Only one," she murmured, and they dressed at last on the dark beach while, among the trees which bordered the meadow, fireflies gleamed like a swarm of old stars falling.

The room was large with small shuttered windows and rough beams showing; a four-poster bed, square and massive, was set in the center of the tile floor. Brass gleamed in the fireplace and the room smelled of smoke and linen, wood and roses.

"It is our best room," said the old man, grumbling and snorting like every French character actor Philip had ever seen. "Feather." He punched the thick mattress. "The *vase de nuit*." He indicated a blue and white chamber pot beside the bed. "Only candles. We have no electricity here." He paused, challengingly, prepared to attack the new age, but they had already surrendered to him and to the room in the stone house, a half mile from their beach.

Since he was always with Anna, Philip had little time to contemplate his own emotions, like a physician taking his own pulse. Yet he was sharply aware that at the center of those easy days there was a pain equal to the delight of loving . . . the dark side of the love, the parallel emotion without which nothing could be measured or identified: no day without night, no life without death, no love without this cold pain, this separateness. For, at the last, he was a creature of his world, time-haunted and future-loving, obsessed with hours and minutes, terrified by days and years

and the loss of youth, the end of the good present in which
he now moved, like a man who dreams and knows that he
is dreaming in a world all his own, where he reigns a god
but, unlike a god, conscious of the world outside his dream,
its noises intruding fitfully, unbidden, until at last, half-
blind and angry, he awakens, the dream scattered in a
hundred fragments by the ruthless light, the significant
design forever gone, only the anguish and the sense of loss
lingering to mock the day.

But his watch was broken, rusted by sea water, and
neither spoke of the hour for many days.

◳

He sat cross-legged on a rock and watched her walk out of
the sea wringing water from her dark hair, her body gleaming white in the sun. Birds chattered in the orchards. Gray
gulls circled over the sea. The sun burned gold and hot in
the sky.

"How brown you are!" she exclaimed joining him on the
sand between their two tall guardian rocks, Gog and Magog
she had called them.

"And you're still white," he said, touching her cold wet
thigh.

"I never tan. I can't think why. I should like to look
like one of those bronze amazons with golden hair. I admire
them so."

"I don't," said Philip, stretching his legs, the short hairs
sun-bleached and glistening on his brown arms and legs,
only the lower belly and thighs still white, the line of
bathing trunks still marked on his skin. "It's like going to bed
with a man, to go to bed with one of them."

"Did you ever?"

"Go to bed with one of them? Oh yes. In my college days
all the girls were six feet tall and liked to engage the boys
in various competitive feats of strength. Fortunately, that
was before the days of jujitsu, so all but the slighter boys
got their way . . . the weak ones were either thrown back into
the sea or else raped by their conquerors. One young man
named MacDougall was forced to surrender his virginity to
a giantess from Smith College . . . three time in one terrible
hour in his room while his two roommates, roaring with delight, watched through the keyhole. . . . They had locked the
door so he couldn't escape."

Anna laughed, wonderingly. "It sounds like the end of
213

the world," she said, lying back on the rock, her hair a dark rain cloud against the sand.

🔲

One eminent man of letters (whom many think the first among us) once wrote in a novel that when his hero made love to his heroine the earth moved and celestial firecrackers went off in the void where presumably his audience, a benign eternity, applauded rapturously each mighty thrust. A lesser, more superficial man of letters (equally celebrated but less well regarded at the moment) chided his peer, saying that nothing of that sort ever happened when a man and woman made love . . . at best they had a good time. To which the great man responded, *"You* could never understand," retiring like any good priest into mysteries which cannot be defined in familiar terms: either one *knows* or one does not.

In Philip's case it would be untrue to say that the course of his life was altered by that moment with Anna: it was not . . . at least as far as one can determine which events do affect character and to what degree. He got out of bed the morning after their first night together as he had got out of bed the day before and as he would get out of bed ten years later. He was the same man in the usual sense of sameness: he did not go out into the street and preach the Word; he made no attempt to proselytize; he gave up nothing he had liked before (including promiscuity), nor was he inspired to become a marvelous artist because, as it has been earlier demonstrated, he had no particular talent and, contrary to a certain opinion, vision alone is not enough in the arts . . . although it may serve one handsomely in life. But in one important sense he was changed. Where before he had believed he now knew, and that, as any mystic will attest, is the difference between night and day. And for the rest of a long life, he would glimpse the fire again and again, always reflected, however, in a woman's eyes. Yet never the way it had been the first night when, briefly, his flesh and bone, memory and will had been consumed and he became a part of all that is.

🔲

When the Duc de Lyon et Grénoble died, twenty years ago, his vivacious widow, who was then only sixty, moved into a small but stately house on the Faubourg St Germain, selling her husband's hôtel to a speculator who made several

214

apartments of it, in one of which, as we have already noted, Mr Edmond Twill now resides steeped in his own rich atmosphere of drugs and debauched street boys, no trace of the stern Duc or his still handsome Duchesse remaining in that old building . . . even the cobwebs in the cellar have been changed for the Duchesse is very mean, as everyone knows, and she is supposed to have taken the family spiders and mice with her when she moved into that smaller establishment where she has re-created an imperial atmosphere that is the despair of all the Bonapartists, none of whom, not even the Murats, has been able to equal it in grandeur or in authenticity.

Needless to say, the better Royalists have very little to do with her and she, in turn, has nothing to do with any member of the Republican government, excepting always those old friends who have blundered into high office: for those unfortunates, she gives small teas in her boudoir, not allowing them, however, to attend her carefully chosen receptions or those formal dinners where she entertains the relics of the Empire and the older members of that world of high fashion which used always to amuse her before she became deaf and blind. She is, according to Charles de Cluny who insists he knows, a hundred and seven years old. No matter what her age, it is a fact that she was on intimate terms with the Empress Eugénie and dined with her once a week until that lady's death. The Duchesse has had no close woman friends since, although her friendships with men are still much talked of; she is known to have been the cause of a number of duels, suicides, divorce cases, as well as the lifelong love of one lyric poet's short-termed existence. She is now living with her onetime coachman, a portly silver-haired gentleman who is seldom in evidence although early callers report that he brings her breakfast to her each morning on a tray, with a bouquet of fresh violets across the morning paper.

Philip and Anna were led by de Cluny to the center of a gray and silver drawing room where, directly beneath a chandelier, the Duchesse stood, a straight small figure with bright red hair held in place by a fillet of green velvet, in the style of the 1880's, modified somewhat during the early years of the twentieth century to set off a figure which had once been handsomely proportioned but now had grown thick at one end of the torso and grotesquely frail at the other, where the narrow shoulders were hung with discolored pearls as filmy and as dark as the eyes which darted this way and that, not seeing, the world shut out by white-ness . . . having attained certain Alpine peaks, thought Philip poetically as he studied those dim eyes, she had been blinded by the glare of light on glaciers.

"Charles?" Her voice was surprisingly full for one so old; loud too from deafness. "Did you bring me the young people? Ah yes, here are their hands. She is a lovely blonde with white skin and he is a fat American boy. I can always tell by hands. Such a comfort to have some communication with the living since, obviously, I have none with the dead . . . although many of my friends think they can talk to the dead, I don't: all nonsense. Besides, why should one want to talk to an absolute stranger with whom one has nothing in common? 'I am Yvette, a midinette, and I died in Seventy-four. . . .' " She mocked in a high voice, still holding the hands of the lovers in her own, her touch as smooth and as dry as old silk.

"Fortunately, everyone I used to know is dead, including the ones who attended séances. They certainly realize *now* what nonsense it all was. Well, go on . . . there are other young people here, I think. Bore one another." And with a shadow of what must have been a brilliant smile, she let go their hands abruptly and they found themselves in a room full of strangers of whom none were young. They sat in a brocade love seat next to a spinet where a tired-looking man played Mozart with a faded grace, the thin elegant sounds lost in the party's chatter.

Above the mantel was a portrait of the Duchesse as she had looked when Bismarck entered Paris. On the spinet, on every table, were miniatures and photographs of an earlier time: a lock of Napoleon's hair, dark brown and lusterless in a heavy case of gold and crystal, a silver rattle which had belonged to the King of Rome, Murat's spurs and the baton of the first Duc, all preserved under glass with yellowed cards identifying them for those casual visitors who had strayed, like Philip, into this drawing room with no real knowledge of what it meant, of what it had been in other more vigorous days, when ladies sewed golden bees onto handkerchiefs for French boys who were to die far from home.

Anna was finally taken away by an old acquaintance and he was left alone by the spinet with de Cluny, who smiled and bowed continually at figures across the room, talking to Philip at the same time.

"Love of unfamiliar, outworn ways is a weakness, I

suppose," he said genially, bowing very low at a poorly assembled mass of lace which passed close by, exuding a musty odor like a closed room suddenly opened. Philip half expected the ambulatory lace to be attended by reverent outriding moths.

"It's natural," said Philip.

"On the contrary, most unnatural. Have you noticed the hatred with which lower-class people (and much of the middle class, too) regard the past? One sees it at a cinema where they laugh derisively at the costumes of another time and on those occasions when confronted, in school or in the theater, with some classic literary work, they respond with confusion and anger, mocking the language not only of the past but, worse still, of all art, since they are as afraid of the new as they are of the old. No wonder one loathes the mob."

"But why loathe people who don't share your taste? It seems bigoted to say the least."

"Taste is another thing. No, I don't really mind if the working classes mock Corneille but I do mind when they attempt, as they periodically do, to destroy all art, to reduce the great to their own level. That is the terrible anti-human constant in all our affairs and that is why I, for one, do loathe the mob. The people who deposed Aristides and poisoned Socrates. . . ." He kissed a dingy alabaster hand which emerged for one brief moment from yards of faded yellow silk.

"Odd isn't it how each age has its panacea . . . its banner, as it were. In the Middle Ages it was Faith; in the eighteenth century, it was Reason . . . later, it was Progress. . . ."

"And what, I wonder, is it now?"

De Cluny smiled. "I know."

"What?"

"I don't dare say."

"That's hardly courageous."

"Love!" said de Cluny, bringing one long finger down on the keyboard of the now deserted spinet. An eighteenth-century E-flat tinkled faintly, like a derisive echo in the air.

"That has never been the ideal of more than a few," said Philip sternly.

"I'm not speaking of amity or charity or the brotherhood of man. I am speaking of sexual love. Think for a moment: man is no longer the center of the universe as he once was, or thought he was, which is the same thing. His displacement began, in modern times, with Copernicus and ended with Darwin. The idea of a personal god who watches over man with a worried eye, giving out marks for deportment and arranging celestial bliss or eternal discomfort for the good and the bad, is dying in the West. While a belief in the universals of Aristotle has been succeeded by a conception of relativity . . . morality is relative and variable, change is constant and the Protagorean conception that man is the measure of all things is, in practice, if not in orthodox belief, quite general. Where, then, is man? The universe in his own image has been succeeded by a universe in its own image *containing* him, and he is now beginning to perceive what two thousand years of Western culture tried to hide: that his race is not the central adornment of the universe and that its control over nature is as precarious and as limited as its control over itself. Man is important only to himself. The fiction of a partisan deity has become so transparent that even the most uneducated are able to see through it, to see the infinite impersonal void beyond this world, this single particle in an indifferent galaxy . . . child of earth and of starry heaven indeed! I doubt if even the most eccentric, the most persuasive mystic will ever again be able to personalize the void, to subordinate it to this one race as our fortunate ancestors did. Man has nothing except himself; so, without hope of heaven after death or of Utopia on earth, he is left nothing but games like art and power, the satisfaction of various hungers and, of all the games and of all the hungers, the most exalted, the most godlike is the sexual act since, in human terms at least, it is the most important of all our deeds: continuation of life, while as sensation, there is nothing to compare with it, in the vigor of one's youth at least. And of all the old gods of the West, Venus alone is regnant. Two can face the void with less terror than one. The moment of orgasm fills the dark with light, or seems to, which is enough, I think. Everywhere in the West, one sees this sudden preoccupation with sex, in our literature, in art, in science . . . there's even a new philosophy of sex with men like Lawrence and Freud attempting to define it, either mystically or empirically. One knows now that love is the last illusion, the only magic, and unlike other pleasures . . . the exercise of power, mysticism, the creation of works of art . . . it is physically possible for nearly everyone while in a spiritual sense (or whatever word one wishes to use to characterize so tenuous a state of being),

218

it is a challenge to the few, a proof of virtue, a temporary defeat of the impersonal reality, black magic in an age of science."

"That only leaves death to be accounted for," said Philip, thoughtfully.

"Death accounts for us, not we for it," said de Cluny, as the room was split in two by Zoe Helotius.

Philip moved close to the room's center where Zoe paid court to the Duchesse and the party paid court to Zoe.

"Darling Hélène, I'm late. I came as soon as I could but I was in the house of X and you know how difficult it is to get away from them." The reference to X was sufficiently lofty to impress even the oldest of the Bonapartists.

"I can't hear a word you're saying, Zoe,"—complained the Duchesse which was obviously not true since Mrs Helotius' voice could have penetrated walls of lead.

"Darling, can you hear me now?" The voice reduced the room to silence.

"Just barely. You must learn to speak without mumbling. When I was a girl, we were taught elocution by La Meynard of the Comédie-Française. 'Speak up,' she used to say. 'Speak up!'"

"My childhood was less privileged!" bellowed Zoe, and then, ignoring the old lady's occasional remarks about her diction, she gossiped and Philip, among these relics of the first Napoleon, thought of Madame de Staël and her loud progress through these same drawing rooms a century ago, in search not only of lions but of ideas.

"She is lovely," said Charles, admiringly.

"You think so? I think she's terrible."

"I meant Anna."

"Oh. I thought you meant Mrs Helotius. Yes, she is."

"Did you enjoy your trip to the sea?"

"How did you know?"

"I know everything."

"Yes, very much."

"I knew in Cairo this would happen."

"So did I. Do you think she did?"

"Certainly. What do you intend to do now?"

"I don't know. I haven't thought. Go on, I suppose."

"He'll be coming back."

"We haven't discussed the future."

"Sensible. I hope you'll know what to do when the time comes, however."

"When *what* time comes?"

"The moment of choice. There's always one in every relationship."

"I don't like generalities. You know, as well as I do, there are no rules to these things."

"True, but I know better than you the nature of the choice *you* must make . . . if only because I am older and once selected, long ago, impetuously, my own way."

"Which was not the right way?"

"Right, wrong, it makes no difference; we die in any event. No, I should say one chooses what one must, of course, but I believe there is an instant of free will, a moment when one can assume direction. The trick is to recognize that moment."

"I'm not sure I follow you."

"Don't follow me! That's precisely it. There's your answer."

"There will be war, Hélène!" shouted Zoe.

"More what, my dear?"

"I have it on the best authority . . . within ninety days. Then the end. Pouf! No more Europe. Nothing. Where will *you* go?"

"Know what?"

"I shall die with the world I have loved. I will not desert. Never! I shall be at Antibes, waiting. I shall wear all my jewels and, when *they* come, I shall receive them on the lawn. They will drive their tanks through the boxwood and over the roses, the pink ones named for me, and I shall be drinking champagne with the Duke of Windsor on the terrace when they shoot us down!"

"I haven't been to Antibes in twenty years . . . it was a new resort in those days. I went there with Paul Avril. You remember him? He dedicated his *Titania* to me. They do it now at the Comédie I hear, But I no longer attend the theater. Crowds confuse me, except here in my own house."

"No, none of us will survive this war . . . and who will want to? Who?"

"New? What, my dear, is new? You are naïve, but it's your charm, Zoe. Never let them take it away from you."

"Call me Cassandra! I see what I see."

"But I love the sea as much as you and perhaps, if these treatments I am taking work, I may be able to visit you at Antibes."

"I should love that, Hélène."

"They're giving me the glands of sheep. Imagine! To be a sheep, after all these years."

"Ninety days, Hélène; that's all we have. Ninety days. One really doubts if there is Someone above."

"Love? But, my dear Zoe, *who* loves you? And how nice for you. Tell me, I must know."

"You see," said Charles, turning to Philip, pausing in their journey across the room, beneath a portrait of Marie-Louise.

"Yes, I think so."

Through black lace and black broadcloth, he saw Anna at the far end of the room, waiting for him.

Chapter Twelve

"*IT IS FIFTH NIGHT:* the moment of revelation . . . the hour of truth!" Glenellen paused, arms outstretched, glowering at the crowded room. The worshipers stood or sat in a dense circle about him, leaving hardly any space around the empty throne before which he now stood. Two young women, hearty in tweed, guarded the Green Door.

There was a sigh of anticipation, a murmur of excitement at this pronouncement. One young man near the bookcase fainted from tension while, in other parts of the room, there were several audible moans of religious fervor, including one resounding "Hallelujah!" from an American night-club singer, a New York Italian girl who had attempted, with complete success, to pass herself off as a Negress, thus insuring a considerable following among the credulous French.

Then Glenellen, red-faced and tense, stepped to the Green Door and stood, head bowed, in front of it, waiting. The silence was broken at last by the ringing of an alarm clock; then the dinner bell tolled and the Green Door slowly opened, revealing Augusta, completely nude, a tall pale figure with primary and secondary sexual characteristics of unusual variety. With a serene smile the beloved figure moved through the cheering worshipers to the empty throne. But then, before the first Statement of the Day could be made, a dozen gendarmes shouting "Exhibition! Exhibition!" broke into the room.

The noise was deafening. Most of the young women jumped out the window (the shrine was on the second floor of an eighteenth-century building) while several of the young men fainted and were severely trampled by the panicky worshipers and the no less hysterical gendarmes who rushed this way and that, shouting Republican sentiments, invoking *Legalité* as they tried unsuccessfully to arrest the fleeing Augustans, all of whom, within several minutes, had got out the door, excepting those vigorous young women who had sprained their ankles on the hard pavement below and the young men who had fainted and lay now like corpses after a battle, while the gendarmes hammered on the Green Baize Door behind which Glenellen and Mr Norman together protected the cowering Augusta as she lay on an iron cot, shuddering convulsively, the various articles of worship covered with a torn linen sheet.

"Go away!" shouted Glenellen. "This is sacrilege! This is a private institution! I shall go immediately to the British Ambassador if you persist! Do you hear me?"

The gendarmes continued to batter at the door, demanding the arrest of Augusta, professing shock at the obscenity of the exhibition they had witnessed.

"You had better let them in, Ayre," said Mr Norman quietly.

"Never!" shrieked Glenellen, moving an old wardrobe against the door. "Desecration!" he roared at the gendarmes on the other side, but they were too busy with their hammering to hear the solemn curse which, presently, he thundered at them, leaning against the wardrobe, one hand clutching his chain of office.

Mr Norman sat down on a three-legged stool, the only furniture in the room besides the cot and the wardrobe. Calmly he lit a cigar and then, exhaling, a model Englishman in a confused moment, he looked about the small airless room curiously, at the shrine which until now none but Augusta had seen. Dust was everywhere and the single window with its dirty panes of glass had obviously not been opened for many years while on the floor, on the bed, on the window sills, lay old candy wrappers and tag ends of food, fragments of stale cake and biscuits while several ominous floor-level holes in the wall suggested that Augusta shared her feasts in much the same way the saint from Assisi had shared his.

"That should hold them," said Glenellen, his curse completed, his last thunderbolt launched at the gendarmes who had found some sort of battering ram and were now, at regular intervals, hitting the door, splintering it methodically as flakes of plaster fell from ceiling and walls upon the motionless figure of Augusta, like a corpse beneath her sheet, and upon the two Englishmen who conversed quietly, pausing only when the regular noise of the battering ram crashed through the shrine.

"What shall we do when the door finally goes?" asked Mr Norman.

"Fight them with our bare hands," said Glenellen grimly.

223

"Come now, Ayre. Neither of us could handle an angry child, much less the pride of the gendarmerie."

"A token resistance, then . . . we will not surrender easily."

"I suppose they'll book us on some charge or another."

"Martyrdom!" exclaimed Glenellen, his face transfigured for an instant as he considered grace.

"Should the movement triumph we will of course be included among its first martyrs but should it not prevail we shall have wasted our time in unnecessary humiliation."

Glenellen looked at his companion sadly. "You too, Clyde?" he whispered.

"I was speaking realistically, my dear old friend. You know that. I shall never desert you . . . although I have at times disagreed with your methods in the conduct of the Missions . . . especially when you deposed dear Edmond from his post as Bursar, even though I begged you not to."

"You should never have taken his side."

"At a time like this . . . a climacteric, as it were . . . I should not think it advisable to be too finicky."

"Let me tell you, Clyde, since you wish to discuss the squalid affair of Edmond's fraudulency, that you yourself have been, on more than one occasion, accused of selling audiences with Augusta and, worse still, of receiving a retainer from a certain Brazilian for the Privilege of the Braces."

"*I* sell audiences! It is fortunate indeed that you are my old friend, or I might forget myself."

"That it is you, dear Clyde, who are the offender, justifies or, rather, ameliorates the deed and precludes penalty."

"Penalty!" A large section of plaster, shaped like a map of France, fell to the floor at Glenellen's feet. Augusta whimpered and turned her face to the wall.

"Remember Savoy!" said Glenellen furiously. "The House of Savoy! Remember? Did we desert Umberto, the first gentleman of our adopted country, our rightful lord, for this? That we end by selling audiences to the Incomparable, dirtying our fingers for the sake of ready cash, exploiting our co-religionists. . . . Oh, I should rather have remained a Communist and cursed the bourgeoisie than such an Augustan!"

"Don't turn on me, Ayre. I won't have it. I won't! You forget, I am a believer too, more devout than you. . . ."

"Stop it, Clyde! You know you're not. You have no vocation."

"I have."

"And *I* say you haven't."

"I shall lose my temper with you, Ayre, if you don't watch your tongue."

The mirror on the wardrobe came loose and smashed on the floor. There was a shout of triumph from the gendarmes on the other side; they renewed their battering.

"You bore me, Clyde."

"Is it possible?"

"Listen to me, Clyde. Don't interrupt and stop glowering at me like an idiot."

"Great heavens! . . . has it come to this?" Mr Norman was genuinely anguished.

"Yes, my dear, all this . . . and more. Fret all you like because from now on I shall be quite serene, undisturbed by these outbursts. . . . I find you ludicrous, Clyde. Do you hear? Absolutely ludicrous."

"Then it is over. . . ."

"You say you are more devout than I . . . such insolence. Prove it. Tell me one vision you have had which might substantiate your pretensions."

"Now you wrong me, Ayre; I'm sorry. I said I was *as* devout as you . . . I didn't say more, did I?"

"I don't care if you did."

"When we served Umberto you would not have spoken to me like this. You know it. You no longer care for me, Ayre. Augusta has drained you of all humanity."

"I do not like your faults."

"If you were a friend you would overlook them."

"If I were sufficiently insincere, I suppose I could pretend not to see the Eiffel Tower."

"I am tired," sighed Mr Norman, with the gesture of one rehearsing for a crucifixion. "I hope the gendarmes come soon and take us to the station. I can't bear your carping, your hatred . . . this morbid concern with my imagined faults. I'm too weak, too exhausted to bear all this."

"Oh, Clyde! Clyde!" Glenellen turned to the window as the top panel of the door splintered above the wardrobe.

"I can't bear your contempt, Ayre . . . your indifference."

"I'm not indifferent, Clyde. I was ill-tempered when I said that."

Mr Norman rose from his three-legged stool, tears in his eyes. "I am happy you said that. Give me your hand."

"Gladly." They shook hands gravely, too moved to speak, as the wardrobe toppled over and landed with a crash at

225

their feet. Through the shattered upper panels of the door they could see the gleaming vandalous faces of the gendarmes, outlined by shreds of green baize.

"To the barricade!" shouted Glenellen, throwing the stool through the gap in the door. But the shrine was occupied by the blue-uniformed men at whose loud center Glenellen still struggled, while the recumbent Augusta shrieked like a tropical bird and Mr Norman, wringing his hands, was led away.

◙

Regina returned to Paris on a bitter and lugubrious February day when all alliances seemed purposeless, all motives suspect and the immediate prospect of a war was not only possible but, in the general apocalyptic mood which prevailed, desirable: a fitting climax to the grayness, a last proof of Lucifer's victory so many millennia before in that not so dubious battle on the plains of heaven.

They met in her rooms at the Ida, to Philip's amusement, aware as he was that in the corresponding suite on the floor above Anna Morris occasionally received him, though as a rule they met at his hotel, now nearly empty, the visitors from the West gone back to school, to jobs, to mother and to real life.

As they talked, he could hear the faraway sound of the wind as it assaulted the mansard roof of the hotel.

"Did you get my letter?" she asked.

"No, did you write?"

"Twice . . . to American Express."

"I never go there. I told you . . ."

"I forgot. I said nothing in particular. Like a good politician I never commit myself on paper!"

"How is your husband?"

"Very well. . . ." She laughed. "I was almost going to say 'thank you'! I wonder why we are so formal?"

"Well, we've been separated by quite a few months . . . nearly a year of them."

"The year is almost over, Philip."

"Time to go home."

"To what?"

"I wish I knew. To whatever I was before, I suppose."

"You feel unchanged?"

"I'm afraid so."

"You've had no revelation after all?"

"No, and now that the year is gone I see how foolish it

226

was of me to have ever thought I could so arbitrarily resolve all doubts and make a final choice, just like that."

"That's one discovery, at least."

"Perhaps, but not much of one. I find it demoralizing to
realize that there is no such thing as future time, only a
long present . . . that all acts are essentially meaningless,
except of course to one's self. . . ."

The dialogue proceeded, as it always did between them:
from the general to the particular, from the sensibility to the
reason and back again. Philip, unknowing, went further in
it than he ever had before. If he had gained little in this
precious year, he had lost a great deal. What had been only
a vague awareness of the long present had at last become a
conviction and he was no longer alarmed by this knowledge
since it was, finally, the point from which the temporary
arrangement of matter that was himself surveyed the material world, without guilt or shame, afraid of death but
resolutely concerned with life, preferring harmony to vision.

Snow began to fall. The sky turned black before
the sun had set, and the river stopped. Frozen birds fell in
the icy streets and shattered like porcelain figurines on the
sidewalks. A number of people died of exposure that evening, as they always did when the winter was hard, while one
of the energetic philosophers of the day published a novel,
produced a play and composed a dozen pamphlets suggesting
that although there was no God, no governing spirit, one
should still act and, in the act, forget that all was meaningless: constructing not a philosophic system, as the philosopher
had hoped, but reporting merely what the majority of the
more thoughtful people of the day felt, paradoxically,
offering himself as a figure to be believed in and, to an extent,
as paradoxically, some did believe, rendering black February less a burden.

"I shall be here for a few months," said Regina, as the
dialogue came to its usual indecisive end.

"Until the first of May?" asked Philip, smiling.

Then, carefully, soberly, they duplicated their former
passion and both found it wanting, though Philip as always
was attracted to her, against the advice of his reason, and she
in her turn, though loving, seemed concerned with something
else, something unspoken and as yet undeclared.

The moment ended when a windowpane broke and the
room was filled with an ice-cold wind on which, like the
white petals of frozen flowers, snowflakes whirled for one

brilliant moment; then the wind upset the lamp and the room went dark as the light bulb smashed and the lovers fled.

㊉

Jim found his way with some difficulty down the dark hall to his own room where, in the circle of red and blue light from a single paper lantern, his bed was illuminated, like an altar awaiting sacrifice, in this case his own body, pale and lean as, quite naked yet not shivering, not noticing the cold, he did what he had been forbidden to do: he took the long wooden pipe out of its hiding place in the medieval chest and with steady hand lit the blue flame of the burner. There was only one pellet left, he remembered . . . almost the only thing he could remember, he thought, suddenly happy at the familiar odor, redolent of past pleasures, the smoke rising in a pale slender spiral from the blue flame to the faraway ceiling, dark and menacing, where the ghosts and villains and all the unbeloved outrages awaited the extinguishing of the blue flame . . . when he would float away from its comforting light to them, to the shadows above, to the night-mare world of the ceiling across which he must journey, occasionally floating, sometimes running, other times strug-gling to move even a hand, a finger, as the dreary shadows held him tight above the room, embraced his body with a loving greed, draining it of will and memory, even of pleasure, so that when he was released he fell like the dis-carded husk of a locust from the dark ceiling to the bed below, and what was left of him could hear the dry crack-ling of the rest, like brown paper rustling in a Virginia kitchen: it was June again and like a faded, cracked movie, sometimes too fast, sometimes too slow, he saw himself speak to this person, speak to that person, saw lips move in question and response . . . a silent movie, for the dialogue did not matter since he knew the order of the mass already; and though he might try feebly to exert his will and change the course of ancient events he could never intrude upon that flickering cinematic world which viciously unreeled, over and over again, leading him each time to the same delight and to the same despair as it had done since that first day when there were indeed voices and the trees were green, not gray and white, and he'd been out on location and had accompanied that slim hard figure with its helmet of short wiry curls down to the edge of a river, the camera of mem-ory taking it all in, mercilessly, blackmailing him for life with that one image to which, at last, he came, dry tears in

228

burning eyes, as he saw the bodies touch by firelight and then, with a sense of loss, he moved on in time through a world of faceless men, until the act of violence turned everything about, and he saw with terror that each of the faceless men had now assumed identity, the egg-smooth whiteness of their featureless faces covered with masks: some were vultures, others sheep, others eagles; some were lions, and several apes, while one of them with the monstrous face of a toad nuzzled him until he felt a scream rise like a tide from his groin to his throat, only to die on his lips when he saw himself, as he always did, with terror and eternal astonishment, reflected in the gelatinous globule of the toad's eye, and his own face was as smooth, as white as the shell of an egg: the worst was over then. The film ran backwards at great speed and he blinked his closed eyes, growing dizzy in the flickering light.

"Do you think he'll remember he asked us to come by?" asked Stephen.

"I don't know. He seemed all right to me." They knocked at the door again. He heard them knocking but he could not speak or move. The good part was next, he remembered.

Stephen opened the door and, followed by Bill, entered the bedroom. The flame still flickered in the rusty burner and by its blue light Jim's body looked as if it had been rolled from some deep sea's bottom to a reef; Stephen almost expected to find seaweed in his hair and the mark of shells upon his skin.

"Is he dead?" whispered Bill.

Dead, dead, dead: what an ugly word it was, thought Jim, contented in his paralysis. Yes, he wanted to say, I am dead. Then, among the soft clouds of his other dreaming, he wondered: am I dead? is this what it is after all? an old movie winding forwards and backwards forever. . . . "I am not dead!" he shouted; but he had no voice. The now caressing clouds held him in their arms and stopped his voice: no sound in a vacuum.

"I don't think so," said Stephen, and he put his hand on Jim's breast and felt through warm skin the slow thud of the heart. "No, he's on the stuff again."

"Didn't the doctor say it would kill him?"

"Sooner or later."

Not dead, he thought, delightedly. That was a relief, and he viewed the clouds about him spitefully, contemptuously. They were his still; he was not theirs. Lovely Stephen, pretty Stephen, come lie with me.

"I'd better cover him up," said Stephen. "He'll freeze to death."

"He looks all right," said Bill, as they pulled the blanket over him.

"You'd think he would look worse, considering what he's done to himself," said Stephen, turning off the blue flame, changing the character of the room, banishing much of the horror as warm red lanternlight replaced blue.

He remembered, as they talked, that he had asked them to come see him that evening but somehow time had got muddled and he now had a distinct recollection of having seen them earlier, that the evening in question had come and gone some weeks (months?) ago and that they had had a pleasant time and the conversation, not to say the circumstances, had been very different from this. He tried to offer them a drink but he was facing in the opposite direction, he discovered sadly, and it would never do to attempt communication with his back to them and all those shadows between. He was grateful for the red light as opposed to the blue: it made all the difference in the world. He felt now as though he was at the warm secret center of an odorless velvet-leaved rose through whose petals sunlight came, ruddy, diffused, penetrating his blindness like an intimation, a prescience of light to a new-formed eyeless embryo still safe at home.

"Doesn't look like the sanitarium did him much good," said Stephen.

"Poor kid," said Bill. "He was like a ghost this afternoon."

"No memory. You remember he couldn't think of our names? And he talked so slow, as though he'd forgotten how to talk."

No memory! At the heart of the rose he chuckled silently, stirred even, like an uneasy foetus anticipating birth. Was it not enough that he *knew*? Was it necessary for him to *remember* as well?

"I don't think those shock treatments do any damn good. You remember. . . ."

"That guy in the Army, in the hospital? Shocked his mind clear out of him . . . poor bastard."

"Do you think he'll die?"

"Who, Jim? I don't know."

"The doctors all say that if you keep on after a certain point you never get off the stuff, you just dissolve."

The red stuff of the rose melted about him and he was

alone in the dark again, the voices of the two Southern boys, gentle and soft, far below him, as he floated upon a dark tide which transported him quickly away from the viscous carmine puddle where the rose had been. His arms and legs were without sensation; he wondered if they were still attached, or was it only a memory? an odd fantasy that in some other existence he had been a creature with two legs, two arms. Where was he going? he wondered lazily, as layer after layer of darkness opened to receive him.

"Seems funny for a boy like him to have ended up like this," said Bill, looking at one of the Balzac volumes on the table: "*Louis Lambert.*" He read the title aloud, automatically.

"I know," said Stephen, considering the melodramatic fate which had so logically, if not tragically, befallen Jim. "Well, we'd better leave him a note to say we're going back to the States."

"If he'll remember our names when he sees it."

"If he can read." Stephen wrote the note carefully, explaining that they had come, as invited, but that since they had found him asleep they had gone away without disturbing him. And so this was good-by, they were going back home to school. "If you should ever be in Spartanburg, S. C.," he wrote in big firm letters, "look us up anytime. Yours truly, Steve and Bill. . . ." Followed by their addresses.

"I don't guess there's anything more," said Bill, looking down at the face of the dreamer. "Looks like a baby, doesn't he?"

"Well, he's not much older than us."

"But he's taken it every way, one time or another."

He was not aware when they left. He had long since ceased even to hear their voices. He was only interested now in trying to recall who and what he was and why, disembodied, he should be caught in all this darkness, with no physical sensation except that of motion . . . forward, outward, away from the tiny red light below.

Then he understood what was happening and he was terrified, preferring any pain, any unpleasurable sensation or anguish, to dissolution, to the enfolding darkness. He tried to speak, to move, to turn back, not wanting to die. He stared fixedly at the red point in space until, slowly, it drew him back to it, grew larger and larger until the leaves of the rose held him once more safe inside. He had a moment of peace, of satisfaction, before the old movie began to unwind once more; and it was June again and his father and mother moved jerkily as the faded strip of memory displayed its images, the light behind as full and as constant as the images themselves were cracked and dim with use.

▣

"We *must* have her, Zoe."

"But, Julia, she won't fit."

"You'll have to *make* her fit. You have been at her house twice this year and she's not been to yours *once*."

"But she can't see . . . she can't hear."

"She knows, however, that she *is* where she is."

"Would the Murats come if I had her?"

"The Duchesse always attracts the Bonapartists, you know that."

"All right, darling, put her name down." Lady Julia Keen wrote Lyon et Grénoble in her tiny but vigorous hand while her employer, Zoe Helotius, occasionally patted the quart of dry mud which made her face look like a mummy in danger of unraveling. The bed where she lay was shaped like a ship, with an enormous gold Eros for a prow. The remains of Zoe's breakfast (Holland rusk and weak tea) decorated the night table.

"Now, what about the Windsors?"

"Well, what about them, Julia?"

"Will they be in Paris in time for the party, and will they come?"

"They will not be here in time," said Zoe evenly, like a chief of government who has just lost an important minister in a cabinet crisis.

"I . . . I'm terribly sorry, Zoe."

"That's all right, Julia. These things must be faced squarely. It never does to cry over spilled figs." (In moments of crisis she tended unconsciously to relate all things to the source of her wealth, the rock on which her fortress stood.)

"It seems like only yesterday. . . ."

"Never look back, Julia. It doesn't pay. Go on, go on: that's my motto. If one were to stop each time fate dealt one an unkind blow one would remain stationary. We will invite . . ."

"*Him?*"

"Yes, Julia." For a moment the mummy seemed almost to smile with triumph.

"What a thrill! And her?"

"She will come too."

"But how . . . I mean, well, when?"

232

"A week ago. It was all arranged. I was saving it as a little surprise for you."

"And what a surprise! The biggest, absolutely the biggest of all."

"I know." The earlier dereliction was forgotten.

"I could not be more thrilled," said Lady Julia, writing two names under Lyon et Grénoble.

"Back to work," said Zoe, holding her arms up like a mantis praying, so that the veins in the backs of her capable hands would grow smooth.

"Regina Durham?"

"By all means," said Zoe. "Is the husband here?"

"Not until May."

"Too bad. The politicians one wants always come if Rex Durham is about."

"Now darling, what shall we do about the young man?"

"What young man?"

"Mrs Durham's."

"Oh I remember. He's with the Embassy."

"No. He doesn't work. He was in Capri. . . ."

"I know, Julia. I *do* remember things, you know. There are times when you treat me like an utter fool."

"Zoe!"

"Yes, by all means have him."

"But there is a complication."

"I should have known, Julia, from your tone, that you were planning a complication for me. What is it this time?"

"Anna Morris."

"What about her?"

"And Philip Warren."

"Who is he?"

"I thought you said you remembered."

"You mean Regina's friend?"

"I do indeed."

"And he is Anna Morris's lover now?"

"He is indeed . . . and she is coming to the party too."

"Now that's very interesting," said Zoe, waving her arms like a man signaling a ship with flags, exercising the wrinkled wattles of flesh which hung from her sturdy bones, attesting to that age which her face, thanks to certain miracles of quasi-medical science, did not reveal at all. "You think there might be a scene, Julia."

"I doubt it."

"Then we are safe if we have all three."

"I should think so. I felt you should know, however."

"But, of course. Now that you mention it, I have heard talk. I must say, he's done well for himself. Is he a gigolo?"

"I don't believe so. He has money."

"I wonder what his charm is?"

"He's quite good-looking, and young."

"That combination is easily come by if one has money, if one is Regina Durham."

"And then I've heard . . ." And Lady Julia lowered her voice although they were alone and, flushing slightly, she whispered something into Zoe's ear. The only word an eavesdropper might have overheard was "butterfly." The ladies laughed heartily or, rather, Lady Julia did for because of the mud Zoe could only snort, blowing a cloud of fine dust the length of the bed. Then the telephone, hidden in Madame de Maintenon's chamber pot, rang. Lady Julia answered it. Her eyes grew round with delight and her voice became warm and personal; then she put her hand over the mouthpiece and hissed, "It's *her*, Zoe . . . the Duchess!"

"My God!" Zoe sat up abruptly and the mud cracked and crumbled about her ravaged shoulders as she seized the telephone.

For three days during mid-April there were violent storms. But when at last the sun shone winter was gone and Philip began to contemplate departure as he read the various letters from home which suggested, mildly yet with an underlying urgency, that he return to the valley where his life was to be.

"What did you do all winter?" asked Sophia curiously, as they drank coffee on the rue de Rivoli, a glimpse of new green in the Tuileries Gardens across the street, its fence of gold-tipped spears bright in the sun.

"I wonder that myself," he said. "When you ask me like that, abruptly, I can't think of a thing. I have an image of myself reading English novels in the bathtub."

"That's something," she smiled.

"I have some recollection of having kept a diary."

"Now that's very interesting. . . . Why only a recollection, though?"

"Because I've kept journals off and on all my life, but I continually lose them and I've never written in one more than three days consecutively."

"What did you write in this one?"

"What would I have written, is more likely. Because the

234

more I think of it the less sure I am that I *did* keep a journal during the winter . . . but if I had I would probably have done what I've always done: commented on whatever I happened to be reading, what conversations I had overheard, what profundities occurred to me while crossing the Place de la Concorde, dodging automobiles, late to an appointment. I've been late recently, to almost everything."

"Sounds as if you were at least having a social success."

"I suppose I intended it to sound like that; actually I've seen very few people . . . mostly Americans, at that."

"Like Mrs Durham?"

"How did you know?"

"I've been here a few days," said Sophia, with as much malice as her ordinarily serene detachment would allow.

"I've seen a little of her . . . these last few weeks."

"Poor Regina," said Sophia.

"Why poor?"

"Her husband is such an oaf."

"At least he leaves her alone."

"Perhaps," said Sophia mysteriously.

But Philip refused to challenge her and they spoke no more of Regina, which did not displease Sophia who was now eager to discuss the character of Anna Morris.

"I like her very much," said Philip, wondering what had so abruptly caused the usually impersonal Sophia to confront the character of other women with that same intensity which she ordinarily reserved exclusively for facts, for generalities, for the contemplation of those syllogisms which gave her such pleasure.

"I have known her such a long time," said Sophia, "such a very long time that I suppose I am too close to her to know what I think."

"Yet," said Philip to himself.

"Yet," said Sophia, unconscious for once of the effect she was having, "I can't help but feel that she has been somewhat dishonest emotionally."

"Dishonest?"

"I think that's the word. It's not that one objects to her having affairs. Most women in her postion do these days. Rather it's her prodigality. I mean, each time she goes to bed with a man it can't be as earth-shaking, as unique an experience as she maintains it is. Oh, there've been so many! Each time you would think that at last she had found the half for which she had been searching all her life; then, a month later, there's someone else."

"You make her sound more frivolous than she is."

"Deluded. No human being could survive that intensity which she claims she experiences each time."

"She is serious," said Philip.

"I'm quite sure she is . . . resolutely so. I question only her sincerity . . . or her reason."

"Not everyone is alike. Perhaps she's exactly the way she seems. Some people are."

"I remember she loved a general once, a young man, and she followed him about everywhere . . . it was a great scandal."

"How did it end?"

"The way it always does."

"And how is that?"

"He lost interest. The man always does. Men aren't constructed for such intensity, simulated or not. Poor Anna . . . she is always deserted in the end."

"Which proves her sincerity."

"Or bad judgment." Then, having said what she had wanted to say, realizing instinctively that she had perhaps gone too far, she spoke of other things, amiably, recalled mutual acquaintances, asked even about Charles de Cluny, as though they had, at one time, all three, been the best of friends.

He told her that he planned to go back in the spring.

"Will you be sorry to leave?" she asked.

"No, I don't think so."

"But you *have* enjoyed it?"

"Oh very much . . . even if I can't remember what I've done."

"You'll remember later."

"I often do."

"That's right. But a bad habit: not to appreciate the moment except in recollection."

"I'm not so sure."

"But I am, for me at least. Do you look forward to going back home?"

"I think so. I don't really know. I have a terrible feeling that nothing matters, that it will make very little difference whether I spend the rest of my life in Egypt poking about in the dirt or whether I have a political career in New York."

"It seems very different to me."

"Not when I think of death . . . not when I think there

236

is no reason to be alive . . . but I *am* alive, of course, and don't want to die."

"Afraid of hell?"

"No."

"Of pain?"

"Not very."

"Of what?"

"Of *nothing*. Isn't that enough to fear?"

"One could learn to prefer it," she said. He laughed at her until he saw that she was serious; he tried then, out of politeness, to present an argument that would support her curious nonsensical announcement, discussing gravely with her the inadequacies of the alien garment of the flesh which they both wore with such distinction, each aware of that day when awareness would be lost in the whole reality: the flesh gone and the breath properly contained in the larger breathing of the world.

He told her about the International Typewriter Company which maintained an enormous factory near his home town of Hudson. The paternalism of this institution (so low has the father fallen in American life that his social function, when recognized at all, is identified with tyranny) has assumed significant proportions. Total security is offered in exchange for total resignation to the order. Wages are high. Company-owned houses, all alike, are sold to workers on easy terms. No union is allowed even to contribute to the delicious harmony which prevails between pater and his children and, when a child wishes to remain home a day to endure or to feign an illness, a registered nurse is sent him post-haste, by broomstick, by magic carpet, to make sure that he is really ill and not playing hooky, as the children of even the very best, the most indulgent fathers will do on occasion. In every lavatory of the new glass-and-chrome factory, in every hall, in every office, there is a placard which enjoins each boy and girl to REMEMBER, signed J. Branson Etting, their father, himself the eldest son of the grandfather of them all: the noiseless International Typewriter. "Now, more than ever," quoted Philip to himself, as he discussed the penultimate phase of that eccentric yet occasionally colorful civilization into which he had been born, so near the end . . . yet so near the beginning, he suddenly thought, with some surprise, of still another, of something else again, as yet unknown: I am the alpha and the omega, the first and the last, the beginning and the end. But which? Or did it matter?

Sophia thought not.

◫

The hour of the equinox was celebrated in such a way that what Philip had suspected might be true was proved true, that repetition for the first time in his life became confirmation rather than the familiar boredom which he had inevitably experienced with everyone and everything, more soon than late. Could it be that this body was in some way different from all the others he had known? that this head which he now held cupped in one hand was really so strange: a round globe of bone wreathed in dark hair and containing a mystery which he did not know, would never know . . . thus, through ignorance, was he held by an attraction far more intense than the usual center, the dark groin where the other mystery resided, the one he had always known, the center from which he had at last successfully strayed to the true center, to that unseen mythical altar before which only kings are anointed, adjured and crowned.

"Nor am I jealous," said Anna suddenly.

"Jealous?" They had been silent for some minutes as their racing hearts quieted in unison and their breathing grew more easy, less quick and harsh. "I don't know what you mean."

"Oh, but you do." She sat up on one elbow, the pale light of early spring across their bodies, across the gray-cold, winter-old city and its gardens and the fields far, far beyond the gates of St Denis. Would there be lilacs soon? he wondered touching her breast carefully, like an unobserved boy in a museum caressing the stone fantasy, the dream lover of a Greek two thousand years dead, the marble evocation of his pain, serene and unbemused among strangers in a distant city, fondled by a boy.

"You mean about Regina?" he asked, falling back upon the crumpled pillows, his arms crossed upon his chest like a Crusader on his bier.

"About Regina. You knew her first."

"But not as well."

"She's doing everything she can, you know."

"Everything?"

"To win you."

"But why?"

"Don't you know yet?"

"I'm afraid not. I've often thought about it, of course . . . why should she be so interested in me?"

"Because she loves you."

238

"Now you're making fun of me. I'm not that vain. Women like that never fall in love, or if they do they would love a completely different sort of man . . . a Rex Durham."

"And me? What sort of man would I love?"

"I wonder."

"You?"

"Yes, I think so. For a while."

She looked away and when she answered she spoke to the pale daffodil light on the wall. "I never end it," she said softly. "I am always there when the other leaves . . . when you go back next month, to your real life. . . ."

"This is it, right now."

"You've made me talk of the future," she laughed. "What a bad influence you are! I don't believe in the future. There's no such thing."

"But there is."

"There is change in the present and when you leave, the present will change for us both."

"I could stay."

"No, you couldn't."

"I suppose not."

"But I am vain enough to like hearing you say it."

"Why can't I see you in America?"

"Because . . . oh, so many reasons. Perhaps you won't want to. Perhaps *I* won't want to. And then, I won't be coming back for some time."

Philip sighed and wondered what to say, wondered what he should feel . . . it would be nice, he thought, to be able to have definite responses to everything, to know always not only what one should feel but, more important, what one did feel.

"On the other hand," said Anna sharply, suddenly out of character, "you will be seeing a great deal of Regina when you go home."

"I suppose so," said Philip, almost resenting this display of less than godlike emotion. He had created her, after all, he suddenly realized with some wonder. The body he held in his arms, the perfect response to all his needs on every level, had not existed except in his own imagining. She was not real and he knew it now. The perfect love had been himself, loving himself; the arms of a stranger whom he had never known had held him while his own reflection had come between their two bodies, like a silver mirror or like an old curse: you will never know any other, never walk through the reflecting glass to the true world, to the one outside. Who

239

was she then? he wondered, suddenly frightened at having revealed so much to a stranger: was she a spy? a blackmailer? some sort of saint? or, worse yet, a patient fool who mocked him from behind the smooth implacable glass which separated them. Where am I? He touched the iron bedstead ... was it iron? Who am I?

"Philip."

"Yes."

"What do you want?"

What do I want? "Knowledge."

"Of what?"

"Of everything, of someone else, of you."

"But you know me."

"Never. You are I."

She smiled. "Haven't you always known that?"

"No, no, no."

"Isn't that what you wanted?"

"To know myself?"

"To know yourself and through yourself to know me?"

"Or the other way around."

"It is the same."

"But it shouldn't be." Not even the iron of the bed was real. "I want something more than that, more than myself."

"There's nothing more, Philip. There's only you."

"No one else?"

"Only when the illusion becomes so intense that you forget yourself. . . ."

"Like St Malo?"

"Like that . . . and, then, I am dreaming, too, at the same time. You are I . . . I made it all."

"But not the same thing."

"Never the same."

"That could be unbearable."

"It could, but it won't be for you, as long as you imagine me."

"Or Regina?"

The iron was cold and smooth beneath his hand; it chilled his fingers at the same time the warmth of his flesh made the iron less cold. Then the room grew warm with light and through the window he saw the sun.

Chapter Thirteen

DURING APRIL the letters began. At first they were wistful; by the end of May, however, they had grown urgent and he knew that the time had come for him to make his choice to return, if he could, to the summer valley and the gray river of home.

▣

Zoe Helotius who had no secrets (other than the central one concerning her obscure birth) had, nevertheless, one peculiarity which none of her intimates suspected, not even Lady Julia. Like most people with a private fancy, a secret life, she was enormously cunning and resourceful and consequently no one was aware that she talked to herself. Most people on occasion will think aloud but Zoe differed from the majority in that she was quite aware that she was talking to herself and since she was essentially a conventional woman, she was ashamed of her habit; even so, whenever she was alone she would address herself, in baby talk, as "Tiny Tot," an adorable slyboots of a child who was often naughty but always forgiven and indulged. On those busy days when social engagements followed one another too closely, Zoe would grow nervous and irritable, like an addict deprived of drugs, craving desperately the company of Tiny Tot to whom she could confide her latest plan or some bit of gossip, with whom she could share her brilliant triumphs and her glum defeats. When she could bear this separation no longer, she would abruptly leave even the most celebrated of her guests and hurry to the nearest bathroom where, seated on a commode or on the edge of a bathtub, she would commune with Tiny Tot, apologizing abjectly for not having come sooner, for having neglected her darling duck, her fig, her *choux fleur*, her only love.

Needless to say the party for the birthday of the British King (which is celebrated in June) occupied Zoe's every moment for several weeks, enraging the spoiled Tiny Tot who exacted, on the rare occasions when she and Zoe now

241

met, elaborate apologies for her creator's dereliction. On the afternoon of the party, Zoe suddenly broke off a spirited debate with her caterers and hurried to the ladies' retiring room of the Bain de Ligny. Here, alone at last, in front of a Venetian mirror, she crooned to her love, her fig.

"I've been a brute . . . I know, I know . . . a beast . . . you must forgive . . . that's a darling, a true lamb . . . I couldn't endure it another minute . . . five days away from you, I know. Can you ever forgive me? Please . . . please." And she was forgiven at last, as she always was. Then, briskly, she discussed the arrangements for the fête.

"It will be better than the Eiffel Tower . . . I feel it, I do, Tiny Tot . . . you'll be so proud; just wait and see, my darling. It will be Mummy's best, her very best. It took courage not to rent the Tower this year but nothing lost is nothing gained as they say. It will be an evening like no other! I have done the whole boat like a Byzantine pavilion, like a Venetian palace . . . and there'll be gondolas in the pool and banks of flowers; then, at midnight . . . yes, you've guessed it, darling, your favorites: fireworks! and a portrait of *him* in rockets as the orchestra plays 'God Save the King.' There'll never be another party like this in our time . . . my masterpiece: and everyone is coming. Yes, darling, yes, yes! Yes! and she will come, too . . . yes, yes and even her! Imagine! A triumph . . . everyone! And when it's over what stories I shall have to tell my darling Tiny Tot, my own dear. . . ." And at this point Zoe Helotius' voice became low and guttural as she murmured endearments in her native tongue, a language which she'd not spoken in thirty years, except in private to Tiny Tot.

Lady Julia put her head in the door of the ladies' room, which had been decorated to resemble an Ottoman harem. "Zoe, the conductor wants to go over the music with you . . . and also the costumes for the musicians . . . they never arrived."

"One minute more, Julia, and I'll be done." She pretended to examine an eyebrow as Lady Julia withdrew: the only person in the world who had even the slightest intimation of Tiny Tot's existence. Zoe was aware of her secretary's suspicions and she often trembled at the effect an exposure might have on her darling who was now listening raptly as she completed the list of those who were to come that evening, the important dozen guests . . . the less important five hundred who were to be scenery, props, supernumeraries.

"Oh, and there may be trouble . . . yes, a marvelous scene,

242

perhaps. Regina Durham—I've told you about her, haven't I?—is coming and her ex-young man who is now Anna Morris's young man, but Anna's husband will be here, too. I hope I shall have time to watch them. Julia will know, in any case, and when she tells me I'll tell you *all*, word for word, my darling, the moment I know. I've already made up my mind that at twelve-thirty, after the fireworks, I will sneak in here for a quick, comfy chat . . . I know how restless you get when there's a party. Now be a lamb while I talk to the musicians, and remember that you are my own love, no matter what anybody says."

回

The Bain de Ligny is an enormous barge on the Seine, moored to a quai on the left bank. Inside the barge is a swimming pool of filtered river water with a narrow sun deck on four sides, two storeys of cubicles, a restaurant and a bar. During the summer the Bain de Ligny is very popular with city-bound Parisians and tourists who swim there by the hundreds during the day; at night it is deserted. But not this night, for Zoe had indeed transformed it into a new Venice, a new Byzantium, a new Babylon with glowing lanterns everywhere and burning torches held by half-nude Algerian boys while garlands of flowers festooned *papier-mâché* arches supported by delicate fluted columns of gold-encrusted plaster. In the pool (illuminated from beneath by jade-green lights) gondolas plied languidly back and forth, to the music of a symphony orchestra whose members were dressed, for some curious reason, in early dynastic Egyptian costumes.

At sundown the guests began to arrive. The costumes were exotic though not always Venetian as the invitation had suggested. The moon was full at the black sky's center and a warm wind made the torches gutter dramatically, a flickering light upon bright jewels and festive eyes.

Philip arrived alone, in Venetian costume, wearing a mask like the other guests. His identity, however, was quickly checked by two non-Venetian thugs who examined his invitation carefully. Then he was allowed to present himself to Lady Julia who stood just inside the gate, by the pool; she greeted him warmly. "How marvelous you look, Mr Warren! I'm sure you must've been an Italian in another life."

"You never can tell," said Philip inadequately, but Lady Julia, a column of scarlet satin, was gone: a pillar of fire by

243

night, thought Philip, moving toward de Cluny who stood near the bar, talking to a massive lady.

"Charles!"

"How did you recognize me? I thought I was invisible." The heavy lady giggled and retired. The orchestra began the "Nutcracker Suite."

"A sixth sense," said Philip, glancing at the other's spidery legs which black tights did not flatter.

"Lovely party."

"Very."

"Lady Julia just told me that she sent to the south of France for a thousand fireflies but they arrived dead. . . ."

"It might have been too much."

"Perhaps . . . the last impiety: 'When the flower of pride has blossomed, death is the fruit that ripens, and all the harvest reaped is tears' . . . as the Greeks would say."

"A grim message for such an occasion." Then Philip saw Regina; she was seated alone in a gondola which was moving toward them; by torchlight her black gown glowed with tiny pearls and on her head diamonds flashed messages of light in some exotic code.

"Who is that?" asked de Cluny, impressed.

"A friend of mine," said Philip, excusing himself. Proudly he helped her from the gondola.

"I saw you," she said. "From the other side." Beneath her black mask, she smiled.

"Well met by moonlight," said Philip; and they sat down on a white wrought-iron bench beneath an arch of pink camellias and new ivy.

"What a job she's done," said Philip conventionally.

"I wonder if the orchestra intends to play *all* the 'Nutcracker Suite'?"

Two unidentified couples paid brief homage to Regina. At last alone, Regina said, "I've seen so little of you these past few weeks. Have you been busy?"

"Oh yes," he lied. "I've been seeing all the sights of the city . . . places I hadn't bothered to visit before."

"Are you leaving, Philip?"

He nodded. "Next week."

"Then the year is finally over."

"It seems like only a month ago that I came to Rome, not a year."

"Are you ready now?"

"For what?"

"Our plan . . . I can go back when you do. Rex is expecting me next week."

Philip did not answer.

"It will be so easy, believe me . . . and it will happen soon . . . if only because I haven't the time Rex and I had when *we* started, years go."

"Tell me why you want all this."

"Because I lost Rex," she said the truth at last. "Lost or shed him . . . it's hard to say which. Now he lives one life and I lead another, an aimless one. He has no use for me any more: his career is made."

For the first time Regina had touched him; he took her hand awkwardly and held it, not knowing what to say.

"You wonder perhaps why I don't have a career of my own . . . I sometimes wonder that, too. It would make it so easy if I did, if I could be self-sufficient; but I can't. I can only act through the man . . . I live only through him." She smiled. "Don't mistake me, Philip, it's not love I want. . . ." And she lost him for good.

"I was the wrong choice," he said gently. "We want different things. I want a private life, not your public one." And he let go her hand.

"She did this, didn't she?"

"Who?"

"Anna."

"I don't think so."

"She did . . . she did," said Regina, as though her own anger gave her pain, as though she had, like some furious scorpion, turned on herself. "Would you give up the world for someone like her?"

"No," said Philip coldly. "I wouldn't. I'm not giving up any world, except yours . . . one which I never had, in any case. She had nothing to do with it." But did she? He could not be sure.

"Don't listen to her, Philip. You'll find she's wrong . . . believe me you will. I know. I've seen all this before."

"You don't understand, Regina. You take so much for granted."

"You'd better go to her then. I understand she's here tonight."

"I suppose I should." He got to his feet.

She caught at his sleeve. "I didn't mean that, Philip. Please stay!" But he pulled away from her and stepped out of the camellia-decorated alcove onto the deck. Torchlight made her diamonds burn like a fire of ice. "Philip!" But he was gone, separated from her by a band of chattering ladies in harlequin masks.

◙

"A triumph, Zoe! a triumph!" exclaimed Lady Julia.

"I know," said Zoe, gentle with pride.

"They all came."

"Are you surprised?"

"No . . . yet I had hardly dared to dream. . . ."

"Even our wildest dreams become, on rare occasions, reality," said Zoe who was saving this particular line for Tiny Tot but saw no harm in rehearsing it now with Julia.

"I know . . . I know. Oh, darling, who are those two young men over there? sitting next to the bar . . . the ones who are wearing old clothes."

"They are Americans, Julia. Anne brought them. They are writers."

"Oh . . . how odd they look."

"We live in a changing world, Julia." On this philosophic note, the ladies parted.

◙

The Duchesse de Lyon et Grénoble rode in a gondola, back and forth across the pool; she was dressed in the wedding gown of the first Duchesse of her name, an intricate tent of yellowed satin and Brussels lace. Tonight she was enjoying herself immensely, humming toneless arias from forgotten operas, not always sure precisely where she was but pleased at being in motion, on water, with a gondolier to whom she occasionally gave irrelevant commands that he ignored as he poled their frail bark across the chartreuse pool which reflected, like fire in an opal, the light of torches, the gleam of rainbow lanterns.

◙

Standing at one end of the dance floor, watching the couples waltz, de Cluny observed that he seldom minded those tyrants who treated their subjects as though they were animals since, after all, men *are* animals but he did object to those new tyrants who treated their subjects like machines, which they were not: the one sin against the Holy Ghost. Philip agreed; then, catching sight of a Tintoretto girl, he deserted de Cluny and danced until the disagreeable scene with Regina had been forgotten, and the girl was claimed by a bearded Moor.

246

Philip wandered up to the second storey, to a long balcony overlooking the pool, one which had been transformed into an avenue of laurel and adorned with Renaissance interpretations of classic deities, white upon the green which skillfully hid dressing-room doors. At the end of the avenue a figure in gray, a woman, stopped him and said. "Good evening, Philip."

It took him a moment to guess who she was for the light was green and dim and, too, he had not expected to find Sophia here.

"I couldn't resist it," she said, as though apologizing.

"Nor I, said Philip. "How have you been?"

Slowly they walked the length of the avenue and then, as slowly, they walked back to the spot where they had met. "Do you look forward to leaving?" she asked.

"Very much . . . I was getting to the point where I could absorb nothing new here. And then I'm a little homesick, too. There is a lot to be said for living in a country where the people speak your language."

"I suppose there is." Sophia paused before a broken Hermes. "What will you do back home?"

"Practice law . . . in the town where I was born."

"A quiet life?"

"Who can tell? Perhaps. I don't think of the future any more. Everything is finally here, in the present."

"I believe that, too. Will you go into politics, do you think?"

"I may," said Philip, surprising himself a little. "I think I might like it . . . but who can tell?"

"Who can tell?" sang an American night-club singer, engaged for this one song: "Who can tell that I'm in hell and not so well and not so swell for the wonder of you and me, the blunder of you and me, the wonder of you you you."

"Do you know?" she asked suddenly.

"I think so."

"Is it clear at last?"

"Very nearly."

"And you? Are you certain?"

"Yes, I know it now."

"In terms of what?"

"Of people. . . ."

"Regina!"

"Not Regina. I never took her seriously."

"But you take the world seriously."

"There is nothing else."

"The idea, each time. . . ."

"That, too, but in proportion."

"Earth smothers fire."

"Fire comes from earth."

"Don't!" she said abruptly. "Don't listen to Regina. The other is more important."

"I know what I need. No one loses what he needs."

"But men do."

"And your way is wrong, too . . . for me, if not for you. I can't tell. No one ever really knows about anyone else . . . and that's the point."

"What point?"

"Discovery of someone else . . . recognition . . . all that."

"But you just said no one ever knows another. . . ."

"No one does . . . but each should try: and, finally, there is illusion which is so much better than knowledge, as any lover will tell you."

"I don't understand."

"I do but I can't explain. But suppose . . . suppose that I was born on an island without people: I should be an animal then, without a language, without words, without reason . . . an animal with a certain instinct for survival, and nothing more. So, in a real sense, I would never exist until I had been identified, until I saw myself as my own kind saw me. But if others should come to the island and give me words and attitudes, I should know who I was, not in ultimate terms of course but in terms of them, the only terms there are. Then, for better or worse. I should exist, created by them; and I would know that some would be attracted to me for my face or my manner and others would be hostile for the same reasons. Of course at the deep center I should always be the island animal, volatile, instinctive, nameless, but I should have a new, more important life in terms of others . . . and, finally, at some point, if I'm in luck, I would find another like myself, a stranger for whom I would exist in a new and terrible way . . . the way she will exist for me and then, for moments at a time, we shall identify with one another, the true coupling of those island beasts. . . . Do you see? do you see what I mean? do you see why I can never go back to the island?"

"You came from the world."

"No, I am an islander, and I know where the island is even now . . . on dark days I see it clearly, inviting me to return, to lose the myriad faces and all hope of another, to live alone, like Prospero with his dreaming. I am tempted; but I shall not go there now."

"Is the woman Anna?"

"Yes . . . no."

"What sort of answer is that?"

"I'm not sure what I mean. She was the first I knew. . . ."

"You are a fool!"

"Through her I knew what it could be like . . . isn't that enough?"

"It is all the same."

"Except where before there was one there are now two; a difference."

"She'll never leave her husband."

"Why should she? I may never see her again after to-night."

"I don't understand."

"You?—not understand?"

"You tell me she had done a miracle, that you are finally touched, no longer tempted by withdrawal. And then you leave her, too."

"Strange, isn't it?" said Philip joyously. "She understands."

"She always does."

"Why do you sound so bitter?"

"Only sad. . . ."

"Look! The fireworks!" Philip hurried to the end of the avenue of laurel and stood on the upper deck looking down at the pool where, from a raft, fireworks were being set off. The lanterns had been put out and it was dark, except for the light of occasional torches and the fountains of fire on the raft, the exploding constellations in the sky.

回

In her gondola, the Duchesse heard the noise of fireworks near by, caught a gleam of light through her gray-filmed eyes, and she asked querulously, "What is it, boatman? don't mumble. What's happening?" But the gondolier, a Paris tough in an embroidered vest, knowing that she was blind and deaf, did not answer, his eyes on the spectacle.

回

Alone for a moment, Zoe whispered, "Look at them, my darling . . . look! better than last year, better than the Eiffel Tower. And the rose, see? The rose all in rockets . . . for you, for my own darling Tiny Tot who loves roses and beauty . . . all for you, *mignonne*. Soon I'll leave all these people and we'll talk . . . and what news I have for you! You'll never guess. But here comes Julia."

When Philip turned to speak to Sophia he found her gone. The avenue of laurel was deserted; one of the marble figures, which had been insecurely fixed to the wall, had fallen face forward upon the deck, wreathed all in withered laurel, like funeral flowers. He moved down another balcony, one which was light and airy and hung with fern and roses. Here couples made love by the light of rockets. Suddenly, the King's portrait appeared in the sky and the orchestra played his anthem. For a moment there was silence. Then a gondola caught fire, to the delight of everyone, and by its ruddy glow Philip continued his progress down the balcony, watching lovers hide among the fern and rose.

She was waiting for him at the end of the balcony, in a grotto of shell and starfish, of seaweed and mother-of-pearl. She was unmasked, in white, with a summer flower in her gleaming hair. As he looked at her by firelight, saw her smile, the silver mirror dissolved before his eyes, dispelling its ungrieved ghosts like smoke upon the night, and beyond her in the dark, a promise at the present's furthest edge, a dreaming figure stirred and opened wide her golden eyes.